Critical Acclaim for Allison Brennan's Novels

Stalked

"Once again Brennan weaves a complex tale of murder, vengeance, and treachery filled with knife-edged tension and clever twists. The Lucy Kincaid/Sean Rogan novels just keep getting better!"

—RT Book Reviews (4½ stars, Top Pick)

"The novels featuring Lucy Kincaid and her cohorts are marked with deep characterizations and details of the workings of investigations by private eyes, the police, and the FBI. . . . Catch the latest in this series as Lucy continues to evolve in strength and wisdom."

—Romance Reviews Today

Silenced

"Brennan throws a lot of story lines into the air and juggles them like a master. The mystery proves to be both compelling and complex. . . . [A] chilling and twisty romantic suspense gem." *—Associated Press*

"The evolution of Lucy Kincaid from former victim to instinctive and talented agent continues in Brennan's new heart-stopping thriller. . . . From first to last, this story grabs hold and never lets go."

—RT Book Reviews (Top Pick)

"An excellent addition to the Lucy Kincaid series. Lucy and Sean continue to develop as complex, imperfect characters with a passion for justice. . . . The suspense was can't-put-it-down exciting." *—Fresh Fiction*

"A fan of Allison's for many years, you always know what you are getting . . . a great story with love 'em or hate 'em characters and perfectly placed plot twists in every book."
—Shannon Raab, *Suspense Magazine*

Original Sin

"Brennan shows a deft command of all things both normal and otherworldly in crafting one of the best tales of its kind since Dean Koontz and Stephen King were still writing about monsters. There's no shortage of those here and the result is a new genre classic."
—*Providence Sunday Journal*

"Allison Brennan pens a chilling tale in *Original Sin,* the first in her Seven Deadly Sins series. [It] will keep you up all night—whether it be from the horror or because it's such a page-turner." —*Sacramento Book Reviews*

Cutting Edge

"Both the nature and nurture sides of the 'what makes a psychopath' argument are on display in Brennan's chiller. . . . Leave it to Brennan to deliver the creepy and deadly. This is definitely the stuff of nightmares."
—*RT Book Reviews*

Fatal Secrets

"In this chilling thriller, Brennan explores the consequences of sliding from fierce commitment into obsession. . . . A master of suspense, Brennan does another outstanding job uniting horrifying action, procedural drama, and the birth of a romance—a prime example of why she's tops in the genre." —*RT Book Reviews* (Top Pick)

Also by Allison Brennan

STOLEN

Allison Brennan

Minotaur Books
New York

STOLEN. Copyright © 2013 by Allison Brennan. Excerpt from *Cold Snap* Copyright © 2013 by Allison Brennan. All rights reserved. Printed in the United States of America. For information, address St. Martin's Press, 175 Fifth Avenue, New York, N.Y. 10010.

www.minotaurbooks.com

ISBN 978-1-250-04247-7 (hardcover)
ISBN 978-1-250-02240-0 (e-book)

Minotaur books may be purchased for educational, business, or promotional use. For information on bulk purchases, please contact Macmillan Corporate and Premium Sales Department at 1-800-221-7945 extension 5442 or write specialmarkets@macmillan.com.

First Edition: June 2013

10 9 8 7 6 5 4 3 2 1

ACKNOWLEDGMENTS

Many people have helped me with the Lucy Kincaid series, and I greatly appreciate their time and effort in providing information, details, and support.

First and foremost, I couldn't write this series without the support and editorial guidance of my amazing editor, Kelley Ragland, and her team, espccially her fabulous assistant, Elizabeth Lacks. Special thanks go to Andy Martin and Matthew Shear, who warmly welcomed me into the Minotaur and St. Martin's Press family. And thanks to my calm, reasoned agent, Dan Conaway from Writer's House, who took me by the hand in the middle of my career and made the transition easy.

The Lucy Kincaid series has been greatly enhanced by the continuing input from the good men and women of the Sacramento FBI office, in particular Special Agent Steve Dupre and Special Agent Jim Abbott. Jim, who graduated from the FBI Academy in 2009, helped make Lucy's experience as real as possible in both *Stalked* and *Stolen*. And when I told Steve that I'd written myself into a hole in a previous book by giving my character Sean Rogan a crime with a ten-year statute of limitations, he immediately said, "Bank fraud." Steve, you saved my butt. A thousand thank-yous! Thanks also to media representative Kurt Crawford at Quantico, who not only gave me a tour and answered a myriad of questions (some of which I'm sure would have gotten me into trouble had I not been a writer), but has made himself available by e-mail. And a very special thanks to SWAT Team Leader Brian Jones, who always made sure to include me in training scenarios and introduced me to more men with guns than I dreamed possible. If there are any errors or omissions, it's solely my fault.

Dr. Doug Lyle has always been a wealth of information and has helped me with medical details in all of my books, and former cop Robin Burcell has helped with numerous, practical details (like how and when to shoot from the hip in Lucy's novella *Reckless*). That both of these generous professionals are also authors tells you how wonderful the writing community is.

My family has always supported my writing career, and without their support I wouldn't be able to do what I love. My husband Dan has been a rock. My kids have provided me with inspiration and laughs. And my mom has always been my first reader. Love you all!

A round man cannot be expected to fit in
a square hole right away.
He must have time to modify his shape.
—Mark Twain

PROLOGUE

Three weeks ago

Sean Rogan's brother Duke had always known exactly how to twist the knife to make Sean feel like shit, but this time Sean stood firm. It wasn't like he had a choice.

"You haven't changed," Duke said, breaking a long, awkward silence. "You're still the arrogant, irresponsible hacker you were in college."

Sean's jaw tightened so painfully that when he opened his mouth to speak, he heard it pop. "You don't sound surprised."

Duke glared at him. "I'm not."

Sean wasn't above lying when it was necessary, but he hated lying to people he cared about. This time, he didn't have a choice. He couldn't tell his brother the truth. If Sean had any hope of saving his future life with Lucy, he had to let Duke believe Sean had willingly broken the law.

He just hadn't realized that, for years, Duke had been waiting for this. Waiting for Sean to fail.

Duke ran both hands through his hair. "I'll find a way to fix this. But dammit, you went too far this time."

"No."

"You don't think hacking into a pharmaceutical company and stealing files is going too far? You owe me an explanation!"

Sean hated disappointing his brother, but what could he do? "I need you to trust me. Please, Duke."

"You violated my trust."

"No, I didn't. You never trusted me to begin with."

Duke stared at Sean, the vein in his temple visibly pulsing. "Maybe," he said through clenched teeth, "because you've done nothing to earn my trust."

Sean's stomach sank. It didn't matter that Duke had said it in the heat of an argument; he meant it. He'd never trusted Sean.

"I quit," Sean said.

He knew it would come to this, that he'd have to quit RCK, but that didn't make this conversation any easier. Purposely destroying his relationship with his brother, regardless of the reasons why, physically pained him.

"I'm not accepting this! You will make this right."

Sean said, "If you trusted me, you would give me the benefit of the doubt."

Duke's fists were balled, and Sean didn't know if his brother wanted to hit the wall or him. Probably him.

"You really believe that?" Duke said. "That I would let you destroy RCK because you have a misguided sense of loyalty to a criminal like Colton Thayer?" He shook his head. "I never knew you."

Duke was right: He'd never known Sean. Never tried to understand why Sean sometimes couldn't resist crossing the line. To Duke, it was about the act, not the reasons. For Sean, it was always about motive. And his motives had always been solid.

And this time, his motive was to clean his slate so he could have a future with Lucy.

"You're right," Sean said. "You don't know me."

The sound of the front door closing startled Sean. No

one had the front door code except his partner, Patrick Kincaid, who was upstairs avoiding the fight, and Lucy. He glanced at his watch. It was already six thirty? Where had the afternoon gone?

"Sean?" Lucy walked into the living room and looked from him to Duke and back again.

"Lucy—" Sean went to her side. He whispered, "I need to talk to Duke. Can you wait for me in my office?"

Concern clouded her dark eyes, but she said, "Of course."

"No," Duke said from behind Sean. "If you won't listen to me, maybe you'll listen to your girlfriend. You're not only destroying your life by going down this path, you're taking her with you."

Lucy put her hand on Sean's forearm. "Why don't you meet me at Dillon's when you're done?"

Sean was relieved. He didn't want to lie to Lucy, and having this conversation with Duke in front of her was going to make everything worse. "I'll be there as soon as I can."

"You don't get it," Duke said.

He turned and faced his brother, furious that he was dragging Lucy into this. "I do get it. I've changed my mind. I don't want Lucy to leave. I want you to go."

"You've put our entire company at risk. I can't ignore it this time."

"I've never asked you for favors."

"Don't do this, Sean." Duke's voice cracked. He had finally realized that Sean was serious. Now Sean had to hammer in the final nail.

"I've never lived up to your expectations, because I can't be your clone."

"I've never wanted you to be me, Sean. You just have this knack for finding trouble, and you've never grown out of it."

Sean's fists clenched and unclenched. "We're done."

"No—"

"I'm done. The business, the job, everything. I'm *through.*"

Duke slapped his hands down on the dining table. "You always try to justify your mistakes!"

"Therein lies the problem," Sean said. "I didn't make a mistake. But you won't have to worry about my business decisions anymore. I no longer work for you."

Sean needed to get away. Seeing his brother glare at him with such contempt hurt more than he'd thought. He turned to Lucy and the love and trust he saw in her face helped, but he hated not being able to tell her the truth either. She took his hand, her eyes asking questions, but her actions showing that she was on his side.

He wouldn't have been able to do this without Lucy. She'd told him time and again that he was her rock; what she never understood was that she was *his* foundation. Without her, he would never have had the courage to do the right thing when doing the right thing was going to be dangerous to his reputation and freedom. Risking his life had never been a problem; risking jail time had him nearly in a panic.

But he reminded himself that all this, the fight with Duke, quitting RCK, was for a greater good. He had to focus on that.

"Let's go," he said to Lucy.

Duke grabbed his arm and turned him around. "Don't walk out on me. You're part of RCK, you can't just leave."

Sean shrugged Duke's hand off. "Good-bye, Duke." He took Lucy's hand and started down the hall to the front door. He had to get out now. He'd come back later for his things.

He had expected a confrontation with Duke, but not in person. Not like this.

Sean and Lucy went outside. Duke's rental car was

blocking his Mustang. He swore, angry and frustrated. Driving always calmed him down.

"I drove home with Kate after classes and walked here from their house." Dillon and Kate lived three blocks away.

It was just now dark, a beautiful autumn evening, but Sean couldn't enjoy any of it. He squeezed Lucy's hand hard as they walked down the block.

"Sean—"

"Tell me you trust me, Luce."

"You know I trust you."

"I'm taking a security job in New York."

"Is that why Duke's so mad?"

"No. He believes something that isn't true, and I'm not going to waste any more breath explaining." The irony was that Sean had *wanted* Duke to know he was working with his old hacker buddy Colton Thayer. It was all staged, at least on Sean's part.

Duke, though, hadn't been acting. His brother had flown three thousand miles to confront Sean in person. And that made everything much, much harder. Because the lack of trust, the blatant disapproval, couldn't be faked face-to-face. Sean would never forget the contempt Duke showed for him. "He's never trusted me."

"That's not true."

"I wish I were wrong."

"Is this job—permanent?" Lucy's voice hitched, and Sean realized he'd laid this all on her abruptly, nothing like he'd wanted. He'd planned to tell Lucy tonight over a romantic dinner. Patrick was leaving on a late flight to Chicago for an assignment and wouldn't be back until Sunday; they'd have the house all to themselves.

He shook his head. "A few weeks. A month, maybe." He stopped at the corner and touched her face. "I'll be done long before you graduate."

"Who are you working for?"

This was where it was going to get sticky. He'd promised never to lie to her, and he wasn't going to start now. "I can't share any details. It's a strict confidentiality agreement. But," he said quickly, "when I'm done, I'll tell you about it, okay?" He breathed a bit easier. None of that was a lie. He would tell her. He hoped she'd forgive him for keeping her in the dark.

She smiled, but it was unsteady. "We've never seriously talked about what's going to happen when I graduate—"

"That's still a couple months away." He wanted to tell her he'd follow her wherever she went, but right now he couldn't. He didn't know if he'd survive the coming weeks. He didn't know what would happen with RCK, or Duke, or his life. The future was uncertain, and he just needed to get through the next month. "Let me finish this job, Lucy, then we'll make plans."

She nodded, but Sean wished he knew what she was really thinking. She trusted him, and that trust and love were going to help him more than she'd ever know.

He kissed her, as if it would be the last time, though they had all night. "God, I love you, Princess."

"I love you, too." She smiled, but concern clouded her expression. She was trying hard not to show it, but Lucy was an open book, at least to him. "Happy birthday."

"Didn't we go camping last weekend for my birthday?" She sighed dramatically. "We're never going to be able to go on vacation, are we?"

Their camping trip in the Shenandoahs had been a complete bust because they'd ended up being drawn into the search for a missing child, only to discover a major criminal enterprise set up in the middle of nowhere.

"We've tried to plan a trip, and that ended up with you discovering a dead body," Sean said. "Then we tried for spontaneity, and again . . . you discovered a dead body." He kissed her on the nose. "Next time, we'll lock ourselves in a hotel room and order out for room service."

"You'd get bored with me." But she smiled.

"Never." Sean needed Lucy now more than ever. "Good thing I don't leave for New York until Monday." He frowned. "I might not be very good company right now."

He desperately needed to get out of this depression after his fight with Duke. Sean had to keep this night light and fun. Force himself to put the future aside. Lucy was perceptive, and he didn't want her picking up on more than what he'd already told her.

"Dillon and Kate are out with friends," Lucy said. "Instead of a restaurant, why don't we go to their house? I'll cook."

His eyes widened in shock. "You cook?"

She hit him on the arm. "Don't ever let my mother hear you say that." She kissed him. "Tonight's for you. No other people, no conversation. Trust *me*, Sean. Tonight is just for us."

He glanced down the street at his town house. Duke was getting in his car. He wouldn't be coming back.

Good-bye, Duke.

CHAPTER ONE

Present Day
Saturday

Theft came in all shapes and sizes, from grand to small, from violent to peaceful. For Sean Rogan, the most satisfying robbery was stealing from someone who was a criminal, because the victim would never report the break-in. It was also the most dangerous.

The safest theft, and almost as satisfying, was stealing information so the victim never knew they'd been targeted. This was the type of crime where Sean excelled and why his former mentor and friend Colton Thayer had for years wanted him to rejoin the group. It was why Sean had quit the family business. Now there was no turning back.

The target was the CEO of a pharmaceutical company, Pham-Bonner Medical Solutions. PBM was primarily a cancer research company, but they also had their fingers in many other medical pies. They created low-cost vaccines for common diseases, for example. And they had a small division that experimented with vaccines and cures for biological weapons, like anthrax and ricin.

A week before he quit RCK, Sean hacked into PBM to pull vaccine documentation because Colton believed they'd accidentally contaminated a shipment of vaccines with a bio-toxin and were working double time to cover it up. He had some circumstantial evidence pulled from news feeds and press releases, but Colton wanted to destroy the company because he blamed them for the death of his brother, Travis.

The problem was Colton couldn't break through their network, and he had been reaching out to Sean to take the job. It was blatantly illegal, something Duke would never have approved even if it wasn't at the behest of Colton, but the assignment gave Sean an in with Colton. A way to regain his trust.

What Sean found was far more worrisome than a cover-up that hadn't actually resulted in any deaths. It appeared that PBM was not only researching cures for bio-toxins but also creating a bio-weapon themselves. They had a government contract to provide vaccines to low-income communities, but Sean could find no contract that gave them permission to experiment in biological weapons.

Unfortunately, there were only hints and no solid evidence or documentation accessible through their network. That meant Sean needed to go on-site.

The safest way to get on-site was to clone a badge. That's what this exercise tonight was for. The only problem was that Sean didn't think Colton's philanthropic concern about a private company creating biological weapons was the only reason Colton wanted to get inside the building. Ten years ago, it would have been enough. Today, Sean knew that Colton was working for someone else. Someone whose identity Colton wouldn't confide to Sean.

Sean took a long, slow breath as he straightened his bow tie. After tonight, there was no going back.

Skye Jansen walked up next to him and looked at their reflection in the hotel mirror, her dark lipstick glistening against her perfect, straight teeth. "You're still gorgeous in a tux, Sean."

He caught her eyes in the reflection. "Stop."

She gave him a fake quizzical look, her chin tilting
defiantly. There was no doubt in his mind that Skye knew
exactly what she was doing, but she'd never admit it.

"Aren't *you* uptight, sugar."

He stepped away from Skye, not overly concerned
about his appearance. The tux was a fail-safe—in case
he was caught, it would be better if he appeared to be a
guest at the museum charity event and not a thief. But he
wouldn't be caught. This was something he was particularly good at.

Correction: He wouldn't be caught if everyone on his
team did their job right.

This was the third crime Sean had committed in as
many weeks, all in preparation for the big job at Pham-
Bonner Medical. Sean hoped he'd learn exactly what
Colton had planned before Thursday night's job; otherwise he'd be going in blind. He was already getting nervous. He'd known Skye, Colton, and Hunter Nash since
college, but two were new to Colton's group and Sean didn't
trust either one of them. He'd been quietly checking into
their backgrounds, but so far nothing stood out.

What really bothered Sean was that Colton had far too
much money to spend on this project. The overall plan
sounded like Colton, but the execution required access to
a gold card. Colton had never been one for having big
bucks. U.S. Senator Jonathan Paxton was the gold card—
yet Sean's friend hadn't said anything about his benefac-
tor. This greatly worried Sean.

For now, he needed to focus on the job, because one
mistake would cost him his life—or his freedom. Sean
valued both.

Skye took a step toward him and stroked her long fingers down his back. "Sean, honey—"

He turned around and was face-to-face with his ex-
girlfriend. She was still beautiful, blond hair tight with

wild curls that tumbled down her back. She'd maintained the lithe dancer's body she'd cherished, and ten years had turned her even more confident and sexy. She didn't flinch when he crowded her. Her green eyes darkened as she smiled seductively and put her hands on his chest, her red fingernails shining in the light. She leaned up to kiss him.

He sidestepped her, avoiding her lips, and walked across the hotel room.

Skye was his past. His long-ago past. Proximity didn't change the fact that they had been over for ten years and he had no urge for round two.

"Oh, Sean," Skye sighed dramatically. She smiled at her reflection and smoothed out her already-perfect makeup.

They were in the hotel next door to the museum where their target was attending a private charity event, and this was their best shot at getting to CEO Joyce Bonner. They'd considered her house, while she slept, but she had state-of-the-art security and dogs. They also didn't know where she kept her badge at home—could be in her bedroom while she slept. Plus, her two children lived with her— one an adult, one a minor. The presence of other people made things sticky. Colton wasn't violent; in none of their jobs in college, and none since from what Sean could deduce, had anyone been physically hurt.

Going after Bonner's badge at the charity event had been Skye's idea, and it was just like her—big and bold. And smart.

"Sean, I hope you have your head in the game."

"It's always in the game," he said. "I'm just not going to take your crap anymore."

She rolled her eyes. "Oh, baby, you are so wrong about me."

Hardly.

Skye's phone vibrated on the dresser. She picked it up and responded to the text. "I'm on, babe. Don't be late."

He didn't say anything but watched her swish out in her red beaded dress. He checked the time. He had twenty minutes before he had to be in place. The hotel had a museum access hall open during regular hours but closed during evening events. He'd determined that route was the easiest to breach.

He took out his cell phone and called Lucy.

"Hello," he said when she answered.

"Sean, hold on." He heard her excuse herself, the clink of dishes and utensils, the hum of voices in the background. Dinner at the FBI Academy's cafeteria.

A moment later, Lucy said, "It's good to hear your voice."

"You stole my line. Sorry to interrupt dinner."

"I'm done. Just chatting."

"How's everything?"

"Good. We're past the mid-point. Nine more weeks. It feels surreal."

"You're going to graduate top of your class."

She laughed, a deep and genuine tone that Sean loved to hear, especially when he was with her. He hadn't seen her in three weeks, since the weekend before he moved to New York. He missed her more than he could say.

"I'm sorry I had to cancel our plans this weekend." He'd hoped to get away to see her—he needed the connection to his real life, to the life he hoped to regain when this was over. But now that Colton had set the schedule for the week, Sean wouldn't be able to leave.

"You're busy, and it gives me more time to study. We have a PT test on Tuesday and the big legal test on Wednesday. That's the one I'm worried about."

"You'll ace it."

"I wish I had your confidence. What about you? Are you enjoying New York or just working?"

"Mostly working."

"Have you seen Suzanne?"

He'd avoided FBI Special Agent Suzanne Madeaux for the three weeks he'd been in Manhattan. He and Lucy had met Suzanne last February when he was looking for his runaway niece and tracked her to New York. Since, he, Lucy, and Suzanne had become friends, and Lucy had told Suzanne that Sean had taken a job in New York. Twice Suzanne called him to meet for a beer. Sean had ignored the first call, then told her the second time he was swamped with work. She'd asked questions; he evaded and could tell she was irritated. As long as she was only irritated and not suspicious, Sean thought.

"We haven't connected. My hours are erratic."

"Are you okay? You sound down."

Lucy was perceptive—Sean should have known better than to call her. He forced a smile into his voice. "I'm only depressed because I had to cancel on you, princess. I miss you."

"Miss you, too. Since you're busy, why don't I fly up to New York next weekend and we'll have dinner?"

"Sounds extravagant."

"I planned on spending the night."

He laughed, even though he realized he could never allow Lucy to visit him in the city while he was still working for Colton. It would jeopardize everything, and he couldn't risk her finding out what he was doing.

"I'll see if I can swing it," he said. "But I should only be here for a couple more weeks." He hoped it was shorter than that. It might be over after Thursday. Or that operation might be just another move in the game.

"Talk to you tomorrow?"

"Same bat time, same bat channel."

She laughed. "I love you, Batman."

"Love you, Batgirl."

He hung up. His chest was tight and his eyes burned. *You didn't lie to her.*

Not lying didn't mean he was telling the truth. He

didn't want to deceive Lucy, but he couldn't avoid it. Not now, with so much at stake. He had to give Lucy a clean slate. He had to make amends for his past. All of it, the good and the bad.

He leaned over the dresser, his palms on the cool, glass top, and breathed deeply. Ten years ago deception had come easily for him. Even now, when he shouldn't be committing a crime, the thrill was electric. The danger drew him in; bigger and harder challenges enticed him. He'd grown bored with RCK long before he quit. Even opening his own office in D.C. with his best friend, Lucy's brother Patrick, had become predictable. Sean feared there was something wrong with him that he only felt he was valued when he did the impossible—when he hacked unbreakable systems, when he manipulated situations to obtain information that was unobtainable.

He had always lived larger than life because that's what gave him his edge. But now? It might be his downfall. He had thought he'd put this life behind him, that when he came back he'd be no good at any of it.

He was better than when he was twenty. Smarter. Sharper. More focused.

And there lay the biggest problem. He craved the adrenaline rush that came after a successful job. He didn't hate living on the edge. And that terrified him. Because he loved Lucy more and didn't want to jeopardize the amazing relationship they had.

But today he had no choice.

He pushed back from the dresser and avoided the mirrors in the room. He double-checked his equipment and secured the small cloning device in his pocket. Anyone would think it was a cell phone.

He left his doubts and fears in the hotel room and went to do the job. Calm and focused.

And no small bit excited.

He took the elevator down to the ballroom level and

mingled with a wedding party through the foyer until he reached the tunnel-like hall. He glanced at his watch. Right on time. He dropped a jammer behind a potted plant, which would disrupt the nearby cameras so he could slip in and out without being detected.

Once in the tunnel, Sean used an employee badge Evan had swiped to access the private hall that led to the museum. Sean moved smoothly through the museum foyer toward the restrooms, where Evan palmed him the PBM badge as they passed and left without a word.

In a bathroom stall, it took Sean only four minutes to clone the badge and verify there was no hidden security code.

He pocketed the badge and walked back through the foyer. When two patrons smiled at him, he returned the smile and pretended to admire a horrendous metal sculpture. People paid good money for *that*?

When the couple moved on, so did Sean, heading toward the coatroom. The coatroom was between the main entrance and the tunnel access, but the employees could access it through the rear corridor. There were no cameras there, only security on individual doors.

When they'd had the final planning meeting for this operation, Evan had told Sean that the museum used a standard digital card-key system for their employees that worked on all private doors. So when Sean lifted the badge to the panel—the badge that had already opened the door from the tunnel to the museum—he expected the lock to pop open.

It didn't. He scrutinized the panel and realized it was different from the panel he'd accessed earlier. It appeared to have been upgraded. He glanced at the other doors on this wing, and they all had the same security panel, which was different from the panels in the public parts of the museum. Why didn't Evan know about the two layers of security?

Sean examined the panel and realized that the equipment was built by a small, elite company called Hawk Electronics, who worked almost exclusively for RCK. No doubt the security on this door was an RCK system and there was nothing "standard" about it except its appearance.

One of the key components of RCK security systems was that every access was logged—there was never a hidden back door. Even admins would be logged. Sean had an admin clearance; even if Duke had locked him out, he had his own backdoor admin account. His brother would get an email that indicated that an admin had bypassed security—when, where, and how.

There was only one way around it, and Sean hated to do it. But he had no choice—there was no other way into the secure coatroom without being caught on-camera. And they couldn't risk Skye being caught putting the badge back in Joyce Bonner's purse, since Skye had already pickpocketed her once.

Sean entered the nearby employee elevator, which had no cameras. He stopped the elevator as soon as the doors shut and took out his small palm computer. He logged in through the RCK back door that he'd created, maneuvered directly to the RCK server, and wrote a program that would manipulate the admin e-mail system. Instead of messages going to Duke and the RCK webmaster, all admin e-mails would go directly to Sean for the next ten minutes. The breach would only be found if someone sharp was specifically looking for it, and then they'd only see that the admin system had been compromised—they wouldn't see Sean's blind e-mail, because it would self-delete.

He unlocked the elevator, checked the halls, and went back to the coatroom door. He used his admin code to get into the room and slipped to the side as the coat girl came in with two more jackets. She hung them up and left, not noticing Sean standing in the corner.

He didn't dare breathe heavily. Skye had sent him Bonner's coat-check number—81—and Sean found her long brown mink in the proper slot. Since Bonner was left-handed, he slipped the badge into the left pocket.

Sean was out in less than two minutes, but he'd exposed himself to the one person who might catch him—his brother.

Evan was going to pay for his screwup.

CHAPTER TWO

FBI Special Agent Deanna Brighton once had a career that was headed for the stars. She'd graduated from Quantico when she was twenty-six, after four years as a CPA. When she was twenty-eight, she'd developed a state-of-the-art tracking system to trace illegal financial transactions over the Internet, pooling her unit's resources with the cybercrime unit to create what she'd billed as an impenetrable, foolproof net over child pornographers and terrorists, all in one tight, brilliant program.

"I had everything," she muttered to herself. "Until you."

She stared at the thick, worn, unofficial file that she'd been building for years. The official FBI record—the portion that wasn't sealed—was thin.

The faded tab mocked her: *ROGAN, SEAN TYLER.*

Sean Rogan had hacked into her program and destroyed her *life*. The arrogance of his actions, that it was *no big deal* for him to destroy sixteen months of hard work in one day, should have been enough to put him in prison. But he had walked away after a couple of days in jail and a slap on the wrist. That she'd managed to get him expelled from Stanford was no real consolation for the damage he'd done to her career.

Deanna's boss had been furious with her because he'd backed her claims that the system was ready to go wide. After Rogan hacked it, her boss had shut down her program and disbanded her task force. Her colleagues ostracized her because the failure had been public and embarrassing to their unit. She was lucky she hadn't been fired.

That was twelve years ago, and she'd hated Sean Rogan ever since.

Deanna had no idea how thick Rogan's sealed files were. That's the benefit of having friends and family in high places—your crimes were erased. That he also had high security clearance unnerved her, because she'd never have approved him to empty the garbage at FBI headquarters. That his clearance was higher than *hers* hurt, a twisting hot pain in her gut that the agency she had dedicated her life to trusted a criminal more than her.

She'd spent the last twelve and a half years, since she'd crossed paths with him, building her own file on Rogan. It was largely conjecture and most of it had no legal meaning. But she was learning everything about him. She *would* catch him breaking the law and it would be so obvious that not even the director of the FBI himself could keep Sean Rogan out of prison.

And if she had to, she'd turn to the media.

She'd tracked Rogan from California to Boston and back to California, but getting the FBI to transfer her had proved difficult. She was always a year behind him. When he moved to D.C. last year she asked for a transfer; the closest she could get was New York City. She took it.

It was fate that Rogan was now in Manhattan. And good news for her that her informant told her something big was about to go down with Colton Thayer's gang of cyberthieves. She'd been tracking Thayer because he was a connection to Rogan. This was no coincidence. Her gut told her Rogan was going to make his big play—and she planned on being there to slap the cuffs on him. She couldn't wait to read him his rights—again. Because this time, he would face serious charges and she'd have cause to open an investigation into everything he'd done in the last twelve years.

Her partner, Steve Gannon, walked by her cubicle, briefcase in hand. "Go home," he told her. "It's late. It's *Saturday*."

She smiled thinly and shook her head. "I want to get this done."

"You're not still going over that security tape?"

"Two days before Sean Rogan arrives in the city for an undetermined stay, my informant tells me he's working with Colton Thayer again and something big is in the works. Then we catch him on tape during a routine surveillance? That's no coincidence." They'd caught Rogan entering the stock exchange even though he had no business there.

"Nothing went down at the exchange that day."

"But there's no record that he's living here. No apartment, no utilities in his name or in the name of RCK East. He's *here,* but he's off the grid. What's he doing? I guarantee it's not legal."

"We have no tangible proof that Colton Thayer is breaking the law, and no proof that Rogan is involved if he is."

Steve was right, but just because there was no proof didn't mean they weren't guilty. They were guilty of *something*.

She had to keep Steve on her side. She and Steve had been working together on the white-collar squad since she'd been transferred earlier this year. Though she had four more years in the Bureau than he did, he was the lead agent. He was well liked among everyone in the division and others in the building, while she had continued to make enemies among her peers. She tried to be likable, but she was smart and tenacious and confrontational. And White-Collar generally attracted the type of agents who didn't want to make waves, who didn't want to go out into the field, but preferred to catch bad guys the old-fashioned way—through the paper trail.

She was different. Driven. Bureaucrats didn't like "different."

"Look at these." She slid over a file of pictures she'd taken of Rogan over the last month. "Rogan has met with Colton and his team multiple times." Colton's house, a couple restaurants, walking in Central Park with the blond woman. "If I just had the resources for full surveillance—"

"You pitched your idea and lost. Can your informant get you more? Something tangible? A location or plan?"

"I'm working on it."

Colton Thayer had been on the short list for a myriad of thefts, but nothing stuck. Sean Rogan had been the computer genius behind Thayer when they were at MIT, and though they had hardly spoken in nearly ten years—at least that Deanna could find—that all changed two months ago. Something was going on, and she was going to catch them. She'd turn Colton Thayer on Rogan in a heartbeat—she didn't care about Thayer; he was an ideologue, a hacktivist who wanted to make a political statement. Rogan was far more dangerous.

He was going to pay for damaging her career.

"Deanna—"

"Go home, Steve. I'm fine." She forced herself to relax and smile. "Really, I won't be here more than an hour."

He hesitated. "Just don't get obsessed about this guy. He's not worth throwing away your career."

Steve walked away and Deanna breathed easier. Rogan had almost ruined her once; she was certainly not throwing away her career in pursuing him. He was bad news and would embarrass the FBI when all his crimes came out and she could prove the higher-ups had protected him. It was only a matter of time before she found someone to turn. Steve Gannon was a good agent, but he didn't understand the problem that Rogan had created within the Bureau. He was protected because the principals of RCK, Duke Rogan and JT Caruso, were chummy with the leaders in national headquarters. Deanna had figured that out through old-fashioned research. Caruso had been in the Marines with the assistant director, Rick Stockton, who had the ear of the director himself. Rogan was married to an FBI agent in Sacramento. Sean's partner, Patrick Kincaid, was related by marriage to several key FBI personnel. But now that Sean had split with RCK, he was fair game. Deanna would build a case against him that was so completely watertight he would suffocate. She couldn't wait to watch him fall.

Once Steve was gone—and Deanna was sure he wasn't coming back—she reopened a file she'd recently uncovered. She didn't want to explain to Steve how she'd gotten it, because he already thought she was obsessing on Rogan.

Lucy Kincaid.

Rogan's girlfriend was his Achilles' heel.

Deanna had learned about Kincaid nine months ago when Rogan had come to New York and worked with one of her colleagues, Suzanne Madeaux, on the Cinderella Strangler investigation. Deanna had only heard about it after the fact—White-Collar didn't talk much with the violent-crimes squad. But she'd read the entire file and found an interesting note about Lucia "Lucy" Kincaid, an FBI candidate assisting on the case. At first Deanna hadn't thought there was a personal connection—"Kincaid" had been tacked onto the name of "Rogan-Caruso" a few years back, and Deanna had already dug around into Rogan's partner, Patrick Kincaid. But then she learned that Lucy was romantically involved with Rogan.

Deanna had to be very cautious about how she investigated the Kincaids, because every file she came across was secure. To ask for permission would have alerted her boss that she was pursuing something beyond her scope, and she didn't want to be told to stand down. She'd have to defy the order; she would rather do it quietly and ask for forgiveness rather than permission.

But because she didn't want anyone to know she was looking into Lucy Kincaid, it took Deanna months to investigate her. She'd put together a stunning dossier on the new FBI recruit.

Kincaid was an agent at the FBI Academy at Quantico, set to graduate in December. She had a background in both forensics and psychology and had graduated in the top 10 percent of her class at Georgetown, then earned a master's in criminal psychology. She'd worked a variety of jobs from congressional aide to assistant pathologist at the Washington, D.C., Medical Examiner's Office.

She'd also been instrumental in putting a former FBI agent in prison for conspiracy to commit murder.

All this was surface information. Every time Deanna tried to get more than the most superficial intelligence, she hit a brick wall. Sealed records, missing files, redacted passages. Lucy Kincaid had secrets. Lots of them. How could the FBI have allowed her to go through the Academy when she was romantically involved with a known computer hacker? And from what Deanna had uncovered, they were pretty serious—serious enough that she figured the best way to get to Rogan was through his girlfriend.

Deanna again looked at the surveillance photos she'd taken in the park. It didn't look like Sean was all that exclusive. She hadn't actually seen Rogan making out with Skye Jansen, but they'd been an item in college. Maybe Rogan broke it off with his girlfriend. That would be even better—Deanna would turn the bitter ex-girlfriend's screws tight until Lucy Kincaid snapped and spilled everything to her about Rogan's new game. And if not? One look at these photos and Lucy Kincaid would tell Deanna everything. A woman scorned looked to revenge. Deanna pulled out the most damning picture and smiled.

Her personal cell phone rang and she smiled even wider when she recognized the caller ID. She'd almost given up that Special Agent Meredith White would do the right thing.

"Deanna Brighton?"

"Hello, Meredith. Thank you so much for calling back."

"I gave a lot of thought to our last conversation. Did you tell anyone I spoke to you?"

"No one. I promise, this is between you and me."

"Last month I had a visit from someone in headquarters reminding me that the application process was confidential and asking if I'd spoken to anyone about it. They told me if I said anything I would be reprimanded."

Deanna's mind churned. Why was headquarters hammering this point? Sure, the panels were confidential, but Deanna had served on a hiring panel for a year and it was no big deal.

"I assure you, anything you tell me is between us." Deanna thought ahead: Meredith was scared, but she was willing—Deanna needed to give her a bone. "I'm investigating Ms. Kincaid's boyfriend, and I believe there may be a security breach. No one in my office, outside of my boss and partner, knows I'm working on this case," she lied smoothly. Steve knew she was pursuing Rogan, but didn't know to what extent. And her boss had only given her permission to spend a limited amount of time on Colton Thayer—she hadn't even told him about Rogan's connection. "I haven't told anyone about our initial contact," she said. "As you know, Rogan's family is connected to headquarters. I need to keep this investigation under the radar until I have incontrovertible proof, or he'll walk again."

Silence. Had she said too much? Sounded too eager? Deanna backtracked. She added, "I probably shouldn't have told you all that. But I want you to trust me, Meredith. I won't get you in any trouble." She held her breath, waiting.

Meredith said, "Tomorrow. Central Park West, across from the Museum of Natural History. Juan agreed to meet with you, and doesn't want to run into anyone from the Bureau."

Deanna's heart raced. "You ask for my confidentiality yet you told someone about our conversation?"

"I'm in D.C. Juan Martinez is assigned to the JFK regional office. He was transferred last month right after being questioned by someone from national headquarters. He thinks his transfer had something to do with the hiring panel—we were disbanded prematurely."

"Who is this girl?" Deanna asked. "The daughter of a director?" Deanna knew she wasn't but hoped Meredith would share some inside information.

"She has a lot of friends in a lot of places. Tread carefully."

Deanna was sick and tired of nepotism and special favors. She'd never gotten a special favor in her life, never had anyone watch her back or protect her. Everything she'd gotten she'd earned—and then to have a weasel like Sean Rogan take everything she'd earned the hard way was unacceptable. He would pay. So would his girlfriend. Deanna would make sure Lucy was kicked out of the Academy if she didn't help put Sean Rogan in prison. No one was above the law. Especially a cop.

"Natural history museum. I'll be there."

She hung up, heart racing. Giddy and nervous. She was close; she felt it in her gut. Once she had the goods on

Lucy Kincaid, Deanna would leverage that into evidence against Rogan. If Deanna had to take down Lucy Kincaid before she could take down Sean, she would do it. Collateral damage.

Kincaid should have never gotten involved with a criminal in the first place. Whatever happened from this day on was now Lucy Kincaid's choice. She could choose to side with a criminal and lose her career and her freedom, or she could choose to do the right thing and keep both.

CHAPTER THREE

Sean was the last to arrive at Colton Thayer's carriage house, an hour after the heist. He strode over to Evan and pinned him to the wall. "You knew it was an RCK security system."

Evan deadpanned him. "I did not."

"Bullshit."

"Knock it off." Hunter was ever the peacemaker. "Colton is going to be here any minute."

Sean stared at Evan. "I'm happy to explain to Colton how Evan jeopardized our operation."

Evan pushed Sean and Sean let him walk away. He didn't know how much time he was going to have before Duke showed up in New York. Sean was good—one of the best—but it was an RCK system, a system he'd helped design. If Duke smelled a breach, he'd be on a plane immediately. He wouldn't be able to prove it was Sean, but Sean hadn't made a secret of being in New York. Duke wasn't an idiot; he'd track Sean down, because the lack of evidence would be damning.

"I didn't screw up anything." Evan strode across the polished wood floor to the bar. He opened the mini-fridge and took out a bottle of champagne. "It was a success, all around."

He popped the cork and everyone, except Sean, gathered around the bar for a glass.

Sean went to the kitchen and retrieved a beer.

Though everything had changed, including some faces, Sean felt like he was back in college. It would have been so easy for him to stick with Colton ten years ago and continue down the wrong path. There were things about their group that Sean missed. The friendship. The excitement. The adrenaline when they collectively figured out how to hack into a system. Sean had become smarter, sharper, and better because of what he'd learned—what they all learned, together. Because of Colton, Hunter, and even Skye if Sean wanted to be honest with himself, he was who he was today—for better or worse.

Yet . . . this wasn't college. Evan was new, and Sean didn't care that he'd been with Colton for the last two years—Sean didn't trust him. Carol was even newer to the group and sleeping with Colton. Sean was now considered the outsider, practically a stranger.

He glanced over at Hunter, who was sitting across the room, in the corner of the sectional sofa, not really paying attention to the confrontation. Hunter was smarter than all of them, but he was the stereotypical anti-social nerd. He didn't know how to talk to people on any level other than his. He had a limited wardrobe, and it was Sean who had convinced Hunter when they were in college that daily showers were a necessity. It's not that he was a slob; it's that he didn't think about personal hygiene. Hunter was a good guy and shouldn't have been working for Colton on the wrong side of the law. He could have been making good money at any technology company, except for one roadblock: fear. He liked his longtime group of friends and knowing what was expected of him. The world terrified Hunter. He had a conspiracy theory about everything.

Sean drank half his beer before he rejoined the group in the living room. Skye sauntered over to him with a glass of champagne. "This is for you."

"I'm fine." He held up his beer and sipped.

"You were amazing," she said. "Like old times."

"This isn't old times." He stared at Skye. It was hard not to let the past creep in and take over. He'd thought he'd loved Skye when they were together. They were both wild, adventurous, and the adrenaline-fueled sex was mind-blowing—but he didn't know what love really meant when he was nineteen and Skye was twenty-one. Lust plus excitement didn't equal love.

"You used to be so much more fun, Sean." She pouted and ran a finger over his lips.

Sean brushed past her and walked over to the bar. "If Duke comes to New York, he's going to figure out I hacked the system."

Evan stared at him with ice blue eyes. "Not if you're any good. No one should know there was a breach at all. Unless you screwed up."

Sean regretted losing his temper. He had to learn self-control with Evan or risk everything he'd been working toward for the past month.

Hunter grinned at something Skye said to him that Sean couldn't hear. "We rocked," Hunter continued. "It was just like our Indiana Jones days. Remember the system around Professor Houston's museum?"

Skye's eyes twinkled. "For the time, it was state-of-the-art."

"And Sean and I had to work the two separate systems simultaneously to take it down. Even one second off and we would have been busted."

"But you did it," Skye said. "And we returned the artifacts the professor claimed he never found."

"That guy was weird," Hunter said. "Who wants ancient bones in their bedroom, anyway? Creepy."

"The museum that funded the project," Sean said. "Though you're right—Houston was a freak."

For more than two years, the group had been inseparable. Sean, Skye, Colton, and Hunter. But all good things changed—or came to an end.

Sean leaned against the back of the couch and smiled down at Hunter. Hunter would have fit in well at RCK—as long as he never went into the field. He remembered everything he saw and could monitor simultaneous feeds and transmissions better than anyone else Sean knew. Hunter had saved their bacon more than once in his role as surveillance master.

Skye sat down next to Hunter and linked her arm through his. "My favorite job was breaking into the police commissioner's house and reclaiming the drugs he'd stolen from the evidence locker, then putting them back. That was exciting."

"And dangerous," Sean reminded her. "I still think we should have turned him in, not saved his ass."

"It wasn't saved," Hunter said. "He still lost his job over the scandal, but at least those drugs didn't make it out on the street."

"Let's take the champagne and go to the roof," Carol said. She grabbed a second bottle and led the way. Sean retrieved another beer and followed.

It was eleven in the evening and New York was bright with lights. The Upper East Side was quiet and peaceful—a place Sean could easily see himself living. In fact, the narrow carriage house was the type of house Sean could picture for himself and Lucy. Five stories, on the edge of the city, close enough to never feel disconnected, but far enough on the edge for privacy.

Ten years ago, he and Skye, Colton, and Hunter had done a lot of jobs together, things Colton set up. Good jobs—illegal, but not for their own personal gain. Sean had been so invested in their projects, especially after what happened at Stanford. He'd learned a lot about trusting the authorities—namely, they weren't trustworthy.

Colton was picky about which assignments they took and they spent more time planning than anything, but for four geniuses who were bored in school and with life, all with chips on their shoulders, the ability to circumvent any computer system was heady. They all thought they were gods, and in some ways they were. They saw a virtual world that could be controlled and manipulated, easier than people. They didn't want or need recognition, except among one another. They went out of their way to avoid attention, or the media.

At least, in the beginning.

"Remember the time we shut down the traffic lights?" Skye said as she lounged under a heat lamp and looked at the night sky. The lights from Manhattan erased all but the brightest stars.

"Showed the city that they had a security hole a mile wide," Hunter said.

Colton had a thing for hacktivism—hacking into secure systems to show weakness but not stealing anything. Colton took jobs primarily to keep them all in the latest equipment and to pay for the carriage house, but what he liked best was exposing flaws in systems. Making money was second to making a point.

"You'd think after Nine-Eleven they'd have tightened up the network," Carol said, "but Colton said it was just as vulnerable."

"It hasn't gotten much better," a voice said.

They turned and watched Colton Thayer walk across the roof to where they were celebrating. Colton was barely five foot nine, but he walked tall and dressed well. Sean had been accused of using his charm as a weapon, but

Colton had charm down to a science. When he smiled, you'd believe anything he said.

Until Sean had moved to New York three weeks ago, he hadn't seen Colton in ten years. They'd talked on occasion—primarily when Colton was trying to recruit Sean for a job—but he had done his best to keep his past firmly rooted in the past. He'd never taken a job until now, because Sean knew that as soon as he was back inside, there would be no leaving.

Colton was hard to say no to.

Sean had mixed feelings about this entire operation, and the primary reason was because he didn't want to hurt Colton. He'd helped Sean through the darkest time of his life, when his brother Duke had all but abandoned him after his expulsion from Stanford. Duke had pulled strings to get Sean into MIT even though Sean had told him he didn't want to go. Colton had listened when Sean doubted everything he believed and missed his parents more than when they'd first died. Colton had been Sean's rock, and he would never forget it.

Sean smiled and sipped his beer. "We missed you at tonight's festivities, C.," he said.

Colton smiled broadly, which lit up his entire face, from his green eyes down to the dimple on his chin.

"You're finally back where you belong, Rogan."

CHAPTER FOUR

The adrenaline rush from the heist had faded by the time Sean arrived back at his apartment.

He went up to his fourth-floor corner flat, a spacious, two-room apartment with windows on two walls. He liked the place, which he'd leased under a shell company, but hadn't spent much time here. Most of the work he did was on the second floor—in the studio the FBI had rented under an assumed name for FBI Special Agent Noah Armstrong.

Sean grabbed a stack of mail off his counter as a cover, in case he'd been followed. It was clear the level of trust between Evan and Sean was mutual—it didn't exist. Even though Sean had gone a roundabout way home, he couldn't be certain he wasn't followed. He swept continually for any electronic surveillance—but good old-fashioned foot-work could be just as effective.

Sean took the mail and went downstairs to Noah's studio. It was well after midnight, but Noah wouldn't sleep until Sean checked in. Sean could have called, but he needed to tell Noah what had happened—much more than what he was willing to share over the phone.

"Here's mail that was delivered to my box again," Sean said when Noah opened his door.

"Want a beer?"

"Sounds great." Sean shut the door behind him. Noah tossed the envelopes on a chair and went back to his desk.

Sean said, "Didn't you say *beer?*"

Noah gave him a look that Sean couldn't quite read, then walked over to his refrigerator and grabbed a bottle for each of them. Sean wasn't surprised that the beer of a "brewer" and "patriot" was Noah's drink of choice; it suited the former Air Force pilot.

Sean sat at the table and Noah sat across from him. "What happened?" Noah asked.

The FBI loft was one large, sparsely furnished room. Functional. The bed and couch were almost incidental—no television, no radio, only a laptop, printer, and tidy desk. Noah did most of the work at the secondhand dining table. The file cabinet was new, and Sean suspected all the drawers were full. He wondered how many of the files related to his past.

He said, "We have a problem."

"Have?"

"Evan set me up. The museum's internal security is an RCK design. I had to reroute admin protocols for the duration of the job. I covered my tracks, but I helped design the RCK system. If someone on their end is specifically looking for a breach, they'll see it and there's nothing I can do."

"Will RCK know it was you?"

"They won't have proof, but through the process of elimination Duke will know."

"We'll cross that bridge when we come to it," Noah said.

"I don't think you understand. My brother knows I'm the only one who can break into the admin system. He may not come to the conclusion immediately, but he's going to be suspicious. Especially since he's been trying to keep tabs on me since I quit."

"How do you know he's been tracking you?"

"He's been calling Lucy to find out when she talks to me. He tried to get my phone number from her, but she respected my wish not to talk to Duke while I'm working here. I have a trace on my RCK computer in D.C. He's been pinging it to see if I've been logging in remotely and bypassing his servers. And then—"

Noah put up his hand. "I get it. He wants to know what you're up to. There's nothing we can do about it now without reading him in, and Stockton wants to hold off as long as possible. You said yourself you think it's all going down on Thursday."

"It's only going to end if we have the evidence against Paxton."

"It's going to end when I say it ends."

Sean stared at Noah. They weren't friends, but they weren't enemies.

Noah said, "Why do you think your buddy set you up? Maybe he really didn't know."

"Evan is not my buddy," Sean said.

"You're supposed to be on the same team, aren't you? Working for Thayer?"

Sean conceded that point. "Evan knew. He denied it, but he knew. It was a test—to see if I would reveal RCK trade secrets as well as embarrass RCK. If it gets out that one of RCK's key security people has gone to the dark side, it will destroy everything Duke has worked for."

"Just Duke? What about you?"

"Corporate security is all my brother. It's his division."

"I'm sorry." He didn't sound sorry.

"Duke's not stupid, Noah. Eventually, he's going to figure out I'm working for Colton. He'll interfere, thinking he's protecting me."

"Let's hope it's after we're finished."

Sean had never pegged Noah as a wait-and-see guy, but even he knew they were in so deep there was no pulling out. It was more his tone that irritated Sean. After everything that happened this past month, now Noah copped his authoritarian nature?

"What's your problem?" Sean asked.

"I don't have a problem." Noah was focused on the spreadsheet in front of him.

Sean grabbed it, and Noah clasped his hand around Sean's wrist.

"Let go," Sean said.

"Drop it."

They stared at each other a moment. Sean let go of the spreadsheet, now wrinkled, and Noah let go of his hand simultaneously.

"You haven't liked me from the minute we met," Sean said. "Though you never told me, I assumed it had something to do with one of my brothers, because we'd never crossed paths before."

"You've always known I've had issues with RCK and the gray areas you play in."

Sean shook his head. "This was personal."

Noah smiled, but his pale blue eyes turned icy. He sat back in his chair and sipped his beer. "You want to play shrink now."

Sean said seriously, "I want to live." He leaned forward. "What scares me is that you are the only one in a position to protect my ass and sometimes I get the feeling you want to take me out yourself."

Noah didn't blink. "The past isn't important, Sean."

"Don't lie to yourself. The past is *always* important. Do you think I'd be here now if it weren't?"

Noah said, "You're here *now* to earn your get-out-of-jail-free card."

Noah didn't even try to keep the contempt out of his voice.

Sean abruptly pushed back from the table and stood. His chair fell backwards. "You really don't know me, Special Agent Armstrong."

Sean left the apartment. Why had he let Noah get inside his head like that?

He needed to talk to Lucy, but it wasn't safe to do so. But he couldn't go up to his too-small, too-claustrophobic apartment where he'd just think about the past. The good, the bad, and the very, very ugly.

He left the building to clear his head but feared he'd made a serious mistake trusting Noah Armstrong.

Noah had baited Sean on purpose, and he regretted it.

He was letting his personal feelings cloud his interactions. How could he not? Rogan-Caruso Protective Services had a long-standing reputation worldwide, long before "Kincaid" had been added to the masthead. Sean's three older brothers had built the company from the ground up after the deaths of their parents. They had their fingers in a lot of pies and didn't always play by the rules. Noah had been an officer in the Air Force for ten years, and rules were there for a reason. Noah had indirectly butted heads with Rogan-Caruso operations, so when he met Sean nearly a year ago he assumed he was just like the others. Especially his brother Liam, whom Noah had dealt with several times overseas. Rogan's parents were inventors who created gadgets for the military, and after their deaths Liam and his twin sister had taken over the overseas operations until they left RCK to start their own enterprise.

When Noah had first met Sean, he'd seen Liam in him. Arrogant. Cocky. Manipulative. But Sean had something that Liam didn't, and it took Noah months to see it.

Honor. It's what separated Sean from his brother, what made Noah not despise him. Unlike his brother, Sean had proved he was willing to risk his life for others. Noah didn't always like how Sean got results; he didn't like private security companies like Rogan-Caruso-Kincaid taking the law into their own hands. But in the end, Noah reluctantly looked the other way because sometimes the system failed and RCK could right wrongs.

Besides, he'd wanted Sean as part of this investigation, knowing full well what he was getting into.

But everything Noah knew about Sean made him wonder if he had really changed. He'd fallen comfortably back into his old gang. There were crimes he'd committed that he could never be prosecuted for because the statute of limitations was up. And these new crimes were protected by Sean's current immunity agreement with the FBI. Sean was a lucky guy in so many ways, skirting past the law, making his own rules, using his wits and charm to get his way. The potential hiccup in his life plan— going to prison for a nine-year-old crime—was being cleansed as they spoke, simply because there were worse bad guys than Sean.

For ten months, almost for as long as Noah had known Sean, Noah'd been quietly investigating U.S. Senator Jonathan Paxton. No easy feat considering that Paxton was a senior-ranked member of the Senate Judiciary Committee, which oversaw the FBI. But there were too many questions after two former FBI agents with a connection to Paxton went to jail for running a vigilante group that targeted sex offenders. Paxton had funded the front organization, and while so far the white-collar division hadn't been able to find any financial evidence that he had paid for hits, Noah's gut told him Paxton had been involved.

But neither of the agents was talking, and terms of their plea agreements allowed them to remain silent. Noah thought they'd gotten off far too easy, but he understood the pressure that the U.S. Attorney's Office was under. The agents had killed known sex offenders—brutal rapists and child molesters who had been released early. The media attention, not to mention finding a jury pool that would convict, were both obstacles the Justice Department didn't want to deal with during an election year.

But Noah thought there was far more to the scheme than killing sex offenders. After talking to Paxton in the course of another investigation over the summer, Noah got the feeling that Paxton was involved again in something very shady. Only it was impossible to get a warrant on a hunch and Paxton would use the law to his advantage.

In the course of his off-book investigation, Noah had learned that Paxton had paid Colton Thayer a substantial sum of money for consulting. Research into Thayer revealed that he'd been the subject of multiple investigations for hacking and high-end cybercrimes. Investigations that had been stalled because of lack of evidence.

And he had gone to college with Sean Rogan.

That's when Noah took his suspicions about Senator Paxton to Assistant Director Rick Stockton. And Rick had decided to bring in Sean.

Noah wasn't 100 percent confident that Sean was even now squeaky clean. He feared Sean's past not only was going to continue to resurface but also would taint the one thing Noah knew Sean cared more about than himself: Lucy.

And for that reason alone, Noah was willing to do whatever it took to save Sean.

CHAPTER FIVE

Sunday

If Deanna weren't so determined to put Sean Rogan in prison, she might have enjoyed Sunday afternoon in Central Park.

She sat on the bench directly across from the museum and glanced around. She didn't know what Juan Martinez looked like, but by the name she assumed he was Hispanic. He'd most likely be alone. She was ten minutes early, so she tried to relax and enjoy her surroundings while keeping an eye out for Martinez.

The leaves in the park were starting to turn, just hints of gold and orange. Autumn happened so fast—it seemed that just yesterday the park had been green. Now it was multi-colored. When was she going to sit still again? When the park was dead in winter?

Today was even more beautiful because she would have the information she needed to do her job.

An attractive Hispanic man wearing Dockers and a crisp white polo shirt approached from the north. He sat next to her. Younger than she expected, in his early thirties.

"Deanna," he said in greeting.

"Yes. Juan Martinez?"

He assessed her, nodded. "Let's walk."

They rose from the bench and started along one of the paths leading into Central Park. It was more crowded than Deanna liked, but what could she expect on a clear autumn day?

"I almost didn't come," Juan said, "except I promised Meredith. And, ultimately, it's the right thing to do."

Deanna had plenty of questions, but she started at the beginning.

"Meredith told me that you sat with her last year on the D.C. hiring panel."

"Correct. From September until March. It was supposed to be a one-year assignment, but they disbanded our panel in March."

"Because of Lucy Kincaid."

"That wasn't explicitly stated, but both Meredith and I felt that because we voiced our concerns over the process we were reassigned."

"And this was Kincaid's second panel, correct?"

Juan nodded. "The first rejected her application on a two-to-one vote; so did we. The third panel member, Nolan Cassidy, was originally from the Sacramento office, where Kincaid's sister-in-law works as the SSA of Violent Crimes. I don't believe he was impartial, and I felt he should have recused himself even though he said he'd never met Ms. Kincaid, nor had he worked directly with her sister-in-law."

"Still reeks of nepotism." Deanna stepped aside when two teenage bikers came up the path.

"I almost quit when Hans Vigo stepped in and overruled our decision."

"Assistant Director Hans Vigo?" Dr. Vigo was way up the ladder and currently served as liaison between national headquarters and Quantico. He was well known among field agents because of his longtime stint in the Behaborial Science Unit and the three years he taught at Quantico.

"Dr. Vigo told us our decision was overruled and that we weren't allowed to discuss the proceedings with each other, or anyone else. It was quite heavy-handed, and left a bad taste in my mouth."

"I'd feel the same."

"Then, nearly two months ago, an agent from the D.C. office came to both me and Meredith and asked if we'd told anyone about what happened, and then reiterated that we were forbidden from discussing it."

"And had you?"

"I didn't, but Meredith had. She didn't admit it, but since I knew I hadn't talked about it with anyone, and there was no reason for Cassidy to do so, it had to be Meredith. She's worried about her career. She's only a couple years from retirement; she shouldn't have to stress over an upstart newbie agent who gets a pass on the process because of who she knows."

"You're loyal to Meredith."

"I'm angry that the process has been perverted. As far as I'm concerned, Lucy Kincaid shouldn't be a federal agent. I hope the instructors at Quantico see the same problems with her that we saw." He glanced at Deanna, then motioned toward a bench across from the stone bridge that crossed the north part of the lake near 77th Street. It was quiet here under the shade of an oak tree. The few people who passed them didn't pay any undue attention.

"You told Meredith that you were investigating Kincaid's boyfriend, Sean Rogan."

"Yes. I have been tracking him for years, but only recently have I uncovered a solid lead."

"Tell me about the investigation," Juan said.

Deanna didn't want to share, because this was where her involvement could get dicey. Deanna's boss knew she was looking at Colton Thayer for mortgage fraud, but she'd created that cover story so he'd give her some room to work. Technically, Thayer's crimes would be covered under the cybercrime unit, but every time she'd tried to get back on the squad she'd been stymied—because of what happened at Stanford. So she made up a scam and her boss gave her some room to build a case.

But there was nothing on Thayer, at least related to white-collar crime. She falsified enough reports to give a hint of something fishy without having enough evidence to turn over the case to the U.S. Attorney's Office. Her boss had bigger cases to manage, so her Thayer investigation slipped under the radar.

She told Martinez, "There have been a series of thefts in Manhattan that we believe are tied to Colton Thayer, a known computer hacker. He's hard to track—Cybercrime has been working on him for years. His M.O. is to stay clean for long stretches of time. Because I have a background in accounting, I've been kept in the loop." Mostly true. "Thayer and Rogan were at MIT together and suspected of a whole host of cybercrimes, but nothing was ever proved and the statute of limitations has long since passed. However, Rogan has been in New York for the last three weeks and has been seen at Thayer's residence."

"You suspect they're working on something together? Like what?"

"Right before Rogan moved to New York he split from his brother's security company. The only reason I learned this is because Rogan had high-level government security, which was suspended by RCK. However, Rogan had access to top-secret projects RCK was contracted for with both our government and defense contractors."

Juan frowned. "I know a bit about Rogan, from our interviews with Kincaid. He doesn't seem to be one for treason."

Deanna couldn't lose Juan now, not when she was so close. "But he *is* one for power and money. Probably not treason, but he can use his skills and knowledge to hack

into any system he wants. Without his brother to rein him
in, he's gone rogue. His involvement with Thayer proves it."
That was Deanna's theory. "And Thayer had a recent in-
flux of cash. It appears to be legit, but my team is going
through it with a fine-toothed comb." Meaning her. She
had no team—she was in this all on her own, with Steve
Gannon's help on occasion.

But she felt in her gut that this was it, this was her last
shot. Taking down Rogan would fix her career and rebuild her reputation, which was still damaged even after
all these years. She had nightmares about the continuing
snickers and comments. How she'd stood on the stage at
Stanford, in front of two hundred law enforcement professionals, and right after she had proclaimed that *her*
system was foolproof, Rogan had hacked it and exposed
one of his professors as a pedophile.

There were even some who said Rogan should have
been hired to fix the security. Like he was some sort of
white-hat vigilante.

But she'd prove he was a criminal. She might even get
a promotion to SSA. Her own squad to run. Vindication.

Juan asked, "Do you think Lucy Kincaid is part of his
scheme?"

"Not that I know of," Deanna admitted. "She's been at
Quantico for the last ten weeks, but she and Rogan are
still involved, and I know he's guilty."

"If you have proof, why hasn't he been brought in for
an interview? Or indicted? Do you have a grand jury
working on this?"

Juan's questions were all good, too good, and Deanna
hedged. "I don't have any authority to go after Rogan right
now, not unless I can connect him to Thayer. That's where
Kincaid comes in—I want her to tell me what's going on.
Either she's a total idiot and doesn't know what her boyfriend is up to, or she's part of it—and either way, she
shouldn't be an FBI agent."

Juan scowled. "You're right about that."

Deanna gained confidence. Laying out her suspicions about Rogan hadn't helped her case with Martinez, but tying it back to Lucy Kincaid gave Deanna the bait she needed to hook him.

"I need leverage. If I'm going to get her to turn on her boyfriend, I need to understand her. Unfortunately, her file is full of holes, redacted, or sealed."

This was where Deanna hoped she had played her cards right—that Juan would tell her everything he knew about Lucy Kincaid and why he had voted against her hire.

"I'm not surprised you haven't been able to learn anything about Kincaid," Juan said. "My read on her is that she wouldn't care one way or the other about financial schemes or computer hacking. Her sole purpose for being an FBI agent is to work sex crimes. She has a vendetta. She's psychologically unstable, though she hides it very well."

That information was more than Deanna had expected. She pushed. "A vendetta? Why?"

"When she was eighteen, she killed her rapist. He was unarmed. Essentially, it was vigilante violence on her part—which is almost funny, considering that she put another FBI agent in prison for allegedly orchestrating a vigilante group."

"Fran Buckley." Deanna remembered the case. "I read in Kincaid's thin file that she'd worked with Buckley for a predator watchdog group."

Juan nodded. "I believe that Kincaid is volatile and potentially dangerous to herself and her partner. She received little psychological counseling after her rape, and none of it on record with the FBI. Her rape was a traumatic event to be sure—it was digitally recorded and shown live on the Internet. I don't blame her for killing her attacker—I think anyone in the same situation would have been justified. Except that when she emptied her gun into his chest, he was not a threat to her or anyone else. It was overkill."

"She killed him in cold blood?"

Juan nodded, his lips pursed. "Kincaid has a master's in criminal psychology. Her brother is a forensic shrink who is close personal friends with Dr. Vigo, who's the one who cleared her psychologically. There are ethical and moral problems with Dr. Vigo doing the assessment. I think they conspired to rubber-stamp her acceptance because she's this wonderchild to them. But there's no way they can know what she will do when put in the line of fire. There's no way to know how she'll react. She has a history of panic attacks, but you won't see that in her professional record. She discussed them with the panel.

"I'll admit," Juan continued, "she has an impressive background with a lot to offer—just not to the FBI. We don't need any more wild or rogue agents. Kincaid's brother is married to Kate Donovan, who was a fugitive for five years, but suddenly, because of her connections high up in the Bureau, she's teaching cybercrime at Quantico after a six-month suspension? Hans Vigo was her training agent, and he's the one who overruled our panel to get her sister-in-law into the program. There's something not right about this whole thing."

Deanna's head was spinning with the many connections, but this was all good stuff. Kincaid was definitely the weak link. If she wanted to become an FBI agent so badly she'd break all the rules to get there, then she'd turn on her boyfriend in a heartbeat to protect it all.

"What would encourage her to talk to me about her boyfriend? What scares her?"

"Losing her slot. She was so determined, so certain she was going to be at the Academy, I'm pretty sure it was already established that if our panel rejected her she would still be admitted."

"Arrogant," Deanna mumbled. *Just like her boyfriend.*

Juan nodded. "She's already been reprimanded by her class supervisor at Quantico. She's been before the disciplinary panel twice. Both times, a slap on the wrist. No expulsion."

"How do you know?"

"I have friends." He didn't elaborate. He handed her a thick envelope. "These are my notes. We weren't allowed to keep or copy any of the files, and though Kincaid's file is sealed, we were allowed to review it during the hiring process. This is what I remember as important."

She took the envelope, resisting the urge to hug Juan. She would dig into this file tonight and find the nugget that would force Lucy to help her.

Or she'd be going in front of the disciplinary panel again. And maybe this time get her ass booted.

"Thank you," she said.

"I will deny speaking to you, Deanna."

"I'm not going to tell anyone. I didn't even tell my partner that we were meeting. You're doing the right thing." Deanna squeezed the envelope again, almost disbelieving that she finally had something tangible to work with.

Juan stood up. "Kincaid is a wild card who plays by her own rules. On one hand, she appears to do everything by the book, but it's clear she's had people helping her every step of the way. On the other hand, she's both smart and deadly, and has proved she'll do anything to further her goals. I don't know how she got everyone wrapped around her finger, why they look the other way when she goes off on her Nancy Drew investigations, but that is what makes her dangerous. I hope you're right about Sean Rogan, and that she is helping him. Because an overt crime that can't be buried by the powers that be is probably the only thing that will get Lucy Kincaid kicked out of the Bureau."

CHAPTER SIX

Sean had found the Irish pub on Lafayette shortly after he rented the apartment in New York, and it had become his favorite place to think. Or not think. His apartment often felt like a prison with Noah downstairs watching and pushing him. Intellectually he understood why he was on Noah's bad side, but sometimes, like last night, it hit him hard.

Sunday afternoon, like now, when it was too late for lunch but too early for dinner, was Sean's favorite time of day. Most of the patrons were fixated on football and didn't give him a second glance. Which was good, because he wasn't in the mood for small talk.

He ordered a Harp on tap and stared at his phone until Colton finally responded to his text message.

I'll be there in twenty minutes.

Sean breathed deeply, slowly let it out. After last night's near-miss with the RCK security system, Sean needed to know the truth. He was tired of Colton playing the *trust me* card: Sean didn't trust him. Not anymore.

Unfortunately, Sean wasn't sure his old friend was

going to give him the answers he needed. He'd been pondering the endgame all day while helping Noah dig deeper on Evan Weller and Carol Hattori, until Noah's bad mood chased him from the building.

Sean knew as soon as Colton walked into the pub, but didn't make a motion to wave him over. Instead, Sean watched Colton in the mirror as he casually crossed the room, more observant than he appeared. Colton had been raised by a single mother after his father left when he was seven and his brother Travis was three. His mom worked two jobs to afford to live in a better school district, and Colton had gone to MIT on a full scholarship. It had been hard on the Thayers. Travis had died when they were kids, and his death had deeply affected Colton to the point that now, two decades later, his choices still related to Travis. Sean knew Colton had subconsciously replaced Travis with him—Travis would have been thirty this year, just like Sean.

Colton sat on the barstool next to Sean. "You've grown soft." He gestured to the lighter brew. The bartender walked over and Colton asked for a black and tan, Guinness over Bass ale. He and Sean had drunk the concoction at their favorite bar in college.

Sean said, "I'll have one as well."

He drained the rest of his Harp and pushed the empty pint forward.

Colton grinned. "It's really great to have you back."

"I told you before, it's temporary while I get my life straightened out."

"I know what you said."

"Evan nearly screwed the entire operation yesterday."

"Evan told me what happened."

That surprised Sean. "Everything?"

"That he didn't know it was an RCK security system until yesterday and he was afraid you'd pull out if you knew."

"That's bullshit."

"I don't think he's lying."

"That makes one of us."

"Why would he jeopardize the operation? I've done my research, Sean."

"I don't know why. Maybe he's as sick and tired of Skye flirting with me as I am and wants to take me out."

Colton snorted. "We need you on this, Sean. You're the best."

"You keep saying that, but I don't even know what you have planned. I really don't like being kept in the dark. Based on what we learned from PBM and what you're telling me, I can't see the big picture. That's why I need to take a step back."

Colton didn't say anything until after the bartender delivered the two pints. Then Colton sipped, carefully placed his drink on the coaster. "You used to trust me."

"I did."

"Did?"

Now Sean had to spill what he suspected. Noah thought the move was risky, but if what Sean knew was the truth, Colton would expect him to ask. And if he was wrong? That meant there was someone else with information that could land Sean in prison.

"You ratted me out to Senator Jonathan Paxton."

Sean was watching Colton's reaction in the bar mirror. He wasn't surprised at the mention of Paxton, but he looked confused.

"Ratted you out for what?"

"You set me up so I'd have no choice but to work for you," Sean said. "You used him to get to me."

Colton became agitated. "I don't know what the hell you're talking about, Sean."

"Are you denying you know the senator?"

Colton looked into his beer. "I still don't know what you're saying, Sean. I would never turn on you."

Sean pushed back his growing guilt for lying to Colton about why he was here.

"Did you tell Paxton about what happened ten years ago?"

"Of course not! I would never betray you like that." He looked pained at the accusation. "Sean, don't you believe me?"

He sounded sincere, but Sean couldn't be certain. He hadn't worked with Colton in years. Things changed. People changed. Why would Colton go through such lengths to bring Sean into the group?

Colton's face fell. "You don't."

"Paxton knows about Robert Martin and his company."

"Impossible."

"C., he blackmailed me into stealing something for him. In July, he said that he knew of a crime I committed where the statute of limitations was still eight months from expiring. The only thing still over my head is that."

"I swear to God, Sean, I said nothing to Paxton about Martin or Martin Holdings. I would never betray you."

Sean believed Colton, and it killed Sean that he had to lie to him. Sean knew Colton as well as himself—he would protect Sean's secret to his grave. Sean regretted doubting him.

"Did you tell anyone else? Someone you trust?"

"No one. I swear."

"But you do know Paxton."

Colton nodded, sipped his beer. "I haven't told the team yet, but he's the one who hired me for this job."

Sean had no cover, no secrets other than his purpose for joining Colton's group. It was the only way this under-cover investigation could work—Sean publicly left RCK and reconnected with his old friend, who brought him back into the fold. Three weeks ago, there was nothing to do, no jobs, just meeting the team. Now everything was happening double time.

Sean kept his voice low. "Why would he pay you to break into PBM?" This was the information that Noah had been searching for for months. Sean kept his voice even and pretended his only interest was in finding out how Paxton knew about his crime.

"He wants to prove that PBM took government money and didn't do what they claimed."

"We proved that when we hacked into the network."

"We need physical proof."

"He's a fucking United States senator," Sean said. "He can get any proof he wants with a snap of his fingers."

"Shh!" Colton frowned, then said quietly, "You know that if the senator went through proper channels, PBM would be tipped off and have time to destroy evidence."

They'd been down this path before. Finding evidence only to have it destroyed before the proper authorities got their warrants and their act together.

"Did you tell him about the bio-weapons?"

"No."

"Why not?"

"Would you have wanted me to?"

"No." Sean glanced at his friend. Colton was keeping something back. "What aren't you tell me?"

Sean was having a hard time buying the story and didn't think Colton was that gullible, either, though everything he said had a ring of truth. And if Sean didn't know what kind of manipulative, murderous bastard Senator Paxton was, he might have let it go. But Paxton didn't fork over this much of his own money to expose government waste.

Sean said, "There are far better ways of proving a company misused public funds than hiring a known computer hacker to get the evidence. He's a *senator.* He can put together a committee, go to the FBI, start a federal investigation, whatever he needs."

"It's more complicated that that."

"Paxton has his own rule book, and you can't believe anything he says. He's a killer, Colton. And if you don't care about that, care about how he uses people. He blackmailed me!"

"You should know me better than that, Sean. Of course I don't trust him—I don't trust any politician—and I'm certain he has his own agenda, but on this project, our purposes are aligned. And he has money."

"See, this is what I'm having a hard time understanding," Sean said. "I see why *you* care, but why Paxton?"

"He has his reasons, I have mine, but we both want the company destroyed. And it will save lives, Sean. You care about that."

"You haven't proved it to me yet. You haven't told me anything beyond what we found last month in the files."

Colton looked pointedly at Sean. "You used to take my word on it."

"Yes, I did." Sean stared back.

"I need you, Sean. I need you with me, one hundred percent."

Sean drank his beer. He didn't know why Colton needed him—Hunter was as good as Sean, probably better if it came down to it. Evan was competent, even though Sean didn't like him. Skye was smart and had her own assets. Why bring Sean in?

"You're the only person I've ever trusted, Sean."

His heart twisted. Colton wasn't lying. That Sean was made him feel like shit.

Colton lowered his voice. "I'm finally in a position to prove that Pham-Bonner Medical killed Travis and covered it up."

Colton had never accepted that his brother had died of

leukemia. He understood that Travis had the disease and would probably die, but after Travis went on experimental drugs, he deteriorated and died three months sooner than the doctor's worst prognosis.

"Shit, Colton—"

"That's why I need you. The next step of the plan—we need to get into PBM."

"And where does Paxton fit in?"

"I couldn't do it alone—the cost of the equipment alone is astronomical."

"But you've been doing well."

Colton shrugged.

"You've given your money away."

"Maybe a little too much."

Colton had always been generous to a fault. Other than the carriage house on the Upper East Side, he'd never spent money on himself. He never forgot his roots in South Boston, even though he'd painstakingly worked to lose the accent. With Colton, it was feast or famine.

"Tell me," Sean said. A sick feeling crowded the beer in his stomach. If Colton was playing games with Paxton, this would not end well for anyone. "What's Paxton's plan?"

"I can't tell you."

"Then I can't help you." Sean had to be willing to walk. If he didn't, Colton would be suspicious.

Sean drained his beer.

Colton looked panicked. "I need you."

"You just said you trusted me. If that's true, then I need to know your game plan. I'm not going to risk my freedom. I'm not the same arrogant, reckless kid I was in college."

"It's sensitive right now. I'll tell you everything tomorrow night, once I put the rest of the pieces together."

"How do you know Paxton is the only one involved?"

"I don't care if he has a whole gang of senators, none of them know about *me*."

"You can't be certain."

"Sean, I just told you I can take down PBM and you're squabbling about irrelevant details."

"Not so irrelevant if we want to live free when this is all over. I don't want to lose what I have."

"It's your girlfriend, isn't it?"

Sean hadn't lied about his relationship with Lucy because it would have been too easy to verify, and no way would Sean break it off for this operation. If he broke it off without telling Lucy why, he'd hurt her deeply. And if he brought her into the plan and faked a breakup, she would constantly worry about him and jeopardize her graduation. He didn't know how long Colton had been keeping tabs on him—it could have been since they'd parted nine years ago or only during the last few months. But either way, Sean had to assume that Colton knew everything about him—which was why he had had to officially, and publicly, leave RCK.

"I told you when I agreed to help that Lucy is off-limits."

"It's never going to work between you and her," Colton said.

Sean's jaw tightened. "I said—"

"Sean, I know you better than anyone. We might not have kept in touch since—"

"Another off-limits subject." He didn't want to discuss what had happened after he destroyed Martin Holdings.

"I know what drives you. I know what keeps you getting up each and every day. No federal agent is going to understand that the system doesn't work. That people like us are necessary."

"First, you don't know Lucy. You don't know what drives her. She's not even interested in white-collar or cybercrime; she's driven to put sex offenders and killers

in prison. Something I can get behind and support. Sometimes, the system does work."

"Then why did you agree to come back?"

"You know why." He hadn't spoken to Duke since he
quit. He'd talked to Patrick a couple of times, helping him
adjust to being a solo operation, but Sean wasn't going
to talk to Duke. Sean didn't even know if he wanted to
talk to Duke when it was all over, but he'd figure that out
later.

Breaking with RCK was necessary, but his emotions
were still raw. Sean had been acting. Duke hadn't. Rick
Stockton felt it was absolutely essential that no one at
RCK know about the undercover operation.

"I'm really sorry about Duke. If you weren't trying to
help me—"

"I don't want to talk about Duke, either. He's still my
brother."

"Have you talked to him since—"

"No. But he's *family.*"

"Understood." Colton drained his beer. "I've always
had your back. You're as much a brother to me as Travis
was. You know that."

Sean didn't doubt Colton's loyalty. It was the one thing
Sean had always trusted. He knew Colton was keeping
something back about PBM, but he hadn't betrayed Sean
to Paxton.

Someone else had.

Sean motioned to the bartender for two more beers for
him and Colton.

"Paxton isn't someone you can screw over."

"Let me worry about Paxton."

"I can't."

"Sean, Paxton has far more to lose than either of us."

"Tell me what you know."

"He understands the risks, but once I get into PBM, I'll
have everything I need—" He cut himself off.

"What?"

"I don't want to say yet—"

"Dammit, tell me."

Colton waited until the bartender put the beers in front of them, drank a long gulp, then said, "He just wants one file."

"What file?"

"I don't know what's in the file, but it's in Joyce Bonner's personal safe. He wants it before I expose PBM to the world, in exchange for funding my operation. He has a secret. So do we."

"I really hope you're going into this with your eyes open, C."

"I am."

"If I think Paxton is doing something that's going to screw people, especially us, I'm walking." Sean paused. "I need something from you."

"What?"

"When you know what he's after, tell me. I will never trust that man." He held up his beer. "Deal?"

"Yes." Colton seemed to sag with relief.

"Tell me about Evan," Sean said.

"He's been with us for a couple years. Skye brought him in. He's not as good as you, but he's good."

"Carol?"

"She's been living with me for a year. I love her, Sean, just like you love your Lucy. Why all the questions?"

"I don't want to go to prison."

Colton smiled and relaxed. "You won't. And Sean? It's really great to have you back. It's like you never left."

Hardly. Sean hadn't realized how much he'd changed in a decade. While the adrenaline high was still incredible, he had far more to lose. Things—people—he wasn't willing to sacrifice.

He needed to dig deep into PBM and figure out why the pharmaceutical company was important to Jonathan

Paxton. Because there was something else going on and Sean couldn't figure out if Colton knew and was keeping Sean in the dark or was truly ignorant.

Jonathan Paxton was the last person Sean would ever trust.

CHAPTER SEVEN

Sean sat in the bar for another thirty minutes after Colton left, researching on his smartphone any connection between Paxton and PBM or their principals. He'd already looked into PBM and they were squeaky clean, at least as clean as a corporation could get. There was no active federal or state investigation, per Noah.

Nothing jumped out at Sean, but he made a note to investigate their cancer trials from two decades ago. Colton wouldn't say PBM had given his brother unproven cancer drugs if he didn't have something solid to base his accusation on. Sean needed a copy of Travis's medical reports, and that was treading in a delicate area.

There was no reason for Paxton to fund a big project like exposing PBM simply to expose them. Sean knew it in his gut. It all centered around this mysterious file that Paxton wanted Colton to steal.

Sean believed Colton when he said he hadn't told Paxton about the information on a possible bio-weapon—it was likely that a military development company or the government could have a private medical research company like PBM developing such a thing. That was the kind of political statement Colton would love to make, and he wouldn't trust a politician with the knowledge. Everything made sense, except Paxton's involvement.

"Colton," Sean mumbled as he left cash on the bar for the bartender, "what have you gotten yourself into?"

He left the pub and turned east down 19th toward his apartment. The late-afternoon sun played across the old buildings, and Sean wished Lucy were here to share the beautiful day with him. He stopped at the corner and was about to cross with the light when he glimpsed a reflection of a woman stepping into a doorway. He glanced discreetly over his shoulder and noticed her black, low-heeled shoes—she was waiting, not entering the building. He couldn't see anything else to identify her. He crossed the street but turned north, away from his apartment.

Did Colton put someone on him? Colton knew where Sean lived; he hadn't made it a secret. Or did Paxton hire someone? That would make more sense.

Sean turned into a corner grocery and bought a water bottle and pack of gum. While he paid he looked at the reflection in the curved mirror behind the cashier. He couldn't make out any details outside the store but caught sight of a blondish woman in a beige blazer and dark slacks. The shoes were low black pumps, like the ones he saw in the doorway. It was her. She passed the store, but Sean suspected she was waiting on the other side. She looked like a fed, the way she moved, the way she dressed—what if she was Paxton's mole?

He grinned.

The clerk said in a thick accent, "I say some-ting funny?"

"No." Sean put his pennies in the tray next to the register. "I just thought of a joke."

This was going to be fun.

* * *

Where the hell was Sean Rogan going?

After her meeting with Juan Martinez, Deanna had crossed Central Park and staked out Colton Thayer's carriage house. She often found herself in the area, hoping to catch a glimpse of Rogan, but while she sometimes saw him entering, he always seemed to elude her when he left.

She'd followed Colton this afternoon and was pleasantly surprised that he met with Rogan. She only popped into the pub for a minute, exiting immediately, not wanting Rogan to see her. She didn't think he'd recognize her, but she didn't want to take the chance. She sat in the Starbucks down the street and watched the door with an eagle eye. Colton left first, nearly an hour after he entered. She expected Rogan to leave immediately, but he didn't. In fact, he didn't leave for another thirty minutes, and she'd feared he had skipped out the back. Just when she was about to give up, she saw him at the corner.

Deanna nearly had to sprint to catch up with him. He crossed the street, turned north, and entered a grocery store. They were on the border of SoHo and the West Village, two neighborhoods, either of which he could live in. All she had on him was that he had been in New York City for the last three weeks.

What she wanted was his address, so she could search his place. Not legally, but she was beyond that at this point. She needed a direction, some tangible proof of what he was up to, and then she'd find a legitimate way to get the information before going to her boss.

Rogan seemed to be walking in circles. He went around the same four blocks twice, going in and out of stores without purpose. He took the subway and she followed. One stop later, he got off.

She was hot and crabby, and chasing a crook around New York wasn't her idea of fun on her day off. Either she confronted him or she walked away. He obviously knew he was being followed.

She approached him and he stepped into an art gallery without looking at her. Dammit, she would have rather talked to him on the street. Maybe she should leave it alone—she had no cause to arrest him. She just wanted to find out where he lived. She could demand ID and then fib and say she thought he was someone else. That might work—he had to produce identification to a federal agent. That way she could legally get his address. He might recognize her, but it had been twelve years since Stanford. She'd changed a lot, including longer, lighter hair.

She stepped into the gallery and scanned the room, hyper-alert for any movement. There were more people than she expected. She wasn't surprised when she realized it was a gallery of famous cartoon stills.

She didn't see Sean anywhere. An elderly employee, dressed all in black with a red-and-white name badge, approached with a warm smile. "May I help you find something? We're closing in ten minutes, but I can—"

"No," she snapped. The employee stopped smiling. Deanna took out her badge. "I'm Deanna Brighton, Federal Bureau of Investigation. A man walked in here, six foot one, dark hair, blue eyes, wearing a light blue polo shirt and jeans."

The employee looked both concerned and worried and glanced around. "Is there a problem?"

"Where is he?"

"I think a young man went into the Seuss exhibit. It's in the back, through the red-and-white-striped curtains."

Deanna strode toward the curtains. As soon as she pushed open the drapes, she was confronted with a roomful of kids, none of them taller than her waistline. Someone in a Cat in the Hat costume was giving the captivated munchkins a tour of the exhibit, which included a car-sized replica of the machine Thing 1 and Thing 2 used to clean up Sally's house.

For a minute, Deanna was transfixed by the whimsical

art, remembering when her dad used to read her the silly books, long after she could read them herself. She'd loved listening to his voice. It stopped when she was eight, and she liked to believe it was because she was finally too old, but she knew it was because her dad had lost hope after he lost his business. Without hope, no one could enjoy Dr. Seuss.

She blinked, pulling herself out of her memory, and scanned the room. She walked around the periphery and still didn't see Rogan.

Dammit, where had he gone? She rubbed her temples. The headache she'd been nursing at Starbucks was a full-blown migraine now.

There was another curtained doorway and she went through it, but it was a hallway that led back to the main studio. *Shit.* He'd ditched her!

"Did you find him? Is there something wrong?"

She went back outside, ignoring the employee's questions. Her fists clenched and she pounded her sore feet on the pavement.

"Damn, damn, damn!"

Impossible.

Then she saw him in the back of a cab. He tipped an invisible hat to her as the taxi turned the corner and disappeared from view.

Sean had the taxi driver drop him off at Grand Central Station. If the fed got the cab number—and Sean was pretty certain the woman tailing him was a federal agent—she could find out where the cab took him.

From Grand Central he walked around to make sure she hadn't followed in another cab, then ten minutes later took a taxi to the carriage house. He had the driver leave him two blocks away. Sean was certain the fed hadn't followed *him* to the pub; that meant she was following Colton.

Sean went up to the door and used the pass code Colton had given him to enter.

Colton was walking up the stairs. He turned around immediately when the door opened.

"Sean."

He closed the door behind him.

"A federal agent followed me from the pub. I lost her, but I guarantee you led her to me."

"I wasn't followed." He didn't sound confident.

"I'm paranoid by nature. Learned that from Hunter. Are you being investigated by the feds?"

"No, of course not."

"How can you be sure?"

"I check periodically."

"Shit, Colton! Paxton could be setting you up. You get him the information he wants, he turns you in. He turns us *all* in."

Colton shook his head. "He knows I have something that will destroy him."

"What?"

"I can't tell you."

Sean ran up the stairs until he was face-to-face with Colton. "You owe me."

Colton didn't like the threat. "I have our initial conversation videotaped, all right? Taped and safe. He knows it. He won't do anything to us."

"Then who is the fed?"

"What did she look like?"

"Dark blond hair, highlighted, five foot six, one hundred thirty-five pounds. Or so. Forty, give or take." He'd taken a picture of her on his cell phone, but he was saving that for Noah.

Colton said, "Let's go to my control room. We'll look at the security footage from the last couple weeks. If you see her, let me know."

Sean followed Colton to the small room off his office where he had all his security cameras. They sat down.

"It's going to take a while," Colton said. "I'll have Carol put another plate on the table." He smiled. "It'll be like old times."

Not quite, Sean thought, but he nodded. "Old times."

CHAPTER EIGHT

Monday

Sean stared at the ceiling, unable to sleep. The last time he looked at the clock it glared 1:47. Too late to be up on a Sunday night. Monday morning? He should just get up and walk off his anxiety, but he didn't want to leave. He was too wound up, too angry and frustrated, and with all the drunks leaving the bars he feared he'd get himself into trouble.

He'd made his bed. That's what Duke would have told Sean. And maybe he had agreed to help Rick Stockton because he was desperate to purge these demons that had haunted him. Maybe he'd agreed to go undercover because it would disappear his past.

Except it wouldn't. His past had been locked tight until now, and Sean had willingly opened the door. Redemption? Maybe. Maybe that's all this was about. Cleaning the slate for him and Lucy.

But even though he'd agreed to work undercover with Noah Armstrong, Sean couldn't help but think that he'd been manipulated into it.

Over two months ago, the week Lucy started at the FBI Academy, Assistant Director Rick Stockton asked Sean to meet with him. Sean hadn't been surprised or suspicious at first—Rick was a longtime friend of JT Caruso and Sean's brother Kane, who'd together founded RCK. They'd also been Marines and Marines tended to stick together, even if they hadn't served with each other. Sean had always been unclear how the friendships had been forged. Because Rick had the authority to hire private contractors for certain jobs and RCK was on the approved-vendor list, Sean had met with him a few times for business since moving to D.C. last year. He'd also done a few private jobs for him.

But Rick's call was unusual because he hadn't gone through Duke for the meeting; he'd asked that they meet at Sean's house instead of the FBI office and insisted that Sean's partner, Patrick Kincaid, not be present.

Sean made it all happen, his curiosity battling his wariness. Any time law enforcement was involved, Sean became apprehensive. He didn't trust most of them.

And then the kicker: Rick brought Noah Armstrong with him.

Sean had planned on meeting with Rick informally, at the dining table that sat in the middle of the great room next to Sean's pool table. Maybe play a game or two. But when he saw Noah, Sean changed gears and took them upstairs to his office. He sat behind his desk and motioned for them to take either the chair or the couch. Rick sat in the chair across from Sean. Noah leaned against the wall.

"What can I do for you?" Sean sat back, casual, though his muscles were tight. He and Noah had settled their differences for the most part, but they'd never be friends. It was because Sean knew, in his gut, that Noah cared too much for Lucy. Personally cared. He'd never admitted it, to Sean or Lucy, but guys knew these things.

"I'm sure I don't have to ask this, but I need strict confidentiality," Rick said.

Sean dipped his head. "Of course."

"You remember the case Lucy assisted in a few weeks ago, before starting the Academy? The Wendy James murder?"

"Yes." Lucy would have been dead if not for her bulletproof vest. Sean couldn't forget if he wanted.

"Noah came to me with an off-book investigation—"

Sean couldn't help but smile. "Noah, I'm impressed." When Noah looked at him quizzically, Sean added, "You aren't usually one for breaking the rules. There's hope for you yet."

Noah scowled, but Rick almost cracked a smile. The assistant director continued, "I listened to his suspicions, and because I had additional information regarding the suspect, I decided we had more than enough to warrant an investigation. But the problem is information channels. The investigation needs to be quiet."

"Meaning you're investigating someone internally and you don't want them to find out. Got it. But don't you guys have a federal IA or something?"

"I decided to keep this *completely* out of our system. The director approved my operating plan, and he and Dr. Hans Vigo are the only other people who know who we're investigating and why. The director has given me blanket authority to run it as I see fit."

"Don't keep me in suspense."

"We're looking at two people, one we know and a mole in the FBI that we've narrowed down to someone in the New York City regional office." He paused. "We're investigating Senator Jonathan Paxton."

Sean almost laughed. "It's about time."

Paxton was someone Sean would love to make disappear, if he did those kinds of things.

Rick motioned for Noah to explain. "Last January, after we arrested Fran Buckley, a white-collar and cybercrime task force was created who went through all the records of her organization, Women and Children First. She claimed during her plea agreement that all activities were funded through legitimate contributions made by law-abiding citizens who wanted to help stop violent crime—that none of their donors knew what they were doing with the money. There were enough legal successes with their program that everyone was deceived until Lucy found the connection to the vigilante ring.

"There's nothing in the financial records that screams murder for hire. But I interviewed Senator Paxton because he was the de facto head of WCF and he had been raising money for them around the country. I got the feeling that he was holding back. He was definitely angry, but it didn't seem directed at Buckley. I started looking into some of the donors who had given to both Paxton's senatorial campaign and WCF and realized that many had lost a loved one to violence. The donations were all across the board, from a hundred dollars to tens of thousands of dollars. I don't think that any of the donors hired WCF to specifically target a killer, but I suspected that Paxton had his own hit list, created from people he'd met—people he might have bonded with because they shared a tragedy."

Sean didn't say a word. Noah was very close to the truth, but Sean had never been able to prove it. Knowing someone was guilty and having the evidence to prove it in a court of law were very different. And while Lucy had cut ties with Paxton, she had suspected he'd been involved as well. Had Noah talked to her? Had she fueled these suspicions?

Noah was watching Sean closely, and Sean kept his face as blank as possible, though talking about Paxton angered him.

"But I couldn't find anything substantive," Noah said. "I put my suspicions aside until the senator put himself in the middle of the Wendy James investigation."

Sean knew far more about that investigation than Noah thought he did, so he kept to the minimal facts. "Lucy said he was the one who turned the photos of Wendy and the congressman over to the media."

"He started the ball rolling, though I think he was far more involved in manipulating events. I don't have a good grasp on his psychology, but Hans is writing up a profile for me."

"I can tell you exactly who Paxton is," Sean said. "He's a narcissist with a god complex." He almost said more but cut himself off.

Rick said, "That's pretty much what Hans has already told us. He found out more about Paxton when he interviewed Lucy."

Sean leaned forward. "You brought Lucy in?"

"Not into this investigation. But as part of her pre-Quantico interview, Hans talked to her about what happened at WCF and got her to talk about her relationship with Senator Paxton, without letting on that he was the subject of an investigation."

"She doesn't have a relationship with him."

"But she did—she worked for him as an intern for a year; then he got her the job at WCF. They had been friends. I know you're angry—"

"You don't know half of it." Sean stopped himself. Again. He was only going to dig himself into a hole. Unless . . . unless Rick and Noah already knew what Paxton had on him. Unless they already knew that Paxton had blackmailed Sean.

Noah said, "We needed more insight into what motivates Paxton. It's easy to say 'money and power' because he's a politician, but it's more than that. You know that Lucy looks like his dead daughter."

Sean nodded once. He didn't trust himself to speak.

"Hans thinks that Paxton has a driving need to protect

Lucy like he couldn't protect his daughter, and also that
he sees himself as some sort of superhero, a violent Robin
Hood who, instead of stealing from the rich to give to the
poor, kills the guilty to protect the innocent."

"I wouldn't put such a noble cause on his head," Sean
couldn't resist saying.

"Nor would I," Rick said. "But as you know, it's important in criminal psychology to understand the suspect's motivations so that we can figure out his next move.
That's why we're here."

Sean knew what was coming before Noah said it. He
was already thinking of ways to get out of it.

"We need your help."

Sean delayed by saying, "It probably kills you to say
that."

"It does."

Honest. Sean admired that.

"There's nothing I would like more than to take down
Paxton, but I don't see how I can help."

Noah walked over to Sean's desk and handed him a
thin file. "Over the last few weeks, since I shared my suspicions with Rick, we've learned that Senator Paxton paid
your old friend Colton Thayer a large sum of money for
'security consulting.' We know that Thayer has been under
suspicion in the past for cybercrimes—generally hacking,
but instead of stealing information he exposes company
corruption. Proving it has been far more difficult. He's
never been indicted."

Colton was good. He wouldn't be caught. But that he
was under suspicion wasn't good.

"Paxton is up to something," Noah continued. "He's
taken more trips to his home state of New York this year
than he has in past years."

Rick said, "When Noah came to me with information
about Paxton's involvement in the vigilante group, it took
some digging, but it became clear that someone in the

FBI was feeding him information about our investigations. He was able to steer clear of sex offenders who were already on our radar, and target only those who no one was tracking."

"Why do you think the mole is in the New York office instead of D.C.?"

"Paxton is extremely careful, but we traced some suspicious communications to the main Manhattan office. We can't dig deeper electronically without bringing in more people, and right now I don't know who I trust to do it."

"Because a lot of cops don't think that there's anything wrong with knocking off child molesters and rapists," Sean said.

"It's more than that. This isn't just about vigilantes anymore. Thayer has no ties to violent or organized crime. He's a hacktivist. Why would Paxton hire him?"

"I don't know." But Sean had been thinking about it since they mentioned Colton's name. Now Sean knew where Paxton got the information he used to blackmail him. He'd suspected, but now it was practically proven. Would his closest friend do that to him? What was Sean even thinking? He hadn't seen Colton in nearly ten years. People change.

"That's why we need your help," Rick said. "We want you to go undercover for us."

"You want me to spy on my old friend."

"We want to know what he's doing for Senator Paxton. And Sean, we know he's been calling you."

Sean slammed his fist on his desk. "You've been investigating *me?*"

"No. We've been investigating Thayer. He's called you multiple times. But you've never called him."

Even if Sean had, they wouldn't see the record. Sean would have used a secure phone. That Colton hadn't done the same made Sean wonder if he had grown overly confident or sloppy. "I haven't seen Colton in nine years. Not since I graduated MIT. Don't you think it's kind of suspicious that I just waltz back into his life?"

"Why was he calling you?" Noah asked quietly.

Sean had to deflect them. Distract them. "He's been trying to get me to work for him." That was the truth.

"Why haven't you?"

"Duke. When I starting working for RCK, Duke said I had to cut ties with Colton. So I did."

"But he still talks to you."

"What do you want from me?" Sean asked. "Colton was my best friend during a really shitty time in my life. Yeah, he wants me to work for him. I always tell him no."

"Tell him yes."

"Absolutely not. You're asking me to betray a friend."

Noah said, "You want to take down Paxton as much as I do. Why won't you help?"

Rick said, "You justifiably have reservations about infiltrating your friend's group. I can give him limited immunity if he cooperates."

"You want me to convince him to turn on Paxton? You don't even know why he's working for him."

"Even after the fact."

Sean rubbed his face. "I can't."

"Why?" Noah said.

Noah was staring at him. Sean said, "You said this conversation is completely off-the-record. Is anything I tell you off-the-record as well?"

"Yes," Rick said without hesitation.

Shit. Sean didn't know how to avoid this conversation. He couldn't do what they wanted; he would lose everything. "Paxton has information about my past that could land me in prison. Last month he blackmailed me into retrieving an item that was stolen from his office."

That information was a surprise to both of them. Sean didn't want to tell them, especially Noah, but he felt that he was stuck in a corner. Paxton needed to be destroyed, but Sean couldn't be the one to do it. No matter how much he wanted to.

Sean continued, "There's a crime with a ten-year statute of limitations that is currently nine and a half years old. Paxton knows about it. I don't know what proof he has, if anything, but I can't risk it. As soon as the statute is up, I'll do anything you want to take down that bastard. But until March? I'm steering clear of him."

"I never pegged you as a coward," Noah said.

"Fuck you, Armstrong."

"We don't have until March! This is happening now."

Rick said, "I can give you full immunity."

"Pardon me from being skeptical, but I've been lied to in the past."

"You know me better than that."

"Yeah, well, I also know that promises mean shit when someone higher up the ladder wants to screw you."

"This isn't Stanford," Rick said.

"Do you know what happened there? Really know?"

"Duke told me—"

"Well, Duke has a selective memory. I was told by the FBI that nothing would happen to me if I told them how I hacked into their system. I walked them through the back door I'd uncovered and how I'd mirrored the pedophile's account over their system, and then how I controlled it remotely. It was pretty damn brilliant, especially twelve years ago. I trusted them, but dammit, I should have had a lawyer write up something ironclad, because the next thing I knew, all my computers were confiscated, I was arrested, and then expelled and put on probation."

"The charges were dropped."

"I was in jail for three days. I was kicked out of school. I was threatened by Boston FBI agents for years just because I was on their radar as a hacker."

"You were a hacker," Noah said.

"See why I don't believe you?" Sean said. "My brother Kane doesn't trust many people, but he trusts you, Rick, and that means something to me. But I don't trust the system. I don't trust your boss. You can't protect me if this all gets out."

Noah said, "Rick, can I have a minute with Sean?"

"No," Sean said, but Rick left. "Shit." He rubbed his face again.

Noah sat on the edge of the seat Rick had vacated. He picked up the picture of Sean and Lucy that sat on Sean's desk. Sean grabbed it from Noah's hands and put it out of reach. "Don't go there," Sean said.

"You say you love her, but you have this shit hanging over your head. Paxton blackmailed you? That means he can get to you again."

"He can't. I have something he wants."

Noah shook his head. "It's a game for you; I get it."

"My freedom isn't a game."

"If Paxton can blackmail you now, he'll do it again. And again. When the statute runs out, he'll still hold it over you because he'll threaten to tell Lucy. Or release the intel and embarrass RCK. How many people does RCK employ? Dozens? Not to mention freelance contractors? As soon as Paxton knows your weakness, he'll exploit it until he has you under his thumb permanently."

"Do you know this because of personal experience?" Sean was trying to deflect Noah, but it didn't work.

Noah rolled his eyes. "I know men like Paxton, and I know men like you. Don't give him the power. You're better than this."

"I'm not going to prison. But you'd like that, wouldn't you? Give you a free road to Lucy."

Noah stared at him. "You think I'm trying to get you out of the way so I can have Lucy?"

"Yes." There. He'd said it. Put it out in the open.

Noah leaned back and stared at him. "The thought's crossed my mind."

Sean's fists clenched. He wanted to hit Noah in the worst way.

"But Lucy loves you. I'm not even on her radar. I care for her enough to respect her decision, including keeping you in her life. But if you really loved her—"

"Don't ever doubt my feelings for Lucy."

"You would clean the slate. She's going to be a sworn FBI agent in four months. What if someone else finds out this information? What if they tell her? What if she does or doesn't do something because she thinks she's protecting you? Secrets kill, Sean. You know it. I'm the one who wanted to bring you into this operation. For all the shit you pull, you're one of the smartest guys I know, and you're loyal. I can't do this without you."

If Noah had planned on guilting him into going along with this insane plan, it was working. Noah was right about one thing—that Paxton knew what happened nine and a half years ago meant that someone else knew about it, and there might be proof. Proof that could hurt not only Sean but also Lucy.

"You don't even know what I did."

"Trust Rick to do everything in his power to protect you." Noah paused. "This isn't going to be easy. You'll have to make Colton believe you quit RCK."

"That isn't the hard part," Sean said. "I simply need to quit."

Noah looked surprised. "You want to read Duke into the plan?"

"No. You don't want Duke to know. He won't like it, and I don't want him looking over my shoulder. But I know what to do to set Duke off and give me a reason to quit." Sean pushed a button on his desk and his voice came out through a house-wide intercom. He hadn't realized that he'd already decided to help until now. But Noah was right. He didn't have a choice. He couldn't let Lucy pay for his past crimes. "Rick, you can return."

When Rick stepped back in, Sean said, "The hard part is that Paxton knows what I did. He won't want me working with Colton on anything, but we're at a standstill. If Paxton pushes, I'll push back. I never gave him back what he hired me to steal. It's my leverage on him, and it's all I have."

"What does Paxton specifically know?"

"I don't think he has proof, but he knows enough that I'm nervous that someone has proof." Sean took a deep breath. He hadn't spoken about Robert Martin or Martin Holdings to anyone since he left MIT. It was still a black cloud over him.

"When I was at MIT, Colton and I created a group called Net. We were primarily an activist group that hacked into secure computer systems to expose the weaknesses and embarrass the companies and governments."

Rick said, "Much like what you do for RCK now."

Sean smiled. "Except now I get paid for it, we fix the security problems without publicly exposing the weakness, and they don't call it hacking."

"Hacking is usually a five-to-seven-year sentence."

"We also needed money to buy and build the best computer systems. It's not just skill, but equipment, that made us good. We took a few jobs that weren't exactly kosher—usually stealing from crooks."

"You're going to have to elaborate."

Sean had a lot of examples, but he didn't feel the need to share everything with the feds. He gave them one. "There was a guy the FBI was investigating for insider trading. He was really good; you never would have caught him, not until he was drinking daiquiris on some island in the Caribbean."

"Who?"

"Cyrus Block."

"If I recall correctly, we did catch him. He was given ten to twenty."

Sean smirked. "You're welcome."

Rick didn't comment. But Noah let out a short laugh. He knew what was coming. Maybe Noah wasn't all that bad of a guy.

Sean said, "You wouldn't have caught him if we didn't set him up. We learned about him after he hosted a seminar at MIT on the security of finance systems. He seduced a freshman—he was in his forties; she was eighteen—and she tried to kill herself when she found out she was pregnant. Her parents had sacrificed everything for her to go to MIT; she had a partial scholarship, but they took out a second mortgage on their house to get her there. She was in the same sorority as my girlfriend." Sean stared at Rick and Noah. "He was a fucking asshole."

"Sounds like," Noah said.

"Skye Jansen, my girlfriend at the time, knew everything about finances. Sharp girl. She did some legal research and suspected that Block was involved in insider trading, but there was no proof without breaking some laws. My friends and I came up with a plan to take him down. We hacked into his computer and left a trail of bread crumbs so the FBI would be able to figure it out."

Rick raised an eyebrow. "Our white-collar division is good, Rogan. You don't know that we wouldn't have caught him."

"Some of them are good," Sean agreed. "But I know that it usually takes a tip to alert the FBI that there's something going on. We not only gave you the tip, but we opened the door so you could put him in prison."

"You'd probably be given probation. Maybe fines. Lectured. I doubt you would have done jail time."

"We peeled off one of his accounts."

Rick looked at him quizzically. "Peeled off?"

"The FBI never even knew it existed. We rerouted it before the FBI sting. We set up a shell company to donate the money to MIT on the condition that Trina, Skye's sorority sister, was given a full-ride scholarship. We never kept control over the money, but last I heard, the school managed the funds nicely. It pays out a dozen full-ride scholarships a year to women studying the sciences."

"So essentially, the government would have seized the money under asset forfeiture laws. You stole from the government. That's really a gray area, but I think the statute is up on that. I can check for you. But unless someone has physical proof, I don't see your concern."

"I'm not worried about the Block money. I was giving you an example of the things we did. We did a lot of things like that. I'm not going to go into everything."

Rick looked confused, so Sean got to the point. "Ten years ago—technically, nine years and five months ago—Colton and I hacked into a bank. We'd been emboldened by what happened to Block, and I guess we had it in our heads that we could be Robin Hood, taking from the bad guys and giving to the good. Or rather, returning funds to those who were cheated. I learned a lot from our investigation into Cyrus Block. How financial scams worked, and how to identify them. I won't bore you—"

"It's actually not boring, but go on."

"Colton and I decided to keep this particular job to ourselves. Partly to protect the others, and partly because we really didn't have a plan." This was where it was going to be difficult, Sean realized. Not just talking about Robert Martin but admitting his responsibility in what happened to him.

"Colton and I uncovered a pension scam being run by a company called Martin Holdings during one of our, um, reconnaissance missions. It took us a few days but we learned the company was scamming new retirees—they signed over their pension payments to him, and he invested the money. But we figured out it was a version of the Ponzi scheme. They paid dividends from new investors to the older investors, and skimmed the bulk of the money into offshore accounts. We thought at first it was a large group of money people involved, but eventually learned it was one guy running everything. Robert Martin."

"Never heard of him."

"You wouldn't have." Sean rubbed his eyes. This was where it was going to get hard. But if ever he wanted to believe the cliché that the truth would set him free, now was the time.

"I was twenty. Arrogant—more so then than now. I wanted to punish the guy. He was stealing from the elderly—people in their sixties and seventies who had secure pensions. He was a con artist, he manipulated them. Because of the way the wire transfers were managed, we easily cut off continued payments from the investors to Martin. And that should have been enough for us; we should have set him up for the FBI like we did with Block. But we took it a step further. We piggybacked a virus on one of his international transfers and all the money in that offshore account was rerouted back to his primary U.S. account. We repaid all the accounts with interest, then sent a letter from Martin Holdings to the investors that the company had disbanded and all funds invested had been returned."

"Wait," Noah said. "Transactions that large would be flagged by banks."

"No, because they were business accounts with a history of large transactions. There are ways around every law, Noah. You patch a problem, smart guys will get around it."

"And because what you did was actually bank fraud," Rick said, "there's a ten-year statute of limitations."

"Bingo."

The men were silent for a moment before Rick said,

"No jury would convict you. The prosecution would want to plead out because they know the case would be difficult to prosecute. You're right when you called yourselves Robin Hood. And now with all the companies under investigation for mortgage fraud and pension scams? The Justice Department would never touch the case."

"Maybe. Maybe not."

Noah asked, "Does Paxton have proof?"

"I don't know. I kept a file of Martin Holdings records—the real records, not the doctored files that were open to investors. I put it in a safe-deposit box in Boston. After Paxton blackmailed me, I went there—it's still intact."

"You kept evidence of your crime?" Noah sounded surprised.

"I kept it to keep Robert Martin from doing the same thing again. I sent him proof of what I'd done, and told him if he ever tried it again, I would know—and turn everything over to the FBI."

"Why didn't you do that anyway?" Rick asked.

Noah said, "Because Sean would have gone to jail as well."

Sean shrugged. "There was that. I was on probation, thanks to the agreement Duke worked out with Stanford and the FBI in California. See—I started college early. I was two weeks shy of my eighteenth birthday when I was expelled. Duke was my legal guardian. He made the deal over my objections. So everything I did with Net and Colton in Boston was in violation of my probation. But that wasn't the main reason I never went to the FBI." He took a deep breath and finished his story. "A week after I shut down Martin Holdings, Robert Martin committed suicide."

"That wasn't your fault," Rick said.

"Well, it felt like it. I didn't pull the trigger, but I destroyed his life. I don't feel guilty for what I did, but a man is dead. He wasn't a killer; he was a con artist. I didn't want him to kill himself. I read all the news articles. No mention of the Ponzi scheme, no mention of the pensions, just that he shut down his company after returning money to his investors, then shot himself in the head."

Sean was glad Rick didn't say anything. There was nothing to say.

"I left MIT shortly after that. I was close to graduation anyway; I worked it out with my professors and turned in my finals early. Worked my ass off for two months just so I could get my damn degrees and leave. Colton's the only one who knew what happened."

"And he told Paxton?"

"I don't know." Sean still couldn't believe that his friend would betray him like that. Unless for some reason Colton trusted Paxton more than Sean.

Sean typed in a code on his desk and a hidden drawer popped open. He took out the small vial that held the microchip he'd stolen from Paxton. "This is my leverage on Paxton."

"What is it?"

"It's what he had me steal back from someone who took it from him." Sean couldn't go into the details, because Noah had been involved in the investigation and if Sean told him what he knew, he could be charged with something. Sean didn't know what—obstruction? Withholding information? But it wasn't important to what they were doing now.

"What I mean is, what's on it?"

"I don't know. I wanted to crack the code, but decided to hold on to it for a while and see what happened. And what happened is that Paxton is now in bed with Colton Thayer."

"I thought your curiosity would get the better of you," Noah said.

Sean smiled. "It almost did." He tossed the vial to Noah, who caught it. "Now it's yours."

Rick took the vial from Noah and handed it back to Sean. "Keep it for now. We'll figure out what to do with it, but I think it would help us if you found out what is on that chip. I can't do it, and I don't want to bring in a cyberteam, not this early."

"Sean," Noah said, "are you in?"

He closed his eyes. He was going to regret this, but did he really have a choice? "Yes."

"You know you can't tell anyone. Not your partner, not even Lucy."

"I know." He opened his eyes and looked at Noah. "But I need to be the one to tell her, when the time comes."

"Of course."

Sean wasn't going to lie to Lucy, but she was at Quantico for four months. He hoped this project wouldn't take longer.

Rick stood. "You and Noah work out the best way to get into Colton Thayer's group, then let me know the details. I have already secured two apartments in Manhattan and set up a false identity for Noah."

"It'll take a month or two before I can get back in," Sean said. "Knowing Colton, he'll have a job for me first, to prove I'm loyal. I'm going to use that job to force a confrontation with Duke. It's the only way that Colton will believe I've really left—to be fired or publicly quit."

Sean looked again at the clock: 3:26. He couldn't stop thinking about the woman who'd been following him. The more he thought about her, the more he thought, *Fed.*

Who was she? What did she want? More important, what did she know? Did she know what happened with Martin Holdings? Did she have evidence that pointed to Sean? Why did he care? He had immunity. He had Rick's word.

Except twelve years ago Sean had the promise of the FBI that he wouldn't be arrested for exposing his pedophile professor, but he'd spent three nights in jail. He'd had the promise that he wouldn't be expelled from Stanford, but he was.

Promises didn't mean much. Rick's intent was one thing, but Sean knew that anything could happen when all was said and done.

Noah could have brought someone in and not told Sean. Or was she the mole? Was she following him at the behest of Senator Paxton?

Sean needed to find out, because information was power and the lack of information could be deadly.

CHAPTER NINE

Duke Rogan sat at his desk Monday morning doing the one thing he hated about his job: paperwork.

The last month had been hell without Sean. Patrick was handling all East Coast assignments; it was everything he could do to keep up with the workload, and Duke was turning down new clients until they could replace Sean. He couldn't risk overworking his people and putting themselves or their clients in danger.

No successful business could survive on the presence of one person, but Sean's leaving had definitely hurt RCK in ways that Duke hadn't expected. He'd known his brother was a vital cog in the wheel but hadn't realized he'd been doing the work of at least three people and still had time to play. It was the way his brain was wired—when it came to computer systems, it just didn't take him as long to do the job.

Duke had considered sending Mitch Bianchi and Claire O'Brien, two of his top people, to help Patrick run RCK East. Mitch had the added benefit of being a former FBI agent. He'd even had a preliminary conversation. But Duke wanted Sean to return. He couldn't make major decisions like transferring staff until he had a long conversation with Sean—without emotion.

Duke had gone from being furious with Sean to being worried that he was going to get himself in such deep trouble that Duke wouldn't be able to get him out of it. He was still angry that Sean had put RCK in this position—by both leaving them and potentially damaging their reputation. JT, who'd always sided with Sean even when Duke disagreed, was more than a little livid. JT didn't want Sean to return at all.

"He made his damn bed, Duke, when he decided to work off-book for Colton Thayer," JT had said when Duke told him what had happened. "You can't clean up this mess."

Duke could smooth things over with JT if he could just talk to Sean and find out what was going on. He'd been trying to reach Sean since he quit, but he had ignored Duke. Sean shut off his phone and Duke didn't have a new number for him.

Maybe Duke should have cut Sean some slack when he found out about his reconnection with Thayer. Twelve years ago, their lives had been different. Sean had been both wild and angry after what happened at Stanford. Colton had been there when Duke wasn't. Yet Colton wasn't a good influence on Sean and had been under investigation multiple times. Colton had to have an insider in the FBI to never have been indicted, but Duke didn't know who or how. He'd asked people he trusted, but no one knew much about Thayer.

Duke didn't want Sean sucked back into the life that he'd escaped when he left Boston.

Had Duke not appreciated Sean enough? Was that it? What more did he want? Duke let Sean open RCK East, even against Duke's better judgment that Sean wasn't ready to be on his own. He was still susceptible to breaking the rules, and while skirting the law was Duke's job, he never allowed himself to cross the line. They'd worked too long and too hard to put RCK in a position of importance, and he wasn't going to let the whims of his little brother jeopardize a company that employed forty professionals, from computer wizards to bodyguards to security experts. They had a successful operation. Why didn't Sean understand he couldn't do whatever he wanted?

There was a knock at Duke's door.

"Come in," he said.

It was Jaye Morgan, head of RCK's IT department. Jaye was brilliant and gave Sean a run for his money. The only thing that Sean had on Jaye was confidence and speed.

"I found something weird in the admin log."

"Weird how?"

"I don't know. I would have sent it to Sean, but—"

"I'll take a look. Thanks."

Jaye sat down, even though she wasn't invited, and twirled her long brown hair around her finger. Nerves. Duke forgot sometimes how young Jaye was—she'd started working for them when she was nineteen. She was now twenty-seven.

"Something else?" he asked, knowing what it was but hoping if he plastered his intimidating *I'm too busy to talk* expression on his face she wouldn't ask.

No such luck.

"When's Sean coming back?"

"I don't think he is."

"All you have to do is ask."

"It's complicated." *More than a little complicated.* "And even if I asked—which I'm not going to do—he doesn't want to be here."

"Sean only wants to please you."

"That's in the past." Duke's relationship with Sean had been difficult from the beginning. Sean had always been a borderline genius, but he ran wild when he was a parentless fourteen-year-old. Duke didn't know how to control Sean, not when he could hot-wire cars as easily as he could hack into a bank. Duke had been twenty-five and should have been a brother more than a father. But he did the best he could with what he had. Liam and Eden had moved to Europe after their parents died, and Kane would never return home. Duke and Kane had started RCK with JT, but Kane's specialty was foreign hostage rescue and he spent most of his time in Central America and Mexico. So it had just been Duke and Sean, and they seemed to constantly be in conflict.

Duke had thought Sean had grown up. He'd fallen in love with a smart, driven woman. Duke had no doubt that Sean cared about Lucy, and until he did that job for Thayer, Duke had thought he'd never do anything to jeopardize the relationship. But Duke obviously didn't know his brother. Or maybe he did know Sean, because he'd expected something like this.

"I'm not saying it right." Jaye grabbed more hair. It was going to be a knotted mess. "I mean, maybe Sean doesn't know he can come back. Maybe you just need to open the door and say it's okay and you forgive him."

"Jaye, I'm telling you this because you're practically family. Sean crossed one of the few lines I have. He's not going to admit he was wrong, and he can't come back unless he not only admits it, but tells me how far he went over the line. Thayer is a criminal."

She frowned. "I guess—well—Sean always has a good reason for what he does."

Duke stared at her and said slowly, "Not this time."

Jaye obviously wanted to say more, but she left, the frown still clouding her face. Sean's childish act of quitting had really strained relationships in the office. Some of the staff were relieved, because Sean always worked in the gray area and were nervous he would get RCK in trouble. And some of the staff felt a void, both personally and professionally. Sean was a charmer and had a lot of friends. They were practically in mourning. The staff who wanted Sean back and the staff who wanted him out created an unsettling friction.

RCK was never going to be the same.

The receptionist buzzed Duke. "What?" he snapped.

"Special Agent Deanna Brighton with the Federal Bureau of Investigation is on the phone for you. She says it's extremely important. I already tried to send her to JT, but she said she was calling specifically for you."

JT was RCK's law enforcement liaison. JT had built the FBI relationship through his close friend Rick Stockton.

"Did she say which office?"

"No. Caller ID has her in a New York City area code. Manhattan."

Duke's stomach burned. Lucy had told Duke that Sean was in New York, though Duke hadn't been able to track him there.

"Send her through."

Duke let the phone ring three times before answering. "Rogan."

"Mr. Duke Rogan?"

"Yes. Deanna Brighton?" That name sounded familiar now that he said it. He typed it into the RCK database while they spoke.

"Special Agent Deanna Brighton from the New York City field office. White-collar division."

Duke's stomach burned hotter.

"What can I do for you?"

"I need to speak to your brother Sean."

"Why?"

"I'm not at liberty to say."

"I'm not at liberty to share information."

"I understand that he's no longer employed by Rogan-Caruso-Kincaid Protective Services."

"That is correct."

"But he was a principal in the company. How did that work? Can he just walk away?"

"I don't believe that is of concern to the FBI. Why specifically do you want to find Sean?"

"Do you know Sean's associate Colton Thayer?"

Dammit, Duke had known Sean was in over his head from the minute he learned that Sean had hacked into a pharmaceutical company for Thayer. Sean thought he could manage anything that came up, but Colton Thayer was dangerous because he was an ideologue. His causes might be just, but his methods were criminal.

"Yes."

"When was the last time you saw him?"

"Special Agent Brighton," Duke said, "I'm not answering questions unless I know why they are being asked."

"I'm not at liberty to say," she repeated. "Generally, when someone doesn't speak to the FBI it's because they are hiding something. Where is your brother? Are you protecting him?"

There was an RCK file on Brighton. That meant either they had worked with her or she'd come up in one of their investigations. Duke opened it. He didn't need to read more than the first note to know exactly who Deanna Brighton was. It was dated twelve years ago:

Deanna Brighton, FBI special agent out of the San Francisco office, arrested Sean for illegal computer hacking and hindering a federal investigation.

She'd been the agent Sean embarrassed when he exposed his professor at Stanford. Brighton had been furious, and justifiably so. Sean had enjoyed big, public exposures. But that time he'd gone too far. It didn't matter that he'd been party to stopping a sex offender who had a penchant for prepubescent girls; Sean had embarrassed Stanford, the FBI, and Deanna personally when he remotely took over her cybercrime symposium.

"I don't know where Sean is," Duke said.

"You're telling me you don't know where your brother is living? Where he is working? I'm having a hard time believing you."

Duke bristled. He didn't say anything, ready to terminate the conversation.

Deanna asked, "Do you have a current phone number for him?"

"No."

"You're lying."

Duke didn't like anyone accusing him of lying. "I have work to do."

And a flight to catch.

"Your brother is in trouble, Mr. Rogan. It'll help both you and him if you come clean."

Duke rose from his chair. "Is that a threat?"

"I'm stating a fact. I'll find him, and this time I will put him in prison for the rest of his life."

She slammed down the phone.

Vendetta. Duke heard her rage through the phone lines.

"Sean," he muttered, "what are you mixed up in?"

He called JT. "Agent Deanna Brighton in the New York FBI office called me. She knows Sean is working with Colton Thayer. She's investigating them."

"Shit, Duke. You've got to get your brother in line."

"Maybe it's time to bring in Rick."

"If Sean is back in the game, Rick won't do anything to protect him. Your brother is exposing us big-time right now."

Duke rubbed his eyes. "I'm going to New York to find Sean. I'll bring him back."

"I don't want him back. I'll call Rick, but not to ask him

to cover for Sean's crimes. I need to protect RCK above all else. I'm sorry, Duke. I really thought Sean had changed. He's been a valuable part of our team for a long time. More valuable than I realized until he was gone. But I can't condone jumping ship like this and risking everything we've built. You, me, Kane—this is our life, and he obviously doesn't care. I'm telling Rick that Sean is off the rails and disavowing any knowledge of what he is doing. I'm sorry."

"So am I." He took a deep breath and let it out. "Do what you have to. I'll do everything I can to protect the company." *And Sean.*

Sean was his brother. Duke had to give him another chance, or he would never forgive himself if Sean ended up in prison. Or worse.

"Let me know what she does next," Senator Jonathan Paxton told his informant. "But we're running out of time."

"I'm working on it! It's not as easy as you think—"

"Then work smarter. I want Sean Rogan detained before Thursday. It's not just my ass on the line." Jonathan slammed down his phone and immediately began packing a bag. Though it was congressional recess, he'd stayed in D.C. to finish a few projects, take meetings that he'd postponed during the busy end of session, and hold informational hearings related to the Senate Judiciary Committee.

He hadn't wanted to be in New York this week. Now he didn't have a choice.

Jonathan called Sergio Russo, a man who'd done many jobs for him and someone he trusted—as much as he trusted anyone.

"Yes, Senator," Russo said.

"Our cat didn't pounce on the rat."

"She didn't take the bait?"

"Oh, she took it. But Rogan lost her. If we can't put him in jail, then we'll have to stop him some other way."

"Understood."

"I'm coming to New York."

"Are you sure you want to be in the city?"

"I have a cover. But this situation is far too important to leave to chance. If Colton Thayer screws this up, I'm finished."

After everything he'd done for Joyce, she got cold feet. After he protected her, cared for her as if she were his own daughter, supported her ideas and company after her father died, she now decided she didn't want to go through with their plans. If she were anyone else, she wouldn't be alive. But this was Joyce. He couldn't hurt her.

"Sir, maybe it would be best if we let Rogan help."

"I can't risk him finding out the truth. I want him off Colton's team. By any means necessary. Meet me at my apartment tomorrow morning with a plan."

"Yes, sir." Russo hung up.

Jonathan booked the next available flight to LaGuardia, then poured a Scotch while waiting for his car to arrive, not caring that it wasn't even noon.

Sean Rogan had always been an annoyance, but now he was an imminent threat. When Jonathan learned that Rogan had quit RCK and gone to work with Colton Thayer, he knew that smart-ass would be a danger. For a brief moment Jonathan thought it might be a setup, except from everything he'd learned from his people Rogan had had a fight with his brother and quit. His privileges were cut off and he hadn't spoken to anyone at RCK, except his former partner, in weeks.

Rogan's volatility didn't surprise Jonathan. He was an arrogant prick who had a double standard when it came to crime. He questioned Jonathan's motives when his own were just as murky. Working with his old hacktivist group

was right up Rogan's alley and a typical childish man-
uever for someone who didn't get his way.

When Rogan waltzed into Lucy Kincaid's life and
didn't leave, Jonathan had built a file on him. It saddened
him that smart, sweet Lucy had been taken in by the
rogue's charm, but that didn't mean Jonathan couldn't
still protect her. Rogan had lived a life in the shadows,
barely escaping prison on multiple occasions. Without the
protection of his brother Duke and RCK, Rogan wouldn't
last. And his working for Colton Thayer told Jonathan
that Rogan had certainly been playing on the dark side
for much longer than his brother thought.

But Rogan had no love lost for Jonathan, and if he even
suspected what Jonathan had hired Thayer to retrieve,
Rogan would use it to his advantage. He already had the
microchip, and losing that was what had made Joyce nervous.

Jonathan had first tried to get Thayer to cut Rogan out
of the loop, but Thayer made it clear that even though Jonathan was paying him, it was his operation and he needed
Rogan to pull it off. Playing hardball wasn't an option
because Thayer had too much information on Jonathan.

Jonathan didn't like or trust any of them. They'd all
proved to be far more arrogant than warranted and disre-
spectful of his authority. He was a sitting senator in the
United States of America. He would not be played for a
fool.

CHAPTER TEN

Sean dropped a bag of food on Noah's counter. "Well?"

Noah ignored him, typing something on the computer screen.

"I got your groceries."

"Thanks," Noah mumbled without turning his head.

Sean removed a beer from the bag and opened it. He looked over Noah's shoulder. "What are you doing? *Reports?*"

Noah didn't answer.

"Dammit, Armstrong, I've given you nearly twenty-four hours. If you'd just let me do it—"

"Rogan," Noah snapped, "I need to keep Rick in the loop, especially if you want your immunity intact."

"Fuck you."

"Fuck you, too."

Sean almost walked out. He was really tired of Noah's subtle jabs about Sean's long-ago crime. Especially since Noah was the one who convinced Sean to go undercover. Knowing that they'd have to work closely together to catch Senator Paxton, they made an effort to get along. But in the last three weeks they'd begun to get on each other's nerves.

Instead of walking out, Sean stood in the kitchen and drank his beer while eating the deli sandwich he'd bought. He was starved. He'd skipped breakfast, something he rarely did, but he hadn't slept well last night thinking about the woman who'd been following him.

Ten minutes later, Noah sent his report, then grabbed his own sandwich.

"It's true that Pham-Bonner Medical is involved in childhood leukemia research and they were involved twenty years ago when Colton's brother Travis died. Getting his medical records will be difficult, but not impossible. It would be easier with next of kin—but we're quietly working on it."

Noah took another bite, chewed, and swallowed. "Would Colton honestly plan this elaborate break-in just to gather evidence he doesn't know exists about his brother's death?"

"Yes," Sean said without hesitation. "And now that he knows about the bio-toxin they're developing, it's a bigger cause for him. In his mind, the company that killed his brother would of course develop a bio-weapon."

"Hmm." Noah drank some water, then said, "The information you obtained last month is not conclusive about bio-toxins. I don't think he's right about that."

"Colton has been deciphering codes since he could practically read," Sean said. "He made a compelling case."

"You believe him."

"I believe there's something at PBM they've been using in research that makes me nervous. I've put up false paths to prevent corporate espionage—it's one of the things I did at RCK. But this was different. It indicated that the information was only on a closed server. There's no way to access it without a direct connection. I've recommended to many companies who are vulnerable to corporate espionage to keep their networks completely closed. This one isn't like that—they have a completely separate program hidden within the company. Coupled with the codes Colton deciphered, it makes it suspicious."

"I don't think going through with the actual break-in is wise. You have seventy-two hours to find evidence against Jonathan Paxton or I'm going to pull the plug."

Sean was stunned that Noah was getting cold feet. "You can't. I told you, there's something else going on; Paxton wants a physical file from Joyce Bonner's office. He's not an ideologue, unless it involves killing sex offenders. He hasn't told Colton exactly what he wants."

"I don't believe it," Noah said.

"I do."

"Maybe you're blinded by your friendship."

"You don't know Colton."

Noah raised an eyebrow and stared at Sean as if Sean had just confirmed Noah's suspicions.

"If that woman following you is an FBI agent—"

"She is." At least, Sean was almost certain.

"—then why is she following you?"

"That's what you're supposed to find out! Do you have her name?"

"We're running her image, but we have to do it on the q.t. so no one in the New York office is privy. There's no active investigation on you, Colton, or anyone on his team. That's what I was telling Rick when you walked in."

"Maybe it's off-book."

"The FBI doesn't operate like that."

Sean gestured around him. "What's this?"

"This is different."

"Bullshit. You know damn well there are bad agents mixed with the good. What about the mole? Maybe this woman *is* the mole."

"It's possible. But not everyone disobeys protocols."

Sean's fist clenched. "I'm sick of your verbal jabs, Armstrong. You don't like me, you don't approve of me, I get that, but you're the one who wanted me here, so just leave me the hell alone."

Noah walked over to the computer. He pulled a print-out from the printer and handed it to Sean. "Here's the background on the seven PBM board members. I didn't see anything that jumped out as connected to Paxton; maybe you will."

"I'll take it upstairs." Sean grabbed the papers and left.

Sean picked through the information Noah had found on the PBM board members. There wasn't a lot there. He would need to dig deeper to find a connection with Paxton.

Sean's cell phone rang and he planned to ignore it. He glanced at the caller ID.

Duke.

"Don't answer," Sean told himself.

Dammit.

He picked up the phone. "Hello, Duke. I see you tracked down my new number."

"I just had a call from the FBI. You're wanted for questioning related to something involving Colton Thayer."

Shit. That woman yesterday—now it made sense. "Thanks for the heads-up," Sean said. "I'll talk to you—"

"It doesn't work that way, little brother. You messed up big-time when you did that job for Thayer last month. Do you want to spend the next ten to twenty years in prison? I'm not going to be able to bail you out again. JT is officially disavowing you with the FBI. Please, whatever you're doing, stop."

"I'm not going to prison," Sean said. "And I didn't ask you to bail me out of anything."

"If Deanna Brighton has her way, you'll rot in jail."

Brighton! Everything became clear. She'd changed her hair, she'd gotten older, but now that he had her name he couldn't believe he hadn't recognized her yesterday.

"What did she say?"

"She said you were in New York. She wanted your address and number."

Damn, Sean was going to have to lose this number. "And how did you get my number? Did you give it to her?"

"No, but maybe I should have. Give me something, Sean—something to help fix this mess."

Sean didn't want Duke digging around and possibly jeopardizing his undercover work. "Stay out of it, Duke. I have everything under control."

"Like hell you do!"

"I'm not doing anything illegal." At least, not without the okay of his FBI handler. After the fact.

"I don't believe you."

That stung. "You made it clear that if I was friends with Colton, I couldn't work for RCK. I'm not your problem anymore, Duke."

"You're my brother. You'll always be my problem."

And that was the crux of their relationship. Sean had always been Duke's "problem." He'd been a minor when their parents were killed, and Duke had stepped in as his guardian. Not Kane, not Liam and Eden, who at nineteen moved to Europe, but Duke. Sean had both loved Duke and resented him at fourteen. When Sean moved to D.C., he thought Duke had finally realized he was an equal and not the problem child. He'd been wrong.

"No," Sean said, his voice low. "I'm not your problem." He hung up. His hand was shaking when he dialed Noah's number. "I'm coming downstairs. I know the woman who followed me."

CHAPTER ELEVEN

Lucy Kincaid was in the middle of physical training when her class supervisor, SSA Paula Dean, stepped into the gym. One look and Lucy knew she was being summoned. But she waited until Tom Harden, the PT trainer, motioned her over.

Paula was in her early forties, with a no-nonsense manner. She would have been attractive if she didn't hide behind a stern expression and severe hairstyle. She supervised all three new agent classes at Quantico, the newest class having started last month. Lucy was just past the mid-point, starting her eleventh week. They'd had a battery of tests last week and Lucy was relieved she'd passed them all, but the coming weeks were going to be busy and stressful.

Lucy wrapped her towel around her neck and tried to smile, but her eyes went from Tom to Paula's stern expressions. "You need me for something?"

"Grab your bag. I don't think you'll be back today."

Lucy frowned but went to the locker room and picked up her gym bag before following Paula from the gym. "Agent Dean—"

Paula stopped and faced her. They'd had a few rough patches since Lucy had been on-campus.

Paula said, "I'm not supposed to tell you anything, but it's about your boyfriend."

Her stomach sank. "Is he okay?" Of course he was. She'd have heard something from family first if Sean had been hurt—except he'd only spoken to her and Patrick since his birthday. And even when he spoke to her, he didn't sound himself. The split with his brother and RCK had torn Sean up, and she was stuck here, at the Academy, unable to help him get through it. She didn't think he liked his new job. He'd told her it was temporary, but he'd been living in New York for nearly a month and he wasn't talking about coming back to D.C.

The only thing getting her through the long days was her job. She was so busy studying and training that she only had time to miss him at night. And while they talked several times a week, it wasn't enough.

"Two New York agents are here wanting to question you about Sean Rogan."

Lucy immediately thought the worst. Sean often broke rules, but he'd always had the protection of RCK. Without them, had he grown more reckless? He wouldn't—he wouldn't do it because of her. She hoped.

She followed Paula not to her office but to the administrative wing of the building. Paula said, "Sit here; you'll be called in." She gave Lucy an odd look—it might have been sympathy—then left the building.

Lucy remained standing and consciously forced herself to be still—to not pace or bite her thumbnail or her lip. She didn't have her phone—it was in her dorm room—so she couldn't text Sean and ask what was going on. She was worried. She'd spoken to Sean on Saturday night, but he'd been distracted. Why hadn't she pushed him? Why hadn't she trusted her instincts and taken the train to New York and surprised him?

It was several minutes before the assistant chief of the FBI Academy, Lynda O'Neal, opened her office door and said, "Agent Kincaid, we're ready for you."

Under most circumstances, Lynda O'Neal was a hard woman to read—next to the definition of "calm, cool, and collected" was a picture of the assistant chief. But right now, her composure was ruffled. She looked angry. Lucy bit back the urge to apologize, even though this wasn't about her. She'd kept her head down and her class ranking in the top five, in spite of a few distractions. What could Sean have done that two FBI agents would need to talk to her?

She walked into Lynda's office and the first thing she noticed was her file open on the desk. She'd seen it before; with the colored labels on the side she didn't need to see her name on the front to know it was her personnel file.

Lucy didn't recognize the two seated federal agents: a dark-haired man in his early thirties and a blond woman of about forty.

Lynda closed the door and took her seat behind her desk. "Agent Kincaid, please meet Special Agents Steve Gannon and Deanna Brighton from the New York field office. They have a few questions for you." Her voice was tight and clipped.

"Questions? About what?" Lucy asked.

Deanna Brighton took the lead. "When was the last time you spoke to your boyfriend?" She stared at Lucy. "Sean Rogan." As if she needed to make clear who they were talking about.

Lucy didn't say anything. She looked at Lynda, but the assistant chief was looking down at the files and didn't make eye contact.

Why had these agents come all the way to Quantico rather than sending a local agent? Something felt very wrong to Lucy.

"Sit down," Brighton commanded.

Lucy purposefully took the chair immediately across from Lynda. With the agents on the couch, the position gave Lucy a psychological advantage in that they would be looking at Lynda—her supervisor—sitting behind her.

"Answer my question."

"Why do you need to know?"

"Because I'm a federal agent and you're a rookie agent and you're required to answer any questions I have."

Lynda said, "Agent Brighton, I've allowed this meeting even though it's highly irregular. I expect you to talk to my agents with respect."

"I'll get to the point," Brighton said. "We're looking for Mr. Rogan, simply to question him, but he's eluded us. We know he's in New York City. We need his address."

The FBI was looking for Sean. That had to be a mistake. Or a misunderstanding. Or *something* other than an investigation. How did the FBI know he was in New York? *Why* would they know? Why would they need to talk to him?

"Why are you looking for Sean?"

"Do I need to remind you *again* that you're a federal employee and you're required to answer all questions truthfully?"

"I asked—"

"We need his current address. His brother claimed not to know where he was living."

"Claimed?" Did this agent think that Duke was lying? The accusation shifted Lucy from confused to the offensive.

Sean is in trouble.

Lucy said, "I don't know Sean's address, either."

Agent Gannon said, "You're still involved with Mr. Rogan, correct?" His voice was softer than his appearance.

"Yes." Lucy tried to figure out what they wanted. They

probably wouldn't tell her, not if this was an active investigation, yet they were coming to her for information and would assume she'd talk to Sean about this conversation. Was that their purpose? For Lucy to call Sean and warn him? "What do you think Sean has done?"

"Why do you assume he's done something illegal?" Brighton snapped.

"I don't," Lucy said calmly, recognizing the tactic to twist her words to make her flustered. Last year, it might have worked. But Lucy no longer spooked easily. She was no longer always on the defensive. She owed her confidence in part to her FBI training and her experience but mostly to Sean.

Agent Gannon, obviously the good cop in this scenario, said, "The way you can help your boyfriend is to tell us where he is so we can ask him some questions. It's all pretty standard."

"This isn't standard," Lucy said. "Two New York agents coming to Quantico to question a rookie about her boyfriend? Is there an active investigation?"

"We can't discuss any pending investigation with you considering you are sleeping with Mr. Rogan," Deanna said. "We need his address. He's gone off the grid, and people don't just go off the grid when they're law-abiding citizens."

Lucy ground her teeth together, biting back a retort that would have gotten her in trouble. "I told you," she said clearly, "I don't know where he's staying."

"You two must not be that close," Brighton said.

"That's none of your business." Lucy realized she sounded defensive, and by the gleam in Deanna's eyes she'd deliberately baited her. Damn, Lucy had walked right into it.

Brighton said, "If a federal agent is involved with a known criminal, it's damn well my business."

Lynda intervened. "Agent Brighton, Lucy said she doesn't know where Mr. Rogan is staying in New York, and I'm not going to allow you to badger her unless you have proof that she's lying."

"I'm sorry, Chief O'Neal. I didn't mean to badger anyone."

Her tone said anything but.

"I suggest you call your boyfriend and have him turn himself in for questioning," Brighton said. She gave Lucy her business card. "He can reach me at either of those numbers."

Lucy took the card, barely resisting the urge to tear it in half.

"We just need to ask him questions," Gannon said, shooting a veiled glance at Brighton. "He's simply a person of interest. If he cooperates, he won't be in any trouble."

Something didn't add up. Lucy said, "You have his phone number. Call him."

Brighton snapped, "Don't you think we've tried? I know how he operates. He thinks he's above the law. *No one* is above the law."

"I think you're making vague accusations but have nothing substantive, and many law-abiding citizens get nervous when the FBI wants to talk to them about nothing specific," Lucy said. "What *specifically* is going on?"

"And *that* is none of your business, *New* Agent Kincaid."

Lynda stood. "We're done."

Brighton didn't budge. "When you talk to him, tell him to call me."

Warning bells rang. It was clear to Lucy that there was history between Brighton and Sean. She should have seen it from the beginning, but initially she'd been thrown off balance.

Lucy trusted Sean explicitly, but she knew his past wasn't squeaky clean. Was that what this split with RCK was all about? Did this visit by the FBI relate to Sean quitting RCK and moving to New York? Or about the job he couldn't talk about?

Lynda escorted the two agents from her office, then returned. She closed the door. "Lucy, I don't want to see you in any trouble, but you know that lying to a federal agent is a crime."

"I didn't lie. I don't have his address."

Lynda raised her eyebrows in surprise, but that Sean had kept Lucy in the dark didn't surprise her. If Sean was doing something illegal, he would do everything to protect her—including not giving her his address. She hadn't asked for it—there was no need to have it; she knew the move was temporary. But he hadn't volunteered it, either.

"Do you know what that was about?" Lucy asked.

Lynda shook her head. "I tried to get information. I think Gannon would have told me, but Brighton is the lead. She has a bee in her bonnet, as you saw."

"What division?"

"White-collar. I'm not going to ask what you know about it." Lynda was trying to protect Lucy as well, but she didn't want anyone going out on a limb for her. Lucy told Lynda the truth.

"You can ask, but I really don't know anything." She added, "Sean took a temporary job in New York. He said he signed a confidentiality agreement and couldn't discuss anything he was working on. He's been there for nearly a month. I don't have any other details."

"I can make some calls."

"I appreciate the offer, but I know who to call. I should get back to the gym—"

Lynda shook her head. "Make the calls. You won't be able to focus anyway. Paula told you this would take a while?"

It was lunchtime. "Yes, but—"

"Take whatever time you need. Find out what's going on. But remember, Lucy—you *are* a federal agent. If you find out that a crime has been committed, you have an obligation to report it."

In other words, be careful what questions you ask because you might not want the answers.

Lucy nodded and walked out. Her stomach was in knots. Because now everything made sense—Sean hadn't told her anything about what he was doing in New York in order to protect her. He knew she'd be torn between her duty as a new agent and her love for him. But he wasn't a criminal, and the way Agent Brighton spoke made it sound as if he was wanted for more than questioning.

Lucy's love for Sean would always win out, even if he'd gotten into something illegal. She had several calls to make. Starting with Sean.

She walked across campus toward her dorm and was surprised to find Agent Brighton, without Gannon, standing at the edge of the path. Lucy couldn't avoid her.

"You're going to lose everything if you try to protect him," Brighton said.

"If you want to continue this conversation, we should go back to Chief O'Neal's office."

"I'm trying to help you."

"I don't need your help."

"You don't know Sean Rogan like I do."

Lucy resisted the urge to argue or question, but it was hard. Very hard. "I'm not going to talk to you without Chief O'Neal present," she said.

"Then *listen* to me."

Brighton stepped forward and stood only inches from Lucy's face. "I know everything about you," Brighton said in a low voice. "I've read files you think are buried. And it would benefit you greatly if you help rather than hinder my investigation."

Lucy drew in a sharp breath, her heart racing, her skin

heating. "Are you threatening me?" Her voice cracked, but she didn't break eye contact.

"Maybe you don't know your boyfriend as well as you thought." Brighton shoved a large manila envelope into Lucy's hands, turned, and walked away.

Lucy was shaking as she strode to her dorm room, the thin envelope clutched in her grasp.

She wasn't shaking with fear but an anger she hadn't felt for a long, long time. Deanna Brighton was a bully with a badge. Whether Sean had done anything specifically to get under her skin was one thing, but Lucy didn't care what it was. Not anymore. Brighton had taken a big, fat overstep and was definitely screwing with the wrong rookie.

Lucy sat at her desk and stared at the envelope.

Don't open it.

She trusted Sean. More than anyone, more than even her family. Sean had loved and supported her like her family always had, but he'd also been honest and given her back laughter, when she thought it was gone from her life forever.

She'd never thought she'd truly recover from the brutal rape seven years ago. But she did. She survived and regained her will to live; she created new dreams, including to become an FBI agent and fight people like the man who'd hurt her so deeply. She had a focus, but on her steadfast path she never thought she'd learn to relax, or have fun, or have any semblance of a normal life. As long as she had purpose, she would be okay.

But until Sean, she had never been *okay*. Sean gave her *normal*. As normal as people like her could be. He made her smile. He gave her back the peace in her heart she'd thought had been destroyed forever. She'd survived on her own but built a hard shell around her. She'd never realized, until Sean, that she despised herself, as if all that mattered was what she did, not who she was. With Sean, she had begun to like herself again. To be proud of her accomplishments. He gave her hope. He gave her back her soul.

And Deanna Brighton wanted to take it away.

If Sean was in trouble, Lucy would help him. If Sean had overstepped a legal line after his fight with Duke, Lucy would make it right. She wasn't going to lose Sean. She was going to fix whatever had gone wrong. Sean never asked for help, but he was going to get it this time.

And ignorance wasn't going to help him.

She opened the envelope. Inside was a solitary photograph.

Sean stood with a beautiful blond woman Lucy had never seen before. They stood in a park, the woman touching his face as if she was going to kiss him.

Lucy's heart sank even as she told herself there was a logical explanation.

There had to be.

CHAPTER TWELVE

Lucy let herself into Sean's house, which doubled as RCK East headquarters. She couldn't shake the uncomfortable feeling that she was being sneaky. Sean was larger-than-life in so many ways, filling the room with his charm and ego. But even though he had an ego, it was tempered with compassion and a hidden desire to be needed.

Lucy had already talked to Patrick and knew he was out of town. That made her feel doubly guilty for what she was doing, because she hadn't said anything to her brother. Until she had more information, she couldn't confide in anyone.

She walked upstairs to Sean's office and booted up his computer. Her heart pounded even though Sean had told her over and over that his house was her house, and he'd given her his security codes. But she still felt like she was doing something behind his back.

The door, which she'd thought she closed, opened. She jumped, but no one was there. She leaned forward and saw Chip, the cat she'd adopted but Sean had been taking care of while she was at Quantico. Chip jumped on Sean's desk and meowed. Lucy petted the cat and squeezed back tears. Why was she about to cry? She didn't know what was going on; why assume the worst?

Before she left Quantico, she'd tried calling Sean, but he hadn't returned her call. She didn't want to talk to anyone else before speaking with him, but the waiting was making her crazy. She needed to find out what the FBI was investigating related to Sean, but she didn't want to send up any red flags. That wasn't going to be easy.

Sean kept his office tidy. His desk was bare, save for things he obviously valued. A glass apple paperweight that Lucy didn't know the significance of and wished she'd asked him. A photo of him and his parents when he was twelve, two years before they were killed in a plane crash. A small stuffed teddy bear Lucy had given him when they flew commercial back from Albany in May, after his plane had been shot down. He'd been whining about not having his Cessna, and she gave him the bear wearing a New York T-shirt. It had had a lollipop in its hands, but he'd eaten that.

And there was a picture of him and Lucy.

She picked it up, remembering when it had been taken. They'd been on one of their ill-fated vacations, this one to Massachusetts Bay. But this was before all hell broke loose, when they'd first arrived and were eating lunch overlooking the water. He'd said, "Smile, princess," and held up his phone to take their picture. She'd laughed, thinking they looked silly, and he took several more. But this was the first.

She loved him. It was as simple as that.

She scanned the photo of the blonde into Sean's computer and ran facial recognition software. It was something Duke had developed for RCK and licensed to private companies that needed tight security. She didn't know how long the program would take.

She checked her phone for messages and found one

from Duke. He'd called earlier, but she hadn't wanted to talk to him before talking to Sean. Now she realized Duke might have information about Sean that would help her figure out what was going on.

Duke immediately took her call. "Lucy, thank you for returning my call."

"An agent from the New York FBI office just came by to ask me about Sean," Lucy said.

"Agent Brighton. She called me this morning," Duke said.

"Do you know what's going on? I couldn't get any information from her, except that she wanted to question Sean about a pending investigation."

"I don't know, but I will find out."

Duke sounded angry.

"She's a piece of work," Lucy said.

"Sean had better watch himself. You need to tell him to get his act together and stop whatever he's doing before I can't help him."

"Why do you assume this is his fault?"

"You're an FBI agent. You know how they operate. And Sean has always skirted the law. I told him I couldn't bail him out anymore, that he has to live with the consequences of his actions. The stunt he pulled last month was the final straw for everyone here. I don't know what mess he's gotten himself into—"

"I don't think either of us knows the entire story." Lucy was stunned at Duke's reaction. Though why should she be? She'd heard the fight between Sean and Duke. They'd both said things that were cutting, and there was also a long family history that she didn't completely understand. She tried to change the subject. "I don't like Agent Brighton."

"For what it's worth, I think it's personal with her. There's a history."

"I thought so."

"Lucy, I care about you. So does everyone here at RCK. Your brothers are key assets for us. They would tell you the same thing: Don't put your career in jeopardy over this. You don't know Colton Thayer and who Sean was ten years ago when they were friends."

Lucy didn't know what to say. Duke was Sean's brother, and it was like he was abandoning him. "I don't think you can judge anything until we know what Agent Brighton is investigating." She hesitated, then said, "Duke, she's been researching my past."

"How do you know?" His voice was soft and concerned.

"Something she said. She was trying to intimidate me."

Duke didn't say anything for a moment.

"Duke?"

"You need to talk to Sean about Deanna Brighton."

"Were they . . . involved?" She couldn't imagine that; Brighton was at least ten years older than Sean.

"No. Nothing like that. It goes back to Stanford."

"The pedophile professor."

"Brighton was the FBI agent who arrested him."

Now it made sense. Brighton's animosity and anger. Her vengeance.

"It wasn't pretty," Duke continued. "She was over-the-top, but Sean was—well, his usual self, with far less self-control. I suspect she's been after him for a long time, and if he's really back in the same game with Colton Thayer, this time she'll get him."

"I don't believe Sean is doing anything wrong."

"Love is blinding you, Lucy."

"I think your anger at Sean quitting is blinding you."

"Do you know why he quit?" Before Lucy could respond, Duke said, "He flat-out broke the law. He hacked into a private company and extracted information for Colton Thayer. They are up to something, and I can guarantee you it's not legal. I hope you can convince Sean to walk away before he gets into a jam he can't charm his way out of."

Lucy hung up because talking to Duke was upsetting her. She considered calling Noah, but he'd told her last time she talked to him that he was working on a complex case and to only call if there was an emergency. She thought of Hans Vigo, except he was on medical leave, recovering from a brutal attack nearly two months ago.

Lucy decided to go to the source and called her friend Special Agent Suzanne Madeaux in the New York City office. She trusted Suzanne to be discreet.

After they had exchanged pleasantries, Lucy said, "I need a favor, and I need complete confidentiality. If you can't help me, I understand. I don't want you to get in any trouble."

Suzanne laughed. "Where you go, trouble follows."

Lucy didn't see the humor. "I'm serious."

"Lucy, we're friends. Lighten up."

"It's complicated, and I don't—"

"Just ask."

Lucy appreciated Suzanne's friendship. She didn't have a lot of girlfriends, and no one she felt particularly close to except Suzanne.

"Do you know Special Agent Deanna Brighton?"

"No. Should I?"

"She's in the Manhattan office. White-collar."

"We have over three hundred agents in the Manhattan office, and I only know one guy from White-Collar because one of his CIs ended up dead in the middle of one of my investigations. I can ask him, though—"

"No," Lucy said quickly.

"What's going on?"

"Deanna Brighton is looking for Sean, and I don't think it's to ask for his help."

"How do you know this?"

"She came to Quantico because she thought I knew where he was staying in New York."

"Why didn't she call?"

"If I had to guess? She wanted to intimidate me. She also talked to Sean's brother, Duke, in Sacramento. I just got off the phone with him."

"Does this have something to do with Sean leaving RCK?"

"Does everyone know?"

"It got around pretty quickly, since RCK is a federal vendor and there are like a half-dozen former agents who work for them. Is Sean in trouble?"

"No," Lucy said quickly. "I don't know," she admitted. "I don't know where he is. I haven't talked to him today and he isn't answering his phone. I'm worried." She scratched Chip behind the ears as the cat purred and stretched on Sean's desk.

"When was the last time you spoke?"

"Saturday night."

"Less than forty-eight hours ago. You don't know what he's doing in New York?"

"He took a temporary job. Not through RCK. He couldn't share the details because of a confidentiality clause, and now I'm worried there might be something more going on. This Brighton—I didn't like her." Lucy didn't want to go into details. Telling Duke had been hard enough, and Suzanne didn't need to know. "I wish I could explain better. Chalk it up to a gut feeling."

"I trust your gut, Lucy. Stop apologizing and tell me what you need. If I can do it, I will."

"I need to find out if either Sean or his friend Colton Thayer is the subject of a federal investigation. It could be Brighton wants Thayer and thinks she can get to him through Sean. But the way she was talking, she thinks Sean's guilty of something."

"I can get the information. But depending on the answer, I don't know if I can tell you. If he's the subject of a federal investigation—"

"I don't think he is. I think she's fishing."

Sean's computer beeped and Lucy resisted the urge to look at the results.

"Let me see what I can find out. Quietly. You're adding some spice to my life—I get to be a spy."

"I can't ask—"

"You didn't. I get it, Lucy. And tell Sean when you talk to him, if he gets jammed up, send me a nine-one-one."

Lucy hung up and closed her eyes. Her heart was racing, and not from her conversation with Suzanne.

Lucy breathed deeply. In and out. It didn't matter who this woman in the park was, did it? It didn't matter, because whatever that picture showed on the surface didn't mean anything—Lucy trusted Sean. Explicitly.

She opened her eyes and viewed the report.

Skylar Jansen.

Skye.

Sean's ex-girlfriend. One of his many ex-girlfriends, but the one he'd had for years while at MIT.

There'd been a weekend months ago when Lucy and Sean had the house to themselves before Lucy went into the Academy. Carefree, relaxing. They'd gone to see a Disney movie that made Lucy smile and Sean laughed like a little boy. They'd come back and made love in front of the fireplace, Lucy drunk with emotion.

"I love you so much," she'd said as they held each other. She was unable to contain her feelings, a rarity for her, since she usually kept her emotions bottled up inside.

"I don't deserve it, but I hope to earn it."

"Earn it? You don't earn love. There's nothing you can do that could take this away from us."

Sean ran his hands through her hair, kissed her, held

her close, a light blanket covering them as the fire danced across the darkened room. "You're the only woman I've ever loved like this."

"You don't have to say that. I'm not naïve. There have been others for you." Many others, she knew, from what Patrick had said when he tried to get her to break it off with Sean when they first started seeing each other. Patrick was being an overprotective big brother, but she'd never been able to completely forget what he'd said. "I'm not as comfortable with all this, with my sexuality, with you, as I know you expect—"

"What?" Sean propped up his head with his hand and stared at her, his mouth a tight line. "Who said I've ever expected anything from you?"

"I just . . . I know you dated a lot—"

"Lucy, I'm not going to go through all the women I've been with, because none of them matter now. They're in the past. You are my present; you are my future." He sounded hurt, and Lucy wanted to fix it but didn't know how.

"I don't want to ruin tonight," she said, her voice catching.

He lay back down and pulled her close to him, so close it almost hurt. He was shaking.

"I don't know what I can tell you that will make you understand how I feel."

"You don't have to say anything; I know—"

"I'm far from perfect. I know Patrick doesn't like us together."

"He's getting used to it."

"He wants to protect you. I dated a lot of women before you. But from the moment you came to my door in January, drenched from the storm, you've been the only one. The only one I love, the only one I want, the only one I dream about every night."

"Sean—" She kissed him. "Please don't. I trust you."

"Then I'm going to tell you something, because it's important. So you understand my love is real."

"I've never doubted."

But Sean didn't believe her, and she'd done that; she'd put that doubt in his head. She was angry with herself because she didn't want to be this way.

"I dated a lot of women, but I never told any I loved them before you, except one. I was in college, and at the time I thought Skye was it. I was nineteen, she was twenty-one, my life had gone through a major upheaval after I was expelled from Stanford, and she helped."

Lucy wanted to cry. She didn't want to hear about his lost love. But she'd started this, hadn't she? She deserved the story.

"I told her I loved her. And maybe, in an immature way, I did. But what I felt then could fill a thimble; my love for you is an ocean. I can hardly breathe thinking of losing you."

Tears stung her eyes. "Sean—"

"You are everything to me, Lucy. Ten years ago I was a different person."

"Sean, I'm sorry."

He kissed her. "You're crying. Luce—" He kissed her damp cheeks. "Baby, please, don't."

"I just love you so much. I never thought I could feel this way. I thought I was dead inside. I've been reborn because of you."

He kissed her over and over, his arms around her, holding her almost too tight but not tight enough. He made her feel safe and loved and, more than that, wanted. He made her feel special. She kissed him, held his face in her hands, and said, "Make love to me again."

They locked eyes as he slowly entered her. Her body was still overheated from their earlier round of sex, but this time it was different. She craved him physically in a way she hadn't before, as if a switch had flipped and she *was the woman she wanted to be for Sean. She wrapped her legs around him and watched his skin glisten in the firelight as they moved together in a perfect, escalating rhythm until her mind shut down and her body spiraled out of control—*

Lucy's ringing phone broke through her memory.

"Hello."

"Hey, princess."

She swallowed and cleared her throat. "Sean."

"You sound surprised."

"I'm sitting at your desk."

"My desk?"

"I needed your computer."

"What's wrong?"

She turned off the monitor. "An FBI agent named Deanna Brighton came to talk to me today. She's looking for you. I can be on the next flight to New York. Just say the word."

"No," he said quickly. "Please—stay put."

"Are you okay?"

"Yes." He wasn't okay—she heard it in his voice—but she didn't say anything. He continued, "She's had it in for me for a while."

"Since Stanford."

Silence. "How do you know?"

"Duke called. She talked to him, too. He's worried about you." And furious, but Lucy left off that part.

"Trust me, Lucy."

"Always."

"I'm sorry you were dragged into this."

Lucy decided not to tell Sean about Brighton threatening her or about the photograph. Instead, she said, "I'm not being dragged into anything. I didn't like her tone. Suzanne is there if you need her."

"I can handle Brighton."

"You must have really pissed her off."

"I have that effect on people."

Lucy wanted him to tell her why, but he sounded rushed and distracted.

"If you need me, I'm here."

"This job has gotten a little sticky. But I'm not doing anything that I'm not supposed to. I promise you that, Lucy."

"I didn't say you were."

"Duke did."

"Your brother's worried."

"I gotta go, Luce. I love you. Be careful."

"That's exactly what I was going to tell you."

"Always, princess."

He hung up. Lucy slowly lowered her phone. He'd been preoccupied. He hadn't even asked her why she was using his computer.

She turned the monitor back on. Time to do a little research. Sean would try to protect her, not to worry her, but she was already worried and she didn't need his protection.

This time, he needed hers.

CHAPTER THIRTEEN

Tuesday

Sean couldn't spend another day working in the apartment with Noah. They'd hardly spoken. Sean had spent the night alternately worried about Lucy and her visit from Brighton, pissed off at the agent, and researching the board members of PBM, trying to find a connection—any connection—to Jonathan Paxton. He might have found something. He wanted to talk to Hunter, without anyone else around.

Sean left early, picked up a breakfast burrito from a corner shop, and ate it while he walked to meet Hunter at Bryant Park, near the library, which was on Sean's list of places to go today.

Sean trusted Hunter. Maybe because he was a big conspiracy nut, but mostly because he was a good guy. Sean wanted to talk to him about Evan and Carol. He was certain that Hunter had done his own research on them when they joined the group.

Sean spotted Hunter walking down the path, looking at his feet, his hands stuffed in the pockets of his hoodie. He hadn't changed since college. Like Sean, Hunter had entered college early, but he stayed longer. Probably had a

Ph.D., or at least a couple master's degrees tucked away. He functioned well in college, where his intelligence and oddities were respected and even encouraged. The real world, outside the safety of the university, terrified Hunter in ways Sean understood, even though he didn't share the same fears.

Hunter hadn't shaved, but he had showered—his shoulder-length hair was damp. "Hey, buddy," Sean said. "I got you a breakfast sandwich."

Hunter grinned. "Thanks."

They walked while they talked, because Hunter wasn't a guy who could sit still for long. "I'm glad you called," Hunter said between bites.

"I was getting stir-crazy. Patience has never been a strong suit."

Hunter snorted and said while chewing, "You can say that again."

"Did Colton tell you I talked to him about being followed?"

Hunter nodded, swallowed his food. "Asked me to beef up surveillance. I plugged in the picture of that Fed. If she comes within a hundred feet of the carriage house, or me, I'll know." He held up his phone.

"You've always been smarter than me."

"Naw," Hunter said sheepishly. He took another bite of the sandwich. "So is that why you wanted to talk?"

"A few other things. I'm worried about Colton."

"Why? I've never seen him happier. Seriously, dude, he's glad you're back."

"I only signed on for this one job."

"He doesn't believe it." Hunter glanced at Sean and swallowed. "You're not lying."

Sean shook his head. "This is important to Colton, and I want to help him." Both were true. "But I can't stay here forever."

"C. thinks it's because of your girlfriend."

"It's because of a lot of things." Sean needed to steer the conversation back to Evan and Carol. "How well do you know Carol and Evan?"

Hunter frowned. "Why?"

"I want to know if one of them betrayed Colton."

"No," Hunter said quickly.

"You're sure?"

He looked pained and fidgeted with his food. "I hate digging around on my friends."

"I wouldn't ask if it wasn't important."

Hunter stopped walking and almost got knocked over by a jogger. Sean guided Hunter to a bench at the edge of the park, where he made him sit down.

"That fed is the bitch who arrested me at Stanford."

"Did you tell C.?"

"I found out late last night. But she knew I was in New York, and she followed Colton to the pub. I don't care what he says, I know she did—we saw her on the carriage house surveillance tapes."

"Yeah, but C.'s pretty good at slipping in and out. He'd know if someone was following him."

"He's distracted."

Hunter didn't say anything, and Sean knew he'd seen the same thing.

"Start with Carol. What's her story?"

"C. met her over a year ago. She was working at a museum."

Sean frowned. "She's not in this business?"

"Not then. But she really looks out for him. And they kind of bonded, because her sister died of leukemia, just like Travis."

Sounded like a setup to Sean.

"And she has no problem with what Colton does?"

"She's totally into him."

"Does she still work at the museum?"

"Part-time. She graduated from RISD in art history or something. She's a real good artist. Those paintings at C.'s place? In the living room? All Carol."

Sean remembered the bold contemporary art. Not his style, but it was certainly high quality.

"She has her work in an art studio someplace. I was there once, but there were so many people—you know—I left early."

Hunter didn't like crowds or strangers.

"Colton trusts her," Sean said, mostly to himself.

"Yeah."

"And Evan?"

"Why don't you talk to Skye? She brought him in. Two, three years ago. Three years is a long time."

Meaning a long time to prove himself as loyal. Three years was how long Sean and Colton had worked together at MIT.

"Oh, I get it," Hunter said. "You don't want to talk to Skye because you used to sleep with her."

"That's not it," Sean said. "It's just been awkward, okay?"

"She looks at you when you're not looking, you know."

Sean had almost forgotten how observant Hunter could be. He often disappeared in a room because he was so quiet. "She knows I'm not interested."

"Why don't you just talk to C. about this?"

"I tried. Sort of. Sean hadn't wanted to make Colton suspicious."

"You know, he's been trying to get you back for a long time, and I think it bothered him that your brother never liked him."

"Duke was family."

"I don't know why you're back just for this job."

"Because I quit RCK and I needed the money." Sean hated lying to Hunter. By the look on his face, Hunter believed Sean completely. "Colton always said I could come back. I never thought I would, but C. was a better brother to me than my own flesh and blood." Right now, that felt like the truth.

"Family's complicated," Hunter said.

"You're telling me." Sean redirected the subject again. "Has C. told you anything about Thursday?"

"I know what I'm supposed to do." Hunter inched away. Almost imperceptibly, but he was getting suspicious of Sean's questions. Damn, he had to be more careful.

"I'm concerned about the people C. is working for." Sean needed to put Hunter at ease. "I think they're manipulating him because he is so desperate for information about Travis's drug trials."

Hunter relaxed. "You don't need to worry. C. has it under control."

"If you say so."

They sat quietly for a few minutes; then Hunter said, "You know, Evan could never replace you. I think C. expected that he would, but he didn't."

"'Cause I'm irreplaceable," Sean said with a wide grin.

Hunter laughed. "Yeah. You are."

"So are you, buddy."

Hunter wouldn't do well in prison, but Sean had already worked out a plan to make sure that nothing came back on Hunter. Sean hoped that he could keep them all out of jail—all he wanted was Jonathan Paxton. But Sean couldn't say anything until after the big job at PBM.

"I dug around on Evan when he first joined. C. asked me to."

"I figured."

"You should talk to him; he'd tell you anything you want to know."

"I will."

"You think Carol or Evan brought in the fed?"

"It crossed my mind."

"I can find out."

"I don't want you getting into trouble. With anyone."

"Sean, you're good. I'm great."

Sean laughed and patted Hunter on the back. "You know, I really missed you."

Hunter threw his wrapper in the nearby trash can. "I wasn't the one who left."

After Hunter left the park, Sean walked the short distance to the main public library to further research PBM and the seven board members. He'd found some leads when he was searching on the Internet, but much of the referenced information wasn't digitized.

So far, nothing Sean had read connected PBM or the board with Jonathan Paxton. There was little information about Joyce Bonner's father, Randall, on the PBM Web site other than the fact that he'd started the company with his college roommate, Jeffrey Pham, and had died ten years ago, leaving his company to his sole heir, his daughter, Joyce.

Sean wanted to learn more about Randall Bonner, who was the same age as Paxton. Because he was a lifelong New York resident and had contributed extensively to the history and industry of the state, the library should have information on him.

Sean read several articles about how Randall and Jeffrey founded PBM, their purpose, what they hoped to achieve in cancer research. Nothing jumped out until Sean found a society page article that mentioned Randall:

> *Randall J. Bonner, pictured here with his daughter, Joyce, and her fiancé, Thomas Lynch.*

It was one of those obvious things that Sean hadn't noticed. He knew that Joyce Bonner had two children, but he hadn't thought about her spouse. He only knew that Lynch wasn't in her life.

Sean pulled up his phone and did a quick search on Thomas Lynch. There were too many. He narrowed it down by connecting Lynch to Bonner.

That's when things got weird.

There wasn't a lot on Thomas Lynch. He was an attractive man on the surface, but he didn't seem to be photographed with anyone other than the Bonner family.

Friends.

Sean scoured all the photos of Joyce he could find, both before and after her marriage. Before her marriage she was surrounded by friends; after her marriage there were only a few photos of her. All were with her husband, her father, or her children.

The photo history showed Joyce changing, from young and laughing to serious and sad. Because Randall Bonner had been part of New York society, there had been plenty of photos—Joyce was catalogued in over fifty photos the year before she was engaged to six the year after she married.

Why had Joyce changed? Because of her husband? Or did something else happen to make her a recluse? Why did she return to her maiden name? She'd changed her last name after her wedding, but her husband had died eight years later, shortly after the birth of her second child, in a boating accident.

Sean went back to the original article about the Bonner-Lynch wedding. Maid of honor, bridesmaids, ushers, yada yada. There were hundreds of people at the church, at the reception; honeymoon in France. An entire two-page spread of photos that Sean almost skipped over until he saw someone familiar:

The lovely bride, Joyce Lynch, dancing with her godfather, Attorney General Jonathan Paxton.

The photo of Paxton was his profile only, and he was twenty years younger. This was taken two years after his daughter disappeared. She'd been murdered, but he hadn't known that at the time.

Joyce was twenty when she married Lynch. Paxton's daughter would have been twenty that year. Paxton and Randall Bonner had been friends. Joyce and Monique, Paxton's daughter, had likely been friends. That was the connection.

Except what did it matter? Why would Paxton want Colton to break into PBM? What could Paxton possibly want in the company? Why couldn't he ask his goddaughter for what he needed? And why would he help Colton take down a business to which he had close personal ties? It made no sense.

Sean rubbed his eyes. He hadn't had enough sleep, and his head ached. He needed a fresh set of eyes, but he couldn't discuss this with anyone except Noah, and right now Sean didn't want to talk to him. Maybe this was what happened to cops on a stakeout—they started as friends and after a couple days ended up wanting to go a couple rounds with fists. Only Noah and Sean hadn't started as friends.

"Back to the drawing board," Sean muttered, and pulled up the information he'd found on Thomas Lynch.

It seemed obvious, at second glance, that after Joyce married Lynch, she'd pulled away from her friends and family. She gave birth to her first child, a daughter, two years after the wedding, and to her son six years later, a month before Lynch died in a boating accident.

Sean looked up all articles related to the boating accident. According to witness reports, Lynch had suffered a heart attack. He'd been sailing with his father-in-law and a family friend.

Jonathan Paxton.

Had Paxton and Bonner had something to do with

Lynch's death? Though Bonner was wealthy, his money was tied up in PBM. Joyce Bonner received half of Lynch's sizable estate, and the other half was divided equally between their two children.

Murder? Sean wasn't surprised. Paxton had killed before, but he targeted sex offenders and other creeps. He was a vigilante. Was he also a profiteer? Had he helped his old friend kill off Lynch for the money? Or was there another reason?

Sean didn't know how important it was, if at all, but his gut told him something was fishy. The only connection he could find between PBM and Paxton was this—and Sean was going to run with it.

He'd been in the library for six hours—it was already mid-afternoon. He hadn't heard from Hunter yet, so he grabbed a hot dog from a street vendor and sat on a bench eating while sending his notes and questions on Bonner, Lynch, and Paxton to Noah. Maybe there had been an investigation into Lynch's death that Noah could find out about. And if not, maybe he had access to financial records regarding the will or the pharmaceutical company. Legal access—because Sean knew he could get whatever he needed if Noah let him hack into the company again. But after their conversation yesterday, Sean wasn't going to push it.

Sean had gotten up to toss his garbage in a nearby can when he saw a familiar face. He glanced again, and the man was gone. This was New York City—lots of people—maybe it wasn't someone Sean knew. And he didn't get a good look, just a feeling of familiarity, and as he tried to remember the face, he drew a blank. He'd only seen the man's profile.

Still, Sean couldn't be too careful. He walked the three blocks from the library to Grand Central Station, then took a train into Brooklyn, went window-shopping, saw a stuffed animal that looked just like Lucy's cat, Chip. On a whim, Sean went in and bought it.

While paying at the register, Sean kept his eye on the window. A man stood across the street, back to the store-front, texting on his phone. Except that was a trick Sean used often when he was tailing someone.

Sergio Russo.

Paxton's hired thug. Russo and Sean had unwillingly worked together once and had an uneasy truce.

The truce was over.

Sean grabbed his bag and ran across the street. Russo saw him and almost bolted.

"Why are you following me?"

"Making sure you're not getting into any trouble."

"Let me rephrase. Why is Paxton having you follow me?"

"I'm sure you know."

Sean didn't know.

Russo said in a low voice, "Paxton will make your life hell if you screw this up."

"Don't follow me." Sean turned and left. Then he smiled. He'd done something to piss off Senator Paxton. Definitely the silver lining for the day.

CHAPTER FOURTEEN

Sean walked into Noah's apartment early Tuesday evening more contemplative than anything else.

"Where have you been all day?" Noah asked. His tone was accusatory.

"Researching and evading one of Paxton's hired guns."

"Excuse me?"

"Did you get my e-mail about Joyce Bonner and her husband?"

"Yes, but who was following you?"

"Sergio Russo. He works for Paxton. His daughter was raped and killed by a repeat offender. Russo attacked him and was tossed in prison. Ripe for the picking by the likes of Paxton. Someone who would have done well at RCK if he didn't have major ethics issues."

Noah didn't say anything. Sean continued, "I must have done something, because when I confronted Russo he told me not to fuck up the assignment. I'll keep my eyes open. I'm not worried about Russo."

"Well, maybe you should be. We have word that Paxton landed in LaGuardia late last night. He's at his apartment on the Upper West Side."

"He's nervous. Coming to town at the same time he has Colton breaking into PBM. Sending Russo to follow me."

"Does he know where you're living?"

"No. I lost Russo in Brooklyn, before I went to talk to Joyce Bonner's maid of honor."

Sean sat down at the table and slid over a file that he'd copied at the library that morning.

"Becca Shuman," he said. "Joyce Bonner's best friend from high school. In her wedding, hasn't spoken to her much since. But she filled me in on the details."

"I hope you have a point," Noah said.

Sean frowned but decided to cut Noah a little slack. "I do. I'll give you the CliffsNotes version. Jonathan Paxton and Randall Bonner grew up next-door neighbors in the same small upstate New York town. Paxton is Joyce Bonner's godfather. Bonner funded Paxton's early campaigns, before he died. They're tight; at least they were.

"Joyce married Thomas Lynch. She was twenty; he was twenty-eight. He was controlling, judgmental, and Becca believed abusive. Their son was born eight weeks early after Joyce fell down the stairs. She told the doctors and police she tripped. They believed her. Becca didn't, but by that point Joyce had stopped talking to her.

"Two months later, Lynch died in a boating accident, and the only witnesses were Paxton and Randall Bonner."

"I see where you're going with this, but you have no evidence that Paxton was involved with the death. What did the coroner say?"

"Body was never found intact. They found a partial skeleton three years later and confirmed it was Lynch through DNA. Paxton and Bonner said he'd complained of chest pains and stumbled overboard. They searched, but couldn't find him." Sean rolled his eyes. "He was thirty-eight."

"And you think it was murder?"

"Heart attack could have been drug-induced, if there even was a heart attack. Randall Bonner founded a medical research company; if anyone could fake a heart attack, it's him. Joyce and her kids got all the money. She put most of her share into the company."

"Why would Paxton try to destroy the company?"

"I haven't figured that out yet."

Noah sighed. "We have nothing, and in forty-eight hours you'll be committing a major felony."

"We have something. We have a connection. And it's not my first felony." Sean wished he knew why Noah was being such a jerk.

"Geez," Noah mumbled.

"I'm going to keep digging around, but I know the connection is here somewhere. What about you? You find anything?"

"More than you on your day out," Noah snapped. "I know that there is no active investigation on you, but Deanna Brighton is looking at Colton Thayer for mortgage fraud."

Sean almost laughed. "Mortgage fraud? *Colton?* Not in a million years."

"But bank fraud's okay?"

Sean bit back an irritated comment.

"That has to be a cover. She must be using a fake investigation to access information on Colton and me."

"You're accusing a federal agent of a serious crime."

"She went to Quantico to question Lucy. She wanted to know where I'm living. She followed me from the pub. The woman is obsessed."

"She's doing her job."

"She has a vendetta."

Noah raised an eyebrow. "You would certainly know a lot about vendettas, wouldn't you?"

"She's taking authority too far," Sean said.

"There are safeguards to prevent that," Noah replied.

"I don't want to argue with you, Armstrong."

Noah stared at him and Sean finally said, "What is it? You're the one who wanted me to go undercover, yet ever since we've been in New York you've been an ass. I thought you'd agree with me about Deanna Brighton. Frankly, I thought you'd mellowed out this past year."

"This isn't about Agent Brighton. I'll take care of it."

"Then what *is* it about? Is it about this case? That you think I'm getting away with something?"

"You are."

"Fuck this, Armstrong. It was nearly ten years ago. And *you* brought *me* into this mess."

"You don't regret it."

"You mean with Martin Holdings? Hell no. That guy was a bastard. He deserved everything we did, and more—and don't tell me I should have gone to the authorities. Because they would have done shit, and you know it. I told you and Rick everything."

"And you'd do it again."

"Yes, I would."

They stared at each other. An impasse, maybe. But Sean was in too deep with Colton not to see this through. Sean had to give Noah something, an olive branch.

Sean's phone rang and he sent the call straight to voice mail.

"I'm not anti-law enforcement," Sean said. "I know too many good cops. You, even." He gave Noah a half smile, but Noah wasn't in the mood.

"And," Sean continued, "I will never do anything to risk Lucy losing her faith or trust in me. I love her too much."

Noah nodded slowly. "That I believe. It's for Lucy I'm doing this."

"What does that mean?" Sean said, a streak of jealousy running through his veins. He'd known for the past year that Noah had feelings for Lucy. It was something Sean, as a guy, just *knew*. And Noah knew Sean knew.

"Are you in love with her?" There, he'd said it. And it hurt. Not because he thought Lucy would return the feelings, but because some people thought a man like Noah—a cop, a military hero, a law-and-order stalwart—would be better for Lucy than a private investigator and semi-retired computer hacker.

Slowly, Noah shook his head. "I love Lucy, but not like you. You don't need to be jealous."

"Lucy respects you. She *trusts* you. If she even thinks—"

"I care for Lucy, but I'm not competing for her." Noah ran his hand over his face. "I'm having a hard time with this case, okay? I've had issues with RCK in the past, when it was just your brothers and JT Caruso running things. You guys think you're all above the law, and I'll admit, after hearing about your shenanigans with Colton Thayer at MIT, I wanted to shut down the whole operation."

Noah turned away and looked out the window. SoHo was bustling with the club scene, and the street below was a major thoroughfare to get to two of the most popular clubs in the area.

"I'll deal with it," Noah said.

"Look, Noah, I'm trying to understand you. I get that you don't like me, that you don't like what I've done, that you think I'm getting away with something. Just because I don't regret what I did then doesn't mean I'd do the same thing now. Maybe that doesn't make any sense to you, but I don't know how else to get you to trust me."

"Ironically, I do trust you most of the time. The law means something to me, Sean. It means more to me than it does to you. Just—do what you need to do, but remember that this is my op, and I make the calls. If I shut it down, it's shut down, got it?"

"Got it." Sean knew this conversation wasn't over, but it was for now. He glanced at his phone. Hunter had left him a message. "Back to work. Hunter called."

Before Sean walked out, he turned to Noah. "What are we going to do about Paxton and Russo? Maybe I should check out Paxton's apartment."

"Stay away from him," Noah said. "He could be here on legitimate government business. Congress is in recess."

"Or he could be here because of PBM."

"I'll check on Paxton."

Sean raised an eyebrow. "Don't you think he'd find it a bit suspicious if he saw you in New York?"

"I've done surveillance a few times," Noah said.

"Really?" Sean said in mock surprise.

Noah shook his head and cracked a brief smile. "Watch your back, Rogan."

"You, too, buddy."

CHAPTER FIFTEEN

Sean listened to Hunter's message as he walked up the stairs to his apartment.

"I found something really weird, and you're the only one I trust. Don't talk to anyone. I'm freaked."

Hunter was paranoid by nature, but that didn't mean he didn't have a reason to be paranoid now. Even Sean had been antsy ever since he cloned the badge, and now that Hunter was nervous—especially after they talked this morning—Sean was doubly concerned.

He hit Hunter's number on his cell phone. No one answered. Hunter didn't have voice mail set up. Sean disconnected. Hunter sounded scared, not paranoid.

Sean grabbed his go bag from his closet and slung it over his shoulder. It had everything he might need if he couldn't return to the apartment.

He tried Hunter a second time; again, no answer. He went down the back stairs and called Noah. "I'm going to Hunter's. He sounds spooked."

"Do you need backup?"

"No—I'll send a nine-one-one if I have a problem. Find out everything you can on Paxton, Bonner, and Lynch—and that boating accident."

"I'm working on it." Noah disconnected.

Though Noah was still Mr. Law and Order, Sean understood him better. It took guts for Noah to bring Sean into this investigation. And he was relieved that Noah wasn't after Lucy. Sean had always worried that if something happened between him and Lucy, she'd turn to Noah because he was there.

Sean didn't want to wait for the subway, so he grabbed a cab to Murray Hill, where Hunter had an apartment that had been in his family for half a century. Hunter said his grandparents had owned the four-story townhome and had sub-divided and sold off floors over the years to pay for their three kids to go to college. Hunter had been the only grandchild. The top floor was still in the family and worth many times more than the original building had been.

Sean had visited Hunter's flat many times when they were in college, even lived in the basement for a few weeks one summer. A hidden staircase went from the top floor to the basement. In the twenties part of the building had been used as a speakeasy during prohibition. The basement had an old bar along one wall, a remnant of its past, along with a tunnel that led to the house three doors over.

Sean buzzed Hunter's apartment. No answer.

Maybe Hunter hadn't called Sean from his apartment. Except that earlier today, when they parted at the park, hadn't Hunter said he was going home? A loner by nature, he wasn't one for crowds and socializing. If he wasn't here, he was at Colton's.

"Come on, buddy, answer," Sean muttered.

He glanced around. It wasn't quite dark but late enough that there weren't a lot of people on the street in this quiet midtown neighborhood. Park Avenue was a block west and bustling.

The door worked on an electronic release, easy for

Sean to pop. He took out his phone, ran through a series of codes, and thirty seconds later the door clicked open. He slipped in and closed the door.

A central staircase on the south side of the building led to each flat with wall sconces faintly lighting each landing. He quietly went up to the fourth floor.

Hunter's door was ajar.

Sean retrieved his gun from his bag and crept into the apartment.

Nothing appeared out of place. Sean tried to convince himself that Hunter had gone out for dinner or run out for beer, or some such excuse, but he knew that wasn't the case.

The apartment was cluttered but compulsively tidy. Hunter was a bit OCD about his space—he collected a lot of junk and arranged it methodically. His Star Wars LEGO collection was displayed in the dining room, complete with staged battles that Sean suspected Hunter, at thirty-one, still played with. Sean liked video games, but Hunter had always been obsessed. He'd designed many but never sold anything. His skills were the back end, not making the game pretty, and Hunter was hard to work with. Like a lot of computer geeks Sean had known over the years.

Except Sean had always liked Hunter. He picked up a LEGO Han Solo and smiled. He'd always liked Han Solo best.

Sean hesitated to call out, in case someone other than Hunter was here.

He walked quietly down the hall, senses fully alert, listening with more than just his ears.

He smelled blood before he opened the door to Hunter's office.

Hunter was dead at his desk, blood pooled under his head, dripping to the floor.

"Shit!" Sean whirled around, pushing back the tortured rage that tore through him at the brutal murder of his friend. He quickly ascertained that no one was in the room.

He went to Hunter's desk—his laptop was gone. His laptop was his life. What had Hunter learned that had gotten him killed? Could Colton have done this?

Sean didn't believe it. Colton wasn't a killer. But Evan—Sean hadn't trusted him from the beginning. Was he willing to kill to keep his secrets hidden?

Sean assessed his surroundings, looking for any evidence of who could have done this. Hunter's cell phone beeped behind Sean, and he turned around. The phone was on a high shelf, charging. It beeped again, a message across it flashing:

Security Alert Code 2

Sean had no idea what that meant, but he remembered that Hunter had said he'd set up a system to alert him if Deanna Brighton was caught in Hunter's security net.

Sean pocketed his gun and grabbed Hunter's phone, hoping he could access the cloud network through it, since the laptop had been taken. Maybe the information that had spooked Hunter was backed up in cyberspace.

A noise from the living room startled Sean. He froze, looked at all possible exits. There was only one. The way he'd come in. The door was partly closed. He went to it, looked through the crack, saw movement, but it was slow and cautious.

Straight across from the den was the kitchen, and the back door that led directly to the basement.

Now or never.

He bolted across the hall.

"FBI! Freeze!"

Sean recognized Deanna Brighton's voice before he saw her. He didn't hesitate. He ran through the small kitchen and opened the escape door, as Hunter had jokingly called it back in college.

Sean didn't trust Brighton, and that she was here, in Hunter's apartment, meant either she already knew he was dead or she'd been following Sean. It made no sense for an FBI agent, even one as crazy as Brighton, to kill Hunter. But she may have staked out the place, waiting for Sean to show up. Either way, he was in trouble and he couldn't risk being out of commission—not when he and Noah were so close to nailing Senator Paxton. And if Paxton was responsible for Hunter's death, Sean would kill him.

You're not a killer.

Maybe not, but under the right circumstances . . .

"Rogan! Stop! I will shoot!"

It didn't help that he had a gun on him, but he was glad he'd pocketed it before she'd seen him. As he ran down the dark, hidden staircase as fast as he dared, he stuffed the gun and phone into his go bag. He was banking on the fact that he knew this building and Brighton didn't.

"Gannon! Catch him downstairs!" Sean heard. Her partner?

She fired her gun into the dark corridor. *What the hell?* She was shooting at him! How was she going to explain a bullet in his back?

He prayed the door leading into the basement office was unlocked. He hadn't thought of it until now, but in the past there had been a lock to keep people from going up-stairs, not from exiting.

Sean considered himself lucky when the heavy wood door creaked open. He immediately closed it and heard another gunfire burst as he slid the bolt.

He saw feet running in front of the narrow ground-level windows. He would be trapped in here, Brighton behind the door, Gannon in the front. They'd call in SWAT. Sean would have to surrender or get shot.

Except Brighton *had* shot at him.

He needed to escape and regroup. There were too many what-ifs and unknowns.

Brighton pounded on the door. "You're making this worse for yourself, Rogan!"

He pushed aside the bookshelf that hid the tunnel. He did his best to slide it back into place, but it was obvious it had been moved, dusty books and papers strewn across the floor.

He grabbed his flashlight. Brighton and Gannon were shouting, but their voices grew faint as he fled.

He hadn't remembered the tunnel being so narrow. It also reeked. By the smell, many dead animals had rotted along this path.

Where did this tunnel lead? When Sean first knew Hunter, the passage had led to a residence, but he seemed to remember the building had been converted into a business. The exit could be blocked and then Sean would be trapped.

But he'd been lucky twice. *Third time's the charm, right?*

He found the door. Pushed hard.

It didn't budge. He shined his light and fought with the knob, but cement filled the seams. Sealed shut. *Shit.*

"What are you going to do now, dumb ass?" he mumbled to himself.

He glanced at his cell phone but had no reception. He typed a message to Noah that would send as soon as he had a signal.

Hunter's dead. Shot in the head. Brighton is here with a partner, Gannon.

She's shooting at me. I'm running but might be trapped.

The last thing Sean wanted to do was shoot a cop, but Brighton wasn't giving him much confidence that he could turn himself in without injury. He was having a hard time accepting that she'd fired as he ran, and he hadn't had his gun out, hadn't returned fire, or given her any cause to shoot.

Escape was his only option.

Sean shined his light around the tunnel but didn't see much of anything except algae growing on the damp brick walls. The foul, dank smell reeked of mold, over and above decaying rodents. The floor, that may have been cement or worn stone, was damp. Water dripped all around, and in the distance it flowed. Pipes? A sewer? He followed the sounds. They became louder as the tunnel narrowed. He'd never been claustrophobic—except when he'd been in jail—but this passage would give him nightmares.

The tunnel curved slightly and cold air washed over him. There must be an opening up ahead. He walked as fast as he dared over the slippery, uneven ground. The passage narrowed as it curved until both his shoulders touched the walls. He shined his light and saw his escape hatch—a slim opening twenty feet away. Sean had to turn and go through it shoulder first, but he made it.

Sean paused in the wider tunnel and shined his light around. An old, rusting metal staircase went thirty feet down. Sean had never explored the underbelly of Manhattan, but he'd heard of it. There were utility doors, subway exits, sewer access, and hidden passageways that led to the river. He just needed to find one that got him far from here.

Rodents scurried away from his light.

Shit. He hated rats.

It was surprisingly warm and noisy as Sean descended farther down into the sewers. Rushing water he couldn't see or feel, behind walls; electrical equipment humming, churning, working 24/7 to keep the city running. A subway train rumbled down unseen tracks, echoing throughout so Sean almost couldn't tell where the sound came from.

He could hide in here, but he didn't know the tunnels well enough to elude a full-scale manhunt. He needed a way out before Brighton could call in a SWAT team or NYPD, who might know ways to shut down parts of the system. He couldn't go back to his apartment; Deanna Brighton might have located him. And until Noah could get her off Sean's ass, he had to disappear. Why had she started an investigation into Colton for mortgage fraud? That made no sense; it wasn't Colton's game. Why was she after Colton and not the rest of the group? Why had she been at Hunter's? Was she primarily going after Colton to get to Sean? Did this have something to do with what happened at Stanford? Dammit, how long could someone hold a grudge?

Would she follow him in here? Not if she was smart, not without backup. But she had proved that she didn't have all her screws in place. Shooting at him—that pissed him off. And scared him. Stupid and against all FBI protocols.

Sean stepped in something wet and sticky, glad he couldn't clearly see it. He kept moving forward. South? He hoped. There was a subway stop at 33rd, and there should be an access point. If he was going north, he was screwed, because north would take him into Grand Central Station. More cops, more people, more cameras.

"You're not thinking," Sean muttered to himself. He reached into his bag and took out his compass. He'd never been a Boy Scout, but he packed like one—thanks to his brothers. Between Kane, Duke, and Liam, Sean had been well prepared to do just about anything—including navigating an old tunnel under New York City.

He confirmed that he was headed south, and the sound of the subway increased exponentially the closer he got.

Sean picked up the pace. The faster he got out, the better off he'd be.

Somewhere behind him, a radio cut in and out. Sean immediately turned off his flashlight.

Brighton *had* followed him.

The tunnel forked; to the left was darkness, to the right security lights and electrical panels.

She was close. Too close.

He wanted to go toward the security lights, but he didn't know if there were locked doors or people or another dead end. And Brighton might be able to see him.

He turned left, feeling his way down the dark tunnel. He went down as far as he dared. He couldn't see anything but didn't risk turning on his flashlight. He took out his phone and set the light to the dimmest setting, then shined it briefly around the tunnel. It narrowed but was passable. There was an old doorway ten feet in. He pocketed his phone and slipped over the threshold.

He heard Brighton at the fork where he'd been standing not two minutes ago. The radio cut in and out again.

"Dammit, Gannon," Brighton said in a coarse whisper. "I'm trying to find the bastard."

Gannon said, "You shouldn't have gone down there alone! Backup is on its way—"

She cut him off and called out into the tunnels, "Sean Rogan! I will find you!" Her voice echoed. "You ruined my career; you embarrassed me in front of my colleagues and my boss! You think you're smarter than everyone, but you're not smarter than me. I know everything about you. I know everything about your girlfriend. I will destroy you both."

Sean's fists clenched. She was baiting him.

Get your head together, Rogan. It won't do Lucy any good if you get thrown in prison. Or killed.

Brighton was moving away. Her radio clicked in and out again.

"What?" she said.

"Torres says get your ass out of the tunnels now. I'm here at the entrance. Backtrack."

"But—"

"Now!" Gannon said. "I'll protect your ass, but you need to get here and secure the scene. We'll get this guy, but you can't take him down alone."

"I'm coming," she snapped.

The radio clicked off, and Brighton let out an angry cry. "Fuck!" she screamed. "I hate you I hate you I hate you!" She fired her gun and Sean jumped but remained in his hiding place. She fired a second time. "Fucking rats. Rogan, you're nothing more than a fucking rat!"

She was losing it. But, by the sound of her voice, she was moving away from him. The radio clicked on.

"Deanna! Report!"

"I'm fine. That bastard shot at me." Sean could barely hear her now.

"I'm coming to you."

"No. He ran; I took cover and didn't see which way he went."

The lying bitch! Sean didn't move. No doubt she'd shoot him before she arrested him.

"I'll meet you."

Sean could hear the echo of voices but couldn't make out the words. He stayed put. She could be setting a trap.

He wasn't going back that way. He waited as long as he could stand, three minutes, and didn't hear anything but water and distant machinery. He shined his light down the dark tunnel and saw a door at the end, fifty feet from his location. E33AC-4.

He had no idea what that meant, but E33 was likely East 33rd Street.

The wall rumbled in front of him, a roar growing louder until his ears rang. His heart raced and he froze. He hadn't realized how far down he'd gone, but that subway train was right next to him, on the other side of the wall. As it passed he took several deep breaths to collect his bearings.

This must be a subway access door, a way for transit employees to get around in the bowels of the system.

He had to risk it. If he spent any more time down here, the FBI would be sending dogs and their head bitch, Deanna Brighton, to track him.

He opened the door. There was a slim metal walkway that hugged the wall. A blue security light shined over the door. The subway track was practically in front of him. How much time between trains? Five minutes? Seven? He couldn't waste any time.

He looked right and left. The train had been moving south, by the sound, which meant it was coming from Grand Central. To the right was the station.

He walked as fast as he could toward the platform. The lights became brighter as he rounded a curve.

He had to find a place to change out of his filthy clothes and contact Noah. He needed to warn Colton. Screw the warning, he needed Colton to tell him to his face that he had nothing to do with Hunter's murder.

A train sounded at the far end of the tunnel. Sean didn't know how much time he had, but he ran. There was a metal door at the end; he prayed it wasn't locked. It looked like it was to keep people on the platform from accessing the walk.

The door was locked, but it was a simple industrial lock. Sean picked it quickly as the train sped toward the station. It wouldn't hit him—he could push his body against the wall—but the driver would certainly see Sean, call security, and the cops would be waiting for him.

The lock sprang open as the train's headlights reflected off the wall across from him.

He stepped onto the platform. A couple looked at him

oddly, but he kept going, ready with an excuse if anyone questioned him.

No one did.

As he strode up the staircase, he pulled on a baseball cap and adjusted the brim low, to make identifying him on security cameras difficult. He exited on East 33rd Street and kept moving. He entered a bar three blocks from the subway and slipped into the bathroom. He changed quickly, putting his filthy clothes in the garbage, burying them at the bottom. He washed his face and hands with water as hot as he could get it.

Sean took a deep breath and left the sanctuary of the john. He scouted the bar, which seemed quiet for a weekday evening. He sat in a poorly lit corner where he had a good view of the room and entrance while having the added benefit of being close to the emergency exit. While waiting for the cocktail waitress to bring him his beer, he studied the mirror behind the bar, coolly assessing the patrons and staff to make sure no one was giving him unwanted attention. So far, so good.

After the waitress deposited his beer, he pulled out his cell phone. Three missed calls, all from Noah. He returned the call. Noah answered on the first ring.

"What the hell's going on, Sean? I got your message fifteen minutes ago, but you weren't answering your phone."

"When I got to Hunter's, his front door was open and he was dead. Bullet to the head, laptop gone. I heard someone in the living room and didn't know if it was his killer. I bolted down the back staircase. Deanna Brighton was there—"

Noah cut him off. "You ran from a federal agent?"

"Noah, she shot at me. I was running, didn't have a gun out, and she would have hit me in the back."

"Are you sure?"

"That she shot at my back? Hell yes, I'm sure. Twice in the stairwell—the bullets will be in the walls—one on the fourth floor, outside Hunter's apartment, and the second somewhere between there and the basement. I locked the door, went out through an old tunnel—the basement had been used during prohibition. Took me a while, but I exited the maze. Then—"

"Meet me and we'll go in."

"No."

"Sean, this isn't a fucking game."

"She called me by name."

"Did she identify herself?"

"Yes."

"And you ran. I don't believe this!"

"Dammit, Noah, she shot at me! Not just in the stairwell, but she followed me underground without backup and she completely lost it. She fired her gun twice more, probably at the rats she was screaming at, and when her partner demanded an update she told him I shot at her! I swear to God, Noah, I did not fire my gun tonight."

"I believe you, Sean, but you still need to come in."

Why didn't Noah understand? "Hunter is *dead*. We talked this morning, remember? I don't know what I said that had him snooping, but he sounded scared when he called me. And now he's dead and his computer is gone. I don't know if Brighton followed me there or was staking out Hunter's apartment or what, but I'm not going back to my apartment, and I'm not going into the FBI office. You have to trust me on this, Noah."

"It must have been a misunderstanding."

"You weren't there," Sean said, drawing out the words. "She is a fucking lunatic. She was ranting about how much she hates me, how I ruined her life. No way am I getting anywhere near that psycho bitch."

Sean glanced around, lowered his voice. "Noah, we're so close; I'm not going to sit in an FBI interrogation room for the next two days while Jonathan Paxton gets away with yet another crime. We found his connection to PBM, now we need to find out what's so important he's willing to risk his career to steal it."

"This has become too dangerous. You're wanted by the FBI—"

"You have to find a way to fix it. I'm going to disappear for the next forty-eight hours."

"Sean, don't—"

"I have to. I'm going through with this. Colton will expect me to, even with Hunter gone." He paused. "I have Hunter's phone."

"You took evidence from a crime scene?"

"I think I can crack his code and get a history of what he was doing on his computer before he died. I might even be able to find out where his computer is."

"Let me think—" Noah sounded as frustrated as Sean felt.

"I'll call you only on the cell phone I gave you, every couple hours."

"I have to talk to Rick."

"I know you don't owe me any favors, and this is a biggie—"

"Sean—if Rick says you need to come in, you need to come in."

"All right." But Sean wasn't certain that he would. Not until he had answers. "Thank you, Noah."

"Be careful, Rogan. I'll see what I can find out."

Sean hung up and drained his beer. It wasn't even ten at night. He really did need to disappear, but he had one person he wanted to see first.

He wasn't confident he'd get out of this alive, and no way was he dying without explaining everything to Lucy.

CHAPTER SIXTEEN

Noah called Rick Stockton while on the way to Hunter Nash's apartment.

"You need to rein Sean in," Noah told Rick after he repeated what Sean had told him.

"Do you think he's lying about Brighton firing at him?"

"Hell if I know." Noah rubbed his eyes and considered the scenario. "I don't want to believe that a federal agent would shoot at an unarmed suspect, or lie about an exchange of fire, but I think Sean was telling the truth. I called a friend in the New York office, and there's already an APB being prepared to send to the tri-state area. He'll be hunted down as armed and dangerous. He's still running."

"I'll fix it," Rick said.

"And Brighton?"

"Until we know more about the mole, it's too dangerous to expose Sean's undercover role until he's back under our protection. Use your best judgment in how to handle Agent Brighton. Use me if you have to. I'll talk to the New York director and have them pull the APB, then call her supervisor and read him in if I think it's necessary. Keep me in the loop every step of the way."

"Yes, sir," Noah said. "I'd like to brief Agent Madeaux—I need someone I trust in the New York office."

"Bring her in, but tread carefully—if the mole thinks we're on to him, he'll change his routine."

"Maybe that will give us a clue as to who he is."

"Maybe we already know—I'm digging around to see if there's any connection between Brighton and Paxton."

Sean had thought there might be after he was followed, until he realized she was the one who put him in jail twelve years ago. But that didn't mean it still wasn't true. If she was as volatile as Sean thought, Paxton might have been able to recruit her.

"Let me know what you learn at the crime scene." Rick hung up. That was when Noah realized that Rick hadn't said he'd call Sean in. Did Rick actually think that Sean on the run was better than Sean under his thumb?

At least Noah had permission to read in Suzanne Madeaux; he'd already asked her to meet him at the crime scene.

Two police cars and the coroner's van blocked the street outside Nash's apartment. Noah didn't immediately see Brighton or anyone who looked like a federal agent. But it was dark, after ten at night, and spectators had lined up across the street.

Noah introduced himself to one of the cops and showed his badge. "Who's in charge?"

"Detective Tucker. He's in the basement with one of your people."

"Thanks." Noah showed his badge to the officer manning the basement door and went down the stairs.

A woman wearing dirty beige slacks and a filthy white blouse was standing next to a plainclothes cop, but she was talking on the phone. Both had their badges clipped to their belts and looked over at Noah when he came down.

Brighton was saying, "He's a pilot, so make sure you

contact all small, private airports as well. He has the means to leave the country; I want to make sure he doesn't."

She hung up and looked at Noah. "Special Agent Deanna Brighton from the FBI. This is a secure crime scene."

Noah identified himself. "Agent Brighton, I need a word with you."

Surprise and anger crossed her face; then she snapped, "I don't have time." She turned to Tucker. "This is a federal case; Rogan is a suspcct in a federal crime. Understood?"

A vein in Tucker's jaw throbbed. He said, "Oh yeah, I hear you."

"Get your people to canvass the area and let me know immediately if Rogan has been spotted. He's armed and dangerous."

"Agent Brighton," Noah snapped, "this isn't your case." He glanced at Tucker. "Detective, our NYPD liaison agent is on her way. I would appreciate it if you can work with Agent Madeaux to coordinate jurisdictional issues and resources."

Brighton turned to Noah. "Sean Rogan is a thief and a killer. I've been building a case against him for years. This is *my* investigation." She was dead serious. She either believed the lie or was doing this completely off book.

"There's no active federal or local investigation into Sean Rogan," Noah said.

"I'm not getting into this with you, Agent Armstrong. You're out of your jurisdiction."

Tucker was watching the exchange with unrestrained amusement. Noah had to put a stop to it.

"Brighton, outside, now."

"I'm leading the search. I've had Rogan's longtime friend Colton Thayer under surveillance, and Rogan is now working with him again. I knew it was only a matter of time before he slipped up, only he did it in a big way. Murder."

She had to have been following Thayer to know Sean was working with him. What else did she know? But Noah couldn't give an inch on this. Sean's life was in danger if every law enforcement agency thought he was a killer who'd shot at a cop. Noah wanted to tell her that Rogan was working for the FBI but didn't. If she was the mole, then Paxton would know what Sean was doing and Noah's entire investigation would be a bust.

Instead, he said, "Assistant Director Stockton is talking to your boss right now. You are free to call headquarters. But the APB on Rogan has already been canceled."

"You can't do that! I walked into the apartment and Rogan is there with a gun in his hand and a dead body at his feet."

Noah prayed Sean hadn't lied to him about the gun.

"I identified myself," she continued, stepping closer to Noah, "and he ran. I chased him into the tunnels. He shot at me."

If Noah hadn't already talked to Sean, he might have believed her—she was a sworn FBI agent. And while not everyone in the Bureau was solid, Noah generally trusted them until they proved otherwise.

But Deanna Brighton had already created a lot of problems, and while Sean was a lot of things, he wasn't a liar.

"I'll get to the bottom of what happened," Noah said, "but you're relieved from this case."

"Like hell—"

Suzanne walked down the stairs with another agent, a thirty-year-old tall, lanky male. "Noah, good to see you again. And Hayden Tucker, I heard you got your gold shield over the summer. Congratulations."

"Thanks much, Suz."

Brighton was staring at them like they were all crazy and she was the only sane person.

Suzanne continued, "I hear we're working on this together." She glanced around the basement, which was crammed with computer equipment and books. "It's crowded down here. Why don't you and I walk through the crime scene and chat?"

"You still mixing it up with DeLucca up in Queens?"

Suzanne groaned. "DeLucca is off-limits." She said to Noah, "Noah, meet Agent Steve Gannon, White-Collar. I'll leave you to straighten out the deets, 'kay?" Her tone was light, but her eyes were serious. She was trying to tell Noah something, and he wasn't certain he got it.

"Deanna," Gannon said, "I talked to Suzanne, and she said D.C. is lead on the case. I think we should take a step back and listen to Agent Armstrong—"

"No! You don't understand. He's up to something big, and then he kills his partner."

She was talking to Gannon, not Noah. The dynamic was interesting, and she was borderline hysterical.

Noah said, "Sean didn't kill Hunter Nash."

She turned to Noah, her light eyes wild. "You don't know that!"

Noah turned to Steve Gannon. "Agent Gannon, I suggest that you convince your partner to leave and go directly to your office."

"Deanna," Gannon said, looking from Noah to his partner, "let's go."

Deanna took a deep breath and forced herself to calm down. "No. Wait. You have to listen to me. Sean Rogan is dangerous. He shot at me. He killed his partner. Don't you see?"

Noah couldn't tell her anything about the undercover investigation, not with her being such a loose cannon. He said, "I'm vouching for him. If you don't report to headquarters straightaway, I'll be taking your badge. Give your Glock to Gannon."

She looked like she wanted to continue to argue. Then she unholstered her weapon and handed it to Gannon. She walked toward the stairs.

Gannon said, "Deanna's smart. Real smart." He was apologizing for her, Noah realized. "She's been after Rogan for a long time, but when he turned up in New York she got kind of obsessed, certain he was into something big."

"How many gunshots did you hear?"

"Two initially. Then, ten minutes later, two more."

"Watch her," Noah said. He nodded toward her gun. "Check the magazine."

Gannon didn't want to. "Why?"

"Do it."

Gannon reluctantly popped the magazine. "Ten."

"Chamber?"

"One."

"Sean didn't shoot at her," Noah said. "She lied."

Gannon didn't seem surprised. "I walked through the crime scene. She said she saw Rogan standing over the victim's body with a gun in his hand, except Rogan ran when she was still in the living room. There was no angle where she could have seen Rogan or the body, unless she stood directly in the doorway."

Noah realized the implications. "Sean wouldn't have been able to run if she was in the doorway while he was still in the room."

It might have been a minor point—he had fled a room where a body had been discovered—but Brighton had already lied about having eyes on him with a gun over the body and about the gunshots.

Noah said to Gannon, "Don't let her out of your sight."

Gannon nodded soberly and left.

Noah called Rick. He was on the phone, so Noah left a voice mail with the new information.

He looked around the basement. This appeared to be a wasteland for old electronics, as if Nash couldn't bear to part with any of his stuff. Ancient game systems, a computer with a floppy drive that Noah barely remembered, a dozen keyboards stacked on a shelf.

A solid wood bookshelf had been moved and behind it was the passageway where Sean had escaped. A splintered door was open, leading to stairs. Noah found a light switch and turned it on. Only one faint bulb burned from the top. He carefully went up the stairs without touching anything. Four flights later and he was in Nash's kitchen. The coroner's team was taking out the body.

Suzanne was talking with Tucker. She saw Noah and said, "No forced entry, single gunshot to the head, approximately two hours ago. Does that clear Sean?"

"I don't know, but he didn't do it."

Tucker glanced at Suzanne and said, "I didn't know the feds were hiring psychics now."

Suzanne laughed, but Noah didn't see the humor in the situation. "Sean said he didn't fire on Brighton; she said he shot at her and she returned fire. Her partner heard four shots total. There are four bullets missing from her Glock."

"He could have used a silencer," Tucker suggested.

Noah didn't need the help. "You have to trust me on this. I'll take full responsibility."

Noah realized that while he'd *wanted* to believe Sean, he hadn't fully trusted him until he compared Gannon's statement to Deanna Brighton's Glock. He felt like a shit about it, too. Sean made it difficult to trust him, but at the same time, he'd been solid while working undercover.

"Noah?" Suzanne said.

"You're in charge, along with Detective Tucker. Whatever you need to tell him is cleared, but need-to-know, okay?"

"Well, this is interesting," Tucker said.

Noah ignored him. "I need everything. Bullets and casings. We're bypassing the New York office—ship everything directly to the FBI lab at Quantico. Sean told me Brighton fired twice in the back stairwell and twice in the tunnels. I'll find out if there are any distinguishing landmarks, but he got out at the subway at East Thirty-third, so I'm thinking that's the outer search boundary."

"You talked to the guy?" Tucker asked.

Noah said, "I'm sorry I can't give you more information, Detective, but I have to get down to FBI headquarters and make sure the APB on Rogan has been voided."

"Proving she's lying is going to be hard," Suzanne said.

Noah handed her Brighton's weapon. Suzanne put it in an evidence bag. "Full ballistics. And report directly to me. Anything you learn I need to know."

"Sean really needs to come in," Suzanne said.

"Her partner told me she didn't see Sean over the body. She lied about that." Noah walked over to the doorway of the den where Hunter Nash had been killed. "If she was standing here, she'd have seen Sean and the body, but then Sean couldn't have escaped." He walked back to the front door. "Gannon said they were in the living room, Brighton went in first, and she saw Sean run from the den into the kitchen. That's where the back staircase is. She might have seen the body *after* Sean fled, but not while he was in the room."

"Shit," Suzanne muttered. "Why would she lie?"

"Because Sean pissed her off twelve years ago and she's been holding a grudge."

Noah was torn between doing what was right under the law and doing what was right to protect both the undercover operation and Sean. If Sean pulled out of Thayer's group now, they'd never get the evidence against Paxton. Did Noah want Paxton so badly that he'd put Sean in greater danger? Or was this truly the only way to find the truth about both Hunter's murder and Paxton's crimes?

Noah said to Tucker, "Can you make sure NYPD knows that Rogan isn't a suspect? No itchy trigger fingers on this. Suzanne, we need to retrace Nash's steps. Find out what he knew that got him killed."

"You think it's connected to your op?"

"Suzanne was a sharp agent. She'd already figured out something was going on. I'm going to talk to Deanna Brighton. If she's been following Sean since he's been in New York, she might know something that will help us."

Suzanne glanced at Tucker and said, "Would you please excuse us?"

Tucker nodded and left the kitchen.

"What?" Noah asked.

"Lucy called me yesterday. She said Deanna Brighton questioned her at Quantico. Wanted to know if Sean was under investigation for anything. What's going on?"

"I appreciate you coming in the middle of this without knowing all the details. I'll fill you in as soon as possible. The basics? Sean is working deep undercover for me and Assistant Director Rick Stockton, a case I've been involved with for nearly a year. I brought Sean in because of his relationship with Colton Thayer, a known hacktivist. But I can't have his cover blown, not yet."

"Lucy doesn't know?"

Noah shook his head. "I need your discretion, Suzanne."

"You got it."

It was late Tuesday night when Sean circled Colton's carriage house. He didn't see any police or federal agents, but that didn't mean they weren't watching the place. They might have learned a few tricks of surveillance. But he knew more. Confident there was no one with eyes on the back, he went up the alley and into Colton's backyard. He didn't care about Colton's cameras.

Sean typed in the security code on the back door. It

opened into the long, narrow garage that could easily hold three cars. Colton had a classic Mustang convertible, and it was parked in the middle, as usual. He rarely drove. The alarm panel beeped—Sean reset it, then called Colton's cell phone.

Colton answered. "You broke into my house." But his voice was humorous.

"Hunter is dead. I don't know if anyone is watching this place."

Colton paused. "I'm upstairs." All humor was gone.

Sean went up two flights to the main living area. Colton came down from his bedroom, followed by Carol buttoning up her jeans. She had on only a bra.

"What happened?" Colton asked.

"Hunter was murdered. In his apartment." Sean glanced at Carol. "We need to talk alone."

"I trust her."

Sean stared at him and remained silent.

Carol kissed Colton's cheek. "It's okay, C. I'll make coffee." She grabbed a shirt off the couch and pulled it on, glaring at Sean.

"The roof," Sean said. It was the only way they could have complete privacy.

"We're a team," Colton said, closing the sliding glass door behind him. "How dare you treat Carol like shit. You're the one who walked away nine years ago." He was hurt, but Sean didn't want to talk about the past.

"Where are Skye and Evan?"

"In their rooms. You know I like to keep everyone close when we're working a job."

Sean pulled out his pocket computer and ran a jamming program. He didn't want anyone, good guys or bad, listening into this conversation. He didn't know if Colton's house was bugged or if someone had a long-range microphone aimed at the place.

Sean said, "What are you up to?"

"Me?"

"Yes. The more I've gone through this plan, the more I realize it makes no sense."

"What more do you want?"

"I want Hunter alive." His voice cracked.

"What happened?" Colton repeated. "Are you sure he's dead? How?"

Sean was usually good at reading people, but he couldn't tell if the grief on Colton's face was real. He had to push Colton for answers.

"Hunter called me tonight and said he found something that scared him. I went to his apartment and he was dead, a bullet in his head, sitting at his desk. His laptop's missing."

Colton sat down heavily. "He had our entire security plan. Everything on the PBM break-in."

Sean wanted to smack Colton. "He's *dead!*"

Sean paced. He couldn't help it. He felt like this whole thing was unraveling and he didn't know how to put together the threads.

"I trusted you from the beginning," Sean said. "I gave up everything, my brother, my business. I'm risking my relationship with Lucy, because you said you needed me. And you're the first person I ever had in my life who believed in me." As he said it, he realized it was true. Other than when his parents died, he'd been at his emotional lowest after Stanford. He'd gone from the high of his success in stopping the pervert to being in jail and meeting his brother's stern disapproval. It had taken years to rebuild that relationship, and then to learn that all the faith and trust Duke had in him had been a lie. Duke expected him to fail.

When Sean said, *Duke, you have to trust me,* Duke had said, *I can't.*

Yet here Sean had been lying to Colton from the beginning and Colton trusted him more than Sean's own brother.

Sean felt nauseous. He sat on a chair and put his head in his hands. Everything was so far out of control, he didn't know why he'd agreed to do this in the first place. He didn't like himself very much as he realized that he'd agreed to go undercover to get the protection of the FBI in case Paxton had evidence of Sean's long-ago crime. And he wanted to nail that bastard of a senator for his threats and blackmail.

You're a selfish ass, Rogan. You used Colton just like Paxton used you.

"Sean," Colton said, sitting down next to him, "I didn't lie to you on Sunday when we met, but I found out later that day specifically what Paxton wants me to steal. I just decided after you told me about the federal agent following you that it would be best to keep it to myself. But—I can't believe Hunter is dead. No one is ever supposed to get hurt. We don't hurt people, Sean."

"We did. Nine and a half years ago, when Robert Martin killed himself."

"That wasn't your fault. I told you then, and I believe it now. He was a crook, and he would have been on some exotic island before the FBI ever caught him."

Sean believed it at the time.

"Nine months ago, Paxton hired me to hack into the Federal Bureau of Prisons and decipher their tracking code. That's when I first tried calling you, remember? Back in February. But you were in the middle of looking for your cousin."

"I remember."

"So Hunter and I figured it out."

"Hunter is just as good, if not better than me." *Was as good.*

"True, but he's easily distracted. Not as disciplined.

Anyway, all Paxton wanted was information on how the prison system tracked and housed sex offenders. I figured out how they were coded and, based on that, where they were housed within each facility. I researched specific prisoners, then extrapolated. I gave him all the data, coded."

Sean wondered if that was the information on the microchip he'd stolen from Paxton over the summer. Except what would prisoner codes have to do with a pharmaceutical company? And all Paxton had to do was get another copy from Colton.

"Then, a couple months ago, he called me about PBM. He said he had information about their research—he knew about Travis and that I was researching PBM drug trials. He said the information was there for the taking."

"And you hired me."

He nodded. "I didn't want to work for him again—honestly, I don't trust him."

"Good."

"But when we got in and saw that the information I need is outside of their network, I knew I needed Paxton's resources. All he wants is a set of files in Joyce Bonner's office. In her safe. And if there's a DVD, he wants that, too."

"Her safe," Sean said bluntly. He now understood exactly why Colton needed him. He'd been their safecracker. "Shit, C., I haven't cracked a safe in years." Not completely true. "I have no idea what kind of system it is, what tools I need—"

Colton pulled his wallet out and removed a card. "Paxton gave me the specs. I know it's something you can hack; it's computerized."

Sean reluctantly took the card with the specs on it. He knew the system. He could hack it.

But he didn't like being kept in the dark for so long.

"Who killed Hunter?" Sean asked.

"I have no idea!"

"Hunter called me, scared, about something he'd un-covered. That information got him killed."

"You don't know that." Colton was grasping at straws, trying to make sense of the impossible. Impossible only because they didn't have enough information.

"Someone outside of our group knows about what we're doing."

"No, that's not possible."

"You have no idea if Paxton is watching us, if he has his own spy inside."

Colton shook his head. "I trust everyone here. You're the outsider, Sean."

Sean's gut tightened. "I have a sick feeling we're being set up. We need to shut this down."

Colton grabbed his hands. "Sean—I can't do this with-out you. I need proof that Travis was killed by those drug trials and they covered it up. I can get it as long as I bring Paxton these files. It's more than a fair trade, considering how much money he's paid me."

It didn't make sense to Sean—if Paxton wanted files from Bonner, why not just ask her for them? He was her godfather! Did Colton know about their connection? And if not, should Sean say anything? If Colton became suspi-cious about how much research Sean was doing on his own, he might cut him out—and Sean would never know why Paxton hired Colton in the first place.

"I'll pay you anything you want." Colton sounded des-perate.

"I'm not doing this for the money," Sean said.

"You never did," Colton said.

"Neither did you."

Sean took a deep breath, slowly let it out.

"I didn't expect to find the bio-weapon," Colton said. "We're going to expose them for what they are."

It was clear to Sean that Colton didn't care about the

toxin. It was just one more reason on a long list to destroy PBM. "All right." Then he considered something. "Did you tell Paxton about the bio-toxin reports we found?"

"No. Absolutely not. Only our team knows."

"You, me, Evan, Skye, Hunter, Carol—that's a big team."

"And, possibly, whoever stole Hunter's computer."

Sean wasn't so sure about that. "Hunter has a fail-safe on his computer. I don't know that just anyone can break his code." He considered what Colton was telling him. "After our conversation on Sunday, I digged a little deeper into PBM. I just couldn't grasp what Paxton could be interested in."

"I told you what."

"Except he's Joyce Bonner's godfather. Long-time family friend."

Colton looked confused.

Sean continued, "So why is he willing to let you destroy PBM? Because if everything goes the way *you* want, PBM will be shut down. At the minimum, embarrassed and under federal and legal scrutiny. And if we're right and they're experimenting with bio-weapons, the media will be all over it. I just don't understand why Paxton would hire you to break into a friend's business."

"Maybe they had a falling-out. Why are you checking into it?"

"Research. After our conversation—let's just say, I've had run-ins with Paxton and I don't trust him."

"I have us covered."

"No one can protect us if this goes south." Except Sean knew that *he* had immunity. His guilt simmered hotter. He didn't want to throw Colton under the bus on this. He'd gone undercover thinking what? That Colton, too, would get a pass? That once Rick Stockton stopped Paxton, he'd let Sean's old gang walk? They would all be in prison.

But what choice did Sean really have?

"Why did he want the prisoner codes?" Sean asked, almost to himself.

"I don't care. I just want to find the answers about my brother. I want to find out if they're developing a bioweapon and expose them to the world. I want to make this company stop hurting people. Stop lying about their good works and getting all the benefit and money for things they don't do."

Colton looked physically pained, like it was his moral obligation to stop PBM.

"Paxton is using you," Sean said.

"I'm using him, too!"

"C., listen to me," Sean said. "Paxton doesn't do anything without thinking ten steps ahead and to the side."

"We go in; we get the files; we look at them before we give them to Paxton."

"This is not going to go the way we think."

"You told me nine and a half years ago after we returned the money Martin Holdings stole from the pensions that it wasn't worth looking over our shoulders for the rest of our lives."

"It's not," Sean said.

"But you also said you didn't regret it. Do you now?"

He hesitated. Did he? Knowing what he had to do now to protect his relationship with Lucy? That he had to lie to Colton? That Martin had killed himself?

Then Sean thought of all the people, dozens of people, who would have lost everything. Not just their pensions but eventually their houses, their valuables, everything they'd worked a lifetime to earn so they could be comfortable and secure during their golden years. "No."

"I haven't stolen any money since then, but there are some things worth fighting for. Travis wasn't the only kid who died in those drug trials—and I'm going to prove it. I'm not a saint, but everything I've done has been to right wrongs. PBM used these kids as a way to get more government money. I'm going to prove it, and the only way I can do it is to go inside. I need to know the truth, the extent of their cover-up."

"That's why I agreed to help you."

"And . . ." Colton paused. "I haven't told anyone, not even Carol."

"Trust me," Sean said, though his stomach burned that he was the least trustworthy person here.

"I'm going to expose this all to the media. It's the only way that I can protect everyone. I'll have proof, but the higher-ups in government will try to keep it quiet."

"You sound like Hunter."

"He may have been paranoid, but with good reason. And I don't want anyone else to get hurt. The only way to protect us is to make sure that the media has everything I have. Right?"

Sean wasn't so sure about that, but he only said, "It's never that simple."

"Maybe not, but it's the best plan I can come up with, and I think it'll work." Colton stared at him. "I need you, Sean. You don't know what it means to me that you are here to help me avenge Travis's death."

"I think I do," he said.

Sean stood up and walked across the roof. He stared into the night.

"I need to go," Sean said.

"Stay here tonight—"

"I can't." He faced his friend. "I have a bad feeling about this job, and I need to see someone before we go dark."

CHAPTER SEVENTEEN

Wednesday

Lucy was studying into the wee hours of Wednesday morning when someone knocked on her door. It wasn't unusual for the new agents to be up late studying, so she assumed someone had a question.

She opened the door and stared, speechless.

Sean.

He smiled, but his eyes were tired and worried and he looked pale, like he hadn't slept or ate.

She took his hand, pulled him into her room, and closed the door.

"Sean—"

He stepped forward and kissed her.

He kissed her with such intensity that it stole her breath away. She wrapped her arms around his neck and he held her tight, his kiss turning into a tight hug, and he didn't let go.

"I've missed you so much," he whispered. His voice caught on the last word.

"What's wrong?"

He averted his eyes. "It's complicated."

"It's about the job in New York," she said. "And Deanna Brighton."

He nodded. "There's so much more."

Lucy took his hand and led him to her bed. They sat down and he rested his forehead on hers. She'd never seen Sean look so defeated.

"Sean, what's happened?"

"I needed to see you."

In the ten months that Lucy had known Sean, he'd never looked so vulnerable. In fact, *vulnerable* was the last word she'd ever have used to describe him, until now.

"I'm glad you came," she said. He relaxed perceptibly and started playing with her hair, twirling the ends around his finger.

She wanted to ask him about the photo and what Brighton was up to and what he'd been working on in New York. Who'd hired him and was he in trouble? But before she could say anything, he asked, "Why do you love me?"

"What?" She blinked. "Why are you asking me that?"

"I know why I love you. You're beautiful." He smiled, tried to make it casual, but his eyes were too serious and he was assessing her every reaction, as if he doubted she could care for him. "Guys care about looks, you know."

"I've heard." She tried to make her voice light but couldn't pull it off. These were uncharted waters for her. It reminded her uncomfortably of the conversation they'd had months ago about Skye Jansen. It reminded Lucy about the photo and the secrets Sean had.

"You're smart, too. Some guys don't care about brains, but I do. Very much."

"I'm glad," she said. "Looks are temporary; brains are forever."

"You'll be just as beautiful when you're eighty as you are right now."

"I don't know about that," she said. She couldn't smile. Sean was in pain. Her chest ached with the need to help him, but she didn't know what to do.

He ran his finger down her neck. "With you, I feel like

tomorrow matters. There hasn't been a moment while I've been in New York that you haven't been on my mind. Thinking about you gives me peace. You make me whole, something I've never had before. Wherever the FBI sends you, I'll follow. I know I've said we'll make it work with me in D.C. and you wherever you go, but I need to see you every day. It's been nearly four weeks since I touched you, Lucy. I'm lost without you."

She put her hand over his heart. "I'm right here." She took his hand and put it over her heart. "You're here."

Sean stared at her. He wanted an answer to his question. She didn't know what to say—how to put her feelings into words.

"Sean, you gave me my freedom."

"Freedom?"

"I don't know how else to explain it." She closed her eyes, collecting her thoughts, then opened them and said with passion, "Until you, I had been in a prison of my own making. Every decision I made was for one purpose: to be a cop. An FBI agent. I never did anything for me that wasn't directly related to my goal. I never had fun. I don't think I saw a movie in years until you took me to see that Pixar movie in February. Remember when we went ice-skating? You make me laugh. You make me want to do more than *this*." She waved her arm around her sterile room. "This is important to me, but I realize now that my goals held me captive. I can achieve my dreams, but they mean so much more to me because I have you to share them with. You help me put everything in perspective. I don't know how, or why, but I don't want to analyze it. It scares me to shine light on it, as if it'll disappear and I'll be left with nothing."

She put her hands on his face. "Until you, I was half-dead inside. You found the part of me I thought was gone forever. I don't lie to myself—I know there's always going to be situations and reactions because of my past, because of what happened, but I process them differently because you freed me. I love you because you make me a better me."

"Princess—"

She kissed him until he was lying down, her on top of him. "Shh," she said. "No more talking."

Sean wanted nothing more than to lose himself in Lucy for the next hour. To spend the night with her, hold her, her love and trust strengthening him.

But he had to tell her the truth. And he didn't have any more time.

"Lucy." Sean sat up, pulling himself from her arms. He grabbed her hands, needing to touch her, craving the physical contact while knowing he was going to have to leave. He wanted to feel her reaction as well as watch her expression.

"It's okay," she said. She smiled slyly. "I can sneak you out later."

"You may have to sooner."

Her smile faltered. "Sean—what's wrong? Please trust me."

"I do. More than anyone in the world. There's nothing I want more than to make love to you, but I have to go."

His tone, his expression, made her stomach drop. "You drove five hours to leave after twenty minutes?" She stared at him, perplexed.

"Well, it only took me three hours. I flew," he said with a half smile that didn't reach his blue, blue eyes. "I had a friend from the base pick me up at the airstrip, and I need to get back to New York before dawn. But I have to tell you in person. It's important."

He could see her mind running through every possible bad scenario. "You could have called," she said, her voice catching.

"I had to *see* you." *Touch you, hold you, kiss you.*

He took a deep breath, stared her in the eyes, and said,

"I've been in New York this past month working under-cover with Noah."

She blinked, her face frozen in surprise. "With *Noah*? Noah *Armstrong*? The FBI?"

He almost laughed at her stunned reaction. "Yeah. Me and Noah, partners. I have some stories for you. . . ." His voice trailed off. "Stories for later. I didn't tell you because I didn't want you to worry. You have so much on your mind right here"—he gestured around him—"getting your badge and gun, I didn't want you to be divided. And I promised Rick I wouldn't tell anyone."

"Rick *Stockton*? Assistant Director Rick Stockton?"

"There's so much to the story, but I'll give you the highlights. Right after you left for the Academy, Rick and Noah came to see me. Noah has been investigating Jona-than Paxton."

Lucy didn't look surprised. In a clipped voice she said, "Why? Because of the vigilantes?"

"Partly." How could he explain? "Paxton found out in-formation about me, about something I did a long time ago. Paxton blackmailed me over the summer to steal something for him, and I did it."

"Why would you give him that kind of leverage?"

"He lied. He said you knew about the vigilante group from the beginning, and I remembered when you went to see him and gave him the locket from his daughter—I was trying to protect you. But he lied; you didn't know."

She shook her head. "I suspected," she whispered. "But I couldn't prove anything."

"Babe, I didn't know what his game was, and I didn't want anything to come back on you. I did what he wanted, found the locket, but I kept what was inside. A microchip. So I had his microchip and he had informa-tion on me and I was going to hold on to it until the stat-ute of limitations was up." Sean sighed. "It was stupid of me, I know, but—"

"Shh. It wasn't stupid. I know how Jonathan operates. I just wish you had told me."

"So do I. I don't want secrets between us, Lucy."

She kissed him. "It's okay, I understand."

"You're not going to ask what I did?"

"You'll tell me when you're ready."

Her love and trust turned his heart inside out. "I don't deserve you."

"Shh. You'd never let me say that to you." She cocked her head. "Okay, what did you do that Jonathan was holding over you?"

"Nine and a half years ago I hacked into a bank and rerouted money a con artist had stolen from pensions." Sean explained about Robert Martin and his scam.

Lucy stared at him blankly. His heart fell. "Don't hate me."

"I don't hate you. But why didn't you go to the FBI?"

He shrugged. "At the time, I didn't trust them. Not after what happened at Stanford, and the way I found out about the scam was illegal."

"But Jonathan found out. Who else knew?"

"That's what I'm trying to find out."

"But I don't understand why you've been in New York."

"Noah uncovered a connection between Paxton and my old friend from MIT, Colton Thayer. Colton has always been trying to get me back into his group. That was my past, and with RCK I couldn't—well, it just wasn't going to work out. But—Noah convinced me to accept his offer."

"What does Jonathan have to do with your friend?"

"He hired Colton. I needed to find out why. Noah needed me, my skills and connections, to pull off the sting. And Thursday night it all comes down. I know Paxton hired Colton to steal something from a pharmaceutical company, but I don't know what or why. I'm not sure Colton's telling me the whole story."

"Did he tell Jonathan about the scam?"

"He says he didn't."

"You believe him?"

"I do. But—someone told Paxton. I think Colton told someone else. Maybe everyone in the group, maybe just his new girlfriend, but he told someone who talked to Jonathan. That's the only thing that makes sense to me. I don't see why Colton would betray me, especially now."

"And Patrick and Duke were in on it? So you really didn't quit RCK?"

"I had to make it real. No one knew. *No one* except Noah and Rick."

"You mean the fight with Duke—"

"It was all real. At least on Duke's end. I helped Colton with a side project and made sure Duke found out about it. I knew he'd blow, and he did. He doesn't know why I did it."

"You need to tell him."

"I can't, not until this is over. And—" Sean looked away.

Lucy touched his cheek, turning him to face her.

"He didn't mean what he said. He didn't know the truth."

"He meant every word. Duke and I have had a rocky relationship ever since our parents died. Up and down. But it's fine." It wasn't fine. Sean would have to work through things with Duke when this was over. He just didn't know how.

"I really have to go, Luce. I'll fill you in on all the details later, but I have to get back to New York. Something happened tonight—a friend of mine was killed because I asked him to research a few things. I have to figure out what he learned that got him a bullet in the head. And that FBI agent, Deanna Brighton, is trying to convince the authorities that I'm the killer and shot at her while escaping."

Lucy's hands tightened around his. "Oh, God."

"I didn't—"

"I know."

Relief flooded through him. Lucy believed him, without hesitation. He kissed her. "It's gotten out of control, but I'm going to fix it. It ends in forty-eight hours."

"I'm coming to New York with you."

"No."

"*Yes,*" Lucy said.

"*No,*" Sean repeated. "Brighton is crazy. She threatened to destroy you. She put an APB out on me."

Lucy said, "She gave me a photograph of you and Skye Jansen."

It felt like a knife twisted in his heart. "Photos? What kind of photos? Lucy, I haven't—"

"I know. They were of you and Skye in a park. You were talking, your heads close together—"

Sean's heart nearly stopped. "Lucy—you can't believe I would ever betray you. I love you. Skye and I were over nine years ago."

"I know. I trust you, Sean."

"That bitch."

"I'm okay. Just full disclosure—I didn't know who she was and I went to your house and used your photo recognition software to identify her."

"Monday night when you were using my computer."

She nodded. "But it means that Brighton has been following you for some time."

"Do you have the pictures?" He needed to figure out when Brighton took them.

Lucy got up, retrieved the envelope from her desk, and handed it to Sean. He didn't look, not yet. He was so angry that Deanna Brighton had tried to put a wedge between him and Lucy.

Lucy said, "If there's a rogue agent out to get you because of something that happened in your past—"

"Lucy, I destroyed her career. She's trying to destroy mine."

"You didn't destroy anything—she's still an agent."

"Nutshell? I didn't do it on purpose. She's the one who created the cybersecurity network I exploited to expose my professor who was a pedophile."

"Duke told me. Her system was flawed. Whatever you did, you don't deserve to be hunted like this. It's not normal for her to hold a grudge for so long."

"She thinks I should be in prison for that stunt."

Lucy nodded. "To her, it's personal. When I found out who she was, I realized why she'd come here and threatened me, why she is so driven to go after you. You need to be careful with her; I don't think she can be reasoned with."

"Noah is taking care of it. In fact, he's the only one who can clear me. I need to get back to New York, though, and find out who killed Hunter. I owe him that."

He pulled Lucy close to him and held her. Just held her. He didn't want to leave.

"It'll all be over Thursday night. And maybe we can go away this weekend."

"Maybe we should lock ourselves in your house for forty-eight hours. Trips aren't very relaxing for us."

"You, me, alone for two whole days?" He smiled. "I'm there."

He could tell by Lucy's expression that she was not only worried but also planning something.

He said, "Luce, I'm deadly serious about this. You can't leave Quantico. Not until I know who killed Hunter and if you're in danger. You're the only way they can get to me, do you understand? I never kept you a secret, I never wanted to bring you in at all, but it was easier to keep the lies to a minimum, so I told them about our relationship. Colton already knew. But if Evan or Skye or Carol—I don't trust any of them—if they need leverage over me, they'll come for you. You're safe here. I mean, I know you can take care of yourself, but—"

"Shh. I understand. I don't want your attention divided. But call me. As soon as it's over."

"Noah's trying to save my ass right now, but I'll have him call you later. Keep you in the loop." Sean grinned. "I think he might actually have started to like me."

Lucy smiled. "You might be stretching it."

Sean forced himself to relax. "I understand him better now. Wait until I tell you how closely we've had to work for the last month."

"I look forward to it."

Sean reluctantly walked to the door. He didn't want to go. He had to.

"I love you, Lucy."

"I love you. Please—watch yourself."

"Always."

She pulled him back into a kiss. "Stay safe," she whispered.

Sean left and Lucy closed the door behind him.

No funny comment, no reassurance that he knew what he was doing. Just a wistful look that told Lucy more than any words.

Sean was worried. And scared.

It took all of Lucy's willpower not to go after him. But she knew him well enough to know if she left Quantico she would be added to his list of worries—as if she'd resent him for jeopardizing her future.

But she *could* help.

She walked over to her cell phone and dialed Noah's number. It went straight to voice mail.

"Noah, it's Lucy. Call me as soon as you get this message, or I'm on the first available flight to New York City."

CHAPTER EIGHTEEN

Noah had left Suzanne and the NYPD in charge of the crime scene and gone to headquarters to meet with the assistant special agent in charge, Gregory Torres. Torres was a fifty-year-old FBI veteran with an impeccable reputation but deemed to be extremely cautious as an agent. He'd been promoted quickly and hadn't been a field agent in more than fifteen years.

Steve Gannon was in his office but not Deanna Brighton. "Sir," Noah said, "I need to speak with Agent Brighton."

"I sent her home after she gave her statement," Torres said. "She was highly agitated and not doing herself or this division any favors."

"Sir, with all due respect, I still need to talk to her."

"Deanna is one of my agents, and we have established protocols in place to deal with conflicting statements. I took her statement, and Agent Gannon's. They don't contradict each other." The way Torres looked at Noah meant that Noah's statement was the odd version of events.

Noah glanced at Gannon. He looked worried, and Noah didn't blame him for trying to protect his partner.

Gannon said, "Just because I only heard four shots doesn't mean Rogan didn't shoot at Deanna."

"The apartment—"

"She went in first. I can't say what she saw or didn't see," Gannon said. "Look, I understand where you're coming from, but you need to know that there's a long history with Rogan getting away with crimes, and Deanna simply wants justice."

Noah wished he could see Deanna's files on Sean. What did she know? Was Sean in deeper with Colton than what he'd told Rick and Noah back in August when they originally came up with this undercover plan? Rick had given him blanket immunity—had Sean used that to his advantage? What else was he hiding?

Noah rubbed his face. He had to look at the physical evidence. He'd been in Hunter Nash's apartment. From where Deanna was standing, there was no way she could have seen Sean in the room like she said. Noah had never seen Sean with a silencer, but he had no proof Sean didn't have one. Sean had no motive to kill Nash. But Sean had taken Nash's cell phone. What if Sean had also taken the laptop?

Noah had to trust Sean's version, even knowing he was letting his personal involvement in the case cloud his judgment. His primary concern was that he didn't know if he was trusting Sean too much—or not enough.

"Sir," he said to Torres, "may I see Agent Brighton's statement?"

Torres opened a file and handed it to Noah. He scanned it. It was consistent with what both Gannon and Brighton had previously said, but there was something missing. "Why were you at Nash's apartment in the first place?"

"Deanna and I have been working on a possible mortgage fraud scheme involving Nash's employer, Colton Thayer. It was on the back burner for a while because we didn't have anything tangible, but when Rogan came into town and Deanna found out he was working with Thayer she—we—began to look back into the case."

Torres frowned but didn't say anything. He was trying to protect his squad from scrutiny from national head-quarters, but Noah suspected that either this was the first he'd heard about the Thayer case or Torres hadn't thought it was an active investigation.

Gannon continued, "Deanna had learned that Nash and Rogan had met earlier in the day, and she planned to question Nash about it." He glanced at Torres, then con-tinued, "She's my partner, she's the senior agent, I knew she was a bit obsessed with Rogan, but she has great in-stincts and I believed her when she said Rogan was here to run a scam with Thayer and his group. If we could catch them in the act, they wouldn't be able to get out of it. She felt Nash was the weakest link."

"How long were you outside Nash's apartment?"

"I met Deanna there right before we went inside."

"You didn't arrive together?"

He hesitated. "No, but she got there at about the same time."

"Armstrong," Torres said, "you're treading on danger-ous ground."

"Did you see Rogan enter the apartment?"

"No," Gannon said. "We met on the street and went upstairs. We saw the door was ajar. We proceeded cau-tiously. It's all in the report."

"Everything except why you were at Nash's apartment."

"He told you," Torres said. "Armstrong, I understand your position and that you work for the assistant director. I can give you latitude, but remember that this is my divi-sion. I'm not going to allow veiled accusations. I will in-vestigate this matter fully, and I assure you that if there was any impropriety on the part of Agent Brighton it will be taken up through proper channels, including the Office of Professional Responsibility."

"I appreciate your diligence," Noah said. But the bureaucracy worked slowly, especially if an agent was going to be up for reprimand or termination.

"Sean Rogan needs to come in and give his statement," Torres said. "As a courtesy to AD Stockton, I canceled the APB, but I still need a statement and explanation."

"Understood," Noah said. "May I look at the files you have on Thayer and Rogan?"

"Gannon, please give Agent Armstrong what he needs."

Going home was a risk even with Patrick out of town, but Sean knew how to avoid surveillance. He drove slowly by his place, and there was no one on the street at three on Wednesday morning. Still, he parked the borrowed car around the corner and walked around through the back, climbing through a loose board in his neighbor's fence. He slipped in through the sunroom, typed in the alarm code, then reset it for exterior surveillance. He wanted advance warning if anyone crossed his property line.

He was giving himself two hours to break Hunter's codes. Sean needed to be back in the air before daybreak, and he planned to land at a small private airstrip owned by an old friend of his who was far off the grid. If Noah couldn't stop Deanna Brighton from tracking Sean, he didn't want to use an airport.

He sat behind his desk and booted up his computer. While he waited, he stared at the picture of him and Lucy, taken when they were in Massachusetts the week before she reported to Quantico. He'd used his phone and loved the photo so much he had it printed.

Her smile was genuine, her long black hair pulled into a curly ponytail, the wind whipping a few strands around her face. He had one arm around her, holding her close to him, the other holding the phone faced toward them. The spontaneous pose captured Lucy's true personality—her beauty, the sparkle in her dark eyes, her genuine smile, devoid of her natural worries and fears. She'd felt safe and loved, and it showed in the photo.

"Princess," he mumbled, caressing the picture.

His computer beeped, asking for his password. "Time to get to work," he mumbled.

Hunter was smart, but Sean had known him for nearly twelve years and he had a methodical way of organizing his cyberlife. To the untrained eye, it would seem both haphazard and highly secure, but Sean cracked Hunter's phone in short order, using a program he'd written. Now the key was to collect the data from Hunter's computer through the external cloud network.

Sean scanned the software on Hunter's computer, all of which he had renamed either to be cute or for an added layer of security. But Sean looked at the back end and realized that not only could he download Hunter's last twenty-four hours of work, he could also physically locate Hunter's computer. Under a game icon named "Carmen"—from the game *Where in the World Is Carmen Sandiego?* Sean was certain—was coding to track Hunter's computer.

Heart racing, Sean downloaded the data and mapped it. He tracked the computer from Hunter's apartment to . . . nowhere. Sean had a route, but someone had disabled or somehow masked the computer. There was no live feed, though Sean had the location of the last ping: an industrial neighborhood in Brooklyn.

Sean wanted to go there himself, but it would take him a minimum of three hours. Time was against him.

He sent all the data he'd collected to Noah before calling his handler.

Noah answered on the first ring. "You promised to keep in contact and this is the first I hear from you? Four thirty in the fucking morning?"

Sean didn't give him any lip because Noah rarely swore, showing that he was both impatient and frustrated.

"I cracked Hunter's phone and traced his computer to Brooklyn. It's off now, completely shut down. I suspect they took out the battery or hard drive, or destroyed it. But Hunter had a trace on it, and I sent you a map of the route it took from Hunter's apartment to where it stopped functioning."

"I see it. What's this? You have it on the move at seven forty-seven p.m.?"

"The killer shot Hunter, took the computer, and left."

"I need FBI forensics to look at that phone."

"I'm still working on following his cybertrail, and I need to figure out how he modified Colton's security system so he would be alerted to a breach."

"This clears you, but I need my people to verify the data. You didn't leave SoHo until seven-fifty-five."

"If someone wanted to make a case against me, they could say I falsified the data because the phone was in my possession. I'll give it up when I know what Hunter found that got him killed."

Noah didn't say anything. Sean jumped ahead. "I'm not in New York."

"I know. Lucy called me. What the hell were you thinking, going to Quantico? There was an APB on you—"

"So you took care of it?"

"Yes and no."

"What does that mean?"

"It means you're not wanted by every law enforcement agency out there, but you need to come in and give a statement. As soon as possible. Deanna Brighton has pled her case. I proved she lied about you firing at her, but she's saying that her partner wasn't able to hear all the shots because you used a silencer."

"I didn't fire my gun at all," Sean said through clenched teeth.

"I believe you, but you need to make a statement nonetheless."

"After tomorrow night."

Noah sighed. "Get some sleep. Meet me at FBI head-quarters at noon."

"No."

Noah said, "This isn't up for debate."

"I'm not going to blow this cover. I'm not going to let Jonathan Paxton get away with whatever he's planning. If we don't stop him now, we'll never stop him. What if he had Hunter killed? What if Hunter found out something about the FBI mole?"

"What if Colton Thayer killed his friend?"

"Colton isn't a killer."

"Sean, listen to me—"

"I'll write up a statement and e-mail it to you."

"It doesn't work like that."

"The last time I went to FBI headquarters voluntarily to give a statement, I was arrested. I spent three days in jail and was expelled from school. Everything they promised me they reneged on. I'm not letting them do that this time. Deanna Brighton tried to fabricate evidence; who's to say she won't try it again? And there is that little matter of the statute of limitations—I'm not going anywhere near anyone who can put me in prison."

"You need to trust me," Noah said.

"I do." Sean wasn't lying. "But I'm not coming in. You'll get your report, it will satisfy everyone except Brighton, and I'll let you know when I'm back in New York."

CHAPTER NINETEEN

Noah had had little sleep, fueled by coffee and protein bars, when he met Suzanne and Detective Hayden Tucker at NYPD's midtown precinct.

He had grown increasingly frustrated through the night. While Gannon tried to be helpful, it was clear to Noah that Brighton had manipulated the younger agent into going along with her thin investigation of Colton Thayer on mortgage fraud. In addition, they could find no notes on Sean at all, making Noah think Brighton had cleared out her desk.

Noah briefed Tucker and Suzanne about the laptop and how Sean had tracked its location.

"Boarded-up warehouse in Brooklyn?" Tucker said. "Makes me itchy, not knowing what we're facing. I'll call in some uniforms to help secure the facility."

Tucker admitted he was intrigued by this case. "So your guy is a criminal informant? From what Brighton said last night, Rogan is bad news."

"Rogan isn't a CI," Noah said. "He's a private investigator." He hesitated. "This is need-to-know, Tucker. Our operation is ongoing."

"Understood."

Noah gave the official version that he and Stockton had worked out. They'd both agreed that if they needed to reveal any information, they wouldn't mention anything about a U.S. senator under investigation. "Rogan knew the victim and a group of hackers when he was in college ten years ago. When it came to our attention that his old friends were up to something, he agreed to go undercover and help determine if their plans were a threat to national security. Since the timeline was so tight, we couldn't develop an inside man."

"Your colleague was emphatic."

"She has a history with Rogan."

Tucker glanced over at him. "They were involved?"

"She arrested him for hacking twelve years ago when he was a student at Stanford. The charges were dropped." More or less. "I need to fill in my boss." He sent Rick a message, and was a little surprised when Suzanne filled Tucker in on the details of Sean and Brighton's history.

Tucker said, "So he caught a pedophile but embarrassed the Feds and Brighton in the process." He grinned. "Sounds like I'd like him."

"He has his moments," Noah said and hit *send* on his message to Rick.

Thirty minutes later, Suzanne, Noah, Tucker, and six uniformed officers were outside the boarded-up warehouse that was the last known location of Hunter Nash's laptop.

Though dawn was breaking, the narrow streets were dark and poorly lit. Suzanne pointed out security cameras on the corners of the building. "Those aren't cheap. There could be more."

"They look new," Tucker said.

"If there was ever a time to have Sean here, now is it," Noah muttered. There was no doubt that Sean would be able to disable the cameras remotely. He had an uncanny knack with all things electronic.

"They'll know we're coming," Suzanne said.

"Then let's not keep them waiting."

"Warrant?" Tucker said.

"I have probable cause," Noah said. It was thin, but he would stand by it. "Besides, the building owner is unreachable and the business is closed."

"Just cover my ass with my boss if this goes south with the D.A."

"You got it."

Tucker instructed his men to cover the two exits and then took two officers with them to the main entrance.

Noah glanced at Tucker and he nodded. Noah pounded on the door. "FBI—we're coming in! Keep your hands where we can see them!"

They entered the building with flashlights and guns drawn. It was filled with wooden crates and not much else. It hadn't been used for anything business-related in quite some time.

They split up, NYPD going to the left, Noah and Suzanne to the right.

In the back of the warehouse was a row of makeshift offices. In the first one, they found a body.

The white male had been dead for several hours. He had cuts and bruises on his face and hands, probably from a fight, but he likely died from the bullet in his chest.

On the desk sat Hunter's computer, or so Noah suspected. He sniffed. In addition to the blood, there was a burnt smell. Like burning metal.

He slipped on gloves and inspected the computer. The bottom looked, literally, fried—the case was warped and it looked as if the computer had overheated to the point of self-destruction.

Noah wondered if it was Nash's fail-safe, to protect against any unauthorized access, or if the killers had destroyed the computer because of evidence inside.

While Tucker and his cops cleared the building, Noah

looked through the office without disturbing any potential evidence. A printer was in the corner, but there was no computer. Newly installed wiring was evident. The file cabinets were also new, and they were empty, though loose papers littered the cement floor.

"Someone got out fast," Noah said.

Tucker joined them. "We're clear. How did they know we were coming?"

"I don't think they did," Suzanne said. "This body has been dead at least six hours, could be longer. And he was severely beaten before he was shot."

"Which means," Noah said, "he was killed shortly after the computer was destroyed."

"Maybe he screwed up," Suzanne suggested.

"Like killed Nash when he was just supposed to take the computer?" Noah frowned. "Maybe."

"What are you thinking?"

"Sean swears that Thayer isn't a killer, and I've studied every crime he's been accused of in the last fifteen years. He's never been violent. I don't see him shooting a longtime friend in the head, then torturing this guy."

"Got in with the wrong group," Tucker said.

Suzanne had a theory. "Maybe the people he works for were pissed he busted the computer. Maybe they took it because they needed something on it."

"That's likely." Noah suspected that Senator Paxton had ordered several murders, but Noah didn't think the senator had killed anyone who wasn't a known criminal. If Nash had uncovered his plans, would Paxton have ordered a hit?

It didn't feel right. But without more evidence, it was a theory Noah had to pursue.

Noah searched the victim's body, even though procedure required that he wait until it had been checked by the coroner. He didn't have time.

He pulled the man's wallet. "Timothy Alan Corbett,

New York City address. Thirty-four." He handed the wallet to Detective Tucker. "Is this address nearby?"

Tucker nodded. "It's in Queens. If this guy is connected to Nash's homicide, my people should take a look."

"Agreed," Noah said. "If you find anything at all—"

Suzanne nodded. "I'll go with Hayden. Keep Noah in the loop. This isn't my first rodeo."

It was after dawn, much later than Sean had planned to leave, when he finally cracked Hunter's system. He smiled, though his success was bittersweet.

"I'm going to miss you, pal," he said to himself. He wished he hadn't cut ties with Hunter or Colton. Now there was no going back. Colton wouldn't forgive this betrayal when he found out Sean was working for the feds.

Sean reviewed the logs and saw that after he'd told Colton that Deanna Brighton had been following him, Hunter had changed the security system so that anyone who walked past Colton's house was photographed and the file sent immediately to Hunter's iCloud server. When Sean cracked the phone code, he had access to the iCloud and pulled down the images to his desktop.

He disregarded people on the sidewalk unless they stopped. He was particularly interested in anyone who watched or approached the house.

Only one person showed up who Sean didn't know. Tuesday, late morning, only a few hours after Sean and Hunter met in Bryant Park.

Sean didn't recognize the well-dressed, trim, blond stranger. From where his head matched up to the doorframe, Sean guessed he was about six feet tall. He looked like an accountant or businessman in his mid-to-late thirties.

Sean couldn't see who opened the door, but the stranger entered. He left fifty minutes later.

Sean had to take a risk. He called Colton.

Colton answered the phone, groggy. "What?"

"Are you alone?"

"Carol's sleeping."

"I sent you a picture. Look at it."

"Just a sec."

Sean heard a door close, a computer being booted up. A moment later, Colton said, "Who's this?"

"I don't know. I cracked Hunter's security. When he changed the security after Deanna Brighton followed you from the carriage house—"

"After you *think* she followed me—"

"He had pictures of anyone near the house sent to his external server. It's a fail-safe, in case your system was tampered with."

"No one touched my system."

Sean wasn't going to argue with him. "This is the only person who went inside. He was there from eleven thirty yesterday morning until nearly twelve thirty. You don't know who he is?"

Colton said, "Hunter was spying on me?"

Sean squeezed his temples, his headache going from throbbing to pounding. "No," he told Colton. "After Hunter beefed up your security, I talked to him. Someone tipped Brighton off about you and I working together again. No one knew I was in New York except for you and the group. I didn't say anything to Hunter that I didn't already tell you. What do we really know about Evan and Carol?"

"Carol is not a spy!"

"Hunter said the same thing. He said he'd check old surveillance feeds and see if anyone on the team had met with Deanna or if he could spot her staking out the carriage house. Phone records, GPS tracking, anything he could get. Hunter accessed this photo thirty minutes before he left me a panicked message. I think he knew who this guy is."

"I wasn't here yesterday."

"Who was?"

"I—I don't know. I didn't think anyone."

"Can you check the logs?"

Colton typed. "No one came in or out yesterday during that time."

"Obviously someone did. And they hacked your security to erase it."

"I'll recover it."

Sean doubted that would work. If the hacker was good enough to manipulate the logs, they were good enough to destroy them. "You can't let anyone know what you're doing."

"Who would betray us?" Colton said.

Again, the guilt ate at Sean's gut. But he wasn't the one who met with this stranger, and he wasn't the one who killed Hunter.

"If you want out, I understand." Colton's voice was defeatist. "I never kept evidence on you. Never. You can walk free and clear."

"I didn't help you because I thought you'd turn over anything to the feds. I helped you because we are friends." He felt grossly uncomfortable playing both sides, but if he told Colton now about the undercover operation, Colton would ice him out. Sean focused on the end goal: stopping Paxton. And now finding out everything he could about this man.

Sean said, "I'm not leaving you in the middle of this mess. I think you're in danger."

"I'm willing to take the risk. This is more important than me."

Colton would not budge. Sean had no choice: Not only did he have to stop Paxton, he also had to protect Colton.

"I'll be back in three hours. Don't tell anyone about this. Please, Colton—keep this between you and me."

"I promise."

Noah took the subway back to his apartment so he could shower and change. He'd been up all night, except for the hour he slept on the floor of Suzanne's cubicle. When he'd been an Air Force Raven he'd slept in far worse conditions, but he was no longer as young as he once was. At thirty-six he was feeling the effects of too little sleep.

The shower woke him up, followed by strong coffee. He was sitting at his desk finishing his cup when his phone rang. It was Sean.

"I'm on my way back to New York. I found something on Hunter's phone. It's a picture taken outside Colton's late yesterday morning. A guy I don't recognize, but it was after Hunter downloaded the photo that he left me the message."

"Call me as soon as you land. Stockton is here; he wants to shut this thing down, but is willing to give you time with Colton to see if he'll turn state's evidence against Senator Paxton. Can you do that?"

"I don't know," Sean admitted. "But we still have thirty-six hours—have you gotten any closer to finding out who killed Hunter?"

"His security cameras went directly to his laptop. We found it this morning, at the warehouse you told us about. Destroyed. Dead guy there. Timothy Corbett—name ring a bell?"

"No." Sean hadn't found any security footage from Hunter's apartment on the cloud server.

"He was beat up and shot. NYPD is processing the scene. Suzanne and the detective in charge, Tucker, are at Corbett's apartment."

"I'm going to talk to Colton as soon as I get there."

"Don't do anything without talking to me."

"I'll play it by ear."

"Sean—" But he'd hung up. *Dammit!* Noah's phone vibrated and he got the image from Sean. Blond, thin, late thirties. Noah didn't know him. He sent the image to Rick Stockton, then left for FBI headquarters.

It was going to be another long day.

CHAPTER TWENTY

Noah arrived at headquarters before Suzanne. He took the time to go over his notes and looked at the preliminary reports from the Hunter Nash shooting. Noah hoped to get Deanna Brighton into an interview room later this morning—while he understood that the Office of Professional Responsibility might be getting involved, he had urgent questions that needed immediate answers.

Noah had a hunch that Paxton's mole might be Deanna Brighton. Paxton found ways to use people with grudges, and if Deanna was vulnerable—possibly by having broken the law in her pursuit of Sean—Paxton could manipulate her far more easily. What Sean had said about Sergio Russo yesterday—how Paxton used a father's grief to turn him into a hired gun—could also apply to someone like Agent Brighton, who felt cheated somehow when Sean didn't go to prison for his crime at Stanford.

Somehow it made a twisted sense—if Paxton knew that Sean was working for Colton, he had to believe that Sean was going to try to screw him. What better plan than to get Sean out of the operation by having an agent with a vendetta detaining him?

Noah realized he might be the one to blow Sean's

cover. There was no good reason for Noah to be in New
York when he worked out of D.C., and Paxton knew Noah
worked special projects for Rick Stockton. If Russo followed Sean, he might see Noah and make the connection.
Or, the mole might have already talked to Paxton, which
made Sean's position more precarious.

If Paxton called Colton off the PBM break-in, then
Noah would know that someone he'd met in the last
twenty-four hours was the mole. It would certainly narrow down their search. He'd bring each and every one
of them into interrogation with him and Rick Stockton,
search phones and computers, whatever it took to find
out how Paxton was getting inside information, and
why.

Ultimately, it might be the best way to shut down the
operation and bring Sean in safely. Noah hoped that the
next call he got was from Sean telling him Colton was
backing down and had evidence to force Jonathan Paxton
to cut a deal.

The flip side was that even if Paxton suspected it was
a setup, he might go through with it and find a way to
wiggle out of any crime. The senator was very good at
that. Noah hadn't had time to track him down yesterday
after Sean's confrontation with Russo, and then Hunter
Nash was killed. There was no way of knowing if Paxton
was at his New York apartment. Rick Stockton was sending two trusted agents from national headquarters to
keep an eye on Paxton, but they were still en route, ETA
noon.

An e-mail from Sean popped up on Noah's computer.
The message was clear:

> *Here's my statement. It's complete and accurate.
> I swear to it under penalty of perjury and whatever
> else is necessary.*

Noah clicked on the link, expecting a Word document to open; instead, he got a video file.

Sean was certainly audacious.

Noah stared at the video and listened to Sean's recounting of everything he'd done from the moment he left Noah at five to eight on Tuesday evening until he escaped out of the tunnel at East 33rd Street.

Then Noah started it again and took notes.

Noah's cell phone rang. It was Rick Stockton.

"Did you get Sean's statement?" Rick asked without preamble.

"Just watched it, sir." *Incredible.* But Noah didn't know whether to pat Sean on the back or deck him. He wanted to do both.

"Get it to Brighton's boss and her partner. Have Agent Madeaux massage this through NYPD at her discretion. In case there are any doubts."

"I told Sean to come in. Again."

"And is he?"

"No. I'm concerned that he's been compromised. If the mole is any good, they'll know I'm working for you and run my name by Paxton."

"I share that concern, and I'll add one more to it. Duke Rogan landed at JFK this morning. Came in on the red-eye. Find him. If Sean's cover isn't blown yet, his brother may jeopardize it."

"Sean's not going to listen to me. But he'll listen to you." Noah hoped.

"I've thought about it all night. And ten minutes ago I would have agreed. Except we IDed the man in the photo you sent. Kurt LeGrand."

"Never heard of him."

"I'm forwarding you his file. It's thin. He worked for a financial services company, Avery and Block, that went down for mortgage fraud to the tune of tens of millions of dollars. The owner killed himself two years ago, two principals are in prison, but the money has never been found."

"And LeGrand has something to do with the missing money?"

Noah didn't quite see how this all factored into the current operation. Pharmaceutical secrets and mortgage fraud?

"He's been flagged and our white-collar division has been watching him ever since. But he hasn't done anything that makes us think he has the money, and he cooperated in the investigation. His financials have been completely audited, and he's clean."

"According to Sean, Colton Thayer doesn't know him."

"We only have bare-bones background information on him. He's thirty-eight, born in Boston, graduated from Boston College with a business degree. Father was career military and died in a training accident when LeGrand was twelve. Mother remarried and moved out of the area when LeGrand was seventeen, but he lived with friends and graduated from high school with his class. As far we know, he has no real relationship with his mother. Had a series of finance-related jobs in Boston, then New York, then took the job with the ill-fated Avery and Block. For the last two years he's run his own financial consulting business. Lives in White Plains, New York. Does well, above average compared to others in his business, but like I said, he's been audited and he's clean."

"Are there any ties between LeGrand and Senator Paxton?"

"Nothing on the surface. I'll dig around. Maybe Thayer is working two separate jobs, and keeping Sean in the dark about this one."

Noah rubbed his forehead as he sipped tepid black coffee. "I still think we should pull Sean."

"Let's give him a couple hours. He's talking to Thayer, right?"

"Yes."

"Hold on." He put Noah on hold again, but it was only for half a minute. "Noah, Lucy Kincaid is here. She says she spoke to Sean."

"He visited her last night. I talked to her this morning. She knows what's going on." That also bugged Noah. Sean had always said he wanted to be the one to tell Lucy about Martin Holdings and this undercover investigation, but he agreed to wait until it was over. Did he think he wasn't going to survive? Did he know something he hadn't shared with Noah?

"I'll explain the situation to her," Rick said. "What's the status there?"

"The same. We have thirty-six hours to shut this down."

"Keep me informed every step."

"And Sean?"

Rick hesitated, then said, "Keep him in play. He's in the best position to find out what's really going on. Give him everything we have on LeGrand, and order him to check in regularly. Find his brother and read him in; make sure he stays put and doesn't interfere. If Senator Paxton slips away this time, next time will be that much harder."

"Understood." Noah hung up and rubbed his eyes. He sent a note to Suzanne asking if Brighton was in the building. He didn't like how her boss wouldn't let him talk to her last night. He wanted to corner her. He'd get a better read if he was face-to-face.

He wanted her pulled, put on administrative leave, anything to keep her away from Sean Rogan for the next thirty-six hours.

Lucy was surprised that Rick Stockton himself came out to bring her to his office. "Thank you for waiting," Rick said.

"I appreciate you seeing me; I know you're busy, but I need peace of mind."

He nodded. "Please sit down."

Rick didn't sit behind his desk but in one of the visitor chairs, motioning for Lucy to take the other.

"Sean told me that he's working undercover for you."

"What do you want to know?"

"Between Sean and Noah, I think I have the big picture. I want to help. Tell me what you need me to do."

"I pulled in Suzanne Madeaux to partner with Noah. You're still at the Academy."

That didn't come out right, Lucy realized. She backtracked a bit. "I already got permission from my class supervisor for time off. I can't concentrate knowing that Sean is in danger. And if I can help—"

"How?"

"Anything. Background. Research. Sean said Agent Brighton lied in her statement and—"

"Hold it. That shooting is under investigation. You can't go anywhere near it, considering your relationship with Sean."

"You're right. I'm sorry. But background checks, reverifying information, tracking e-mails, phone records, grunt work. I need to do something." Rick stared at her for a minute. She sat straight, prayed she didn't look as desperate as she sounded. "I understand I should be at the Academy right now, that if I take time off I could jeopardize my slot. I'm willing to take the risk."

"We just identified a new player in the mix, and we don't know where he fits in. He's a financial advisor who worked for a company that was under investigation for mortgage fraud when the owner committed suicide. Now he's a private consultant. No red flags, not a lot in his background. My assistant is verifying his information; you can help her. Your psychology background will be an asset."

"I'll get on it." She stood, then turned to face him. "I need to ask you something."

"I'll answer if I can."

"When you and Noah asked Sean to go undercover, he admitted he'd committed a felony. Is he taking this risk so he doesn't go to prison?"

"Sit down."

She sat, clasping her fingers to resist fidgeting.

"This is between us, Lucy."

She nodded.

"Sean's crime could have landed him ten to twenty years in prison. He would have opted for a jury trial, I'm sure, and he may have gotten off because his crime is one of those gray areas."

"Because he hacked into the bank and returned the funds to the retired investors the Martin Holdings company stole from."

Rick almost smiled. "Yes."

"If Sean didn't tell you what he'd done, you would never have known."

"Someone knew."

"Jonathan Paxton."

"Yes."

"And that's why Sean's doing this." Sean was the most loyal person Lucy had ever met; it had to be killing him to investigate his friends. "So Sean played Robin Hood nearly ten years ago, and no one ever pursued him? The FBI didn't suspect anything?"

"No crime was reported, and if it had been, there wasn't any evidence."

"What about the other people in the company?"

"Sean doesn't think that anyone with Martin Holdings knew he did it, and suspected that Robert Martin was the sole person responsible. I looked into the company and they disbanded days after Sean dealt with them."

"And the principals?"

"That's tricky—Sean didn't know who they were; there were no names attached, and the Martin Holdings company was held by another company, and so on. I don't think he cared to follow the path—the answers would have been there—but now, they're gone. I've had some of my best people looking at it for the last two months, since Sean told me about it, but it's nearly ten years old and data is stored differently now."

"But someone knew, and told the senator."

"We don't know how the senator found out. But Paxton blackmailed Sean." He paused, then said, "If Sean hadn't agreed to go undercover, I never would have investigated his crime. I promised him that on the condition of him coming clean. It was ultimately his decision."

"He didn't want it hanging over his head. Paxton could have used it again and again—"

"He didn't want it hanging over you, either."

Lucy knew that was true, but hearing Rick tell her that Sean's primary reason for risking his life and his reputation was to protect her career twisted her with guilt. Sean should have known she'd love him no matter what he'd done in his past. Her career meant nothing to her without Sean to share her life with. He should have told her from the beginning, when Paxton first blackmailed him. She was angry with both him and herself that he hadn't, but maybe she hadn't made it clear to him that he could trust her explicitly.

Why do you love me?

Sean was one of the smartest, most confident people Lucy had ever met, but he had an irrational fear that he didn't deserve her. That fear led him to take these risks, as if by being bold he could earn her love, when he'd already won her heart many times over.

"I'm glad Noah is watching his back," Lucy finally said, uncomfortable with the scrutiny that Rick placed on her.

"Sean does a good job taking care of himself, but we all need backup."

"I'll move heaven and earth to protect him, Lucy."

She nodded and mustered up a half-smile. "Direct me to my temporary desk. I'm ready to get to work."

CHAPTER TWENTY-ONE

Deanna had no intention of returning to FBI headquarters, not this morning. Everyone was running around like *she* was at fault when all she'd done was her job.

Why did everyone think Sean Rogan was innocent? He was guilty of *something*. He always had been. That saying, that tigers can't change their stripes? That was Rogan. He was a hacker twelve years ago; he was a hacker now. He destroyed lives and didn't care who he hurt.

What really bothered her more than Rogan's brazen disregard for the law or that he'd *run* from her after being caught red-handed at a murder scene was that everyone in her office had accepted an outsider's word over hers. She didn't care that Agent Noah Armstrong worked in the D.C. office, or that he was some rising star, or that he was vouching for Rogan.

The whole thing felt wrong. Something was going on and she was being kept out of the loop.

She jogged to work out her anger but didn't feel any better. After showering, she pulled out her files on Sean Rogan. She needed to think two steps ahead. Where was he going to turn up next?

If she only knew where he lived, she could wait for

him. Or, better, search his apartment for a clue about where he was hiding out. If she could just get him in interrogation she'd get him to slip up.

She rubbed her head and took a sip of coffee. Her cell phone rang. It was Steve Gannon.

"What?" she answered. Even Steve was treating her like some sort of pariah. And he'd been the most supportive of her quest for justice. In fact, he'd been the one who told her that Sean Rogan was in New York in the first place, and yet now Steve was acting like she had some sort of obsession. What if the roles were reversed? He'd be doing the same thing she was if some bastard like Rogan had irrevocably damaged his career.

"Are you okay?"

"I'm working from home today. Torres told me not to come in."

"I know; I'm just worried about you."

"I'm *fine*." She paused. "What's going on at the office? Is Agent Armstrong still pulling the wool over Torres's eyes?"

"Well, they haven't put the APB back on Rogan, but he hasn't come in. He gave a statement about the shooting. I'm not supposed to give it to you, but—" He stopped. "Okay, I just e-mailed it. Just—it was dark in the stairwell; there was a lot of stuff going on. Maybe you remembered things differently—"

Deanna's chest tightened. "Are you doubting me, too?"

"No, I just—"

"You don't believe me. It's his word against mine, and no one believes me! I'm the federal agent; he's a known criminal!"

"Deanna, you're a great agent. Don't let this jerk take you down."

"I don't plan on it. Thanks for the heads-up." She hung up her phone, not wanting to hear the pity in Steve's voice.

She clicked on the video link. Rogan was sitting at a

desk; there was a diploma that was out of focus on the wall behind him, but she squinted and figured out it was his, from MIT.

He began, "My name is Sean Tyler Rogan. It is Wednesday, October 24, at five ten a.m. I'm making this recording as a statement to the events as I know them that occurred on Tuesday, October 23."

Women found Sean Rogan attractive, but not Deanna. She saw the slime beneath his fake charm and dimples. His blue eyes might seem soulful or fun or whatever he wanted someone to see, but she saw dark ice, all the way to his heart. He might have been seventeen when she arrested him, but he had a hefty juvenile record that didn't just end when he turned eighteen, no matter what his brother Duke said.

Sean continued, "I started to run when I heard someone walk into the apartment, unsure who it was. I knew of the back staircase and tunnels from my previous visits to Hunter's house. I heard a female identify herself as FBI, but I continued to run because I didn't know if the person was telling the truth. There had been an FBI agent following me around New York for the last few days without making an attempt to communicate."

Liar! He'd avoided her, slipped away. *Bastard.*

He claimed he didn't fire his gun but admitted he had a gun in his backpack.

"Smooth," she said. "Real smooth, Rogan."

He explained how he hid down a narrow passage, in the dark, while she called out for him.

"I heard two gunshots and the female call out that I was a rat like the ones she was seeing in the tunnels. I feared for my safety, and remained in hiding until I was certain she had gone. I slipped through the maintenance door leading to one of the subway tunnels, and exited.

"I did not kill my friend Hunter Nash. He was dead when I arrived. I didn't touch his body. I did not fire my gun at all on Tuesday, and I did not aim or fire my gun at any person, including the FBI. I'll come to FBI headquarters in a day or two to answer any questions you may have. You can reach me through my attorney."

Attorney? What attorney?

That was it. Three minutes and he was done? No one was allowed to give a statement like this. He needed to be interviewed, asked questions, held accountable for his actions.

And he was getting away with it.

She cried out in despair, her fists clenched in frustration. Her phone rang again and she almost ignored it.

She was glad she didn't. It was her informant.

"Um, Deanna?" the skittish voice said.

"Yes. Do you have something for me?"

"You, um, wanted an address. On that guy, Rogan."

"You have it?"

"Yes." The informant gave her an address in SoHo. It wouldn't take Deanna more than fifteen minutes to get there, even in morning traffic.

"Thank you. Is he there now?"

"Yes."

She smiled. "Thanks." She hung up and grabbed her gun.

This time, Sean Rogan would not get away.

Duke took the red-eye from Sacramento to New York and landed at 9:05 a.m. East Coast time. He hadn't slept well on the plane, which didn't surprise him. He'd left his pregnant wife at home—even though Nora was only five months along, because she was forty, her pregnancy was considered high-risk. He had friends both at RCK and in her office promising to keep an eye on her, but Nora was a workaholic and even on desk duty she would work overtime if he didn't call her at six every night reminding her of the time.

Duke hadn't planned on coming to New York, but Sean had changed his phone number again and was unreachable. Worse, Lucy didn't know anything, but she, too, had been questioned by Agent Brighton. Lucy was just as worried as Duke.

Duke wanted to throttle Sean—how could he put Lucy through this? How could he get involved with Colton Thayer again? Sean was a smart kid, too smart, but with the brains came arrogance and a superiority complex. Duke had thought Sean had really grown this past year, but he was mistaken.

He called Jaye as soon as he landed. "Did you find out where he's living?"

"It's six in the morning here."

"Jaye, please."

"I found him. It wasn't easy—no utilities, no rental agreement, nothing—but I backtraced his laptop based on the anomaly I found in the admin code I told you about Monday, then located the most active center. It's spent a lot of time at an apartment building in SoHo. I'll send you the address. I don't have an apartment number, though."

"You're amazing. I'll find him."

"Maybe he has a good reason—"

"Don't make excuses for him, Jaye," Duke said. He was over and done with Sean's excuses. Everyone thought that because he was "cute" he should be cut some slack. Or that because he lost his parents when he was fourteen, he should be forgiven for his indiscretions. But this was more than an indiscretion—this was a crime—and Duke didn't really care why Sean had fallen back into his old hacktivist group; that he had would put him in prison. Or worse. He was going to lose Lucy, and it would break her heart. Sean's actions would do major damage to RCK across the board. Sean had risked not only his career and Duke's career, but also the careers of everyone they employed.

*Selfish. He never thought of how his actions were go-
ing to impact anyone else.*

Duke took a cab to the apartment building. It was non-
descript, with a buzzer door. He walked around to the underground parking and waited until he had an opportunity
to slip through the security door when a car left, the driver
distracted as she put on lipstick while driving.

Sean's Mustang was in the slot for 402. He was here.

Duke took the elevator to the fourth floor, not knowing
exactly how he was going to convince Sean to cut ties
with Thayer, but he was willing to do anything. Or he'd
call the cops himself.

He stopped outside Sean's door. Would he do that?
Call the police on his own brother? He thought of all the
times that Sean had risked his life for Duke and their clients. All the times when Sean had figured out the flaws in
security that had helped grow RCK into a premier cybersecurity firm. He'd risked his life flying into a forest fire
to save Nora. Selfish? No. Sean wasn't selfish.

A risk taker. Loyal. Arrogant. He was working with
Thayer because he thought that not only was the cause
just, but they'd get away with it.

Duke had to convince Sean that he wouldn't get away
with it. Duke didn't want to see his brother in prison. He
wouldn't do well. The few times he'd been in jail, never
more than a couple of days, Sean had lost it. What would
happen if he was in prison for years?

Duke knocked on the door of apartment 402. Sean
didn't answer. Duke knocked louder but heard no movement. *Sleeping?* Possibly, especially if he'd been up late.
Duke picked the lock and slipped in.

He announced himself so Sean wouldn't think there
was an intruder. "Sean, it's Duke. Sean—are you here?"

Duke found a light switch and flipped it on. The apartment was sparsely furnished. A large living area took up

the corner, a kitchen was against the wall, and a small, separate bedroom was to the right. Sean's computer was here. He was not. Neither was his phone, keys, or wallet.

Duke searched the place. It was not only sparsely furnished, but there were only a few changes of clothes and not much food. Sean wasn't using the space to live, at least not to do more than to sleep.

He turned on Sean's laptop and realized this wasn't his primary unit—this was new. Sean had full security protocols on it. Duke tried the RCK security key; it didn't work. If Duke wanted to crack the code, it would take time.

He searched deeper in the studio, all the places Sean might hide something he didn't want Duke to find. In high school, it had been computer disks that stored computer viruses and malware that Sean had created—for the joke, not data corruption. Like the time he hacked into his high school's network after his favorite teacher was fired for some charge that Sean thought was bogus and he had every computer in the facility spontaneously rebooting for two days.

But Duke found nothing personal, nothing that told him where Sean was or what he was up to. Duke would just have to wait.

The front door sprang open and Duke jumped up. He backed up when he saw two large men enter. "Sean Rogan, it's about time you returned home," one said.

The other frowned. "That's not Rogan."

"Looks like him."

"It's not. Rogan's younger. And taller."

Duke didn't have a gun on him and he hadn't found one in Sean's apartment.

"Take him."

Duke sidestepped the first guy and tripped him. The second guy pulled a gun. "I'll shoot you now, let Rogan find you as a warning."

"What do you want?"

"None of your fucking business, but I know who you are. Look just like him—you're the brother."

Goon number one got up and grabbed Duke. Duke decked him.

"Keep him quiet!"

The second guy pistol-whipped Duke and he fell to his knees. "Shut up," the guy said. He pulled a zip tie tight around Duke's wrists, then stuffed a rag in Duke's mouth. "I'll kill you and resort to plan B; don't doubt it."

Duke squeezed his eyes shut and tried to clear the ringing from his head. The two men stood on either side of the door, talking quietly. It was clear they were waiting for someone. Sean. And by the bits and pieces of their conversation, he was on his way.

There was a knock on the door. Why would Sean knock on his own door?

The knob turned. The men on either side of the door had their guns out. The door pushed open. Duke saw a blond woman standing in the doorway. She had a gun in her hand. Who was she? She looked familiar—why did she have her gun out?

Duke grunted, trying to warn her, and she turned to face him.

One of the goons slammed the door shut behind her. She turned, brought her gun up, but he easily disarmed her and shot her three times with her own gun.

She fell to the ground, in death her face a mask of surprise.

Deanna Brighton. The FBI agent.

Duke didn't know who these men were, but they were far more dangerous than the types Sean usually worked for.

The goon dropped the gun next to her body. The other guy said, "What the fuck? Everyone in the building heard that!"

"Grab the brother; let's go."

"You were supposed to use the silencer. It's all fucked to hell, Billy. And why do we need him?"

"This is Rogan's brother. Leverage, Tommy. Rogan is already on the run; he might not come in even when the cops find the Fed's body. With the brother, we'll make him an offer he can't refuse."

"Like he ever had a choice," Tommy said, pulling his mask back over his face.

Duke fought, but his fight was short-lived. One of the goons hit Duke over the head, and as he slipped from consciousness he felt his body being dragged across the floor.

CHAPTER TWENTY-TWO

Sean landed his friend's plane later than he'd planned. It was nearly eleven in the morning, and fog had kept him from lifting off until after nine. He'd dumped all his cell phones in D.C. and picked up a burner phone on the way, just in case someone was tracking him. Before he did, he got the message from Noah that they'd IDed the blond guy outside the carriage house. Kurt LeGrand. Sean didn't know him by name or appearance, and when Noah said LeGrand was a financial consultant, nothing popped, either.

Sean was surprised when Colton was waiting for him at the private airstrip.

"How did you know I was here?"

"When you called me last night, I triangulated your call from here. I figured when you returned, this is where you'd land."

"Why didn't you think I was going to leave for good? A fucking federal agent was shooting at me for no reason."

"Deanna Brighton. She's had it in for you for years."

"How do you know this?"

"Because a few months ago she summoned me for an

interview and had a bunch of questions about you. She's
only been in New York for a year or so."

Sean stared at him, disbelieving. "Why didn't you tell
me?"

"Because you were still working for Duke. There's no
way she could touch you; I figured she was just blowing
smoke. I didn't think she was dangerous. Based on her
questions, I realized she'd been trying to put you back on
the wrong side of the law for some time, but had nothing
to go on."

"You should have told me on Sunday after I was followed."

"I didn't know it was Brighton."

"It would have been a good guess!"

Colton shifted uneasily on his feet. "I didn't want you
to leave."

Sean didn't know what to make of Colton's lies and
misdirection. "What's going on here?"

"I told you—I told you everything."

"Only after I pulled it out of you." Sean wasn't getting
anywhere with this. "When did Brighton first talk to you?"

"Beginning of August."

That was right after Paxton blackmailed Sean. The
timing was not a coincidence. "She's in bed with Paxton,"
Sean said.

Colton's brow wrinkled. "They're having an affair?"

"No—Paxton blackmailed me about Martin Holdings
at the end of July. It's no coincidence that Brighton starts
asking you questions about me in August. Did she have
any evidence about Martin Holdings?"

"No. But—she did say something suspicious. That she
knew you were a criminal and she would prove it."

"And even with a federal agent with a personal vendetta against me you wanted me on your team?"

Colton motioned for Sean to walk over to his BMW.

"Sean, remember in college, it was the day Travis would have been twenty. I wasn't in a good way: My petition for records using the Information Act was denied, and then I was almost caught hacking into the PBM facility."

"I remember. I covered your tracks so they'd think it was a network failure."

"You did more than that. You saved my life." He stopped walking and faced Sean. "I was so depressed. It was Travis's birthday and I failed him."

"You've never failed him."

"You said that, and other things, but mostly, I realized I'm not the only one. You'd never told me about what happened to your parents until that night. I knew they'd died in an accident, but I didn't know it was in a plane crash; I didn't know that you were supposed to be with them."

Sean looked away. He hadn't ever told anyone else about that, not even Lucy.

"Yet you became a pilot. You faced your fears. And what you did at Stanford took courage."

"It was prideful," Sean said. "Looking back to Stanford, and to what we did in college, we didn't do it to change the world. We did it because we could. We did it for the rush."

Colton didn't say anything for a minute. Then, "Maybe part of it was the rush. But you can't tell me you didn't believe in what we were doing."

That was true. "I was never as noble as you, C. You always believed in the greater good. You would have gone to prison for what you believed in. I didn't want to go to jail."

"You're selling yourself short, Sean. Most of what we did no one ever knew. Just us. How can you say that's prideful? Maybe—personal satisfaction?"

"I learned from what happened at Stanford that I didn't need public accolades."

"It's because of you that everything I earn I put into Travis's charity. Real research to end leukemia. It's why I don't have a lot of money, why I took this job. Senator Paxton funded me and I'm getting the proof that Pham-Bonner Medical is responsible for Travis's death. You taught me to stand up for those who cannot stand up for themselves. You never backed down, Sean."

"I did—"

"No, you didn't. You just didn't think I knew."

Sean was wholly uncomfortable with the praise Colton was heaping on him. He had been lying to Colton for the past month, and now Sean felt worse. "Don't make me into something I'm not," he said.

"There's no one I would rather have with me when I find the evidence of what PBM did to Travis in my hands. You're the only one who understands what this means to me."

"I'm a danger to you right now," Sean said. He almost told Colton everything. Noah wanted Sean to read Colton into the investigation and get him to help, but considering the truth about Travis was at stake, Colton would not do it. And could Sean stop Colton from learning the truth? "I shouldn't go to the carriage house, and I can't go to my apartment," Sean said. "I don't know if the feds are looking for me, or what."

"Well, I've been manning the police chatter and there's no APB out on you. Maybe she wasn't able to identify you at Hunter's."

"She knew exactly who I was," Sean said.

He and Colton got into the BMW and Colton sped off. He didn't say anything and Sean feared he was getting suspicious. Sean would be.

Sean said, "Do you know who killed Hunter? Any idea at all?"

"I wish I knew."

"It's connected to what we're doing."

"Maybe PBM found out about our plans."

"One of the reasons I went to D.C. was to run facial recognition on that guy who was at the carriage house yesterday. His name is Kurt LeGrand. He has no connection to PBM. You didn't recognize him, but do you know the name?"

"No."

But Colton had hesitated just a bit. Sean didn't know if Colton was suspicious by nature or if he did know LeGrand.

"Someone met LeGrand at the carriage house, Hunter saw him on the camera, and now Hunter is dead."

"Then it's a good thing that we're changing the plan. If PBM suspects we're going to break in, we have to move up the timeline. We're doing this tonight, Sean, not tomorrow. I didn't tell anyone yet, but they're all waiting at the safe house."

"Safe house?"

"Completely secure, no communication, in or out." He glanced at Sean. "If you want out, tell me now."

Sean should. But he couldn't. He had a bad feeling that one of the others was about to double-cross Colton. Someone needed to watch his back. If nothing else, Sean owed him that.

"I'm in."

Noah looked at the phone message from Sean:

We've been ordered to power down. Will try to reach you later.

Sean had told Noah they'd be powering down twelve hours before the operation, but a day before? Did Colton suspect someone was a traitor? Was Sean in danger?

Too many unanswered questions, too many unknown variables. Noah wished he could pull the plug, but there was no way to reach Sean. And Noah doubted that Sean would back down now that he was so close to getting the goods on Paxton.

And this new player Kurt LeGrand made everything more complicated.

Suzanne ran down the hall toward where Noah was using a small desk on the fringe of the violent-crime squad. "Noah, we have shots fired at your apartment building. NYPD is on the scene, one dead female inside unit four-oh-two."

"That's Sean's apartment." Noah grabbed his gun from his drawer and holstered it. "Any word on Duke?"

"We know his flight landed and he used his credit card to take a cab, but we're still waiting to find out where he was dropped off. NYPD can get it faster than me."

"My bet is on Sean's apartment. He wouldn't have come to New York unless he knew where to find his brother."

If Duke could track down Sean, someone else might be able to as well.

Suzanne drove to the apartment in SoHo. "Any ID on the victim?" Noah asked.

"The coroner is en route. I explained to the lead detective that this is connected to an FBI case, and he's keeping a lid on everything." She glanced at Noah. "You don't think Lucy is in town?"

"She's in Stockton's office in D.C. Rick isn't letting her come up. It's safer for everyone if she helps from headquarters."

"So she's involved?"

"Not until last night when Sean paid her a visit at Quantico and told her everything."

"Why would he do that?"

Noah had wondered the same thing. "My guess? He knows this just got a whole lot more dangerous. From the beginning he told me that he wanted to be the one to tell

Lucy. He didn't like keeping her in the dark, but agreed it was for the best."

"He thinks he might not have another chance."

"He will. No way in hell am I letting him get killed." Noah had brought Sean into this; he was responsible for him.

"Where's Sean now?"

"I don't know."

"How can you not know?"

"This is Sean we're talking about!" Noah slammed his fist on the dashboard. "Don't you know a shortcut or something?"

Suzanne's knuckles whitened on the steering wheel. "Don't take it out on me."

Noah let out his breath. "I'm sorry." His jaw was tight and he thought of a dozen different ways he could have gone after Jonathan Paxton without bringing in Sean Rogan. Yet all of Noah's other plans had holes. Was this one any better?

"I saw his video. Bold."

"That's Sean for you." *What woman could be in Sean's apartment?* Noah had a sick feeling. He called Rick Stockton. "Did you get my message about the body?"

"Yes, are you there?"

"ETA three minutes," Noah said. "Where's Duke?"

"I just spoke to JT Caruso in Sacramento. RCK staff tracked Sean down through a wireless signal on his laptop, and Duke was heading to his apartment straight from the airport."

"His flight landed more than four hours ago."

"JT hasn't been able to reach him since he landed. The last person who spoke to him was a staff member, Jaye Morgan, just after nine a.m."

"I have to go," Noah said, and hung up on the assistant director.

"That didn't sound good."

"It's not. Sean's brother is missing."

Suzanne parked behind the coroner, and both she and Noah walked in through the garage.

Suzanne pointed to a black Mustang. "Isn't that Sean's car?"

"He wasn't driving yesterday."

They showed their badges to an NYPD officer manning the elevator, then took the lift to the fourth floor. The coroner had just released the body for transport, and his assistant was bagging it up. But Noah saw who it was.

"It's Deanna Brighton," he said.

"Oh shit," Suzanne said.

Detective Hayden Tucker was already on scene. "I got your call, Suz, and my boss cleared me to take jurisdiction because of the connection with Hunter Nash, since this isn't my precinct. Frankly, when the responding detective found out the feds were involved, he was happy to pass it to me."

"I appreciate it," Suzanne said. "What do you know so far?"

"First, I got my boys pulling all the surveillance in the building and any street cameras, so hopefully we'll get something from that. Shots fired at ten thirty-seven this morning. First responders on scene at ten forty-eight. In eleven minutes, the shooter cleared out."

"What's been going on for the last two hours?"

"We had to wait for the coroner to arrive. Nasty pileup in the tunnel. Couldn't touch the body except to confirm that she was dead. The address was flagged; that's how you were notified." He handed Suzanne the victim's wallet and badge, which were in an evidence bag. "I recognized her as soon as I arrived, but you were already on your way."

"Her gun?"

"Not here." He motioned for one of the uniforms to

bring him over another evidence bag. "We found this phone. It's been ringing, but we haven't answered it."

Noah took the bag. The last missed call was from JT Caruso.

"I think this belongs to Duke Rogan, Sean's brother. He flew in this morning."

"We only have one body." Tucker looked from Noah to Suzanne. "Are you certain Sean Rogan didn't return?"

Noah wasn't certain of anything. "I know he was in D.C. early this morning. I don't know where he is right now."

"This was the fed who claimed he shot at her. Why would she come here without backup?"

"Good question." Noah had several more, including finding Sean, Duke, and Brighton's gun.

"Suzanne, call her partner; I need to talk to him ASAP. Get her address, I want to check out her apartment. Did she have a phone on her?" he asked Tucker.

"Didn't find one."

Noah said, "We'll need all calls in the last twenty-four hours in and out of her FBI-issued phone and any personal phones she has in her name."

"I'm on it." Suzanne stepped away.

Tucker was listening to his earpiece, then said to Noah, "My boys said the security footage was jammed from ten twenty-five until ten forty-five. They might have something from the neighboring building and are looking at the tape now. They also got confirmation of a man slipping into the garage at ten-oh-eight a.m."

Noah would bet that was Duke. "I want a print, but I suspect it's Sean's brother."

Noah walked around Sean's apartment. Like Noah, he hadn't really personalized it, but there was a picture of Sean and Lucy on the desk. His laptop was gone, but that didn't surprise Noah. Sean probably had it with him.

There were holes in the wall that had been patched, but Noah didn't remember those being there last time he was here.

Duke had dropped his overnight bag in the entry; it had been kicked aside but left behind. Why did the killer take Duke instead of killing him? Why kill a federal agent?

Noah motioned for Suzanne.

She said without him asking, "I had a cop check out Deanna's car; her phone wasn't there." She hesitated, then said, "Torres wants to see you in his office ASAP."

"I don't have time."

"Make time. We have a dead federal agent in a civilian's apartment, someone she claimed shot at her yesterday. He's planning to put the APB back on Sean, and I held him off until you talked to him, but—"

He put his hand up. "I understand. What about Gannon?"

"He's at headquarters."

"First, we stop at Brighton's apartment." Noah looked at her. "You *do* have her address, correct?"

Suzanne nodded.

"Let's go."

Noah called Rick Stockton on his way out and told him everything they knew. Rick said, "Shut it all down. Bring Sean in."

"I can't reach him. He's gone dark."

"If you have to go to Thayer's house and arrest them all, do it. We need to consider that Duke has been kidnapped."

"I have another idea. I'd like to bring in Senator Paxton."

Rick didn't say anything for a minute. "Are you sure? You only have one shot at him."

"I'm sure. But first, I want to follow up on a theory. If it pans out, I'm going to have the two agents tracking Paxton bring him to headquarters."

"I'll tell the team to keep eyes on him."

"Any information about Kurt LeGrand?"

"Not much, but we're working on it. Check in every thirty minutes, Agent Armstrong. Find out what the hell is going on."

CHAPTER TWENTY-THREE

Lucy could find next to nothing on Kurt LeGrand, which was suspicious in itself. He seemed to have a clean slate, hardly what would be expected of someone involved with a hacktivist group like Colton Thayer's.

She put together a time line on the whiteboard because she was visual—she preferred to see everything at once.

She found no connections whatsoever between Paxton and LeGrand. She had LeGrand's work history, residence, and schooling—everything looked normal. The most interesting thing about him was that he'd worked for a financial services company that had been investigated for mortgage fraud. This wasn't unusual, especially now. Many companies had shut down because they had been built on fraud or one of their employees had played fast and loose with the rules.

Lucy didn't know a lot about white-collar crime, so she carefully read over the FBI file on Avery & Block.

The case was pretty standard for mortgage fraud. The company had padded mortgages with fees, kickbacks, and a private mortgage insurance scam that cost banks and homeowners millions of dollars—money that all went directly to the company owners. Two principals had gone to prison for the scheme, even though the bulk of the money hadn't been recovered. The FBI found no evidence to support their suspicion that the funds had been sent to one or more offshore accounts.

The file referred to a whistle-blower, but didn't identify him by name. Lucy flipped through hundreds of documents before she found the whistle-blower's identity:

Kurt LeGrand

She didn't know how this information was important, but since he was somehow involved with Colton Thayer and possibly Senator Paxton, it was at least interesting.

Lucy called the U.S. attorney who had prosecuted the case, but no one was available to talk to her. She left a message and looked at her time line for LeGrand.

College, employment, residence.

He'd graduated from Boston College sixteen years ago, at the age of twenty-two. He'd then worked as an accountant in a major firm in Boston for four years. But there was a two-year gap between when he left that company and when he moved to Manhattan, where he worked for the stock exchange for four years, before taking the position with Avery & Block.

She circled the gap on the whiteboard.

What did he do during those two years?

She went back to her notes on Colton Thayer. There was no connection between Thayer and LeGrand other than the fact that they'd both been born in Boston. They were five years apart, never went to the same schools, the same college, or worked for the same employers. Thayer had never done freelance work for LeGrand or LeGrand's employers, either. LeGrand moved to Manhattan the year Thayer graduated with his master's from MIT and Sean graduated with his bachelor of science.

Something tickled at the back of her memory. Something Sean had told her last night, or maybe it was something Noah had said when she talked to him. About why Sean left MIT.

She left her cubicle and walked briskly down to Rick's office. His secretary wasn't out front, and Lucy hesitated. She didn't want to bother him, but her gut told her there was something odd in LeGrand's career path. She knocked on the door.

"Come in!" Stockton called.

Lucy stepped in and approached his desk. Though she had known the AD for a year and they had mutual friends, she was still a little intimidated. He exuded authority.

He asked, "Find something?"

"It might be nothing."

"You wouldn't be in my office if it was nothing."

"It's more what I didn't find. There's a two-year gap in LeGrand's employment history. This might not be unusual, except that according to his credit reports, he maintained the same lifestyle he had during his four years working as an accountant. There's no inheritance that I could find.

"The other interesting thing that I found was that he was a whistle-blower for a case that was investigated by our Manhattan office. A mortgage fraud case. Two people were prosecuted and pled out. They're in prison for ten-to-twenty years."

"And this guy"—Stockton tapped the photo—"turned them in?"

"Yes. I wanted to talk to the FBI agent in charge of the investigation, but because it was in New York I didn't think I should make the call. I left a message for the prosecutor on the case."

"What do you need?"

"I'd like a list of employees with Avery and Block, plus they should have a background on LeGrand as part of the case file. Especially if he gave testimony and was vetted by counsel."

Rick nodded. "I'll make a couple calls. What else?"

"The FBI accountants indicate that there is anywhere from six to ten million still unaccounted for."

"And you think LeGrand has the money?"

"If he does, he's not spending it. He lives within his means. He was paid well by Avery, but wasn't on the board and made no major decisions for the company."

"Dig as deep as you need. Use my name if you have to. Find out everything about this guy. Did you find any connection to Senator Paxton?"

"None. I even searched Paxton's campaign contributor reports. LeGrand has never donated to his campaign. He's made no reportable political donations at all. I checked the files on Paxton's favorite charities, including Women and Children First, and LeGrand isn't a donor. I don't think they know each other."

Lucy continued, "I'm running the people LeGrand could have met with at Thayer's house—Hunter Nash, Skylar Jansen, Evan Weller, and Carol Hattori—to see if there's a connection to any of them."

"Don't forget Colton Thayer."

"I ran him first. Nothing. They're both from Boston, but no overlap in any area."

"Dig into the others and call if you find anything—I'm leaving."

"Is it that late?" She looked at her watch. It was only three in the afternoon.

"I'm going to New York."

"Sir, could I come with you?" she asked spontaneously.

He raised an eyebrow. "You have to report back to Quantico tomorrow morning."

"I know, but—"

"Lucy, sit down."

She swallowed uneasily and sat.

"I know this is hard on you, with Sean undercover and not being able to get involved. That's why I let you work here today. But I can't give you another pass. Noah and Sean know what they're doing. I'll keep you informed. Stay with your brother tonight; I told Chief O'Neal you'd be back by eight o'clock tomorrow morning."

Lucy knew she had asked for special treatment, something she'd never wanted to do. And only last month she'd had to face the Office of Professional Responsibility because she uncovered a drug operation while camping in the middle of nowhere. It wasn't finding the drug operation that put her on the hot seat—it was shooting a drug dealer. She was on thin ice, and it didn't matter how high she was ranked within her class or how well she scored on her tests, there were too many people watching her, waiting for her to screw up so they could kick her out.

"I'll be there," she said. "Can I stay here for the rest of the day? I still have files to go through, and your analyst, Dorothy, is meeting with me at four."

"Be my guest. Dorothy is the best analyst in my office. She retires next year and I'm going to miss her. I'll make sure Noah updates you. But just because Sean went dark doesn't mean anything's wrong. The nature of criminals is that they don't trust anyone."

"Sean's not a criminal."

"But he's working for one."

CHAPTER TWENTY-FOUR

Noah walked through Deanna Brighton's apartment, increasingly horrified by her evident obsession with Sean Rogan.

The small, two-bedroom apartment in New Jersey had a view of the New York skyline and would have been considered typical for a single, female, fifteen-year veteran of the FBI. Tasteful, uncluttered, and feminine.

Except for her office.

Deanna slept in the closet-sized bedroom and the larger master bedroom was her office. One wall was covered with corkboard pinned with newspaper articles about RCK, specifically Sean Rogan. She had sticky notes on each one with questions like, "Who paid him?" and "How did he get security clearance?" Stacks of files lined another wall. She had information about RCK, their employees, Sean's assignments.

One section was devoted to everything related to Sean's case at Stanford. She had a tape of the symposium where he'd hacked in and exposed his professor. Half her documents related to her failed project.

A day planner on her desk highlighted when and where she'd tracked Sean since he'd been in New York.

Noah flipped to early October, when he and Sean first arrived. Two days *before* they moved to SoHo, she had a notation:

> *SR working with Thayer again.*

No one knew about that outside of Sean, Rick, Noah, and Colton Thayer's group. Unless Thayer had told Paxton, and Deanna was Paxton's mole.

Deanna seemed far too volatile to be the mole, but if she was set on arresting Sean she might work with Paxton to make it happen. It would also make sense that Paxton wouldn't want Sean involved in stealing from Joyce Bonner's pharmaceutical company, because Paxton knew Sean didn't trust him.

Noah rubbed his face. The theory was too convoluted, but there was some truth to it—if Paxton had Sean arrested, then he wouldn't be a factor in the PBM theft. Except why would Paxton kill Deanna and kidnap Duke Rogan? Paxton was a lot of things, but he wasn't a cop killer.

"Noah, you need to see this."

Suzanne walked over to where Noah sat at Deanna's desk and slipped a file in front of him. "This doesn't look like her handwriting."

Noah opened the file. It was a copy of handwritten notes that appeared to have been taken at Lucy's FBI panel. There were things in here that weren't in her permanent file and some that were hand-copied from her file.

Noah knew about Lucy's past—ten months ago, when she was a murder suspect, he'd had access to even her sealed file. She'd be horrified that the information about her abduction and rape seven years ago had not only been written down by members of her panel but also given to someone else.

"'Mentally unstable'? 'Dangerous'?" Suzanne turned

away. "I don't want to see any more." Then she said, "I didn't know about the kidnapping."

"I did," Noah said. He wasn't reading the notes so much as trying to figure out who wrote them. By the end he ascertained that it had to have been Juan Martinez, because the note-taker referenced things that the other two panel members had said.

That's why Deanna went to talk to Lucy—she thought Lucy was the weak link. Deanna had threatened Lucy, but Noah didn't realize with what until now.

"She has surveillance photos of Sean, mostly with his pal Colton Thayer. And a blonde."

Noah glanced over. "That's Skylar Jansen, part of Colton's crew. Sean's ex-girlfriend."

"What was Brighton doing?"

"Trying to catch him in the act."

Noah looked at Deanna's planner. She hadn't written anything down for today, but there was a notepad next to her desk. He lightly rubbed a pencil over it and brought out Sean's address.

"Someone called her and gave her Sean's address."

"We can't track her phone. The battery is out; it's the only explanation."

"Did she have a personal phone?"

"We can't find that, either, and the carrier has no signal. There's no landline into the house, but that's not unusual. I don't have a landline either."

Noah said, "I need a team over here to box everything." He picked up Juan Martinez's file. Suzanne saw but didn't say anything. Noah should leave it as part of the evidence, but he didn't want the notes to become part of the investigation.

He looked around again, trying to put himself in Deanna Brighton's shoes. He couldn't imagine himself so obsessed with trying to catch someone that he would surround himself like this. And it wasn't for murder or child molestation or some other heinous crime that often had Noah working 24/7. Deanna believed Sean was guilty of cybercrime—essentially, computer fraud. But ultimately, she was obsessed because he'd humiliated her twelve years ago.

"If Deanna isn't the mole," Noah said, talking out loud, "she must have an informant in Thayer's group. Unless—" He stopped himself.

"Oh, come on, Armstrong; you can't hold back on me."

"How well do you know Steve Gannon?"

"I don't. I'm Violent Crime; he's White-Collar. We have hundreds of agents in the building."

"He had to have known about this obsession. She couldn't keep it to herself, not with the amount of time she spent tailing Sean."

"You're accusing Gannon—"

"I'm not accusing anyone."

Noah pulled out his phone. He had a hunch—but if he was wrong, he was going to put Sean in greater danger. "Rick, I think I know who the mole is. I need a little leeway to interrogate Deanna Brighton's partner."

"How much?"

"As much as I need."

Rick said, "Okay. I hope you're right. I really didn't want to believe that Senator Paxton could kill a cop."

"If I'm right, he wanted Brighton to arrest Sean. And when she was close, someone else took her out."

"Colton Thayer?"

"Him—or someone on his team. Kurt LeGrand fits into this somehow—it can't be a coincidence that the day he shows up at Thayer's house, Hunter Nash turns up dead."

"LeGrand was a whistle-blower on a major mortgage fraud case two years ago. I'll send you what we have, but so far it's not much."

"I'd bet my badge that he's dirty."

* * *

Lucy was reading the assistant U.S. attorney's files on Avery & Block. There was so much information she could hardly absorb it, so she focused on Kurt LeGrand's testimony.

"Weren't we supposed to meet in the conference room?"

Lucy jumped and glanced up. A well-dressed, petite woman with white hair and reading glasses on a silver chain around her neck stood at the edge of Lucy's desk.

"Mrs. Conner?" Lucy glanced at her watch. It was a quarter after four. "I'm so sorry; I lost track of time."

"That's okay; I do that all the time. I took the time to look at your boards to bring myself up to speed on where you are. You've been busy."

"I only have today." She gathered up the files she was working on and followed Dorothy Conner down the hall. Everyone Dorothy passed smiled and greeted her. She was obviously well liked and respected.

"Rick Stockton filled me in." Dorothy opened the door. They were set up in the smallest conference room but had less chance of being booted. "I've been working on this project since the beginning."

"The beginning?"

"Since Rick agreed to Agent Armstrong's undercover plan. Neither of them trusts many people, but I've worked with Rick since he joined the Bureau right out of the Marines, twenty years ago. When he was promoted to assistant director, he brought me with him."

"He said he'd assigned his best analyst."

She smiled. "He's sweet."

Sweet wasn't a word Lucy associated with Rick Stockton, but she trusted him. If he said Dorothy Conner was the best, then she was.

"I'm going to miss this place," she said.

"Miss it?"

"I'm retiring next year."

"But you don't have to retire, right? There's no manda-tory retirement age for analysts, correct?"

She laughed lightly. "Next April, I'll have worked for the Bureau for thirty-five years. I'll be sixty-two next month. I'm more than ready to spend time with my grand-children."

"Grandchildren?"

"I have three. Two boys and a girl. They live in Colo-rado with my son and daughter-in-law, who just found out she's expecting number four in May. I want to be living there in time for the birth."

"I can't argue with that," Lucy said.

"Good, because Rick has tried to convince me to stay, and he can be extremely persuasive. But I can withstand his charms." She motioned to the boards Lucy had set up earlier. "This is all good."

"I was hoping that before I have to go back to Quan-tico tomorrow morning I can figure out the connection between Kurt LeGrand and Colton Thayer."

"You're basing that on the fact that Mr. LeGrand was at Mr. Thayer's house."

"Yes. According to Sean, Colton denied knowing him."

"But you think Mr. Thayer might be lying."

"Sean doesn't think so."

"But you do."

"I can't say. I haven't met him."

Dorothy nodded. "I've gone through all the financials from Avery and Block and talked to the AUSA who pros-ecuted the case. No one can find the money, and that was the big sticking point in the government's case. But there was no doubt that they had the mortgage scam in place and were profiting from it. The money disappeared."

"What I can't find is what LeGrand did for the two years he was in Boston after he left his accountancy job, before he moved to New York and took a job on the stock exchange."

"That's where I can help. If he filed taxes during those years, I'll know who was paying him."

"Unless it was under-the-table."

"There are usually other clues. Most people don't overtly cheat the system. They generally underreport, such as receiving bonuses and not reporting the income, or pad their allowable expenses."

"Don't we need a subpoena for his tax records?"

"Yes, except he already gave us permission."

She frowned. "I don't understand."

Dorothy pulled out the Avery & Block file. She flipped through to documents in the back and pointed to IRS Form 8821. "As part of the FBI investigation into LeGrand's claims, he gave permission for the FBI to pull his tax records for ten years prior. They never pulled them, but we have the authority, and I put in the request, then called a friend of mine at the IRS who processed the request immediately."

She flipped through several files. "Here are his returns for the second of those two missing years. That was the first year he authorized us to inspect."

"I never would have thought of this."

"You would have if you'd encountered this before. You look at that; I'll go over the Avery and Block files. Fresh set of eyes." She slipped on her reading glasses.

The two of them read silently for several minutes. At first Lucy didn't see anything suspicious on LeGrand's tax return, which was now nine years old. He'd filed as self-employed. Paid taxes on a net income of $52,300. Had what looked like reasonable write-offs.

Though he was self-employed, he only reported income from one entity. Lucy made a note of the company name, address, and tax ID number. "It looks like he worked for Obsidian Trust and Equity."

She turned to the computer and typed in the name. Nothing came up.

"Lucy?" Dorothy said. "Look at this."

She pointed to a computer-generated printout. It was extensive, listing all payments by Avery & Block the year prior to the FBI investigation.

"What am I looking at?"

Dorothy pointed to a name midway down the third page. *Jansen Tech.* The payment was for $10,000 and the memo read: *Final Payment Network Upgrade.*

"Jansen," Lucy said flatly. "Skye Jansen works for Colton."

Dorothy glanced at her watch. "It's after five; I won't be able to pull any business filings to confirm."

"I'm certain it's her. It's the connection—Colton told Sean he wasn't at the carriage house when LeGrand showed up. He said he didn't think anyone was there, but Skye is living there."

"What do you think Skye Jansen has to do with Le-Grand? What's her motive? Mr. Thayer and his group are hacktivists, according to Rick, and not violent. Could she be working something on the side?"

Lucy didn't doubt it. "I need to get this information to Noah."

"Wait—" Dorothy flipped to another folder. "I can't believe I missed this the first time. Rick asked me to quietly run one of the New York agents against all the names in this case. Here he is again."

"Who?"

"Agent S. Gannon. He was one of the investigating agents in the Avery and Block case."

"Does he know LeGrand?"

"I don't know—he was a rookie, but it's one more connection."

Noah was on the phone with the FBI personnel office when Suzanne stopped in front of his desk. "I see. Yes. Please fax everything you have. Thank you." He hung up.

Sometimes, being right didn't feel good.

"What was that?"

"Let's walk and talk. I have Steve Gannon in an interview room."

"Torres agreed?"

"Rick Stockton intervened. I was on the phone with the personnel office. Guess who gave Gannon one of his letters of recommendation?"

"I don't have to. Paxton."

Noah glanced at her. "Is that a guess?"

"A guess from these." She handed him a slim file. "His phone records. He called the senator's private cell number several times this month, including last night."

"Thanks." Noah stopped outside the interview room. "Do you have anything else?"

"I'll be quick." She took a deep breath, then dove into her report. "First, Tucker came back from Corbett's house—the dead guy in the warehouse with Nash's laptop? Nothing of interest, but they snagged his computer and it's in our tech unit with a priority. We're checking e-mails first, then will go into the rest."

"Good."

"However, Corbett has a record. We have a list of his known associates. He's just a gun for hire, so he didn't do this on his own. Spent a few years in prison, has been relatively clean since he got out two years ago."

"Anything come up yet on his associates?"

"No, but Tucker has every cop in Queens shaking the trees. If anyone knows anything, we'll know it."

"I appreciate their help."

"Yeah, well, I'm the one who has to pay them back."

She didn't seem too upset about it. Suzanne went on, "Then, I got a call from a friend of mine in Trace. Twenty minutes before she was killed, Deanna received a call from a burn phone. We can't get the number."

"How did she trace it?"

"We don't have Deanna's phones, but we can still track incoming and outgoing calls." She handed him a slip of paper. "I weeded through the crap and came up with this interesting number from Saturday."

Meredith White.

"I know her."

"Thought you might. Her name was in Deanna's notes on Lucy."

"She sat on Lucy's hiring panel." This might explain why Deanna went to Quantico to talk to Lucy and how she obtained the notes from the panel.

"I've been going through all Deanna's shit, and it's pretty sad and scary how obsessed she was with Sean. I'm no shrink, but it borders on psychotic."

Considering that she'd shot at Sean without provocation, Noah had to agree.

"To be honest, I don't see Steve Gannon killing his partner, or any cop for that matter."

"He could have set her up."

"Why?" Noah didn't buy it. He held up his phone. "Text me if you learn anything else important to the interview. I'm going to talk to Gannon."

Noah stepped into the room and put the file in front of a nervous Steve Gannon. He sat down across from Gannon and said, "We know you've been talking to Senator Paxton. We know that you've known him since before you were hired into the FBI. We also know that he gave you a letter of recommendation. I will remind you that you are a sworn federal agent and if you lie to me you'll make the situation worse. Cooperate, and I'll make your cooperation known to OPR."

At first Noah thought Gannon was going to stonewall him; then he let out a sigh and said, "What do you want to know?"

"When did you start talking to Senator Paxton?"

"Since I became an agent. He would call me and ask questions. At first I didn't think anything of it."

"What were the calls about?"

"Mostly chitchat. Then he asked me to look up a few things in the system. Stuff we're not supposed to give out, but he was on the Judiciary Committee and the Public Safety Committee, and I thought he was looking for statistics and anecdotal stories that would help him get the FBI more funding, or change laws. At least, that's what he led me to believe."

"When did you suspect he had another motive?"

"A few months ago. May, early June, I think. He asked me to get him a list of prisoners set to be released. It was way out of my area of expertise—I'm in White-Collar, not Violent Crimes. I said I could get someone in VCMO to do it, and he said absolutely not. That's when I got suspicious."

"But you still helped him."

Gannon shrugged. "I guess. He told me to find a way to partner with Deanna. That wasn't hard—no one wanted to work with her."

"Why?"

"She's short-tempered, arrogant, and not a team player. She cuts corners. Don't get me wrong—Deanna is real smart, and she sees connections faster than most people. She just gets frustrated by the system."

"Did Senator Paxton tell you why he wanted you to work with Deanna?"

"Not at first. But last month he said that Sean Rogan was in New York and he wanted Deanna to find a reason to arrest him."

"And you didn't find that suspicious?"

"I already knew about her obsession with Rogan. She doesn't make it a secret, at least not in our unit. I helped her create a file that showed Colton Thayer was involved in a mortgage fraud scheme so that we could get the time and resources to pursue Thayer, knowing that Rogan was working for him. But Thayer is clean, at least with regards to financial transactions. Cybercrimes had a file on him, but they'd never been able to build even a minimal case. Torres gave us some leeway. But Deanna let everything else suffer."

"Why did the senator want Rogan arrested?"

"He didn't want him working with Thayer."

"Do you know why Senator Paxton hired Thayer to steal information from a pharmaceutical company?"

Gannon was surprised Noah had that information. "You know about that?"

"Obviously, so do you."

"I don't know details. All Senator Paxton said was that his longtime friend was getting cold feet and he was in too deep to back out. I think—I don't have any proof— that Joyce Bonner had something incriminating on him. What, I don't know."

"Do you know what Joyce Bonner was getting cold feet about?"

"No."

"Did you give Deanna Sean's address?"

Gannon shook his head. "I couldn't find him anywhere; Paxton wanted Deanna to detain him. I couldn't follow him—I was doing the work of two agents because Deanna was solely focused on Rogan."

"When you followed him, how did you do it?"

"The only place I knew he would show up was at Colton Thayer's. But he must have the subway map imprinted in his head, because he always lost me in the subway system. To be honest, I gave up."

Someone else—someone who knew Sean would go to Colton's eventually—could have followed Sean. Or put a GPS on him. Someone inside Thayer's criminal family. Or Thayer himself.

And then given the address to Deanna and set her up.

Noah put a tablet in front of Gannon. "Write down everything you just told me. If you've forgotten anything, include it. Everything that you know about the information Paxton wanted you to get, everything about Deanna's obsession with Sean Rogan, everything about PBM. I'll be back in an hour."

But an hour later it was nearly eleven and Noah got a strange message on his cell phone:

Plan moved up 24 hours. Hurry.

It had to be Sean. Noah almost texted back, except that the number was unrecognized and he didn't know if someone else had access to it. He called Rick. "Sean just made contact. They're at PBM now. I need a SWAT team ASAP."

"You got it."

But even so, they wouldn't arrive at PBM for at least forty minutes.

"I'm going now."

"Not without backup."

"Dammit, Rick—" Noah stopped. In a calmer voice he said, "I got Sean into this."

"I'm not going to let you go solo into an unknown, high-risk situation."

"I won't be alone." He hung up, feeling sick. He was a soldier at heart. He never disobeyed orders.

Unless the life of one of his men required it. In war, tough choices had to be made.

And Sean was one of his men now. Noah wasn't going to sacrifice him.

Noah took the risk and sent a text message back:

Trust no one.

Immediately he received a message that the text had failed.

CHAPTER TWENTY-FIVE

Breaking into a secure pharmaceutical company was not an easy task under the best of circumstances, but Sean didn't trust anyone on his team and that made watching his own back just as important as not getting caught.

There had been no opportunity for Sean to contact Noah to tell him that the operation had been moved up until Colton distributed the burner phones as they got in position outside Pham-Bonner Medical. The phones were programmed not to send or receive messages from any number not programmed into the chip, but Sean hacked the SIM card and added Noah's number to the send list.

But there was no way that Noah would get here in time. Sean and his team had it planned down to the minute and should be in and out in twenty-two minutes.

After? They would regroup at the van or, if there was any problem, at the safe house. But Sean was increasingly nervous.

He'd broken into numerous facilities, many more secure than PBM. But most of those assignments were part of his job at RCK, where he was hired to break into a business and identify flaws in security. There was no real threat, though getting caught was never fun.

This time, the guards had real guns, and so did his team. Noah wasn't on the perimeter to make sure that if things went south no one died.

Worse, one of these four people knew Kurt LeGrand and Sean was certain LeGrand was responsible for killing Hunter. Maybe LeGrand hadn't pulled the trigger, but it was no coincidence that Hunter had died right after he updated Colton's security system. And Hunter had been scared, which meant he either knew who Kurt LeGrand was or knew who LeGrand was meeting with. He'd called Sean, not Colton.

Was Sean wrong about his friend? Colton had always been an ideologue. He believed in what he was doing, and while he broke laws, he'd never hurt anyone. His idea of an attack was destroying someone through cyberspace. At worst, he might screw with their finances or steal their identity and make their life hell. But murder? No. Colton didn't even carry a gun—he was the only one unarmed tonight.

The guns were another problem for Sean. Sean hadn't wanted to carry, but both Skye and Evan were, and Sean wasn't going on an operation defenseless if the person he least trusted was armed.

Carol was monitoring from the van, and she had an open line into everyone's burner phones, which they were also using as radios. If Sean had a way of sending Noah the frequency, he could eavesdrop on the conversation. If he arrived in time.

"Time," Carol said.

Colton nodded and kissed her, then motioned for the rest of the team to leave.

It was eleven o'clock on Wednesday night.

They'd discussed the plan for weeks, run through

drills, and initially everything worked better than Sean could have predicted.

They entered through the employee doors in the back. They could have used Bonner's badge, except that Security would be alerted that she'd entered the building. It was safer to hack into the server and take it down for the minute it took them to get inside, then bring the external security back up. Her card could be used on any of the internal doors. While her access would be logged, Security wasn't automatically alerted when internal doors were opened.

The system was fairly sophisticated, but not perfect. They had two guards at all times, one who manned the cameras—the easiest system for Sean to replace with a false feed—and one who roamed. Before Hunter was killed, he had monitored rotations. The guard on foot during the week rarely deviated from his route—that's why they had chosen Thursday night. The weekend guard—Friday and Saturday nights—was unpredictable and seemed to go wherever he felt whenever he felt. But Wednesday should hold the same predictability as Thursday.

They didn't need to talk. Carol was with the van out of camera range monitoring silent alarms and police activity. Skye and Evan split off to obtain the records on the bio-weapon, and Sean and Colton went to Bonner's office to crack the safe and get the information Senator Paxton wanted. According to Paxton, the real records of the leukemia trials that had killed Travis Thayer were also in Bonner's personal safe.

Sean didn't believe they were. He didn't know what Colton was going to do when he found out that Paxton had double-crossed him. Because that was the way Paxton operated.

They had thirteen minutes before the guard would be in this building, seventeen minutes until he had a 50 percent chance of walking this floor. But they were all responsible for getting out and meeting at the car in twenty-five minutes. They'd started a clock from the point they left the vehicle.

Sean usually preferred to work alone, but this time he didn't trust anyone. He didn't like that Evan was off with Skye. Sean had tried to warn her earlier that he didn't trust Evan, but she'd dismissed him.

Colton worked on Bonner's computer while Sean cracked the safe.

The safe was in the wall behind her desk. The standard electronic lock wouldn't be difficult to break with his equipment, but it would take time. He immediately hooked up his handheld computer and ran a custom program. While he did it, he sent Noah another message, taking care that Colton didn't see what he was doing:

Find radio frequency to track our progress.

"I'm in," Colton told Sean.

Sean quickly sent his message to Noah through his handheld computer and then said, "Good. Copy and get out."

"She has access to everything."

"Shh."

"There's a hidden drive here—"

"C.," Sean warned again. He really wished he was alone.

It took his program two and a half minutes to crack the code. He still had nine minutes and thirty seconds before the guard was in the building. There were only two files in the safe, and Sean used a small digital camera to photograph each page. There were also several CDs that Sean copied on a special drive before putting them back. In the back there was a VHS tape.

"C.," Sean said. He held up the tape.

Colton nodded. "Paxton said if there was a tape to get it."

Sean had no mechanism with him to view the tape. There was no label and no way he could copy the data, but he was not going to give it to Paxton without viewing it first.

Then Sean saw the television with a VHS drive on the credenza.

He walked over and put in the tape.

"What are you doing?" Colton demanded.

"We have to know what's on it before we give it to him."

Sean turned on the television and put in the tape, impatiently waiting for it to play.

It was a black and white recording in a private residence. The room was a well-appointed personal office or library. It had an older, grainy feel to it. The recording could be twenty years old, more or less. The camera had been mounted in the wall behind the desk. He could see only the back of the head of the man working at the desk. A younger Joyce Bonner walked in. She came over and started yelling. Sean had the sound off, so he didn't hear what she said.

The man came around the desk and slapped her. She fell to her knees. It was her husband, Thomas Lynch. She tried to get up and he kicked her down. She crawled away and he kicked her again. Sean's stomach roiled at what he was witnessing.

The library door opened and two men came in. One was Jonathan Paxton, and the other Sean recognized from photos as Joyce's father, Randall Bonner. The two men pushed Lynch to the floor and kicked him like he'd just kicked his wife. Lynch said something to Jonathan, who then pulled out a gun and shot him.

"Holy shit," Colton whispered.

Sean took out the tape and said, "No fucking way we're giving this to Paxton. This is our leverage."

"Sean, we have to give this to Paxton so he'll give me Travis's documents."

"You said they were here!" Now Colton's secrecy

made sense. Paxton held the trials back to get Colton to do anything he wanted.

"Shh!" Colton glanced around. "Paxton has them. It's an even trade."

"Shit." No way was Paxton going to give Colton anything. Sean doubted proof of the tainted leukemia trials even existed. It could all have been leverage Paxton used to force Colton to steal this tape.

Colton grabbed the tape from Sean and put it in his own satchel.

"This is my operation." He glanced at his watch. "We're late."

"This conversation is not over," Sean said. But first they had to escape.

They walked out of Bonner's main office, but before stepping into the hall Sean took out his computer to track the guards.

"Carol is tracking—"

"I'll do it myself," Sean snapped. He flipped through the cameras and found the guard still in the adjoining building. He'd probably come through the underground tunnel because the night was frigid, but they still had an extra couple minutes.

Sean continued to flip through the security cams—he saw the live feed while they'd routed a static recording of the facility to the guard station.

He spotted Skye down the hall but couldn't find Evan. "Okay," Sean said, and Colton opened the door. They rounded the corner at the same time Skye came to them. She gave Sean two thumbs-up.

"Where's Evan?"

"Shh—the guard will be back any minute. We need to go."

Sean grabbed her wrist and pulled her close to his face. He said in a low voice, "I warned you he was up to something. What do you know?"

Her eyes darkened in surprise and maybe a little fear. *Good.* He wasn't fooling around. This wasn't a game, and Evan was dangerous. She needed to understand that. "Let go of me!" She pulled her arm away. "Shit, Sean, you're being a jerk."

"I told you I didn't trust him." Sean flipped through the cameras again and realized that something was blocking his feed into the bio-lab. He decoded it and up popped Evan leaving the lab—with a backpack. He hadn't had a backpack when he entered, or if he did, it had been folded in his tool bag.

"What's he doing in the lab?" Colton asked.

"He's not in the lab."

Sean said, "I hot-wired a live feed. He just left the damn lab."

Skye glared at him. "Now's not the time. If you have a feed, where's the damn guard?"

Sean flipped to where he thought the guard would be. "Basement. He's coming up the stairs toward the first floor."

"I'm outta here."

Colton looked confused.

Sean said, "Stick close to me, C. Something's up—with both of them." As much as he hated to admit that Skye was involved with whatever scheme Evan had going, it was clear she was part of it.

Sean wanted to take Evan down now—but Skye was right; they needed to bolt. And Sean needed to know what was in that backpack.

Sean monitored the cameras. As soon as the guard entered the second floor, Sean said through his mic, "Guard is on two."

Sean, Colton, and Skye took the stairs down to the first floor and went out the way they'd come. They waited for Evan to the right of the door in a break area set up for smokers.

"What's Evan up to?" Sean demanded of Skye.

"He's not up to anything."

"Skye, I don't want you to get hurt. You know something."

She smiled. "You do care."

"I just don't want to see you in prison."

"How thoughtful."

The door opened and out came Evan.

"Let's go," he said.

Sean waited until they were outside the camera's range before he grabbed Evan and slammed him against a tree.

"What the fuck were you doing in the lab?"

Evan looked at Sean like he was an idiot. "Let go of me."

Sean pushed him into the tree again. "Tell me what's in that backpack."

"Sean, later," Colton said. "We need to go."

Over the radio, Carol said, "A car is coming down the main road. Two people inside. I can't make out anything else."

"Sean, Evan, now," Colton said.

"Get the backpack, Colton. He took something."

Colton hesitated, then reached down for the backpack.

"Don't touch it," Skye said.

From the corner of his vision, Sean saw that Skye had a gun aimed at Colton. "It would have been easier to do this later, but plans change," Skye said.

Evan made a move for the gun Sean had under his jacket, and Sean put him to the ground, a fist in his face. As Sean reached for his gun, Skye said, "I'll shoot him, Sean."

Sean glanced at her and saw Colton was in her direct line of fire. She had a silencer on the end of her barrel. Evan jumped up and tried to hit Sean, but Sean ducked and Evan lost his balance.

Sean turned to Skye. "Put the gun away! What are you doing?"

"It's now or later," she said, and shot Colton twice in the chest.

Colton fell to the ground and Sean ran toward Skye, not thinking about being shot. She wasn't expecting him to attack and looked startled.

A bolt of electricity hit him in the back. He fell to the ground even as he tried to fight the charge. He'd been Tasered before; he'd forgotten how painful it was.

He looked up at the sky, but his vision was blurred. Skye came into rough focus. She was still holding the gun. He tried to speak, but nothing came out.

"I told you Evan would do anything I said," she said. "You were just naïve enough to believe he was in charge."

"Who's there?" a guard called.

"Go!" Skye ordered.

"Ne-ne-nev—"

"Save it, Sean." Skye kissed him. He wanted to spit in her face, but his body refused to respond to his commands. "You'll do exactly what I want once you see who's waiting for you."

Evan pulled Sean up and half-dragged him down the slope toward the rear of PBM. The opposite direction from where Carol waited with the van. Sean could hear Carol's frantic voice over the radio.

"Shut up," Skye said, tossing her phone and earpiece to the ground. Evan did the same. Skye stripped Sean of all his equipment and dropped everything at Colton's feet.

"Stop!" the guard called. He was on his radio but didn't pursue. Sean knew both guards in the building carried guns.

Two sets of arms picked him up—Evan and another man, someone who came out of the woods at the edge of the property.

Sean's hands twitched, and he was getting his bearings even though he felt like he was going to puke.

"I need. A minute." He needed to buy time. Noah should be here by now, if he'd gotten Sean's message. But Noah wouldn't know where they were. Had he cracked the radio code? Did he know what happened?

Sean reached into his pocket for his handheld computer. He could send a message by feel. But the Taser might have damaged it.

Skye grabbed his wrist and squeezed, pulling it out of his pocket. His small computer fell to the ground. She grabbed it and was about to pocket it when Evan said, "I don't trust him—destroy it."

"But—"

"No buts, Skye. He's a sneaky bastard."

"Fine." She put the device on the ground and stepped on it. The screen cracked.

Evan swore and shot it.

"I think it's dead now," Sean said sarcastically. "That was a prototype, bastard."

Evan hit Sean with the butt of the gun. He fell to his knees.

"We need him alive and coherent," Skye said.

"He's a prick."

She smiled down at Sean and said into her phone, "We need help with the baggage."

"I'm not going anywhere," Sean said.

"You don't have a choice."

When Sean wouldn't cooperate, she motioned into the dark. A man Sean didn't recognize showed himself and, with Evan, they half-carried, half-dragged him toward the road. They must have another car. There was only one way to get in and out of PBM. If Noah was here, he'd stop them.

Sean had no idea what their plans were, or why Skye

had shot Colton and not him, or what Skye meant by needing Sean.

He had to find out what Evan had stolen from the lab. Sean feared the worst: the bio-toxin.

Could he stall? Delay until Noah arrived? Something bigger was going on, far more deadly than Colton exposing company secrets. Even bigger than Jonathan Paxton killing Joyce Bonner's abusive husband.

The feeling was coming back into Sean's limbs. His shoulder, where Evan had Tasered him, was sore and he had minimal use of his left arm, but he had to work with what he had. There were lights and activity at the lab. All Sean had to do was delay.

Into her radio, Skye said, "Get ready, two minutes to takeoff."

Takeoff? What the hell?

"You don't know how to fly."

"You do."

"I'm not flying you anywhere."

She laughed. "I brought my own pilot."

Sean made himself a deadweight. As the men stopped and shifted to pick him up, he elbowed the one on the right—Evan—in his groin. Evan dropped Sean. Sean slammed his fist into the second man's face. He made contact but didn't have enough momentum to force his captor to drop him. Sean pushed him to the ground and they grappled. Sean tried to get his gun, but the man had decent training. *Cop? Military?* Sean fought back but was losing ground.

Skye said, "We don't have time for this bullshit!"

A crack of a gun and instantaneous pain in his ass.

She shot me. She shot me.

His unknown captor pushed Sean off and jumped up. "Bastard," he spat at Sean and kicked him in the stomach.

Sean reached over and found something sticking out of

his ass. He pulled it out and tried to inspect it, but his hand became numb and he dropped it.

"Pick him up," Skye said. "We're about to have company."

Sean's vision blurred, then turned black. The last thing he remembered was the sound of an idling plane.

CHAPTER TWENTY-SIX

By the time Noah pulled into the parking lot of Pham-Bonner Medical the security lights had flooded the main building and he heard on the police band that an emergency alarm had been tripped. "Be alert," Noah told Suzanne.

It was just the two of them; SWAT was still a good fifteen minutes out. Rick was going to have his ass if anything happened, but Noah would deal with that in due time. He warned Suzanne that he didn't have authority to go in ahead of SWAT, but he'd take the hit for disobeying orders.

She dismissed him and was out the door first.

With their guns drawn, Kevlar vests protecting their chests, badges hanging around their necks, and *FBI* in big white letters on the back, no one would mistake them for the bad guys. Still, one of the guards came out of the building with his gun drawn.

Noah shouted, "FBI! Lower your weapon!"

The guard put his hands up.

"Status?" Noah ordered.

"We don't know what happened, but there was a fight outside at twenty-three thirty. My partner heard it when he was doing his rounds. He put on the floodlights and went outside to inspect. I told him to secure the door, but he went out. I tripped the alarm."

"No one broke in?"

"No, of course not. This is a secure facility. This happened outside."

Noah looked at his watch. It was 11:45. He knew that the team had planned to be in and out in twenty-five minutes. They could easily have completed the mission, then had a fight outside. For all of Sean's flaws, breaking into this building wasn't a problem for him.

Noah called the SWAT team leader, "ETA?"

"Fourteen minutes."

He said to the guard, "Wait for SWAT. Do not confront any hostiles. Go inside and secure the building. I need all security tapes ASAP."

The guard looked confused but agreed.

Noah motioned for Suzanne to flank him and they ran toward the back of PBM, staying to the shadows as best they could.

They approached the rear entrance. Pine and maple trees liberally dotted the uneven landscape. In a group of trees just outside the entrance, Noah saw a body, all in black, facedown.

Suzanne sucked in her breath.

Noah circled the area. No one was here. What was he going to tell Lucy? He'd promised Sean that he would watch his back.

Training took over and Noah pushed emotion aside. Though he shouldn't touch the body before ERT arrived, he had to confirm the man was dead. And confirm the identity.

Noah turned the body.

Colton Thayer.

Noah's relief that it wasn't Sean lasted only a moment.

"He's alive," Noah said. "Two bullets to the chest. Call an ambulance."

There were obvious signs of a fight in the area around Colton's body. Equipment had been tossed around—burner phones, earpieces, pieces of electronics. The fight had been loud enough to attract the attention of the guard. But where were the others? Where was Sean?

Noah pulled his knife out of its sheath and cut through Colton's jacket and shirt. One bullet was in his upper right shoulder, the other below it, to the right of his sternum. There was a lot of blood. Noah said to Suzanne, "Go back and get the emergency kit from the trunk. I have to stop the bleeding."

"I'm not leaving you when—"

"He could die! He's the only one who knows what happened here. Dammit, Suzanne, it's an order!"

Noah pushed his hands on the wounds. Colton gasped as he regained consciousness. He tried to talk.

"Hold still," Noah said.

"Sh-sh-sh—"

"Don't talk, Colton."

Was he trying to say "Sean"? Sean could be nearby. He could need medical attention. He could be dead.

"Skye," Colton whispered. "Sh-sh—"

"Where's Sean?"

Colton shook his head back and forth. His mouth moved, but no sound came out.

A scream cut through the trees. "Colton!"

Suzanne's voice: "FBI! Stop or I will shoot you!"

The woman stumbled and fell to her knees. Suzanne ran over and cuffed her.

"Carol," Colton mumbled.

"Suzanne, I need the bag," Noah said.

Suzanne walked the sobbing, cuffed woman over to them and dropped the bag next to Noah.

"Ohmygod ohmygod ohmygod—"

"Shut up or I will put you in the car," Suzanne said. To

Noah, "Ambulance is on its way. It was dispatched at the same time as the police call went out. ETA two minutes."

As Noah pulled out gauze and replaced his hands with the mesh, he heard a plane overhead. It sounded like a twin prop, not far away.

"Is there an airstrip nearby?" Suzanne asked.

"PBM has a small airstrip a quarter mile from here," Noah said. He and Sean had cased out the place once Sean knew the target.

What the hell had gone wrong? Was Sean on that plane? Was he flying the plane?

It was all Noah could do to stay here instead of following the tracks. By the time the paramedics arrived and took over, the plane was long gone.

Local police were right behind the ambulance. He ordered them to put Carol Hattori in one of their vehicles and secure the scene; then he and Suzanne followed the trail that had been left by Sean and the others.

"We should wait for SWAT," Suzanne said.

Noah didn't respond. He knew what he should do and what he had to do.

He moved forward and found, about a hundred yards from Colton's body, another sign of a fight. In the middle of it was a large yellow feather that looked like a small badminton birdie. Noah carefully picked it up by the end of the feather. There was weight to it.

"That looks like a tranquilizer dart," Suzanne said.

"It is. Do you have an evidence bag on you?"

Suzanne reached into her back pocket and opened up the bag. Noah dropped the dart in.

"You think they used that on Sean?"

"Yes." Sean had seen his friend shot. He'd obviously been half-dragged to this spot. There didn't appear to be blood, but he certainly had not cooperated. He'd found an opportunity to fight, and they tranqed him.

Why? Why did they need to kidnap Sean? Why not just kill him?

And *why* had they shot Colton?

Noah and Suzanne followed the tracks all the way to the small airstrip. Another body lay at the edge.

The body moved. Noah approached cautiously and identified himself. It was the guard.

Suzanne helped the guard sit up. "Are you injured? Shot?"

The guard shook his head. "Someone knocked me from behind." He put his hand to the back of his head and came away with blood.

"What happened?" Noah asked.

"I heard a fight outside, saw a woman shoot a man in black; then another man was Tasered. I called to them, and they left through the trees. I went back in to call for help, then pursued. By the time I got to the airstrip, they were loading someone unconscious onto a small plane."

"They—how many?"

"I saw two men and a woman, plus the unconscious guy. Maybe he was dead; I don't know. But I think there was also a pilot."

"Then who hit you?"

He frowned. "I guess there was someone else."

"You guess."

"Noah," Suzanne said quietly.

"Stay with him," Noah said. "I'm going to talk to SWAT." *Not that they can do anything now.*

CHAPTER TWENTY-SEVEN

Thursday

Lucy and Dorothy brought in dinner and worked together until after midnight, when Dorothy said, "The assistant director told me to make sure you left by eight. I've already disobeyed, but midnight is my witching hour. If I don't leave now, I won't be able to make it home. I'm not as young as I used to be."

Lucy smiled and yawned. She rubbed her eyes. "Sleep will help. Maybe I'll see something different in the morning."

"We already have a lot done. We've connected Skylar Jansen with Kurt LeGrand and we've found a discrepancy in his testimony that no one in the U.S. Attorney's Office or on the Avery and Block defense team caught. It's enough to have the AUSA sweating bullets that her conviction will be overturned on appeal."

"You found it," Lucy said. "I would never have seen it."

"Don't sell yourself short, Lucy." They walked out of the J. Edgar Hoover Building together. "You are diligent and focused and asked all the right questions. I have forty years on you." She stopped. "Where did you park? The garage?"

"I took the Metro."

"I'll drive you home."

"You don't have to—"

"Where do you live?"

"Georgetown."

"Hop, skip, and a jump from here. I'm not taking no for an answer."

Dorothy had an assigned parking place in the garage, right next to AD Stockton. She saw Lucy looking at the sign. "It doesn't mean anything except I've been here a long, long time."

"The assistant director thinks highly of you."

"And of you," Dorothy said. As she pulled out of the garage she glanced at Lucy. "You're preoccupied. Why?"

"I'm frustrated," Lucy admitted. "I want to know what Obsidian is, and there is nothing on it anywhere."

"In my experience, which isn't all that limited, there's always something somewhere. It's just a matter of looking in the right place. If Obsidian isn't a business in the United States, it could be that he had a foreign client."

"Or," Lucy said as a thought came to her, "he had a foreign shell corporation set up. Can we get the tax records of the company? They had a U.S. tax ID number."

"We can—with a subpoena."

"Damn."

"The wheels of justice may turn slow, but they do turn. Tomorrow morning I'll get a subpoena."

"You can do that?"

"No, but I can make the right calls and get it done. It's all about who you know—and what names you can drop. Outside of the director himself, 'Rick Stockton' is probably one of the most powerful names that can be dropped. The AUSA will jump."

"Maybe we should ask him first."

Dorothy laughed as she pulled up in front of Sean's house. "Sweetheart, you're adorable. I'll tell Rick what I'm doing, but I'm retiring in six months. There's really not anything he can do to me if he disapproves. And I know Rick very well—he'll do it, on your recommendation."

"Why?"

"Because he trusts your judgment. And if he trusts you, so do I—otherwise I wouldn't have given up my night to help."

Lucy thanked Dorothy and went into Sean's town house.

It was strange being here in the middle of the night without Sean. Without even her brother to talk to. She petted Chip and gave him fresh food and water. Her mind was working overtime, but she felt sluggish.

She showered to wake herself up. She should sleep, but she wanted to explore more of Kurt LeGrand and Skye Jansen's connection to Avery & Block. The discrepancy in his testimony, about how he found the proof of fraud, was a small point, but it told Lucy that he was lying and forgot the lie for a moment.

She slipped on sweatpants and a white tank top from her growing waredrobe at Sean's, then loosely French-braided her hair down her back. She sat at Sean's computer and stared, willing her mind to start working again.

It was one in the morning and she didn't want to call Dorothy, but she *had* told Lucy she could call her with anything.

Lucy dialed her cell phone. "Dorothy?"

"I thought you might be calling."

"Are you still driving?"

"No—I live in Chevy Chase. Already home and in my pajamas."

"I took a shower and thought, what if LeGrand and Skye were responsible for either embezzling or hiding the money from Avery and Block?"

"Hmm. That would explain a lot, except, to be the devil's advocate, the FBI is really good at tracking funds. Where is the money and why didn't the FBI find a trail?"

"Did the three principals accused of embezzling deny taking the money? Or did they admit it?"

"Why would that matter?"

"If they admitted it, then it wouldn't be necessary to talk to them; if they denied it, then we should interview them and figure out if they were lying or maybe the money was stolen out from under them."

"Or they could have been involved in something illegal that they didn't want to admit to. If the FBI can't find the money, then it's harder to get a conviction."

"One of them committed suicide."

"Chester Block. The brothers, Greg and Brian Avery, are in prison."

"Was there a suicide note?"

"If there was, it didn't make it into the FBI files I saw. But all we have are digital files. There are thousands of pages that were part of the trial."

Lucy was on the cusp of the truth, but she was so damn tired that her mind was working too slow.

"The FBI said there was at least six million dollars missing. Is there that much money in mortgage fraud?"

"Mortgage fraud is fairly straightforward. On the surface it's confusing, but in the end it's similar to graft and corruption. They padded their fees, received kickbacks, but the big-money program for this scam was PMI."

"White-collar isn't my strength. What is that?"

"Private mortgage insurance. When a buyer puts less than a certain percentage of money down on the house, the lender often requires PMI in case of default. The beauty of the Avery and Block scheme was that they padded the closing documents with a five-year prepayment of PMI, when in fact that money was going directly to them and not mortgage insurance. The money was rolled into the loans. Then, the real PMI was labeled differently, because they were smart and covered their tracks. So homeowners were being defrauded, as well as banks."

"Let's assume for a minute that LeGrand and Skye took the money and hid it from the FBI. How could they do that?"

"According to the file, the money went missing from the accounts, but on paper all the money was there."

"The money they received from the PMI fraud," Lucy clarified.

"Right. Wait—" Dorothy flipped through some papers. Lucy smiled. She had brought work home with her as well. Lucy really liked this woman. "Block killed himself at the beginning of the investigation, and it was his suicide that prompted the Avery brothers to talk. They pled, said that Block was a figurehead and was distraught over being accused of the fraud. He must have confronted them and couldn't live with the dark cloud. So in guilt the Averys admitted to the fraud, but said the money should have been in the account. The FBI said the money had never been deposited in the account—no deposit history, though the internal accounting records indicate the money was there."

"This is why I'll never go into White-Collar."

Dorothy laughed. "I have a little knowledge of a lot of areas, but the FBI hired me originally because I had been an accountant. There's really only two logical possibilities. Either the Averys never deposited the money, but falsified internal records so their colleagues wouldn't find out, or they deposited the money, but someone else took it and covered their trail by erasing the deposit history."

"Is that possible?"

Dorothy thought for a moment. "Yes—very difficult, but with computers and multiple sets of books it can be done, at least well enough to fool us for a while. You know—if the case went to trial, they would have more analysts looking at the data. But because the Averys pled out, there might not have been as much scrutiny."

"But it is possible. It would have to be an inside job."

"Kurt LeGrand."

"And Skye Jansen. But why didn't they take the money and run?"

"Because they couldn't get to it," Dorothy said, excited.

"You know why?"

"Possibly. I need to make some calls first thing in the morning, but all evidence is with the U.S. Attorney's Office pending resolution."

"Then what happens?"

"The FBI retains the evidence if there's a chance that additional victims will come forward. The FBI has several evidence storage facilities. If it's a current case, the evidence is logged in the relevant office. If it's a closed case, it's stored in a warehouse."

This was it. Lucy felt it in her gut. "Can you find out where the evidence is?"

"Not until eight a.m., but I will." Dorothy paused. "What do you think this has to do with the pharmaceutical company? There's no connection that I can see."

"Exactly. No connection. This isn't about Colton Thayer and the senator. This is about Skye Jansen and Kurt Le-Grand. Sean's in danger. I have to call Noah right now."

"Explain, and I'll call Rick."

"At RCK, Sean's job wasn't to hack into computers from the safety of his desk. Companies hired him to break into facilities to expose their security flaws. He can break into virtually anyplace with enough time and planning. Ever since we found the connection to Avery and Block, I've been thinking, why now? It's been two years. What if there's something in the evidence locker that they need in order to get the money? You said they pled out, but that takes time. I'll bet it was recent, within the last few months, and the evidence was moved into FBI custody. I might be wrong, but I don't think I am."

"I'll call Rick, you talk to Noah."

"Thank you, Dorothy."

Lucy breathed only marginally easier. She tried Noah,

but he wasn't answering his cell phone. She called Sean. His phone went directly to voice mail. She frowned and tried his backup phone.

She heard it ring in his office. She opened the desk drawer and found several phones and a small computer. He'd come here last night after visiting her.

She started going through Sean's desk looking for any information about this case. In the back of his top drawer he had an envelope marked: *Martin Holdings.*

Had he put that here last night? Earlier? Was this the proof of what Robert Martin had done ten years ago to scam all those pensioners?

The envelope was sealed, but she didn't care. She opened it. Inside was a disk. She popped it into Sean's computer. It was password protected.

Of course it was.

She knew his primary security password, but she also knew that he rotated passwords regularly. This wasn't something she could just guess. She tried his main password—he gave it to her every week when he changed it.

Strike one.

Lucy had one idea and hoped it worked. She called the RCK webmaster, Jaye Morgan.

"Jaye, it's Lucy. I need your help. Can you access Sean's computer remotely?"

"Not unless he gives me permissions."

"Can I give you permissions?"

"Do you have his password?"

"I'm on his computer now."

Jaye walked Lucy through how to grant permissions. "Make sure you tell Sean that this was *your* idea," Jaye said. "He gets freaked if anyone touches his computer. You'd think I was going through his underwear drawer or something."

"I'll take full responsibility."

"Okay, I'm in," Jaye said. "What do you need?"

"To access the password-protected disk. I tried Sean's primary password and it didn't work. I only have four more tries."

"You do know that Sean is one of the best."

"I do."

"Fortunately, so am I. I need some information about the disk; then I think I can decrypt it." Jaye walked Lucy through how to get the information. In five minutes, she'd opened the disk on Sean's computer.

"You're brilliant."

"Thank you. What is this? These are account numbers. Wire transfers. Shit, that's a lot of money."

"It's old data." As Lucy said it, she recognized one of the numbers. "I know why Kurt LeGrand set all this up. He knew Sean had shut down Martin Holdings." Sean was in far more danger than Lucy thought. It was one thing to need Sean to break into the FBI evidence locker; it was quite another to want him for revenge.

"You know your brother is on his way to New York."

"Patrick? I thought he was on a job in L.A."

"Jack."

"Why is Jack going to New York?"

"Oh. Shit."

"Jaye, what are you not telling me?"

"Duke was abducted this morning from Sean's apartment. I assumed you knew."

Noah and Rick had both kept her in the dark. Why hadn't they told her? Did Sean know?

Jaye continued nervously, "Um, it's a major security problem for us because, um, Duke is working on a defense contract and, um, well—"

"It's okay, Jaye. It's not your fault." Lucy hung up and dialed Noah again. Again he didn't answer. Desperate, she dialed Rick Stockton's number. He didn't answer. *Dammit!*

She typed up everything she knew and sent the message to Noah and Rick:

Twelve years ago Kurt LeGrand quit his job with the Boston Accountancy Group and started working for Obsidian Trust. Obsidian was a shell company funded exclusively by Martin Holdings. Martin Holdings was run by Robert Martin, who allegedly killed himself after Sean hacked into his accounts and returned the money he stole to the retirees. I think that LeGrand was part of Martin Holdings and either knew then that Sean had been responsible or learned about Sean through Skye Jansen.

Four years ago, Kurt LeGrand began working for Avery & Block. At one point, Avery & Block hired Jansen Tech, Skye Jansen's consulting firm, to work on their networks. I don't have the time line of the mortgage fraud scheme, but it appears that it had been going on longer than LeGrand's employment. I speculate that LeGrand figured it out and he and Skye siphoned off the money from the Averys.

According to the plea agreement, the Avery brothers said that Chester Block, the principal who allegedly committed suicide, didn't know about their scam. They also stated the money should have been in their accounts. It makes more sense that LeGrand took the money and hid it because either he feared being caught or something went wrong and he couldn't access the funds before the FBI started their investigation. He became a whistle-blower, but Dorothy thinks that there was an FBI investigation open prior to LeGrand turning state's evidence. She is also contacting you about the evidence from the investigation and where its physically stored—I think they haven't gone after the money because of the investigation and working out the plea agreement with the Averys. Now that it's over, they want their money.

Sean is in great danger. They need him to break

into wherever they hid the money, probably because it's a system Sean is familiar with. But it's more than money. I think LeGrand wants revenge for what Sean did with Martin Holdings.

None of you are answering your phones; just let me know that you got this message and that you know where Sean is and that he's safe. Make sure he knows that Skye is as much a threat as LeGrand.

Lucy sent the message and tried Jack, but his phone went straight to voice mail. If he was trying to get to New York fast, he'd probably hopped on a military transport. He'd been career Army before he became a mercenary, and he had many friends in the armed forces. Not to mention that all the principals of RCK, except Sean, had been in Special Forces.

She didn't leave Jack a message. No one was responding to her e-mail. What if something had gone horribly wrong? She hated being here, in D.C., when Sean was in trouble four hours away.

And Duke—why hadn't they told her that Duke had been abducted? Did they think she'd do something reckless?

Maybe she would have. He was Sean's brother. Did Sean know? Was he looking for Duke? Did LeGrand need both Sean and Duke to retrieve the money he stole?

"Be careful, Sean," she whispered.

CHAPTER TWENTY-EIGHT

By the time Noah got back to FBI headquarters, it was after two in the morning. Last he heard, Colton was in surgery and the doctors gave him a 20 percent chance of survival. He'd lost a lot of blood and been unresponsive in the ambulance.

The office was unusually active for two in the morning. Rick Stockton was arguing with ASAC Torres when Noah and Suzanne walked in.

"Madeaux, my office, now," Torres said.

"I take responsibility for Agent Madeaux disobeying protocol," Noah said.

"Armstrong," Rick said in warning.

"Sir," Noah said, "my apologies to you, but Sean was my responsibility and he's now missing."

"He very well could have been playing you all," Torres said. "I have an agent dead in his apartment, the same agent who claimed he tried to kill her the other day, and he may have been responsible for killing one of his partners—"

"Sean didn't kill Hunter Nash or Deanna Brighton," Noah said.

"You can't know that," Torres said. "And I did not authorize you to interrogate or detain one of my agents."

Rick said, "I explained to ASAC Torres about our undercover operation, but he's justifiably upset and concerned about a dead federal agent, and another agent who blatantly disregarded orders."

"And I'm concerned about a missing undercover private investigator and his critically shot team leader." Noah rubbed his face. "I need to interview Carol Hattori."

"She's in Holding," Torres said. "What is going on with Agent Gannon?"

Noah motioned for them to step inside Torres's office. Quietly he said, "He's been leaking information about investigations to Senator Paxton."

"Why?"

"Paxton had been tracking prisoner movements, and he wanted to know when certain prisoners were being moved to within federal facilities. Gannon said he gave him information, but didn't know why he asked. That he was a senator and he liked his policies and believed his help was research for more funding to keep sex offenders in prison. Then, when Paxton started asking for more information, Gannon was already in too deep to say no. Paxton used him like he uses everyone else."

"And what does that have to do with Agent Brighton?"

"When Senator Paxton learned that Sean had started working again for Colton Thayer, he used Gannon to first determine that there was an undercover operation, then to get Sean arrested and off the team. Paxton and Sean have a history. Gannon fueled Agent Brighton's personal obsession with Rogan. I don't know how yet, but at some point Evan Weller became her informant. He must have given her some good information, because she believed him when he called her twenty minutes before she was shot to death."

"What?"

"The last call Deanna Brighton received was from Evan Weller, twenty minutes before she showed up at

Sean's apartment," Suzanne said. "We think he gave her the address and set her up."

"That's a master criminal," Torres said sarcastically.

Noah's temper was thin. "Not all criminals are stupid."

Rick intervened. "Noah, take five; I'll have Carol Hattori brought up for an interview. I'll be observing. Don't make me pull you."

Noah left and went to the men's room. He splashed cold water on his face.

Rick followed him. First Rick checked the stalls to make sure they were alone. "Jack Kincaid is on his way. We have a major security problem with Duke and Sean being off the grid."

Noah must have missed something. "What are you talking about?"

"Duke is in the middle of a major Defense Department contract to secure their overseas servers, and before Sean quit RCK he had been tasked with hacking into the Defense Department to find the holes."

"Did he?"

"Yes. And Duke was in the process of fixing the breaches, but the patch isn't complete."

"You don't think that's why they were kidnapped—"

"No. Did you get Lucy's message? She sent it just before you walked in."

"What message? I've been in the middle of a crisis—" Noah took a deep breath. "I'm sorry."

"Lucy doesn't know Sean is missing. She thinks he's in danger because Kurt LeGrand worked with Robert Martin on the pension scam ten years ago and he knows Sean took the money. It's revenge.

"But if LeGrand is working with Skye Jansen," Rick continued, "she could very well know what Sean and Duke do for RCK, and if he thinks he can leverage them with either our government or another government—"

"He will." Noah got it. "And that's why Jack is coming here? He's coming to protect RCK assets."

"I don't know Jack personally, but I know him by reputation. His specialty is foreign hostage rescue, and he has high-level security clearance. He lands at McGuire soon, then will hop a chopper to Fort Hamilton. I expect him at oh-four-hundred."

Noah pulled out his phone and read Lucy's e-mail. "If she's right—what are the chances that LeGrand killed both Robert Martin and Chester Block? She wrote that they were *alleged* suicides. She's thinking LeGrand is more dangerous than a typical white-collar thief. I have to tell her about Sean—"

"No," Rick said.

"Why?"

"Because Lucy has a fatal flaw. If she knows Sean is missing, she'll come here. Her career will be over."

"I don't think she cares."

"There's a reason FBI agents aren't involved in personal cases. She won't be able to think clearly. I want her safe, in D.C."

"She'd be safer at Quantico."

"She's at Sean's place. My analyst Dorothy is keeping an eye on her. She's going to drive her back to Quantico tomorrow morning."

Noah tapped his phone. "This is the most valuable information we've gotten so far. Lucy works best under pressure." But he conceded that she would only put herself in danger if she came to New York. "If LeGrand is really out for revenge, targeting Lucy would hurt Sean more than anything else."

"Exactly. She needs to stay put."

Noah found Suzanne in the hall outside the interview room where Carol Hattori waited for them. Noah needed to get as much information out of her before she called her attorney.

Suzanne was pale and guzzling a bottle of water. She handed one to Noah.

"I'm sorry about Torres," Noah said. "Rick will smooth things over, but OPR may get involved."

She waved her hand in dismissal. "I've faced OPR before. I'm a big girl, I didn't have to follow your lead. I'm more worried about *my* boss than I am about Torres. Maybe the NYPD is hiring—they seem to like me a lot this week."

Noah hoped the situation didn't deteriorate to the point where Suzanne would feel like she had to leave the FBI.

"If the situation gets bad here, you can always transfer to headquarters."

"I'll be fine, Armstrong. Don't worry." She nodded to the door. "Did we let her sweat long enough?"

"Let's do it."

Noah and Suzanne stepped into the interview room. Carol Hattori looked up expectantly, her eyes bloodshot, her tan face unnaturally pale. She was all cried out.

"Is he out of surgery? No one will tell me anything."

"I spoke with the hospital ten minutes ago," Suzanne said. "Colton is still in surgery. But he's holding on."

Fresh tears slipped out. Noah said, "Ms. Hattori, we need you to focus."

"I-I'll try."

Suzanne glanced at Noah and frowned. She sat down and said, "Carol, if you can please hold it together, for Colton. We want to find out who did this."

"I told you. Skye shot him. I don't know why."

"Yes, but you know more than you think you do. We want you to walk through what you heard, okay?"

"Colton said never talk to any cops without a lawyer."

"Do you want a lawyer?" Suzanne said.

Noah wanted to toss her from the interview room.

Suzanne continued, "Because we can do that for you. But it will take time, and Skye may get out of the country. We have two other people in danger."

"I thought they shot Sean, too. You're going to get her, right?"

"If you cooperate, we'll do everything to find and stop the woman who shot your boyfriend."

Carol nodded and glanced at Noah, skittish.

"Agent Armstrong," Suzanne said, motioning with her eyes for him to sit.

He took a deep breath. Suzanne was right. He was wound too tight. "Carol, would you please explain what happened tonight?"

She bit her lip, but it was obvious she wanted to tell someone. It helped that she was emotionally wrung out.

"After Hunter was killed, Colton moved up the plan by twenty-four hours. He was worried that someone in PBM had found out and had Hunter killed. Hunter had the security plans, so Colton changed the time, day, and even how they entered the facility."

"Who was responsible for what?"

"Skye and Evan were supposed to go to the research director's office and copy a specific file that was on hard copy only. Colton and Sean learned they were experimenting in bio-weapons and he wanted proof. Originally, all he wanted was proof that they had killed his brother— his brother, Travis, was in leukemia trials, and he died suddenly after using an experimental drug. The company swore the drug had nothing to do with it, but Colton didn't believe them, and thought they knew that the drug had an adverse effect. But when he hacked in and found information on a bio-weapon, he said there was a bigger cause to fight for."

"Where did Sean Rogan fit?"

"He's Colton's best friend. I mean, I don't know why, Sean just left years ago and that hurt C. But when Sean moved to New York, Colton was so happy."

"What did Sean do for the team?"

"I didn't believe he was as smart as Colton made him out to be, but he is. They needed him to hack the external security feeds. He came up with this brilliant plan to loop the security cameras, you know, like they did in the movie *Speed* about the bus—"

"We're familiar with the movie," Noah cut her off.

"Oh. Yeah. Well, I thought that was just something that they did in the movies, but Sean not only knew how to do it, but said he could cover their tracks and no one would know they were there. And they needed him to crack the electronic safe. Colton is good with computers, but the safe is above him. Sean is an expert safecracker."

Great, Noah thought. *One more list of crimes in Sean's portfolio.*

"And did they get what they wanted? The guards said no one breached security."

"They got in, got everything, and got out. Sean was really angry with Evan. He asked several times what was in the backpack, why he was in the research lab when he was only supposed to go to the director's office. They were fighting wh-wh-when Skye shot C."

"Do you know what was in the backpack? Did Colton tell Evan to take something?"

"No. Colton just wanted proof that they were working with bio-weapons. He thought that more people would care about that than a long-ago drug trial that killed his brother. Colton just wanted to expose them for the corrupt pharmaceutical bastards that they are."

"What did Colton want in the safe?"

"I—I don't know if I should say." She looked down at her hands, her forehead crinkled in doubt.

Noah leaned forward. "Senator Jonathan Paxton is

being arrested as we speak. So it would help us if you know what they took so we can find it."

Her almond-shaped eyes widened. "You know about him?"

"We know he hired Colton to break into PBM and take something from the safe. What?"

"He wanted a file that was in there, plus if there was a tape. From what I heard, Sean kept the files and Colton took the tape."

That meant everything was in the evidence room.

"Did you hear anything else after Colton was shot?"

"I started crying and they shut down communications. The last thing I heard was Skye telling Sean that she was in charge."

"Do you know this man?" Noah slid a photo of Kurt LeGrand in front of her.

She shook her head. "No."

"Does the name Kurt LeGrand mean anything to you?"

She stopped fidgeting. "Yes."

"What?"

"Skye's fiancé is named Kurt. I don't know his last name, but she talked about him once."

"So she wasn't involved with Evan."

"They had a thing, but it was over. They both lived in the carriage house. Separate bedrooms." Tears started running down her face again. "Why would they try to kill Colton? After everything he did for them? Let them live in the house for free? Gave them jobs, legitimate jobs, he didn't have time for? Why would they do that to someone who loved them like he did?"

When the computer beeped, Lucy jerked awake, a sharp pain in her neck. She rubbed the pinched nerve and groaned. She'd fallen asleep at Sean's desk and would be paying for it all day.

It was a message from Rick:

Your information is solid. We're working on it.

She let out a long, heavy breath and stretched. There was nothing else she could do now but wait.

Lucy hated being stuck here, hated not being in the middle of the investigation. She needed to know what was going on, but she didn't want to stop Noah or Suzanne or Rick from doing everything in their power to find Duke. She didn't want to become one of their problems. She just wished that Sean would have called her and let her know he was okay. Just one word. But Noah would have told her if something was wrong.

She frowned. Maybe not. They hadn't told her about Duke. What if Sean was in trouble and they didn't want her to know? Did they not trust her with the information? Did they think she would do something stupid?

She stood and stretched. It was four in the morning. She'd slept for an hour at Sean's desk, but there was no going back to sleep now.

She went downstairs to make a fresh pot of coffee. The alarm panel was beeping on the front door. Had she set it right? Yes—she'd been here enough to know how Sean's security worked. Hyper-alert, she tiptoed to the front door, not turning on any lights. She looked through the security hole. Two men in ski masks stood there, both focused on the lock.

She pressed the panic button on the alarm as they popped the first lock and was about to run out the back when she saw two more men at the back door.

Heart racing, she ran up the stairs to Sean's office. She opened Sean's bottom desk drawer, but his gun wasn't there. She ran to the bedroom and shut the door. No locks. She pushed a chair against the knob and grabbed her cell phone. There was no signal. Could they have jammed it?

What about the alarm? Could they have jammed that, too?

There was a fail-safe in the alarm system; if the power was cut, the police were notified. If the system went down, the police were notified. The panic button was on a dedicated phone line.

She heard people walking downstairs. Someone was on the staircase.

She searched Sean's room for another gun. His favorite Beretta was missing from under his bed, but she found a fully loaded 9mm in his closet.

She tried to calm down, but the fear of being kidnapped by four men was real. She would die before she let them touch her. She couldn't live through another rape. A scream caught in her throat as she stared at the door, frozen, her hands shaking.

They don't want to rape you; they want to take you to leverage Sean. Like Duke. That's why they took Duke. Oh, God, did that mean he was dead? Did that mean they had Sean?

The men were outside the door. She held the gun out, ready to shoot. The police would be here soon. She just had to hold off the men for five minutes. Ten at most.

What if they were all armed? She couldn't kill four of them while being so exposed. *Think, dammit!*

Bathroom. There was a lock on the door.

She ran into the bathroom and slammed the door, barely having time to lock it before they burst into the bedroom. The door wouldn't hold against their strength. She stood in the corner, between the toilet and the shower, gun aimed at the door.

"She's in here!" one of them called.

It took them two tries to break the door open. She aimed and fired. Two bullets at the first masked man. Two at the second. The first attacker screamed and went down, but the second had enough time to back out of the doorway. She was on autopilot, focusing on movement and sound. It was her or them. She did not want to die.

The second man stepped in again and she fired at him at the same time he shot her in the shoulder.

The pain was immediate, a burning pain, and she slid against the tile. A yellow plastic feather stuck out of her chest, blood dripping down her white tank top. She tried to shoot the bastard again, but she had no control over her limbs. He easily disarmed her.

No, no, no.

"Bitch shot me!" The man with the tranq gun back-handed her.

There was more commotion and Lucy was fading. "Don't kill her!" another man said while the fourth shouted, "Out the back, now! Cops have been dispatched. I thought you took care of it."

"No," Lucy muttered.

"The bastard has multiple layers of security."

"You can't leave me!" the first man she shot cried out as another man picked her up. Her mind willed her body to fight, but she couldn't even open her eyes, let alone move her arms.

"You're right," someone said. She heard three gunshots, then nothing.

CHAPTER TWENTY-NINE

Sean woke up shivering.

His eyelids felt like they'd been glued shut, and when he attempted to move, bile rose in the back of his throat. He swallowed and grunted as waves of pain coursed through his body. As his stomach settled, he moved his hands. They were handcuffed. That's when he realized he wore two pairs of bracelets, one for each wrist, and his arms were splayed wide. He was slumped over and tried to straighten himself. The movement brought more pain.

"Sean."

He heard a voice far in the distance. It sounded like his brother. Great, just what he needed, the Good Angel Duke sitting on his shoulder telling him he'd been an idiot.

Wherever he was, he was freezing. It smelled like hay. Moldy hay. A barn? Maybe—there may have been animals here once, but no longer. It was drafty enough to be a barn. No insulation. It was still dark—at least he thought it was. He squinted his eyes open enough to know there was no light in here.

"Sean, wake up."

I know; I know.

He had to get his bearings or he wouldn't be able to

escape. He didn't care how they'd cuffed him, he would find a way out. If his head didn't pound like the world's worst hangover, he might actually be able to think.

"Sean! It's Duke. *Wake up.*"

"I'm awake," Sean mumbled. His mouth was swollen and dry.

Duke is here?

Sean opened his eyes, and while they still felt heavy, he looked around and realized the light was changing. It was dark, no lights, but windows on the far side of the barn faced east and the sun was beginning to come out. What did that make it? Five thirty, six in the morning?

"You've been out for hours."

"They shot me with a damn tranquilizer." He coughed to clear his scratchy throat. A gallon or two of water would go down real good about now.

"What the fuck is going on?"

Duke rarely swore, but when he did it was usually because Scan had screwed up. There was more than simple anger in Duke's tone; an underlying hostility had Sean on edge.

"I don't know." His head pounded and he tried to get his thoughts together. He took a couple deep breaths and moved his limbs. Nothing was broken, but his shoulder was sore from the Taser and his knee was banged up. They probably had dragged him over rocks.

"You don't fucking *know*?"

"What are you doing here?"

A testament to his being disorientated—he just realized his brother Duke should be in California.

"I took the red-eye Tuesday night, first flight I could get after talking to that FBI agent, Deanna Brighton. She's now dead, in your apartment. The two assholes who grabbed me shot her."

He absorbed everything Duke said and immediately understood the implications.

"Brighton was at my apartment?"

"Focus, Sean. Are you sure you're okay?" The first hint of worry in Duke's voice.

"I'll be fine. Why was she there?"

"I have no idea, but they were expecting her."

"Someone sent her there? The mole?"

"Mole? What mole?"

"The FBI mole." But that didn't make any sense. No one knew where Sean lived, unless they'd followed him. Or maybe someone had put a tracker on him. Who? And why would the mole have Brighton killed? Unless Brighton was the mole and Paxton—but why would Paxton kill her? And, ultimately, attempt to frame Sean?

And if they planned on framing Sean for her murder, then that meant they would kill Duke because he was a witness. So why keep him alive?

Thinking wasn't doing Sean's headache any good. He took several deep breaths as a wave of nausea washed over him.

"What have you gotten yourself into this time?"

Good question. He had no idea. Colton was dead; Skye and Evan had kidnapped him. If Noah made it to PBM it had been too late.

"Why are you in New York?"

"I just told you—"

"Give me a sec; my head feels like mush."

Duke didn't say anything for several minutes and Sean took the opportunity to shift and adjust, roll his neck, feel out his body for serious damage. And think.

Duke came to New York because he thought Sean was in trouble with the FBI.

Sean finally said, "It's a long story, but trust me when I tell you I'm not in trouble with the FBI."

"I find that hard to believe, considering."

"There's a lot more to this than you know." How could he explain it?

"You always think you know best. Action before thought. Do you know how many times I've had to bail you out because you didn't think things through?"

This time, there was nothing further from the truth than that statement. Sean had done nothing but think about what he was doing, from the minute Rick Stockton and Noah came to him with their plan.

"I don't want to talk about this here—I don't know who's listening—but you have to trust me!"

"Trust?"

As the sun rose higher, Sean could see his brother more clearly. He was handcuffed to two steel rings on the floor. Sean had no idea what they were used for. Sean himself was handcuffed to a horizontal pole. Maybe something that they wrapped horse reins around or a saddle or something. Sean had never been a horse or farm kind of guy.

Duke was staring at him, disappointment and anger the dominant emotions.

"Duke—"

"I'll never be able to trust you again."

Sean realized that Duke had never thought he had changed, had never believed he would stay on the right side of the law. Worse, Duke believed Sean was responsible for all this—and that hurt. It hurt as much as when he had walked away from RCK and led Duke to believe he was working for Colton again and Duke had said he expected it.

Sean needed to explain to his brother what was going on. The way Duke must think of him—once he knew the truth, he would understand.

Sean didn't see or hear anyone but he kept his voice low.

"We need to figure out their endgame. I need to give you the abridged version of events, because I don't know how much time we have."

Duke stared at him. "You've never taken a job without knowing the endgame. Did you trust Colton Thayer so much that you didn't find out what he was doing?"

"This isn't about Colton."

"Maybe it's always been about you, always trying to prove to the world, to prove to me, that you're smarter than everyone else."

"It's never been about that."

"Bullshit." Duke glared at him. Disappointment clouded his eyes. "You're just like Liam."

Sean hadn't been expecting the comparison to their other brother. Duke hadn't spoken to Liam in years because of major business disagreements. "I'm nothing like Liam."

"You're *exactly* like him. I just didn't see it, because I felt responsible for you. He and Eden created their own business, they played by their own rules, and I understand them. Liam is in it for the challenge and the money, and he's going to be caught one of these days—I thought you'd grown out of it."

"Please listen—"

"I've always listened to you! I always defended you and stood by you because I blamed myself."

"Blamed yourself for what?"

"Your crimes."

"I'm not a criminal."

Duke laughed. Really laughed.

"That stunt at Stanford—"

"That wasn't a crime—"

"Really? You would have gone to prison if I hadn't stepped in."

"I'd never have been convicted. But I was seventeen. I thought what I was doing was right because too often the cops are tied with rules and red tape and that bastard was going to continue to hurt little kids."

"You can tell yourself that."

Sean hated that his brother thought so low of him, but now wasn't the time to fight about it. He buried the pain, because pain and regret were going to keep him from focusing on getting out of here. Instead he focused on his anger.

He said through clenched teeth, "I'm working with FBI Assistant Director Rick Stockton. Ask him when we get out of this mess."

Duke didn't say anything for a long minute. "If that's true, why didn't you tell me?"

If that's true? That Duke even thought Sean was lying angered him more. "Rick wanted this operation to be completely undercover. Only Rick, me, and Noah Armstrong know the truth. Lucy didn't even know until yesterday." Get to the point, Sean told himself. No apologies. There would be time enough for explanation later.

Sean said, "Noah has been quietly investigating Senator Paxton since January, ever since the vigilante ring was shut down and Paxton walked away. Noah learned that Paxton hired Colton, and he and Rick asked me to go undercover to find out what they were doing. I agreed." He didn't feel the need to explain why—if he told Duke about what happened with Martin Holdings, Duke would disregard everything else Sean said and focus on his mistakes.

"Why you? Why not a real agent?"

"Because Colton has been trying to bring me back for years. You know that."

"And that's why you hacked into the pharmaceutical company? Why didn't you just tell me?"

"Because Colton had to believe that I really quit and the only way he would was if you and I had a major falling-out. It had to be real."

"There were other ways."

"We didn't have a lot of time to put this together."

"Why would you do this? This isn't like you, working for the FBI."

"You're right," Sean said, his anger exploding. "I did it for me. I committed a crime nearly ten years ago. The statute of limitations is up in six months. I have full immunity for helping Rick. Does that make you feel better? Knowing that I'm the scum you always thought I was?"

Duke stared at him. Sean had let his temper win and hated himself for it. Sean said, "Paxton hired Colton to steal a file and tape out of Joyce Bonner's office. I helped him."

"Of course you did."

"You don't listen to me, do you? I did it with the full backing of the Federal Bureau of Investigation."

"So you wouldn't go to prison."

Sean didn't want to talk anymore. Not about his reasons for going undercover or what he'd done ten years ago. Nothing he said was going to change Duke's opinion of him.

"Evan and Skye took something from the bio-lab at PBM. I don't know what it is; I don't know what they have planned, or why they kidnapped you, or why they didn't kill me when they shot Colton."

"Colton's dead?"

Sean blinked back sudden tears over the brutal murder of his friend. "Yes."

"I'm sorry."

Duke sounded sincere, so Sean accepted the apology.

"I overhead something that didn't make sense, but maybe it will to you," Duke said. "They're planning to break into a place with RCK security."

"There can't be many," Sean said.

"Maybe two dozen in New York City. Two museums, a chain of banks—probably twenty total banks with the same system within the five boroughs. Several private homes. A college. There's more, but I can't remember all of them."

"They couldn't have known you were here, so how

were they planning on getting me to cooperate without leverage?"

The barn door opened, bringing in a rush of colder air. Skye stood there. "Sean, I have my ways. But I'll admit, having your brother as part of the 'leverage,' as you say, seems particularly apropos. Time to meet the boss."

The way she said *boss* Sean had the feeling she wasn't sincere. He watched her direct two thugs to uncuff him. She thought she was in charge. Maybe she was.

"Be good, Sean, or I'll kill your brother. Understand?"

Sean wanted to slap that smirk off Skye's face. How could she have gone from a fun, carefree college student to a killer? To *Colton's* murderer? That Sean had underestimated her aggravated him. He'd let the past cloud his judgment.

Never again.

He nodded without breaking eye contact. "Yes, ma'am, I understand perfectly."

Noah watched Senator Jonathan Paxton sweating in the interview room as Paxton watched the tape Sean had stolen. Noah didn't need to see it again; he'd already viewed it twice.

Senator Paxton's career was over. His freedom was gone. And as he watched the tape, he knew it, too.

It was just Noah and the senator. Rick Stockton and the SAC of the New York City field office were on the other side of the glass. The FBI director had already been briefed in D.C. But Rick let Noah interrogate Paxton. It was Noah's operation that had yielded the prize. This was what he had been working toward for the past ten months.

But it didn't feel like a victory when he had a dead agent, a dead hacker, and Sean and Duke missing.

Noah had to give the senator credit for maintaining a poker face.

"Rogan," Paxton said with both disgust and a hint of admiration.

"You attempted to get Rogan off of Colton's team because you thought he would look at the tape."

"I was right, wasn't I?" Paxton shook his head. "It doesn't matter anymore."

Noah didn't know if Paxton was playing the defeatist senator in an attempt to gain sympathy, to delay, or to plot out an escape plan. He had the money and contacts to flee, but he was well known. It would be hard for him to leave the country and set up somewhere undetected.

In the back of Noah's mind he realized that Paxton would never go to prison. He'd been a prosecutor, an attorney general, and now a U.S. senator. He'd never be housed with a violent prison population. There were some facilities where he might be safe, but Paxton must have an out plan. A plan that kept him free, even if he was forced to resign.

But Noah couldn't think about how Paxton was going to maneuver out of this mess. Noah needed answers.

"We have plenty to talk about, but right now I need to know what happened at PBM. You hired Colton Thayer to retrieve this tape. We also know that you told Thayer that you had proof that PBM falsified their drug testing related to the experimental drugs that Thayer believes killed his brother."

Paxton started to laugh. Noah stared at him, his jaw tight, not for the first time thinking about taking a fist to Paxton's jaw. Noah wasn't a violent man. He was methodical. Disciplined. Paxton brought out the worst in Noah, and now he finally understood how Sean felt last summer when Paxton manipulated him.

Noah waited Paxton out. He wasn't going to take the bait.

"You have all the answers."

"I'm asking you."

"What's truly funny is that you and Rogan were work-

ing together. You don't even like each other. You're both
in love with Lucy. Rogan plays in the dirt and gets very
dirty, yet you are the shining knight, the former deco-
rated Air Force lieutenant who believes in the system. I
missed it. You're not susceptible to Sean Rogan's manipulative charm. That means—this was all you."

Noah wasn't certain what Paxton was trying to do.

Paxton said, "When did you open an investigation on
me?"

Noah didn't trust Paxton, but he hadn't asked for a
lawyer and he had been read his rights. When he got an
attorney, the information would be available.

"I became suspicious in January after interviewing
Buckley and the others involved in the WFC vigilante
group. They didn't say anything to give you away. But
Buckley wasn't smart enough to pull off the widespread
vigilante project, and your protegé, Mick Mallory, was too
ruthless to be so disciplined. You're both smart and disciplined. But you also had a vendetta. There was one gun
not recovered in Mallory's house. I think you were the
one to put a bullet in the head of the last man still alive
who'd hurt your daughter. The last man who hurt Lucy."

Paxton stared at Noah. There was no more humor in
his icy expression. "What you think and what you can
prove are far different."

"Agent Gannon has already given a statement. He doesn't
know Kurt LeGrand. Do you? Did you set Sean up?"

"I wish I had," Paxton said. "He's been a problem. But
I don't know Kurt LeGrand, and I don't know why he'd
want Sean, unless Sean pissed him off like he seems to
anger everyone he meets. He's an arrogant, condescend-
ing smart-ass."

Noah gave Paxton a half smile. "I don't disagree with
you there. He's also intelligent, loyal, and courageous. He
knew he was walking into a dangerous situation, but he
did it anyway."

"He did it to get the goods on me. Don't label him as noble. He cares about himself, and that's it. I had evidence of a crime he committed, and I bet you pushed him to help so he gets a clean slate." Paxton smiled. "You have a good poker face, but I see that I'm right."

Paxton gestured to the video that was now paused. "If Sean Rogan had walked into that room and saw a woman he cared about being attacked, he would have done the same thing I did. He and I are no different. Never forget that."

"What happened between you and Joyce Bonner that you felt you had to steal this tape?"

Paxton leaned forward. "It's personal."

"What do you know about the bio-toxin that PBM was developing?"

"I'm done here, Agent Armstrong," Paxton said. "I will have my attorney now."

"We believe that Kurt LeGrand was working with two people in Colton Thayer's group and that they stole a bio-toxin from the lab. Joyce Bonner is being picked up by two agents at her house. I will find out what is going on."

"I believe I asked for my attorney, and I still have constitutional rights, Agent Armstrong."

Noah stepped out before his temper finally exploded. Rick Stockton was in the adjoining room on the phone. His face was red, and a vein throbbed in his neck. Noah had never seen Rick so agitated.

"Find out what happened. Now!"

Rick hung up but got back on the phone without saying anything to Noah.

Suzanne stepped into the room with a dark-haired, tan-skinned, forty-something man who immediately drew attention to himself simply by his foreboding presence. He had on a visitor badge and an expression that told Noah he'd seen everything, and worse.

Rick hung up his phone in the middle of his conversation. "Jack."

"Where's Lucy?"

Noah looked from Jack to Rick. He was definitely caught off-guard.

"We have every D.C. cop, every federal agent in D.C. and New York tracking her. We found the van they used abandoned, and evidence that they picked up another vehicle."

Rick turned to Noah and seemed to gather his confidence and command back. "Noah, while you were interrogating the senator, I got word from D.C. that Lucy was abducted from Sean's house. I don't have a full report, but it appears there were four men who broke in, two in front, two in back. There's a lot of video footage on the attack because of the security system. As soon as she pressed the panic button, all cameras in the house were activated. She locked herself in the bathroom, shot two attackers, was tranquilized and disarmed. She was carried out of the house less than two minutes before the police arrived.

"We IDed the man killed in the bathroom. He's Billy Potts, from Queens, a hired gun associated with the man Corbett you found dead in the warehouse. Lucy shot him twice in the chest, but his partner killed him because he was in no condition to run. We have blood from another victim—she shot one of the other men in the arm. If he's in the system, we'll have a DNA match in hours. I called in everyone at the lab to process the scene."

Jack said, "LeGrand. Where does he live?"

"We've been to his apartment; he hasn't been there in a long time," Suzanne said.

"Other property?"

"We're working on it," Rick said.

Jack looked at Paxton through the one-way mirror. He brushed past Noah and went into the room. Noah followed immediately. "Jack—"

Jack Kincaid didn't acknowledge Noah. He walked around to where Paxton sat and slammed his palm on the table. "Did you order Lucy's abduction?"

The shock and confusion on Paxton's face told Noah that he didn't know anything about it.

"What happened to Lucy?"

"I'm Jack Kincaid. Lucy is my sister. And you're involved in this."

"I love Lucy like she's my own daughter. I've always protected her."

Jack looked as if he would deck Paxton. Paxton must have sensed the same thing, because he flinched and leaned away from Jack.

"What do you know about Kurt LeGrand?"

"Nothing."

"How did you find out about Martin Holdings?"

Paxton blinked. "I—"

"Don't lie to me. If those bastards touch her, if they hurt her, I will hurt you ten times worse."

"After I hired Colton Thayer to retrieve electronic files for me last spring, his partner Skye Jansen delivered the chip. She told me that Thayer wanted to bring Sean into the plan, but Sean wasn't doing it. She gave me the information, implying that they would leverage the information to gain Sean's cooperation. I still didn't want him involved, but she seemed to think he was some sort of security god, the only one who could do what we needed. Once he was in New York I had second thoughts. That's it. I swear, I don't know Kurt LeGrand, never heard of him until Agent Armstrong mentioned his name. Jack, believe me, I'll do anything to protect my daughter!"

Jack leaned forward and, only inches from Paxton's face, whispered, "Lucy. Is not. Your daughter."

He turned and walked out. Noah followed.

"LeGrand needs a remote or private place to keep Duke

and Lucy," Noah said. "There's no property under his name or Skye Jansen's or Evan Weller's."

"We're running Obsidian Trust right now," Rick said. "Lucy and Dorothy uncovered the connection between Obsidian, Martin, and LeGrand."

Jack said, "Show me the message Lucy sent last night."

Rick handed him his phone. "We think they need Sean to break into an FBI warehouse in Brooklyn. RCK upgraded the security on all storage facilities last year."

"Why now?" Suzanne asked.

Rick said, "Now that the plea agreement with the Averys is final the evidence will be sent to a remote storage facility."

Jack glared at first Noah, then Rick. "You should have brought RCK into this operation before putting Sean undercover."

Rick straightened his spine. "That was my call, Jack. RCK has a lot of latitude, latitude I helped put in place, but Sean's defection needed to be real. I stand by my decision."

In a low voice Jack said, "Then I will hold you personally responsible if anything happens to my sister." He walked out.

Noah let out a breath. "Shit."

"He's right. I didn't see this coming."

"Sir," Noah said, "no one did. They set Sean up. They had this planned for a long time. If Lucy is right, Kurt LeGrand has been plotting revenge for nearly a decade."

"I—um, better make sure Kincaid doesn't go AWOL," Suzanne mumbled, and left.

"So that's Lucy's other brother," Noah said. "He's nothing like Patrick or Dillon."

"No, he's certainly not."

"He's a lot more like Sean." *Without the charm.*

CHAPTER THIRTY

Sean remained silent on the short walk from the barn to the house. He surveyed the land but saw no familiar land-marks and no other houses. He had no idea how long they'd flown—they'd left PBM after 11:30 last night, and it was about 6:30 a.m. now. As they were in the country, with no sound of traffic, they would be at least thirty minutes from the city. Or they could be three hours away. More.

Sean was brought into the house through the front door, uncuffed. It took all his control not to fight Skye, but that would do Duke no good and Sean thought he might have a concussion from when Evan hit him with the gun. Or his queasiness was the tranquilizer working through his system. He wasn't 100 percent; that was certain. Not being at his prime in addition to not knowing the layout of the property or the type of security he faced meant any escape attempt would be foolhardy.

As soon as he stepped into the well-appointed house, he heard the tick of a grandfather clock. He glanced over and saw it was nearly seven thirty in the morning. He'd been an hour off on the time. He glanced out the door to gauge the sun, so he could keep track.

Evan stood inside the door and scowled. He slammed

the door shut, and Skye smiled widely at Sean. "Welcome," she said.

Sean returned her grin. "Bitch."

Evan punched him in the small of his back. Sean ground his teeth to fight the pain.

Kurt LeGrand entered the foyer holding a bottle of champagne. "Evan, please." LeGrand spoke as if addressing a child.

Sean sized LeGrand up. He wasn't a large man, trim and five eight, nine tops. Fair coloring, well dressed in pressed khakis and white polo shirt. His cold blue eyes were calculating, and Sean knew immediately that LeGrand should not be underestimated.

LeGrand extended his hand to Sean. Sean didn't take it. His captor didn't seem to care and smiled. "I would say thank you for coming, but you didn't have a choice. Sit."

LeGrand motioned through double doors that led to a dining room that was set for four. That's when Sean recognized the smells coming from the kitchen—sausage, bacon, maple syrup. "Sit," LeGrand repeated.

"I'm not hungry."

His captor nodded to Evan and the other male in the room, who grabbed Sean and sat him at one end of the table. LeGrand sat at the opposite end and said "Eric, please bring in breakfast."

Skye and Evan sat at the table and LeGrand said to Sean, "I understand you want to be difficult in an attempt to show you're in charge, or not yield to my authority, so let me explain. Don't piss me off. Don't be an asshole. I will have your brother killed; then I will go through the other people you care about. Your former partner Patrick Kincaid and your girlfriend, Lucy Kincaid. That's pretty much it, right? You're not all that close to many people. Well, now that your best friend is dead."

It was all Sean could do not to leap across the table and put his hands around Kurt LeGrand's neck.

He simply stared, his jaw clenched shut.

LeGrand smiled. "You understand."

LeGrand poured champagne in four classes, then added what looked like fresh-squeezed orange juice. "It's early," he said, "but we have much to celebrate."

LeGrand was near forty, though his manners and demeanor were a generation more mature than those of Sean's peers. To Sean it seemed like an act. Like the house and table was all a stage and Kurt LeGrand with his careful speech was the star. All eyes on him. Everyone took his lead.

Except—

Sean glanced at Skye. She had an odd, smug smirk on her face, as if she had a secret no one else knew. She'd taken the time to shower and change since they were at PBM. The care that LeGrand took in presenting this meal was the same care Skye took in presenting herself.

Why? What was going on with these two?

And Evan—where did he fit in? When Sean first rejoined the group, Skye went out of her way to show him that she and Evan were involved, yet Sean didn't feel the connection between them. But he'd miscalculated. He'd thought Evan was the traitor, when now he clearly saw that Skye was the one in charge. Evan was following orders.

But was Skye pulling LeGrand's strings? Or trying to? Because looking LeGrand in the eye, Sean wasn't certain he was completely sane. Smart, calculating, but he had a layer of self-containment that made Sean think of a grenade. If someone pulled the pin, he would explode.

"A toast," LeGrand said. Skye and Evan held up their glasses. Everyone looked at Sean, and from his expression Sean knew that LeGrand would make good on his threat to kill Duke.

Sean picked up his glass.

LeGrand smiled. "To freedom." He sipped.

Sean pretended to sip. He didn't know if it was poisoned, but he also didn't want to participate in this farce.

"Let's eat," Skye said, breaking a long silence. "Kurt is an amazing chef. Aren't you, sweetheart." She rose from her seat and went over to kiss him full on the mouth. LeGrand smiled when she was done.

"This is all for you, Skye." He looked at Sean. "And *you* let her go. All looks, no brains for you, right, Sean?"

Sean didn't let the bastard bait him.

The bodyguard, Eric, brought the food out and everyone dished up. Skye served Sean.

LeGrand motioned to Sean's plate. "You'll need your strength."

"What do you want from me?"

"So crass. We'll talk business after our meal."

Sean pushed his plate off the table and stood up. "I'm not eating a meal with the people who killed Colton and kidnapped my brother."

The bodyguard pulled a gun and aimed it at Sean.

LeGrand slowly rose from his seat. "Do not insult me in my home. You owe me."

"I owe you nothing."

"You owe me a fortune, and then your life."

Sean stared at him and didn't say anything.

"Do you remember Robert Martin?"

Sean remained silent.

"Of course you do. He was a nobody. I made him. All that money you thought you stole from him? You took it from *me*. He was simply the figurehead."

LeGrand grinned. "Robert Martin. You knew him and you stole every dime from him; then you killed him when he was going to turn you in." He paused. "At least, that's what the evidence will prove."

Sean's mind instantly grasped what LeGrand had said. Robert Martin, the man who had bilked millions of dollars from retirees. The reason Sean left MIT as soon as he could, why he got out of Colton's group. When Sean found out Martin had committed suicide, the guilt had been overwhelming.

And LeGrand was part of the scheme.

"I didn't kill him, and there's no evidence that says I did. And I didn't steal anything from him, or you. I returned the money you scammed from the pensions of retired folks—"

LeGrand slammed his fist on the table. "You would say anything to get off the hook. You destroyed everything I had built, and I will destroy you. Unless you make amends. And that's exactly what you're going to do. You'll regain my fortune for me, and you will do it so your brother and girlfriend will live. If you don't think I can get to Lucy Kincaid, you're mistaken."

Sean didn't believe that LeGrand could, except that there was a mole in the FBI. Sean hadn't figured out who it was, but if Rick Stockton was right, that mole could be a killer.

And as Sean thought about it, he realized that if Lucy didn't know there was a danger she couldn't protect herself. Snipers, poison, bombs—there were ways to get to someone even if they took precautions. It was much easier when they didn't know there was a threat.

"Sit, eat; then I'll explain. But you will not see your brother again, you will not know if Lucy is safe, until you complete the job."

Sean managed to swallow three or four bites of the meal. He didn't know if it was good or not; his senses were dull and he couldn't concentrate on anything except trying to figure out how to escape or contact Noah.

He determined that there were at least six people. Le-Grand, Skye, Evan, Eric, and two unknown men. Eric wasn't the man who'd been dragging Sean before they tranquilized him. He didn't know where the other two men were. And there could be more.

Sean hated not knowing what he was up against. He watched the dynamics between LeGrand and Skye in particular; it was clear that both thought they were in charge. Sean put his money on Skye—she was too deferential to LeGrand. It was a game for her. Evan—he was not the smartest guy in the room, but he was definitely loyal to both Skye and LeGrand from the way he spoke and looked at them. He was too daft to be faking. Eric was a hired thug—did what he was told.

Finally, the others finished their meal and Eric and Evan cleared the dishes. When the table was clear and coffee poured—Sean decided to drink it for a jolt even though he didn't like coffee—Kurt LeGrand began to talk.

"Tonight you will steal back everything you took from me, and more. And if you don't think your family is worth saving, if you think your FBI friends will come and save you—" LeGrand smiled when he saw the rage cross Sean's face. "Yes, I know you've been playing both sides. Haven't figured out why yet, but I thought it was very interesting that the FBI canceled the APB on you after your friend was killed."

The bastard. Sean's hands fisted under the table. "You killed Hunter."

"I didn't pull the trigger." LeGrand shrugged. His disinterest in Hunter's murder further enraged Sean.

"Let me explain something to you, Sean," LeGrand said. "Nine and a half years ago you took my fortune. I've been planning this ever since I found out you were responsible." If Sean hadn't been staring so intently at LeGrand, he would have missed the subtle glance toward Skye. What did that mean? That *Skye* had been the one who told LeGrand? If that was true, that meant that Skye, or LeGrand, had told Jonathan Paxton. Did that mean

Paxton was behind Duke's kidnapping and Hunter's murder?

"It seems appropriate, doesn't it?" LeGrand said. "You stole my fortune, so I'm using you to get it back."

The test at the hotel finally made sense—they wanted to know if Sean could hack into RCK security even when he no longer worked there. So they thought either he was working undercover and had never quit RCK or he could still get around through a back door.

"You need to be put in your place," LeGrand continued. "You're an arrogant asshole who thinks he is better than everyone else; you think you can be the judge and jury. I'm here to not only knock you down a peg, but by the time you're done, no one will believe anything you say about Martin Holdings, Hunter Nash's murder, or your involvement in your own brother's kidnapping." LeGrand stood. "Skye and Evan will prepare you for your task. And one more thing—if you don't do exactly what I say, if you don't get me exactly what I want, not only will your friends and family die, but thousands of innocent people." He grinned. "You didn't think Evan took that bio-toxin for the fun of it, did you?"

He left the room.

Noah joined a half-dozen agents scouring property records looking for any connection to LeGrand or any of the others involved with him.

An analyst burst into the room and announced, "We have a hit on a possible truck matching the description of the one seen in the vicinity of the abandoned van in Baltimore. A state trooper spotted a black king cab with shell abandoned in Scarsdale, New York. There's blood in the back and on the cab."

Noah calculated the time it would take to get from D.C. to New York. It was nearly eight thirty in the morning; that gave them four and a half hours since the abduction.

"That could be them. Send a SWAT team to the location. Check surveillance cameras in the area. Have locals canvass the area for witnesses. I want to know what they were driving, which direction they were headed, how many, when they were last seen, stat."

Jack jumped up and left the room. Noah followed and grabbed him by the shoulder. Jack turned and smacked Noah's hand away. "The only reason you're still walking is because Lucy likes you." Jack's eyes were bloodshot and he looked more dangerous with a day's stubble darkening his jaw.

"You want to be involved, you do this my way. Because the only reason you're not locked up right now is because I need you."

Jack nodded once. He handed Noah a piece of paper. "White Plains. Farm outside the city limits owned by Granite Holdings. Granite, obsidian, they're both rocks. There's an airstrip near the property, and you said earlier that the people who abducted Sean had a twin prop."

"I'm sold. Let's go." Jack turned to lead and Noah stepped in front of him. "This is still a federal operation, and I'm in charge. If you can't take my orders, you're staying."

Jack wanted to argue with him—Noah saw it in his eyes—but Noah didn't back down. Jack saw that, too.

"Yes, *sir.*"

CHAPTER THIRTY-ONE

Skye led Sean down the hall of the sprawling ranch house. She opened doors to a large, masculine library with dark furniture and ostentatious paintings. A computer sat at the desk.

"Don't think about it," Evan said from behind them.

Skye laughed. "Doesn't matter, there's no network connection. No calling for help on this computer, sweetheart. But you need to be debriefed, at least as much as you need to know."

"You killed Hunter."

Anger flashed in her eyes and she slapped Sean. "*You* killed him. *You* had him sneaking around for you. If he hadn't been snooping, he would still be alive."

Sean had suspected, but now Skye confirmed that she was a two-time killer. Even if she hadn't pulled the trigger on Hunter, she'd known about it. Ordered it.

Sean had no sympathy for Skye and what she'd gotten herself into. "Bitch."

She tried to slap him again, but he caught her wrist. Immediately pain in his kidneys from Evan's fist had Sean dropping Skye's hand.

"This is your fault, Sean," Skye said, her voice sounding hurt.

"All I did was help our friend Colton. *My* friend, since you killed him in cold blood." Sean's stomach churned and he didn't know if it was from the beatings or grief.

"None of this would have happened if you hadn't left Boston!"

Sean stared at her. "That was over nine years ago."

"Exactly! You just *left*. You think I didn't know why? You're a fool if you think that only you and Colton knew about the money you stole."

"I gave the money back to the people Robert Martin and your boyfriend took it from. They were retired, Skye. He stole money from old people."

"I don't care about what you did or didn't do, you left."

Even if he explained his reasons, Skye would never understand. Guilt and self-doubt and the need to reconnect with his brother. That Colton's grandiose plans of changing the world through hacktivism no longer appealed to Sean. When it was a game, Sean enjoyed it. But not when it was life or death. Not when he realized the stakes were so high and he was going to lose his soul if he didn't find something good to do with his life. He'd left MIT when he was twenty-one. He was thirty now, and only in the last year had he begun to see his potential. It wasn't his brains and ability to crack virtually any security system. It wasn't even to be what his brother wanted. It was to help people. To love Lucy. To realize that the smaller jobs were the most rewarding. Finding his cousin when she disappeared in New York was far more satisfying than hacking into companies to identify their weaknesses so his brother could create a more secure system.

Sean wanted both more . . . and less.

"You walked away," Skye said. "From Colton. From *me*."

It couldn't be that simple.

"You've never been a scorned woman, Skye. We had fun, I liked you a lot—"

"You loved me, or was that a lie?"

He had told her once he loved her. And at the time maybe he'd believed it. They'd had a great time, but it was superficial. There was no depth.

"I was twenty-one."

That sounded lame.

"That's your excuse? You were too *young*? Do you love that little bitch Fed that you're dating? Now that you're oh-so-mature?"

He couldn't let Skye bring Lucy into the conversation. He wasn't going to cheapen his relationship with Lucy by discussing her with his ex-girlfriend.

"Aren't you supposed to be telling me what to do so you don't kill my brother?" Sean said, keeping his face blank.

"Don't you even care how much you hurt all of us? Colton was lost without you. He was a far better brother to you than your mightier-than-thou guardian who tried to turn you into someone you're not. Colton was never the same after you walked. You got him off his crazy-ass ideas like taking down power grids and hacking into the Pentagon and dumb shit like that—but without you, he just went more off the deep end. More paranoid, obsessed with his brother's death. He was crazy. You didn't see it because you weren't there. I know, he seemed all perfect and fine at the carriage house, but have you been on the third floor? The rooms he won't let anyone into? I don't even think Carol knows the extent of his craziness."

Skye stepped toward Sean, her eyes large and bright. She really believed what she was saying. "I watched you; I saw the excitement in your eyes. The thrill of the job. The adrenaline pumping through your veins until you wanted to do what you do so well. I saw the way you looked at me, what you wanted to do to me. You were meant to live on the edge. You were meant to take what you want because you can. We can have it all. Together."

Sean laughed. "Obviously you and Kurt aren't so close that you can hit on me. And what about pretty boy over there?" He jerked his thumb toward Evan.

"Evan's not my boyfriend. That's just how I got him into Colton's group." She winked at Evan, who stood stone-faced five feet away. "Evan has his benefits. And Kurt—well, I can handle him. But you and me, Sean—"

"Have been over for nine years."

He couldn't deny that many of the jobs they'd worked together were exhilarating, but it wasn't the same as when they were younger. And not once since moving to New York did he want to touch Skye.

"We had it all," Skye lamented. "You were the smart one. You let Colton lead you around with all his pet projects, his causes, which you couldn't have cared less about, but you did it because you looked up to him. He gave you praise you lapped up like an abused puppy, unlike your brother who banished you across country after one little indiscretion."

"This has nothing to do with Duke."

"It has everything to do with Duke! You left us because you needed his approval. You ran back home and begged for his forgiveness. Guilt ate you up. Kurt's partner was weak, he killed himself, and you feel bad about that? Like you said, he took money from old people. You tried to toe the line, but how many times did Duke look at you with disapproval and you felt like shit inside? Like nothing you did would please him. You couldn't redeem yourself in his eyes, no matter what you did or said. But you kept trying. And trying. Yet, the one time a friend asks for help and you give it without checking with big brother, he fires you."

Skye was getting too close to Sean's core feelings, and she knew it. He had to stop her from framing this discussion.

"You don't know me. I came here for Colton, and you killed him."

"Good riddance. He was a thorn. His causes made us no money. He lives on his trust from selling the one good thing he created, and expects us to be grateful for his handouts?"

"Colton cares about—"

"Don't talk to me about caring! I cared about you, but you cared more about your brother who doesn't even like or respect you. And where is he now? I heard what he said. He doesn't believe you, baby. He knows inside you're just like me." She smiled.

"Kurt's going to kill both me and Duke. You know it. And yet you stand here and try to tell me you care?" There was something else going on in that calculating mind of Skye's.

She smirked. "I can stop him."

Sean shook his head. "You have an inflated sense of power."

"And you have none!" Skye pushed him. "Who do you think has been whispering in Kurt's ear for the last five years? Who gave him his purpose after you took everything from him?" She grinned, her face flushed, and she looked crazy. Sean didn't know Skye anymore. Or maybe he did, and that was even more terrifying. Because she would do whatever it took to get what she wanted. She always had.

"So why would I help you when he's just going to kill me?"

"Kill you? He's not going to kill you. He wants you to suffer. Death is too permanent. But I can fix it all because I control the money. Whose idea do you think it was to embezzle from his last employer? They were criminals, and I saw it a mile away. So right before the feds came down on them, I hid the money and Kurt turned whistle-blower. It was brilliant. I learned it from *you*. Deflection. So as soon as we get into the evidence locker, I'll have the control. And it's not like you have a choice. You're wanted by the FBI."

"You're wrong."

"Oh? Then maybe they haven't found the dead federal agent in your apartment yet. Killed when you have no abili—because you were with Colton and now Colton is dead. No one to back you up. And then there's that little thing about your gun . . . hmm, wonder where it is now, don't you?" She smirked. "I think it's off killing someone. And since no one knows where you are, it's very easy to set you up for it."

Sean's blood ran cold. "None of this is going to work."

"I don't even care if you're working for the FBI or against them or whatever idiotic plan you had in your head. You think your little girlfriend is going to take you back after this?" She laughed. "You are the best fall guy. You did everything I expected. Fell right in line."

No way could Sean reason with Skye. He was going to have to play along. And hope that Noah and Rick didn't believe whatever evidence had been fabricated.

And his gun. God, who had they killed with his gun?

"Do you think that breakfast this morning was just to feed you?"

His prints. His DNA. His presence in the house. They were setting him up in more ways than one.

Skye's face lit up. "Oh, I have a brilliant idea. Come with me, partner."

"I'm not your partner," he said.

"Well, maybe not, but when the police raid the house, they'll think you were involved from the beginning." She leaned over and kissed him. He grabbed her wrist and squeezed. Her eyes flashed, but she smiled. She put her hand up to stop Evan from hitting him again.

"When I'm done with you, everyone, even your precious Lucy, will believe that you had this whole thing planned. Remember that. Stay in line, Sean." She said to Evan, "Get the blueprints ready. Sean has a lot of homework."

Evidence? What was she having him steal? She and Kurt LeGrand had stolen from Kurt's employer—had they hidden the money in a place they couldn't get it? A bank? And now they needed Sean to retrieve it? A bank job would take a lot of time and planning to set up. He hadn't hacked into a bank in years.

Kurt LeGrand stepped into the room and glared at Sean. "We have to leave now."

"He hasn't even looked at the blueprints."

"Pack it up. We have the vehicles running. The feds are on their way. Someone fucked up. It's only a matter of time before they find this place. I'm not waiting for them."

"What about Duke?" Skye asked.

"We're torching the barn. That'll keep the feds busy."

Sean clenched his fists. "Don't—I'll do what you want. Don't hurt Duke."

"Who cares about your brother?"

"If he dies, I won't lift a finger to help you."

"Not even to save your girlfriend?"

LeGrand held up his cell phone. On the screen was a picture of Lucy, bound and gagged, unconscious. There was blood on her chest.

Sean literally saw red. He lunged for LeGrand and had his hands around his neck. "You touch her, I'll kill you. I'll—"

A sharp pain in his kidneys had him dropping to his knees. LeGrand kicked Sean in the chest and he fell over.

"Get him in the fucking truck," LeGrand said, rubbing his neck. "We leave now."

Sean's stomach twisted in knots. "You have no idea who you're fucking with," he said through the pain.

"All I know is, I'm smarter and better prepared. By the time the feds figure it out, I'll be so far out of their boundaries they won't know where to start looking."

CHAPTER THIRTY-TWO

Rick Stockton stayed at FBI headquarters while Noah and Jack joined the SWAT unit headed to White Plains. He generally liked his job as an assistant director because he had a lot of authority and autonomy, but times like this he wished he were still in the field.

Rick joined Suzanne Madeaux to interview Joyce Bonner. Bonner had brought her attorney. Rick didn't like it, but he would work around it.

"Ms. Bonner, I don't generally interview suspects or witnesses," he began. "I'm Assistant Director Rick Stockton from the national office. I hope you understand the severity of this situation and that you'll cooperate fully."

"Of course my client will cooperate," her attorney, Harold Grove, said.

"Good," Rick said. "I want to show you a tape." He nodded to Suzanne, who played the tape of Joyce Bonner being beaten by her husband, then her husband being beaten by her father and Senator Paxton. Suzanne paused it right after the senator shot Thomas Lynch.

"My client wasn't in the room when her husband was shot, and as you can see, she was under great duress. I'd like to authenticate the tape and we'll—"

"Senator Paxton has already made a statement verifying the tape. He hired a group of thieves to steal the tape and everything else from your private safe at the pharmaceutical company. What I want to know is what were you working on with the senator."

"My client—"

"Counselor," Rick said, "enough. I know that a biotoxin was taken from the lab. I have two missing civilians and a missing federal agent. I want my people back safe. I want to avert a potential act of domestic terrorism. I want the truth. I don't have time to play legal games."

He slid a piece of paper in front of Bonner and her attorney. "This gives limited immunity if you talk to me now. I'll give you five minutes to read it and confer with your client. If you don't sign it, we'll be placing Ms. Bonner under arrest. If you do sign it, she'll sleep in her own bed tonight."

"My client wants full immunity—"

"I'm not prepared to grant her full immunity." Rick stood up. "Five minutes."

He left. Suzanne followed. He said to her, "I need you to lead the team at the FBI evidence locker in Brooklyn. That's where the Avery and Block documents are stored. Figure out what they want and call me."

She stared at him as if he'd asked her to fly to the moon. "I—sir—I don't know where to start."

"My head analyst, Dorothy Conner, will meet you there. She's not an agent; she doesn't have a gun; you will protect her with your life."

"Of course."

"She spent hours with Lucy yesterday. I think she'll know what they want when she sees it."

Suzanne left, and Rick went back into the interview room. Bonner was arguing with her lawyer.

"Your five minutes is up." Rick sat back down and stared at them.

"Against my advice, my client is agreeing to the limited immunity."

With a shaking hand, Bonner signed the paper. Rick put it back in his file.

"What bio-toxin did they steal and what is the potential damage?"

Bonner said, "From what I could determine from my research partner, they took a supply of mycotoxin. It's not a bio-weapon; we use it for cancer research."

She avoided looking at him and Rick knew she was holding something back.

"It's not dangerous unless it's ingested or injected," she said. "It can't be used as a weapon of mass destruction."

"Unless it gets into the water supply."

"They don't have enough."

"What exactly do they have?"

"Half a liter. It's highly concentrated."

"Tell me why Senator Paxton wanted prisoner codes and locations."

Her eyes widened. "What? You know? Why these games if you already knew?"

It became clear to Rick. That must have been the information on the chip that Sean stole from Paxton. Bonner got cold feet and shut down the project. Paxton didn't trust her, so he hired Colton to retrieve the tape and any documentation about their plan.

Rick pieced it together. "Senator Paxton wanted you to develop the poison so he could mass-poison sex offenders. How?"

"Don't answer that," her attorney said.

Bonner's bottom lip quivered.

Rick slapped his palms on the metal table. *"How!"*

"Through vaccines. We have the contract to provide tuberculosis vaccines for the federal prison system. Jonathan had obtained a list of sex offenders, and we were working on a fail-safe vaccine that would kill them and make it look like food poisoning. But I told him they would trace it to us, and he said he'd protect the company, but I don't think he cared anymore."

"He doesn't," Rick said. "He has tunnel vision. So you threatened him with the tape."

"He was so good to me, Mr. Stockton. My husband—I would have been dead if it weren't for Jonathan. He's my godfather. When Monique disappeared, he became like my second father. But when he found out what happened to her, he changed. He's not bad; he's grieving. What's going to happen to him?"

"Ms. Bonner, focus on this toxin. How can they use it to hurt the greatest number of people?"

She frowned as she thought. "A small water supply, like a water tank. Injections. Up to two thousand people. But if they tried for a bigger target, they would dilute it to the point where people might get sick, but no one would die."

Rick was marginally relieved, though he suspected that LeGrand had a specific target in mind and knew exactly how much mycotoxin he needed.

"What are the symptoms?"

"Similar to mushroom poisoning, though we genetically altered the toxin to be more resistant to environmental factors for transport. Victims would succumb to stomach cramps, vomiting, muscle atrophy, organ failure, and death."

"Do you have an antidote?"

"Yes, there's a binding agent that can be administered, if the victims are diagnosed in time."

"I'm going to send two agents with you to your lab. I want you to give them all the antidote you have and instructions on how to use it. I want your head researcher at my disposal. You are not to leave the country. You are not to leave New York City, except to go to your lab. Do you understand?"

"Yes."

"My agents will collect what they need, then take you home."

Noah had to admit, Jack Kincaid was intensely focused and disciplined. The problems arose because Jack was used to giving, not taking, orders. Three times Noah had to assert his authority with SWAT because Jack responded first.

"Jack, I'm SWAT-trained and was a Raven in the Air Force. Maybe not as cutthroat as Delta, but I do know what I'm doing. I'm also the lead agent, and I said you could come if you accepted that I give the orders."

Jack looked at Noah as if he wanted to say he would do whatever he damn well pleased, but he gave Noah a nod. "Understood."

Noah cut Jack some slack because of the situation. They were on a SWAT chopper heading north of White Plains where a horse ranch abutted against a small airport. Another SWAT unit was on the ground, but the chopper was making better time. Noah deferred to the SWAT leader, Dave Blake, to plan the drill, though he made sure both he and Jack were placed in key positions.

"The bio-toxin they have is liquid—it must be ingested or injected, but we recommend not coming into contact with it. It is not airborne," Noah said, "but we don't know what they may have done to alter it, so use extreme caution."

Noah passed out pictures of the hostages. "They've already killed two of their own, a civilian and a federal agent; consider them armed and extremely dangerous."

The team had line of sight of the house. The copilot said to the SWAT leader, "Captain, we have a fire at the target."

They'd planned to land a half mile from the house and go in on foot, but then Blake changed the plan and said, "Land in that corral one hundred yards from the fire."

"Visual?"

"No one in sight," the copilot said. "The fire is messing with our heat sensors."

"Vehicles?"

"One truck north of the house, stationary."

The SWAT team was made up of six men, plus the pilot, copilot, Noah, and Jack. The pilot stayed with the plane. Noah went with Delta, and Jack went with Alpha.

Blake said, "Alpha, with me to secure the house; Delta, with Agent Armstrong, verify there are no hostages in the barn. We go live in five. Four. Three. Two." The helicopter landed. "Go go go!"

The eight men fanned out from the chopper. Noah led Delta to the barn. When they were in the sky, the fire appeared small; now it raged, the heat pushing them back.

Noah got as close as he could and heard a shout from inside.

"There's someone inside!" he called out to the team. "Cover me!"

The fire could easily be a trap, and two men scanned the area to cover Noah in case he drew fire. His partner, Lance, helped Noah push open the double doors. The fire nipped at them as smoke billowed from the structure.

A man was coughing. Noah could see little through the smoke, but one man was down on the ground. The haystack behind him was smoking. Noah grabbed the man under the arms to drag him out. He was handcuffed to steel rings on the floor.

Noah motioned to Lance to take one cuff and Noah focused on the other. The burning hay filled the barn with thick smoke. He could barely see the hole in the handcuffs. He removed a lock pick and managed to pop the lock quicker than he'd thought. Good thing because the dry structure was beginning to fall around them.

"Got it," Lance said a half-minute later.

Noah and Lance half-carried, half-dragged the coughing victim from the barn as the roof collapsed.

They stumbled over to the fence, out of the direction of the smoke. Noah said in his com, "We need an ambulance!"

Noah had never met Duke Rogan, but the man who lay on the ground in front of him was an older version of Sean. "Duke Rogan?" Noah said.

"Yes." His voice was hoarse from smoke inhalation.

"Don't talk."

Jack Kincaid ran over. "Duke, it's Jack."

"Jack." Duke coughed, smoke coming from his lungs. Noah sent two men back to the helicopter for the emergency medical kit, which included a small oxygen tank.

"Where's Lucy?" Jack demanded.

"Back off," Noah said.

Jack didn't budge.

"Lucy?" Duke shook his head. "I didn't see her."

"Sean?"

"He left. Early. Couple hours later the barn began to burn. I didn't see anyone." He paused to catch his breath. "A truck came; then two trucks left. I didn't see them."

"Give him a minute," Noah said.

"We don't have time!" Jack exploded. He took several steps away and stared at the house.

The medical kit arrived, and Noah let the team medic minister to Duke. He walked over to Jack. "Kincaid, we will find them. Give Duke a minute. He nearly got roasted alive."

Jack turned to Noah. Though his face was hard, his eyes were full of emotion. Lucy had the same dark eyes. Jack didn't say anything, but he didn't have to. Noah felt the same pain and determination.

Duke batted away the oxygen mask a minute later. Noah turned to him and said, "I'm Agent Noah Armstrong. Tell me what you know."

"Do you know about the dead FBI agent in Sean's apartment?"

"Yes. We know you were abducted from there. Kurt LeGrand is behind this—do you know who he is?"

Duke shook his head and took the water that was offered.

"LeGrand's men kidnapped Lucy from Sean's house in D.C. We tracked them here."

"Lucy? What has Sean got her into?"

"Sean?"

"Sean was helping them because they had me. Now they have her? I overheard—they're breaking into the FBI evidence archive in Brooklyn. RCK installed a new security system last year; Sean can hack it, given enough time."

"We have a team at the evidence locker trying to figure out what they want. Do you have an idea?"

"Ten million dollars, at least."

"We don't keep cash in the facility."

"Codes, bank numbers, maybe hidden in something innocuous." Duke took a few big breaths. "Find my brother. He's reckless, and I worry."

"Reckless?" Noah said. "Actually, that's the one word I probably wouldn't use to describe him."

Jack said, "You didn't see Lucy?"

"I didn't even know they went after her." Duke asked, "Is it true Sean was undercover for the FBI?"

"Yes. He got us everything we wanted," Noah said. "More than I expected. We didn't know that Skye Jansen was working with LeGrand to kidnap Sean and force him to break into the evidence locker. She set him up."

"My brother—he has a bad habit of doing the wrong thing. Jack—I'm sorry Sean got Lucy into this mess."

Noah stared at Duke. He was about to say something when Jack knelt next to Duke and said, "I'll forget you said that. Sean's the best thing that's ever happened to my sister, and I'm going to find them."

CHAPTER THIRTY-THREE

Sean couldn't think about his brother. He willed himself to believe Duke was alive, because if he lost him, especially with how they left things, Sean didn't know how he could forgive himself.

Duke was resourceful. He was smart. He'd have been working on getting out of the handcuffs.

Sean had to focus on Lucy.

They were tied in the back of a pickup truck. They'd bounced over country roads for fifteen minutes before they turned onto a smooth highway. Little light came through. The hard plastic cover that topped the truck bed made it impossible to sit up.

At first Sean thought Lucy was dead. She wasn't moving and was tied to the side of the truck with nylon rope. Duct tape covered her mouth. She was barefoot and wore only sweats and a tank top. Sean's hands were tied behind him, but as soon as they locked him in he rolled over to her.

"Lucy." He put his ear to her chest. She was breathing. *Thank God.* Why was he thanking God? Lucy was the churchgoer, not him. What God would let this happen to her? "Hasn't she been through enough?" he whispered.

He needed her to wake up. Whoever tied his hands did a far worse job than they'd done with Lucy. Sean was out of the rope in only a couple minutes. He removed the duct tape from her mouth and Lucy startled awake. She fought her restraints and cried out.

"Shh, Lucy, it's Sean. I'm going to untie you."

"Sean?" Her voice was scarcely a whisper; he felt his name against his cheek more than heard it. She gasped. "My head."

"I think they tranquilized you."

It took Sean several minutes to untie Lucy; then he held her shaking body in his arms. "You're so cold."

"They broke into your house." She burrowed into him, her teeth chattering. Her feet and hands were like ice.

Sean would kill Kurt LeGrand.

He told her everything he knew while he held her as close to him as possible.

When he was done, Lucy said, "Sean, I'm so sorry about Colton. And Duke—but there's a chance he made it, right?"

Sean didn't believe it. "As long as I don't lose you. Lucy, I can't lose you. I'm so sorry."

"This isn't your fault. Don't even think it. Skye set you up. Kurt LeGrand wants revenge because of Martin Holdings."

"Did I tell you that?" He didn't think so.

"I figured it out last night. Rick and Noah know. They're on top of it. And last I heard, Jack was flying into New York because Duke's missing."

"I didn't even think of the security problem Duke's disappearance would cause."

"Let's figure out what we're going to do. We have time—they can't break into the evidence warehouse until tonight." She hesitated, then said, "Is this something you can do?"

"Yes," he said without hesitation. "It won't be easy.

And they're not going to tell me what they want until game time. It's money, but I can't imagine the FBI would leave millions of dollars lying around. And I wouldn't be able to transport it alone."

"It's not money," Lucy said. "LeGrand and Skye worked for a mortgage brokerage that padded mortgages with additional fees and insurance. They found out about it, siphoned off the illegal money, then LeGrand turned state's evidence and became a whistle-blower. The FBI believes between six and ten million is missing, but they don't know where it is or how it disappeared."

"I get it, it's a code or password—"

"Or account numbers. Something that they could have hidden in plain sight that no one would recognize."

"Why didn't they take it with them before the FBI came in?"

"Maybe they didn't realize that everything is boxed up for processing."

"Or they couldn't get to it," Sean mused out loud.

"How many are there?"

"I saw four at PBM, plus LeGrand. One other guy, I think."

"Four were in D.C., but I think they were hired just to get me. One is dead."

"I'm so sorry," Sean repeated. He kissed her forehead. "I know it's not all my fault, but you should have been safe at my house. I knew something was wrong. I didn't trust Evan, but I had no idea Skye was spearheading this. I should never have gone to PBM."

"Why did they move it up a day?"

"After Hunter was killed, Colton panicked. He wanted it over. Then Skye shot him in cold blood. Like they hadn't been friends for twelve years."

Lucy had her hands on Sean's cheeks. He couldn't see her, but he could feel her, taste her; she was here, and she was alive.

"I'm going to get you out of this," he said, his voice cracking.

"*We're* going to get out of this."

"One more thing—they stole some sort of bio-toxin from the lab. I got a glimpse; it's a liquid. Maybe a liter."

"Why?"

"I have no idea."

The truck slowed down and the quality of the light and road changed. "We're in a tunnel," Lucy said.

"Going into Manhattan. One of the guys mentioned a warehouse. They can probably drive right in."

"Brooklyn. They'll want to be close to the evidence warehouse." Lucy kissed him. "Sean, they're going to kill you when you're through. You can't give them what they want."

"I'm more concerned about you. He wants to make me suffer. God, Lucy, if anything—"

"Shh. I know. But I'm alive. We're going to figure this out. And don't forget, Noah and Jack and Rick arc all looking for us. They know about the evidence warehouse."

"But you're their leverage. I don't think LeGrand thought Duke was strong enough leverage for me to do this—but you are. If Noah stops me, they'll kill you. I have to get it for them."

"We'll figure this out."

"I love you, Lucy. I'm not going to let you die."

He felt her staring at him, though he could only make out shadows. He held her close, needing to be in direct contact with her.

"We're not going to die," she said. "Neither of us. We'll find a way out."

"First chance you get, run."

"I'm not leaving you behind."

"Lucy, I can get out of anything if I know you're safe."

"You're not immortal."

"Luce—"

"We're in this together."

"It's my fault we're in this at all."

"Stop it," she said, her hands squeezing his arms. "I don't care how we got here, this isn't your fault. No one could have known that they'd go after me. No one even knew who Kurt LeGrand was until you found the security picture in Hunter's phone."

"I'm just—" His fists clenched and unclenched.

"I understand." She kissed him warmly.

The truck slowed down and spent several minutes in stop-and-go traffic before it stopped and idled for a minute. A metal door rolled up, the truck drove in, then the ignition cut off, and the door was closed.

No one came to let them out for several minutes. Voices echoed in the building, but Sean couldn't understand what they were saying. There was outside traffic, but it was distant, like they were off a quiet street.

"I have an idea," Sean whispered. "I need to get to a phone so I can send a message to Noah. If he has the number, he can trace the GPS signal."

"Skye is smart enough to keep you away from any electronics."

"I'll find a way. I don't even need a phone. A computer, an iPod, anything that has wireless functionality."

"I'll help."

"Lucy—just do what they say. Once I get the evidence, they have no reason to keep either of us alive."

"I know.

The back of the truck opened and the cover folded up. Sean blinked against the sudden brightness. Two large men stood there, each with a gun. "Get out," one said, motioning at Sean with his weapon. "One at a time, Rogan first."

Sean slid out. He looked back at Lucy and saw the

large bruise on her cheek and blood on her shirt and the side of her head. Most of her hair had fallen out of her braid, and she looked both scared and defiant.

He looked at the two goons. "Who hit her?" He noticed that one of the men had a bandage around his arm. "I'll kill you."

The man scowled and said, "Turn around."

Sean complied, only because two guns were pointed at him and these weren't the only two men in the warehouse. In the corner LeGrand and Skye spoke quietly, and the rest of the goon squad were standing near the front of the truck. Four hired guns, plus Evan, Skye, and LeGrand. Seven against two. Sean definitely didn't like the odds.

Sean was handcuffed, not tied with rope this time, then prodded over to where Skye and LeGrand were looking at blueprints.

The warehouse they were in was narrow, with an office up a rickety flight of stairs. Sean glanced over his shoulder as Lucy crawled out of the truck. Her legs gave out as she tried to stand and the goon caught her arm and jerked her up. He then walked her up the stairs to the office.

"Where are you taking her?" Sean demanded.

LeGrand said, "Safekeeping."

Sean stared at the bastard who orchestrated this scheme. "If you hurt her, I'll kill you."

"Your threats are tiresome. Her survival depends solely on you." He motioned to the blueprints. "This is the warehouse you're breaking into." He picked up a binder. "These are the computer and security systems. You find a way in, find the file I need, and a way out without being caught, and Lucy lives."

Sean stared at the documents without seeing anything. He had to get his temper in check; he had to be smart about this. He breathed deeply. "I said I'd do it."

* * *

Rick Stockton listened to Noah's report on what they'd found at the farmhouse outside of White Plains. They'd found Duke Rogan alive. They were leaving one small SWAT team at the house to protect the evidence response unit, and Noah and Jack were heading back on the chopper.

"Was there anything in the house that gives us an idea of where they took Sean and Lucy?"

"Negative," Noah said. "If they had documents, they took them with them. No computers, either. However, I have a team out canvassing the area. We know they were driving two trucks or one truck and a van. We're also looking for security footage near the on-ramps because we know they're heading back to the city."

"Get back quickly so we can plan what to do if we don't find them before the break-in."

"Yes, sir." Noah hung up.

Stockton's phone beeped. It was Dorothy Conner, his analyst. "Agent Madeaux and I are at the evidence warehouse and we think we found what they want."

"Bring it in."

"Mr. Stockton?" Agent Madeaux said. "Um, excuse me, but if it's not here when Sean breaks in, wouldn't that put him in danger?"

"If we can't find him, we'll think of something. But I can't let ten million dollars fall into the hands of a killer with a deadly toxin."

"Yes, sir. On our way."

"Come up with a plan and convince me it'll work." He hung up and rubbed his head.

Ultimately, he was responsible for this operation. He'd authorized Noah Armstrong to investigate Senator Paxton. He'd authorized a civilian to go undercover. The weight of the operation had taken its toll.

He'd served in the Marines for nine years. ROTC in college and five years out of college—the standard four-

year commitment, plus he signed on for an additional
year because he believed in his mission. He'd faced death;
he'd lost friends; he'd killed the enemy. It was more than
a job, it had been his life for a long time.

His people in the FBI were his fellow soldiers. He was
their leader, and when any of them were in trouble he
took it as an attack on his unit. They knew the risks, but
that didn't make losses any easier.

He watched the security tape from Sean's house for the
third time. Sean definitely had a state-of-the-art system.
If Lucy had been expecting trouble, she could have turned
on external sensors that would have warned her if anyone
crossed the property line. But no one expected that she
wouldn't be safe in D.C.

Rick watched as Lucy first tried to leave through the
back, saw men at the door, and ran upstairs. She looked in
two specific places for a weapon—the guns Sean probably took with him to New York—and in the third place
found the 9mm. For a brief moment she aimed it at the
bedroom door, panic etched in every line of her face. But
she beat it back and locked herself in the bathroom, buying time; it had been her only option.

Rick went back over the tape again, looking for any
sign to identify the attackers, but they'd kept their masks
on the entire time.

He went back to the tapes from the FBI building.
They'd tracked the van used to kidnap Lucy because it
had been caught on FBI surveillance. The attackers must
have followed Dorothy and Lucy to Sean's house. The
van was the same van recovered in Baltimore. Smart to
have a second car waiting.

Then he saw it.

Replaying the film from outside the Hoover Building,
he noticed a man getting in on the opposite side of the
van from the camera. Rick couldn't make him out from
this angle, but there was a security camera on the other

side of the street. He called headquarters and asked security to pull the recording and get an ID on the kidnapper.

It was a long shot, but if they could identify the players they might be able to track them through purchases or known associates.

The agent Rick had been assigned while here in New York, veteran agent Maurice Fong, came into the office. "Sir, Ms. Bonner's attorney just delivered the antidote to the mycotoxin. Homeland Security is holding for you on the second line. Agent Madeaux and Ms. Conner are waiting in the conference room when you're done."

"Thank you. Meet me in there."

Rick dealt with the Homeland Security agent and assured him that there was no known terrorist group planning to use the toxin. He had already sent the specs that Bonner had provided, and Homeland Security was all over the PBM lab right now. But Rick took the heat, because he was in charge.

The more Rick thought about it, the more he wondered if the toxin was a smoke screen, something to divert their attention. There were very well-established protocols when dealing with a potential domestic terrorist. Either that or LeGrand had a specific target.

Once Rick got Homeland Security settled, he went to the conference room.

"Show me what you found."

Dorothy said, "I won't go into all the reasoning, but there were more than thirty boxes of evidence. We realized pretty quick that whatever they wanted was account numbers, and that they couldn't be obvious. We found this."

She slid over a small, pink address book.

"An address book."

"It's coded," Dorothy said. "Not obvious at first, but each entry has an address that doesn't exist and the combination of the street address and zip code is what we believe makes up an account number. We haven't quite figured out where the accounts are, because so far none of the combinations match up with known offshore or domestic accounts. I want to take it to our banking experts."

"Absolutely."

"Sir," Suzanne said, "I think we have a plan that'll work if we can't find them before the break-in."

"Let's hear it."

"We make a forgery of this data and transpose the numbers, then put it back. I talked to a friend of mine at the lab and he can get it done."

Rick said, "What about the book itself? It's going to be hard to find one just like it on short notice."

Suzanne reached into her pocket and pulled out an identical book.

"You're a magician," he said.

"No, I just shop at the same cosmetic counter as Skye Jansen. This was a free gift three years ago if you spent fifty dollars on their Spring Collection."

Rick almost smirked. "Fifty dollars?"

"Make-up is expensive," she mumbled. "If we can get this done and put it back before tonight, then we can stake out the building and follow Sean back to LeGrand."

"What if Sean's caught?" Rick asked.

"He won't be," Suzanne said.

"You've drunk the Kool-Aid, that Rogan doesn't fail."

"No, just that he won't fail at this. Not when Lucy's life is at stake, and you know that's why they took her. And we can help ensure his success."

Rick conceded the point. "If he gets in and retrieves the book, then we follow him." Rick let the scenario settle. It could work. It had to work.

"Exactly. We have surprise to our advantage. They have no idea we know what they're looking for, or that they're even going to break into the evidence locker."

"Work out the details with Agent Armstrong when he returns. Dorothy, you take custody of the book and be responsible for the forgery. Have it back here in three hours."

CHAPTER THIRTY-FOUR

Sean already had a plan to get in and out of the warehouse undetected. Because he didn't care if RCK knew he'd broken in, the security panels were easy. The hard part would be avoiding the cameras and the guards. If they let him have a computer, he could do it, but they rightfully didn't trust him. Skye was going to be his partner, controlling the cameras, which would be funny if it weren't so damn serious.

He already knew how to shortcut the project, get in and get out almost immediately. He simply took up all the time Skye and LeGrand had given him to come up with a plan, hoping that Noah could track them down.

No one came.

Sean hated bullies. He hated anyone who put themselves in the position of God with the belief that they alone had control over everyone else. Being forced to work with Kurt LeGrand to break into the FBI evidence warehouse was infuriating; that LeGrand would threaten those Sean loved the most cut him to the bone.

Colton was dead. Duke was most likely dead. Lucy said to have hope, but Duke had been shackled inside that barn when they set it on fire. If he couldn't get out, he'd most certainly be dead from smoke inhalation, even if the fire department got there fast.

Sean couldn't lose Lucy, too. He struggled with his anger and grief, trying to separate them so he could do the job and give Lucy a chance to survive.

He had no idea what LeGrand planned to do with the bio-toxin. To poison water? What was it? How dangerous? Why? LeGrand was a financial con artist and a killer, but a terrorist? Sean didn't get that feeling. LeGrand killed to advance to his next goal, not to make a political or social statement.

"I'm ready," Sean finally said, thirty minutes after he created his plan.

Skye sauntered over and rubbed his shoulders.

"Don't touch me," he said through clenched teeth.

She rolled her eyes and squeezed his biceps. "You're in amazing shape, Sean. Even better than you were in college."

He shrugged her off. "When are we doing this?"

"The staff leaves at five thirty; the guards change at six. We'll wait until they get settled in." She kissed his neck. "Of course, they have the best security system taxpayer money can buy."

Sean knew exactly what kind of equipment they had. Full, random camera coverage so intruders couldn't time a theft. Laser alarms on doorways to critical areas. Electronic shut-outs if an intruder was spotted—both manual from the guard station and automatic if the system detected an anomaly.

The biggest problem was hacking into the internal database to find out where the files were stored. They were on a dedicated computer system accessible only onsite—a standard setup for any RCK security protocol. While Skye had obtained the names of the files, they didn't have any knowledge of how the filing system was organized or, when they found the location, how to access it. There were two armed guards—one at the entrance and one at the inside desk. Skye didn't know how they rotated, if they walked or were stationary.

Once inside, Sean could use one of the access panels to trick the system into thinking it was still up when, in fact, it was down. But the catch was getting inside.

The FBI evidence locker wasn't going to be easy, but Sean found a structural weakness in the building. Recently they'd placed a construction trailer only ten feet from the rear of the warehouse. The trailer blocked the cameras, giving Sean the time to crack the coded emergency exit. Once in, he should be able to do the rest without detection using both a jammer and his skills. LeGrand had top-notch equipment for this job.

"Relax, baby," Skye said. "We have a couple hours."

Sean faced Skye. "I want to see Lucy."

Skye stepped closer. "That's just not going to happen."

"Then I'm not leaving."

"You don't have a choice."

"Why do you care?"

LeGrand approached. "Yes, Skye, why do you care?"

"He needs to be focused."

LeGrand assessed Sean. "You have a plan."

"Yes."

"And it will work?"

"Probably."

"Probably isn't good enough."

"Let me rephrase: There's no other way to breach this building unless you go in guns blazing and know exactly where your data is. I'm not going to set off any alarms, the guard won't see me, but if there's an unknown variable— like a third guard, or a staff member working late, or you gave me the wrong security system to memorize, then I may fail."

"I appreciate your honesty." He motioned to the goon

named Eric. "Tie him up with his girlfriend. We have a few hours."

As Sean was being led upstairs, he overheard LeGrand tell Skye, "The buyer is waiting at his ship. As soon as we get the book, we'll leave. But we need to be at the dock by midnight."

Buyer. Buyer—why use that word? LeGrand wouldn't be selling the account information when it was worth millions.

The toxin. He couldn't access his money here in the states; he needed the bio-toxin to buy passage on a private ship. That was the only explanation that made sense.

If Kurt LeGrand knew Lucy had overheard as much detail to his plan as she had, he would have killed her as soon as Skye left with Sean. Fortunately, his men were talkative even if LeGrand wasn't.

"You seem like a nice girl," LeGrand said, standing in front of her as he checked her restraints. "Sean Rogan is not worth your tears."

She didn't say anything.

LeGrand sighed, walked over to the desk, and finished packing up his computer. "Do you know what he did?" LeGrand said.

She didn't respond.

"You want to be a cop, and you're okay with dating a criminal." He smiled. "You're not my type, but I could like you. Situational ethics and all that."

Don't let him bait you.

"I would never have known it was Sean Rogan who stole my money ten years ago if it wasn't for Skye." He laughed. "A woman scorned if I ever saw one. She pretends to care about me, but I'm not a fool. I'm actually putting a lot of faith in Sean right now. I suspect, when he gets the account codes, that Skye will make him an offer to disappear with all my money. I was planning to go with him because I don't trust her. Except I realized after seeing you and your boyfriend together that he really does love you. And I think he wants to kill Skye. That would actually help me out.

"Still, Evan will keep her in line. He's been my rock, truly. Without his intel I'd never have known that Skye kept pictures of her and Sean under her bed. He's the only one I trust to make sure I get my money. And if he has to kill them both—" LeGrand shrugged his shoulders and grinned.

An involuntary moan escaped Lucy's chest. She bit it back and glared at LeGrand.

"I'm sorry. But Sean Rogan stole the last decade of my life. Do you know how hard it was for me to divert all that money from that old prick Robert Martin? He wasn't stupid. But neither was I. And then Rogan comes in and gives it *back*? Is he insane? Then sends Martin a letter that he has proof, but doesn't go to the police? For the longest time, I thought Rogan just took the money for himself. But when no one filed a lawsuit I realized he did exactly what he'd said.

"It took me years to rebuild from that loss. I didn't know it was Rogan at the time—not until I met Skye. She sought me out. She came up with the plan. I knew my bosses were crooks, so it wasn't too hard to create a third set of books, then turn whistle-blower."

"Why didn't you take the money and disappear then?"

He sighed dramatically. "Skye created the accounts and left the coded address book in her desk. The FBI raided the day before we'd been told, and we lost the book. Two fucking years."

"Why Sean?"

"Because I've been following his career for a long time and I knew he was one of the few people who could break into a secure building like the FBI warehouse. Once I learned where the book was and what the FBI planned to do with the evidence, I intended to blackmail him. Skye had proof he stole the money from Martin Holdings, and I was going to create a money trail so it looked like he kept it. But when Colton convinced him to work on this ridiculous prove-my-dying-brother-was-murdered gig, I came up with a better plan. As I began to understand Sean, I didn't think he would be easy to blackmail. Until I realized he'd fallen in love. Love makes men stupid."

Lucy watched LeGrand closely. The way he talked, the way he specifically talked about Sean. He hated Sean. He had an admiration for his skill, but he hated that Sean was a better thief than him, and he held Sean personally responsible for his own failures.

"I don't take pleasure in having you killed, Ms. Kincaid. Tommy is quite upset that you shot him."

"I wish the bullet had hit his heart," Lucy said. "Oh, he doesn't have one."

"I'm glad you've kept your spirits up." LeGrand's phone rang and he answered, "Hello, darling." He winked at Lucy. "Very good. I'll see you at the slip."

He hung up, picked up his briefcase, and walked to the door. "Your boyfriend made it inside. As soon as we have the book, you'll be dead. I told them you should suffer a bit. Sorry about that. But I want to gut Sean, and this is the best way." He winked. "Good-bye, Lucy."

CHAPTER THIRTY-FIVE

Breaking into the FBI evidence warehouse worked as well as Sean had planned. He supposed he wasn't surprised, considering he did this for a living. But that didn't make the pressure any less intense. Sean was sweating by the time he made it to the main computer room. This was a place most people who worked in the building didn't even know about, but it was the hub of the property, and, ironically, like the private offices, there were no internal cameras. The door was coded, but it was easy to crack with the RCK admin code.

Skye had wired Sean, which was another distraction for him; otherwise Sean could have found a phone and called Noah. Except there was no doubt in Sean's mind that LeGrand would kill Lucy if Sean didn't return with the book.

First, Sean had to find where the evidence files from Avery & Block were stored. The facility was huge—over one hundred thousand square feet. He logged into the main database and it took him a good five minutes to figure out how the FBI catalogued their evidence. Once he understood the structure he searched for the files. He found the aisle number and shelves, then turned to the security console and opened up the programmer's back door. This enabled RCK to monitor the system when they first installed it, but it was never used except for on-site upgrades. Now Sean reprogrammed the system to avoid rotating the cameras in the sector Sean needed to access. The guard shouldn't see any difference in the feeds because it was still randomized, just not in the section of the building Sean would be.

His head pounded by the time he was done. He held his breath as he executed the command, waiting for alarms of a system meltdown, a warning, an intruder alert, anything to show that he'd failed.

Silence.

Either it worked or it didn't, but no one had been alerted to his system changes.

He'd memorized the route he needed to take, but he checked his watch to verify that he was on schedule. He'd told Skye it would take him an hour; she gave him thirty minutes once he entered the facility. He'd used twelve of them reprogramming.

There was no Internet access in the computer room, but because it was an RCK system he could send a message through the hardwired system to the RCK administrator. He had to alert Noah about the sale of the toxin and to tell him where Lucy was being held captive. Though he didn't have an exact address, he had a street and description. Skye hadn't blindfolded him when they left.

Jaye—it's Sean. Please get this message to Noah Armstrong immediately. A bastard named Kurt LeGrand is holding Lucy hostage and forcing me to steal a file inside the FBI evidence warehouse in Brooklyn. He also has a bio-toxin he stole from PBM that he plans to sell to someone to buy pas-

sage on a ship that's leaving at midnight—don't know which port. LeGrand is NOT planning on using the bio-toxin. Lucy is being held in a small two-story warehouse on Kent south of Flushing. It's near a church. I don't have the address, but there's a partial No Parking sign on the roll-up door that has the P missing. She's being guarded by at least three men, maybe more.

Duke's dead. They locked him in an old barn and burned it. Don't tell Nora yet—I'll tell her. If I make it.

There's no way to reach me. Save Lucy.

He hoped Jaye got the message and sent it to Noah. He hoped they went to save Lucy instead of coming here. A lot of wishing.

Sean left the computer room and listened for trouble. He walked as quickly as he dared, relying on the blueprints he'd copied, his analysis of the storage system, and the reprogramming of the cameras. He wasn't trying to hide his tracks—but that hadn't been their request. As soon as someone ran a diagnostic on the system, they'd see the breach. But that wouldn't happen tonight.

The filing system organized evidence by the date the original investigation was opened. There were some adjustments based on the size of the files or if special storage was needed, but this warehouse housed evidence for all federal cases except capital cases or weapons storage.

Luck would have it that Sean found the section immediately. The problem was that while he knew what he was looking for, there were thirty-six boxes of information and data. The labels were not very descriptive. He pulled out the log of information that Skye had given him. He

needed an address book. The address book was coded
with the bank accounts and passwords to access the money
they stole. It should be in the files seized from Block's
personal assistant.

The evidence log was in the first box. He scoured it for
information. That's why he didn't hear the footsteps.

"Sean."

He jumped, reached for a gun that wasn't there, and
whirled around. *Noah?* He put a finger to his lips.

In Sean's ear, Skye said, "What was that?"

"I was swearing to myself," he whispered, staring at
Noah. "I need more time."

Noah nodded, understanding the danger, and didn't
say anything.

Skye said, "You don't have more time. Where are you?"

"With the files. There are thirty-six boxes here and the
log is a mess."

"Keep me posted. You're running out of time."

Noah handed him a pen. Sean turned the evidence log
over and wrote:

> *Skye Jansen is listening. Open mic. They have
> Lucy. Duke is dead.*

Noah read it and wrote:

> *We found Duke. He's okay. Colton is in serious
> but stable condition after surgery.*

Relief flooded through Sean. Both Duke and Colton
were alive. But they were running out of time for Lucy.
Frantically, he wrote:

> *I need an address book that Skye wrote by hand.
> She'll know if it's fake. And if I don't bring it in*

He glanced at his watch.

9 minutes, LeGrand will kill Lucy.
Don't assume anything. I think he'll do it any-
way, but if I give him the address book, it'll buy us
time. I know where Lucy is being held, a building
on Kent south of Flushing.

Noah handed Sean the address book.
Sean mouthed, *Is this real?*
Noah shook his head, then wrote:

It's a perfect forgery, with the numbers changed.
We have our best decoder going through the origi-
nal now.

In his ear, Sean heard Skye's voice. "You have five
minutes to be in my car, and it's a four-minute walk."

Sean said, "I think I found it. Is it a small pink address
book with gold embossing and on the first page it says *My
little pink book.*"

"That's it!" Her voice went up an octave in excitement.
"Get out. Now."

"Tell LeGrand to stand down."

"Just meet me. I have a plan. I'm so excited!"

Sean wrote:

Get to Lucy.

He wrote out a rough map of where she was being kept.

Noah stared at Sean for a long moment and nodded.
"Be careful," he whispered. Then he wrote:

Jack Kincaid already has eyes on Skye's car.
He'll have your back. I'll save Lucy.

Noah handed Sean a small phone. Sean pocketed it, turned, and left the way he came. Noah didn't follow.

Noah had a SWAT team on standby near the FBI evidence locker. The warehouse where Lucy was being held captive was less than a five-minute drive at this time of night. He received a message from Jaye Morgan at RCK with the exact location of the warehouse, including blueprints. He had no idea where she'd gotten it, and he didn't ask. By the time they reached Kent Avenue, only twelve minutes had passed since Noah last saw Sean.

The warehouse was dark, though there was a light upstairs where Morgan indicated there was an office. Likely the office where Lucy was being kept. There was roof access, and Noah sent three of the team to the roof, while he and the other three team members would split and simultaneously go in through the front and back.

Noah gave the go order and the three groups swooped into the facility.

Noah shouted, "FBI! Freeze! Hands where we can see them!"

A quick sweep of the main floor flushed out three suspects sitting on old couches in the corner.

Guns were within reach, but they froze when they saw the men in black with guns aimed at them. Anyone who moved would be leaving in a body bag.

"Smart boys," Noah said as he kept his sight on them until the team from the rear met up with them.

"Back is clear."

"Cuff them," Noah said. He heard the team moving upstairs.

"Hostage is recovered. Upstairs is clear."

Noah ran upstairs, and when he saw Lucy his heart constricted. Lucy was chained to a support beam. She was shivering, wearing only sweats and a tank top that was stained with blood, grease, and dirt. Her feet were bare, her face was bruised, and her lips swollen. He wanted to take her home and put her in a hot bath and take care of her—

He stopped himself. He'd been denying for the past year that he had feelings for Lucy. He couldn't lie to himself anymore. Sean was right. Noah had always thought he would be a better man for Lucy than Sean. He admired and respected her, and he knew he could easily love her. But she loved Sean, and Noah refused to be the runner-up.

And Jack's words to Duke this morning stuck with Noah.

Sean's the best thing that's ever happened to my sister.

Noah wasn't going to stand in the way. And after the last few weeks, he'd accepted that Sean was a better man than he'd ever given him credit for.

SWAT released Lucy and one of the men helped her to her feet. "We've called an ambulance. Do you need help downstairs?"

She shook her head, but accepted the blanket he put over her shoulders. To Noah, she said, "Sean said you'd find us."

"I ran into him at the FBI warehouse." He tried to make his voice light, but failed. "He told me where to find you."

Her lips trembled. "And where is he?"

"He left with Skye. He didn't have a choice; he thought LeGrand would kill you if he didn't return with the codes."

"LeGrand doesn't care about me—but he hates Sean. I know where they went. We don't have a lot of time."

Noah wanted to order Lucy to stay and wait for medical personnel. He looked at her feet, then called Suzanne. "Suzanne, I have Lucy. She needs shoes and a jacket. We're headed to—" He glanced at her.

"Marine Basin Marina. The yacht is called *Rosebud*

and they're meeting a ship out at sea to sell the toxin in exchange for transport out of the country."

Noah asked Suzanne, "Did you hear that?"

"Yes. I'll meet you at the marina. With backup and shoes."

CHAPTER THIRTY-SIX

Skye ordered Sean to drive south on Nostrand while she sat in the passenger seat and logged in to her computer. He remained silent, watching his rearview mirror. He hoped it was Jack following him, because he couldn't see the driver.

As soon as Skye found out the codes were fake, she would order Lucy killed. Sean knew Skye well. She would kill Lucy out of spite and anger.

"Your whole plan was smart," Sean said, "except for the fact that you let the FBI seize your account book."

"That was on Kurt," she snapped. "He should have known as soon as he went whistle-blower the FBI would be crawling all over the place. I only needed one more day—and that day has cost us two years of our lives."

"You should always have a backup plan."

"Really?" She stared at him. "And what's your backup plan now, Sean? You think you can talk your way out of this?" She softened her tone. "It doesn't have to be this way. I have the accounts. We can disappear together. It was eight-point-seven million two years ago. Think of how much money is in the accounts now."

"Depending on the interest rate, you're probably looking at ten mill, take or leave."

"Ten million is a lot of money. We can disappear. We can go anywhere."

"Ten million is a drop in the bucket if you don't want to be caught."

"I already have property waiting for me; I can live on the interest alone for the rest of my life."

She started typing again on the computer. She took out the book and logged in to a secure account. Granite Trust.

She caught him looking and turned the computer away. "I should have known you'd try to manipulate me."

"I'm not doing anything."

"We were really good together."

"We had fun," he said. "But that was a long time ago. Before I knew you were a killer."

"Isn't that the pot calling the kettle black! I've followed your career for years. You're certainly no saint."

"I never killed anyone in cold blood. Colton was our friend."

"Some friend you were. He worshiped you and you walked away. Who stayed? Hmm? *Me*."

"You killed Hunter."

She didn't say anything.

"Dammit, Skye! He didn't do anything to anyone."

"You had him spying on me. His death is on *you*."

Skye went back to her laptop. Her hands were shaking. Was she angry or upset?

Sean looked behind him again. The car was still there.

He said, "This road goes on forever." And it was slow. There were lights and stop signs. It was a residential and business area. "There has to be a faster way to go wherever we're going."

"Shut up. This isn't working."

"You must have typed wrong. Or maybe your lover Kurt took the money a long time ago."

"Don't be ridiculous. He wouldn't have gone through

this elaborate and expensive plan if he had the accounts *and* the decoding key." She'd obviously thought that might have been a possibility.

She stared at the address book and slowly turned pages, rubbing them with her fingers. "This isn't my book. It doesn't feel right."

"And you can tell that after two years."

She pulled out a gun and put it at his head.

"Pull over."

"Skye—"

"Now!"

The phone in his pocket vibrated once. He hoped that meant Noah had Lucy. He had to believe she was safe.

Sean pulled the car over to the side of the road and slipped it into park.

"Hands on the wheel!"

He did as Skye ordered, waiting for the right time to attack.

"I don't know what you did, but this isn't my book. I will kill you. After you hear your girlfriend die."

Sean used his right arm to push Skye's gun hand up, toward the roof, and his left hand to reach over, grab her wrist, and disarm her. He turned her gun on her and said, "Get out."

"I hate you!"

Sean saw movement on Skye's side of the car. *Jack?* Suddenly Sean's door opened. He turned his gun toward his attacker.

Evan.

Evan slammed Sean's head into the steering wheel. Sean dropped the gun; Skye retrieved it. Evan slammed the front door shut, then got into the backseat. He put a gun to Sean's head. "Drive or I kill you."

Sean wiped blood off his nose and glanced around. He saw a shadow disappear and wondered why Jack hadn't helped him. Unless Lucy wasn't safe yet.

Sean put the car in drive. His nose was probably broken; it hurt like hell.

Skye said, "Evan, thank you. I swear, I don't know—"

Evan turned the gun on Skye and shot her in the head. Sean was so startled that he swerved the car, sideswiping two parked vehicles.

Evan had the gun aimed at the back of Sean's head. "I had the car wired. I heard everything. In case you're wondering, I acted on LeGrand's orders."

Sean had no idea what was going on or who was in charge. He glanced in the rearview mirror but couldn't see anything except Evan's scowl.

"Turn right here," Evan ordered.

Sean looked in the side mirrors. There might have been a truck following, but he couldn't be sure.

"If you're looking for your buddy, I slashed his tires. You're on your own. Turn left at the second light and it's a straight shot down to the marina."

Evan reached over and took the pink book, now bloodied, from Skye's lap. "If she's right and this is fake, you're going to be Kurt's little lapdog. You'll get him every dime you stole from him. We don't care where it comes from. I know you can do it, and so does he."

"Fuck you."

"Tough guy."

The truck following them looked like the same one that followed them before. If Evan really did slash Jack's tires, who was that?

Crossing Brooklyn seemed to take forever. They finally emerged at the ocean, the change sudden and welcome.

"Here," Evan said. "Turn at the gate. Roll down your window carefully. The code is three-two-nine-eight."

Sean typed in the code and the gate rolled open.

"Drive as far as you can on the dock, then turn off the car."

Sean did as Evan ordered.

Evan was on his phone. "I have Rogan and the codes. Skye said there's something wrong with the book before I shot her."

He listened, and Sean couldn't hear what LeGrand said.

Evan hung up and said, "Slowly get out of the car. I will shoot you if you do anything other than what I tell you."

Sean got out of the car slowly.

"Keep your hands up," Evan said as he got out of the back. "Now put them on the roof of the car."

Sean complied, discreetly glancing around to get his bearings. The icy wind from the Atlantic Ocean stung his arms and eyes, whipping the water up, dampening his skin. Evan cuffed him, then led him down the dock to the end.

Sean couldn't be sure, but he thought he saw a shadow moving along the dock parallel to them. If that was Jack, how was he going to get to *this* dock? Swim?

Maybe it was his imagination.

LeGrand stepped out onto the deck of a beautiful forty-two-foot cruiser named *Rosebud*. His face was red with rage. As soon as Sean was on the deck, LeGrand hit him. "Evan, take the boat out. Now, Sean Rogan, you will pay for stealing from me again."

LeGrand took the book from Evan as Evan went up to the small wheel room. LeGrand said, "You will find my money or I'll kill you."

"Go ahead. I'm not working for you."

"I killed your brother; I killed your girlfriend; I will kill everyone you've ever known."

Sean had a moment of hesitation. He knew Duke was alive, but what if LeGrand had already killed Lucy?

While LeGrand ranted, Sean pulled a small bobby pin from the pocket seam in his jeans and picked the lock on the handcuffs.

"I want my money!" LeGrand hit Sean again, and he dropped the pin after one side sprang open.

He swung his arm around and the free end of the handcuffs hit LeGrand square in the face. LeGrand fell to his knees. Sean ran to the other side of the deck, but Evan came down from the wheel house and hit him with a metal pole, then pointed his gun at Sean's head.

"Stupid fuck," Evan said.

Sean was on his knees. His chest burned, and he was certain he'd cracked or broken a rib. He couldn't move if he wanted. He took a couple deep breaths and didn't think his lung had been pierced.

LeGrand came up behind him and kicked him to the deck.

"We'll get the money," LeGrand told Evan, "without him."

Sean rolled over onto his back and looked at the gun in LeGrand's hand. Then Sean looked up, at the top of the yacht, and saw Jack. Jack nodded once.

Sean said to LeGrand, "Don't look up."

LeGrand didn't take the bait, but Evan did.

Sean kicked Evan's legs out from under him. Through the pain in Sean's ribs, he fought Evan for the gun. A bullet flew by Sean; then the shadow that was Jack Kincaid jumped down a full story and tackled Kurt LeGrand to the ground.

Sean disarmed Evan and held the gun on him. "Don't move or I will kill you."

Evan lunged for Sean and Sean fired twice.

Evan collapsed.

Sean crawled over to where Jack was holding LeGrand and hitting him in the face.

"Jack," Sean said. "Stop."

Jack hit LeGrand once more, then dropped him. He was barely conscious.

Floodlights lit up the docks and through a loudspeaker came Noah's voice.

"This is the FBI. You are surrounded. Put down your weapons."

Sean looked at Jack and started laughing.

Sean had no idea what happened at the docks after the FBI showed up. He'd been transported by ambulance to a hospital, Lucy by his side. He got X-rays and the doctor said two ribs were cracked, but not broken. Didn't matter, they hurt like hell. He was taped up and ordered not to do anything strenuous. The doctor had wanted to keep him overnight because of his concussion, but Sean refused. It was already six in the morning, he didn't want to stay an additional day. Still, they were running more tests and Sean had to wait in a bed, like an invalid.

At least they let Lucy in.

"Did you see your brother?" Sean asked.

She nodded. "You don't remember him helping you walk to the ambulance?"

"Vaguely." Once the adrenaline from the fight wore off, his brain had turned fuzzy.

"Maybe you should stay overnight—"

"No," he said. "We'll get a hotel. I need you, Lucy."

He leaned up to kiss her, wincing as his ribs protested.

Lucy gently pushed him back down, sat on the edge of the bed, and kissed him. "Don't move."

"Are you okay?"

"You asked me that a dozen times already."

"Tell me again."

"I'm fine. Some bruises, nothing broken. I promise."

He sighed in relief. "I didn't know if LeGrand had made good on his threat."

"He didn't, he's in prison, he will not be getting out."

"Evan?"

"He's dead. And you know about Skye?"

Sean nodded. "I was in the car."

"I'm so sorry." Lucy squeezed his hands.

"She killed Hunter, or sent Evan to do it. She didn't admit to killing him, but she didn't deny it, either. And Colton—"

"Noah said he's out of surgery and in ICU. It's touch and go, but the doctors think he's going to make it."

"What am I supposed to tell him?" Sean wasn't looking forward to explaining to Colton that he'd been working for the FBI.

"The truth."

"It's going to be hard. Colton was my best friend. I betrayed him."

"He will understand," Lucy said. "You'll make him understand."

"Unless he goes to prison."

"Do you think Rick will do that?"

"He might not have a choice."

"Rick will be fair."

Noah walked into Sean's semi-private room. "Rick will be fair about what?"

Sean didn't say anything. He didn't want to talk about Colton with Noah, not now when he was raw and sore and still processing everything that had happened in the last twenty-four hours.

Lucy said, "Are you going to prosecute Colton?"

"I don't know, I'm not the U.S. attorney."

"Noah, please—just tell us what's going on."

Noah sat at the foot of Sean's bed. "We'll talk to him. And depending on what he says and if he helps fill in some holes, he'll probably not do any time."

Sean breathed easier.

Noah continued, "You could help with that, Sean. Talk to him."

"He may not want to talk to me."

"I think you're wrong about that. I'm not saying it's going to be easy, but it's worth it."

Sean agreed. "When he's out of the woods, I'll see him." He changed the subject. "I'm still a little fuzzy on some details."

"Probably the concussion," Noah joked. "Maybe you should wait a day or two. We're still processing a lot of evidence and information."

"Then just this—why did LeGrand have Deanna Brighton killed?"

"To frame you."

"She was the mole?"

"Steve Gannon was Paxton's mole. Paxton feared you'd do what you did—review the tape he'd hired Colton to steal. So he had Gannon, whom he's known for some time, partner with Brighton and feed her obsession with you. And she was obsessed—she had her home office dedicated to you."

"But—that doesn't make sense," Sean said. "Was Gannon also working for LeGrand?"

"No. Gannon said Deanna had an informant close to Colton. Through phone records, we figured out it was Evan Weller. He called her twenty minutes before she was killed in your apartment."

"He sent her there to be murdered?"

"She walked right into it. She didn't call her partner, she wasn't thinking like a cop. They planned to frame you for it. We have Duke's statement—"

"You also have a tape," Sean said.

"Excuse me?"

"I have a camera in my apartment. It's hidden in the kitchen cabinet and covers the door and most of the room. It sends the data to a cloud server. I'll give you the account information so you can see exactly what happened."

Noah stared at him and Sean couldn't read his expression. "I saw holes in the walls."

"Patched holes," Sean corrected.

Noah smiled. "You're a bright guy."

"LeGrand said that they took my gun and were going to kill someone with it."

Noah shook his head. "Evan Weller had your gun on him. Maybe they were planning something, but it didn't happen."

Lucy asked, "Did the Coast Guard apprehend the ship LeGrand was going to meet?"

"Yes. I don't know what's going to come of it, unless we can find evidence that they planned on buying the bio-toxin. That part of the investigation has been completely taken over by Homeland, and I'm glad. It'll be a headache I don't need."

"And does Paxton walk away from this?" Sean asked.

"No. Rick is working with him on his resignation. Prison—I'm not sure."

"But—" Lucy began before Noah cut her off.

"We have evidence that Paxton and Joyce Bonner planned to taint prisoner vaccines with the mycotoxin, but when Sean stole the chip from Paxton, Bonner refused to help. She planned to destroyed the toxin, but made the mistake of threatening Paxton. That's when he realized she had the tape of her husband's murder."

"And you can't put him in prison for murder?" Lucy said.

"I think we can, but he'd go on trial for killing a man who abused his wife. Bonner has medical records from the time of her marriage showing repeated beatings and broken bones. Justified? Maybe. The vaccine scheme is more damaging to Paxton, but it hadn't even been implemented."

"So that bastard is going to walk," Sean said with a long sigh. "This was all for nothing."

"No," Noah said. "He will not walk away free. He's agreed to resign from office. He's facing serious charges. Whether the U.S. attorney works out a plea deal, I don't know. That's out of my hands. But he's not going to be able to manipulate the system again."

"Well, Noah, it's been fun," Sean said, "but our Starsky and Hutch days are over."

"For the record, even though you drove me crazy half the time, I was glad you were with me. I never acknowledged how difficult going undercover was for you. I asked a lot, and you delivered, at great personal and professional risk. I'll never forget it, Sean."

"I appreciate that," Sean said sincerely. Then he smiled and said to Lucy, "See? I *told* you he was starting to like me."

Noah shook his head, but smiled. "Take care of him, Lucy. I might need his help again some day."

That was the best compliment the fed could have given Sean. He nodded to Noah, and watched him leave.

"He's a good man," Sean said.

"I agree. He has a lot of respect for you. You earned it."

"Do I have stories . . ." He smiled. "We're alone at last. Too bad I'm in no shape to celebrate."

Lucy put her head on his shoulder, and he stroked her hair, surprised that his hand was shaking.

"Sean?" Lucy sat up. "What is it?"

"I can't lose you."

"You won't."

"I don't know what to say to Duke. He came by earlier when I was kind of out of it—they gave me a shot of painkillers when they taped up my ribs. It made me kind of loopy."

"Sean—you'll do what is right for you."

"Duke wants me back at RCK."

"You don't want to go back?"

"Would that bother you?"

She stared at him, her eyebrows arched in surprise. "Why would it bother me?"

"Patrick and Jack are both with RCK. It gives me semblance of normalcy. Validation for everything I do."

"Sean, all I care about is that you are happy. For so

long you have done everything you can to please everyone else. Not just Duke, but Patrick, and Noah, and even
me."

"I want to make you happy."

"Sweetheart, I know. And you do, always. If you stay
with RCK, you need to do it because it's where you belong. If you don't think you belong there anymore, don't
stay for me, or Patrick, and especially not Duke. I never
realized how much your choices in life came directly out
of your relationship with your brother. So don't let Duke
factor into your decision."

"You're right, I know—but you will always factor into
my decisions. Because I love you."

"Then let me tell you this: I will support your decision
no matter what. Whether you go back to RCK or not, I
will be here. That will never change."

CHAPTER THIRTY-SEVEN

Two days later

Each footfall down the stairs made Sean's cracked ribs sing in pain. He knew he shouldn't have gone downstairs. But what Lucy had said at the hospital hung heavily around his heart. She was right. He had to make this decision for himself.

Duke stood with his hand on the doorknob. He didn't have any luggage because he had come to New York only with a backpack, which had disappeared along the way. And now he was leaving Sean's town house the same way.

Duke said, "I didn't want to wake you."

Sean shook his head. "No more lies, Duke. No more platitudes. No more hedging."

Sean needed to sit down, but he was afraid if he turned his back on his brother, Duke would leave and they'd never be brothers again.

Sean didn't want that.

"I love you, Duke."

Damn, it was hard to say. Maybe because they were guys, they were *brothers,* they couldn't just let their emotions leak all over the place. But after all this time of trying to be what Duke wanted, Sean realized he'd failed. Not because he couldn't, but because he shouldn't have tried.

"You're coming back to RCK."

Sean shook his head.

"Sean, when I said I was sorry, I meant it."

"I know."

"What more do you want? I can't even tell you how bad I feel."

"Duke—" Sean winced and held his side. "Can we sit down?"

"I should go."

"Don't. Not yet. Give me ten minutes." Why was Sean pleading with his brother? It wasn't going to change Sean's decision. He needed his brother back. Not a boss, not even a partner, but his brother.

Sean hadn't had a brother since his parents died.

Duke nodded and followed Sean into the family room in the back of the house. Sean made coffee. He didn't drink it, but Lucy would want some when she got up. Sean poured himself a glass of milk, then sat in the big chair. He shifted until the pain faded to a light throb.

Duke sat on the sofa. "I'm sorry I said what I did. I was angry and if you'd only told me—"

"Duke, this isn't about that. I know you were mad; I counted on it. It gave the undercover operation believability. I couldn't risk being exposed."

"But that doesn't matter. I shouldn't have lost it like I did. I didn't mean it."

"Yes, you did."

Duke was upset. "Sean, you're my brother. I would do anything for you; you know that."

"This isn't about loyalty. It's about how you see me. I've done a lot of things that were wrong—or illegal—but I did them with full knowledge of what I was doing. I weighed the consequences and decided that I could live with my actions. My priorities have now changed. I have someone in my life who my actions impact, and that's going to factor into all my future decisions.

"I can't work for you. You will always view me as the fourteen-year-old rebel. I told you once I wanted a brother, because my father was dead. I thought when you sent me here, to D.C., that we were equals. But I don't think you can accept that."

"I'm working on it. Sean, I'm proud of you. God, you know I am! You've accomplished more for RCK than anyone. We make a great team."

Sean didn't think he'd ever heard Duke tell him he was proud of him. Maybe Duke had, but Sean hadn't heard it through the criticism that generally preceded or followed praise.

"Maybe, in the future. But ever since Mom and Dad died, I've been living for your praise. After Stanford, I resented you. You didn't stand up for me. You fixed it. I didn't want it fixed. I was willing to take responsibility for what I did because I believed then, and I believe now, that I was right. It was obnoxious, it was arrogant, but it was right to expose that bastard. And the security that supposedly was going to prevent things like this was deeply flawed. I could have gone through the proper channels, but I was seventeen and even if you *had* listened, it would have taken years to effect the change that I accomplished in one day.

"I rebelled again, and I knew it. Working with Colton, with someone who believed passionately in what he was doing, drew me in. Colton isn't a bad guy. He was loyal and honorable, and even though we broke more laws than I'll ever admit to, in the process we fixed problems. I don't regret it—but I'm not going to do it again. Not in the same way. I have too much to live free for. And I think after a while I realized that a lot of my decisions were to spite you. Because I'd disappointed you and didn't understand why. Believe me, I've been thinking about this a lot in the last couple days, after grasping all the games Kurt LeGrand played, things I didn't even know, that affected

me and my decisions. He got a perverse pleasure in hurting me and me not even seeing it. I think I was doing the
same to you.

"After Robert Martin killed himself—after I thought
he killed himself—I did a one-eighty. I did everything to
get back into your good graces, to prove that I was a mini-
Duke. But I'm not you. I used to want to be; I thought that
would make you like me more."

"I've always loved you, Sean. You're my brother. I was
your guardian."

"Because no one else would take responsibility for me.
Kane wouldn't come home. Liam and Eden were off in
Europe. I had no one else. I love you for staying, but it
was your duty and you treated it like a duty. I don't blame
you for that, my God, you were twenty-five, and suddenly
you had a badass, grieving, angry kid you were responsible for. And worse, I had the brains to get into a lot of
trouble. I thought after I graduated from MIT that you
would finally not look at me as a duty and obligation, that
you would be proud of me."

"I always have been."

"You've never told me."

"Of course I have!"

"Not until today. But this isn't about you; it's about me.
I can't live my life to please you. I need to stand on my
own. Patrick is more than capable of running RCK East.
Send him someone. Hire someone. I don't know where
Lucy is going when she graduates, but wherever it is, I
will follow. I'm going to focus on private investigation.
I'm good at it and I can do it anywhere."

"You can work for us anywhere as well—"

"But I don't want to. I need to do this for me. I'm thirty
years old, and if I stay, I will continue to seek your approval and praise. I can't live like that anymore. I don't
like how every time you say 'Good job,' I lap it up like a

puppy. I need to stand on my own. Without your protection, without RCK."

Duke didn't say anything for a long minute. "I would take back everything I said if I could. I hate that I hurt you so deeply."

"I forgive you." Sean smiled, but it felt funny, especially since his eyes were burning. This wasn't good-bye forever, he wanted to say, but it was good-bye for now. Because Sean didn't want to rely on Duke or RCK and it would be so easy to do it.

"After Nora has the baby, in March, I hope you visit."

"I will."

"I need to go." Duke stood up. Sean tried to stand. "Stay." Duke put his hand on Sean's head. "I love you, brother," he said, his voice cracking.

Then he left.

Lucy came down the stairs when she didn't hear voices. Duke was standing by the front door, looking at his feet. He glanced up at her, tears in his eyes. "You have a good man in my brother, Lucy."

"I know."

She hugged Duke, then locked the door behind him and went to the family room where Sean sat in his favorite chair. He looked as upset as Duke.

She sat on the arm of the chair and took Sean's hand. "Are you okay?"

He nodded. "I made the right decision. I'm ready to be on my own. I just didn't want to hurt him."

"Honesty can be painful, but to save your relationship, you needed to tell him the truth."

"I know." He squeezed her hand. "You're okay with this, right?"

"Okay with what?"

"I'm going where you go."

"I can't tell you the weight that has been lifted off my

chest. I think in the back of my mind I expected you to stay here, because I knew how much you loved RCK, and I didn't want to ask you to come with me."

"I love you more than my job."

"It's more than a job for you."

He shook his head. "Without you, it doesn't mean anything. But when I said about going where you go—I mean it literally. I want to spend every night with you. I want *our* place, not your place and my place."

"That's kind of what I expected," she said, confused. "Did you think I wasn't ready for that big of a commitment?"

"I didn't want to presume."

She laughed. She couldn't help it; the way he was talking made her giggle. "Sean, I can't wait to graduate. To find out where we're moving, to find a home we can share, to wake up every morning with you. I love you, Sean Rogan."

Lucy sat on his lap and kissed him. "How are your ribs?"

"Just don't move," he murmured.

Sean considered himself extremely lucky to have Lucy. That she stood by him without question, that she trusted him and his love for her, that even when she learned his darkest secrets she forgave without hesitation. She'd said there was nothing to forgive.

He was scared. Change was scary, because right now his future was both out of his hands and solely in his grasp. He didn't know where the FBI would send Lucy; for the next seven weeks they would be in limbo, waiting for her orders. And then they would go, together, to forge their future.

It was a challenge. And Sean had never shied away from a challenge.

Read on for an excerpt from
Allison Brennan's next book

COLD SNAP

Coming soon from St. Martin's Paperbacks

San Francisco

Patrick Kincaid had a problem: he couldn't say no.

Whatever was asked of him, he did it, usually without complaint. He was amicable that way, and his friends and family knew it. He didn't mind helping out; if he could do something for someone, why not? He had a challenging job he liked, a family he loved, and a few good friends who had stuck around even during his two-year stint sleeping off a coma in the hospital. Life was too short to be stingy with it.

But this time, as he circled the arcane street system in San Francisco that seemed to have no methodology, looking for a parking place in a dense fog, he wished he'd said no.

He would have, if anyone else in the world had asked him to drive two hours out of his way (which took three because of the inclement weather) to hunt down a family friend he hadn't seen since he graduated from high school. He'd have found an excuse or found a replacement. Except, his mother had called. And Patrick had never, not once, said no to his mom. His older brother Connor had told him—often—that he was Mom's favorite because he was her "yes-man."

His job, because he'd chosen to accept it, was to bring Gabrielle Santana home for Christmas. Gabrielle Santana—the girl who'd staged a sit-in sophomore year to protest the expulsion of three students who she thought hadn't had a fair hearing with the school board. The same girl who'd been arrested at seventeen for organizing a rave in an abandoned warehouse in downtown San Diego. The girl who'd been suspended for skinny-dipping in the high school pool. Patrick was three years older than Gabrielle, but she'd done more her freshman year—both good and bad—than he had his entire four years of high school.

The problem was that Gabrielle had called her mother two days ago and said something came up at work and she couldn't come home for Christmas. Now, she wasn't returning her mother's phone calls, or those from anyone else in her family. They were worried, and because the Santanas were worried, Rosa Kincaid was worried. And if Rosa Kincaid was worried and called upon one of her children for help, the worry fell onto them. In this case, Patrick.

"You're already in Sacramento," his mother had said. "It's not that far out of your way to help the Santanas."

She had to have sensed the hesitation in his tone because she gave him the hard sell—and the guilt. Irish Catholic guilt compounded by the fact that he had a Cuban mother. No one said no to Rosa Kincaid.

After fifteen minutes of driving around in widening circles because there seemed to be no street parking in the vicinity, he finally squeezed the rental car into a spot four blocks from Gabrielle's loft in a converted warehouse off Howard Street. At least he was driving in a flat area and not the insanely steep hills that made up so much of the city.

Patrick pulled the collar of his jacket up against the cold, damp air as he walked briskly down Howard. His phone vibrated in his pocket and he reluctantly pulled it out. He hadn't brought gloves. He'd packed for San Diego—where it had been 78 degrees today—not wet San Francisco. He glanced at the text message from his sister Lucy.

Be glad you're in Sacramento—we're stuck in Denver. Airport shut down. Blizzard. Won't get out until tomorrow night, if then. Love you! ~Lucy

He responded that he was on an errand for their mom in San Francisco and would be delayed as well, then pocketed his phone and continued up the hill.

Maybe this side trip had a silver lining. He didn't want to be the fifth wheel stuck in Denver with Lucy with her boyfriend, Sean. It would make it doubly awkward. Patrick wasn't a prude, but Lucy was his little sister, and he would always think of her as his little sister. While he'd grown to accept her relationship with his best friend and partner Sean Rogan, she was *still* his little sister. There were some things he didn't want to think about.

The fog was so heavy a layer of moisture quickly coated his jacket. Driving here, he'd thought of all the reasons why Gabrielle was *incommunicado*. Off with a boyfriend. Working. Drinking with her girlfriends. It was selfish and cruel not to respond to her mother's calls for two days, but it didn't mean anything was wrong. He'd already checked hospitals and her employer. Nothing. The only odd thing was that her employer said she would be out of the office until after the holidays. Patrick couldn't get any other details from the snippy receptionist.

Again, not being in the office didn't mean something was wrong. In fact, that she'd informed her employer she would be out told Patrick there was nothing to worry about.

Except . . . he had to talk to her. Find out what she was doing and give Mrs. Santana peace of mind. Give her a piece of *his* mind, too. He would never have needlessly worried his mom, as a kid or as an adult. He'd been a cop and now worked for the private security firm of Rogan-Caruso-Kincaid, and when he was going to be unreachable for more than a day, he made sure his family knew his plans. It was common courtesy.

He rounded the corner of Gabrielle's narrow street, not wider than an alley. One car could barely fit. The buildings were a mix of very old and renovated. Mostly businesses, with apartments upstairs. In Gabrielle's converted warehouse, the heavy metal door was accessible only by a keypad. A sign indicated that the lobby was open from 6 a.m. until 6 p.m.

Patrick rang her buzzer. No answer. He tried her cell phone number—she didn't have a landline in her name—again, no answer. He looked around for an external security camera and didn't see any. He easily hacked the keypad and the door opened.

Sean had taught him a lot of tricks over the years, and the former cop in Patrick winced at breaking and entering. Though, as Sean would say, he wasn't *breaking* anything.

It took Patrick a few minutes to get his bearings. First, he was surprised at the quiet. Even the traffic from the interstate a few blocks away had dimmed once he stepped inside. Music faintly played from somewhere upstairs. The lobby was a small square with mailboxes—sixteen—built into the wall. Eight of them were larger boxes labeled with business names—a realtor, an interior decorator, and similar white-collar professions. The other eight were narrow and had last names only. Bruce. Carmichael. Santana, in Unit 12.

The building was a mix of new and old, with the warehouse structure built out, but the polished concrete floors made the place feel cold and sterile. The staircase upstairs was metal—new and reinforced, but it also added to the cool interior. It was probably young and trendy, but

Patrick shivered. The building seemed lonely, if a building could feel anything.

On the second landing he found Unit 12 in the far back corner. He knocked on the door and silently swore. It was solid metal. He rang the bell.

No one came.

Patrick tried the door, not expecting it to open, but it did. Gabrielle left her apartment unlocked? Even in a semi-secure building, he'd never leave his door open.

He pushed open the door and glanced around before entering. The entry was small and narrow. It was completely dark. He called out, "Hello? Gabrielle?" then felt along the wall and found a light switch. This lit up not only the entry, but lights in the living room. A short staircase led to a large room with lush, bright throw rugs tossed haphazardly across most of the cement floor. The exterior walls were brick; one was embedded with small, square warehouse windows; the other was dotted with bright and wild contemporary art. The raised, galley-style kitchen included a long, low bar with two benches. The ceiling was more than twenty-five feet high. A spiral staircase led to a loft above the kitchen. Small, but the ceilings and wall of windows made it seem much bigger.

Patrick felt like an idiot standing in the middle of Gabrielle Santana's apartment. Nothing appeared out of place. Two mismatched couches that looked comfortable. Several bean-bag chairs. Scuffed coffee table covered with books and magazines. He tilted his head. One side of the table was definitely shorter.

"Gabrielle?" he called out. "It's Patrick Kincaid from San Diego. Your door was open."

Nothing.

The living room was just that, no work or desk area. He didn't want to roam through her house, he already felt uncomfortable being here. He went into the kitchen and rummaged through a couple drawers before he found a sales flyer. He turned it over, pulled a pen from his pocket, and started writing a note. What was he going to say? To phone home? To call him?

He jotted down his name and number and put it under a magnet for Chinese take-out on the refrigerator.

Still, the unlocked door made him nervous. He went up the stairs to the loft to make sure there was no sign of anyone breaking in.

The loft was two long, narrow rooms, both of which looked down into the living room at different angles, with a bathroom between them. One was Gabrielle's bedroom, one her office. Gabrielle's bed was unmade, clothes strewn all over a chair in the corner, make-up and other girl things covering the dresser. In the den was a couch that had a pillow and sleeping bag open on it. Company?

But there was no blood, no sign of anyone searching the place to suggest a robbery.

He went back downstairs just as Gabrielle—wow, she'd gone from stunning to gorgeous, but he'd have recognized her anywhere—was running up the short staircase from the entry. She glanced at him, green eyes wide with shock, then turned and ran back out the front door.

"Gabrielle! It's Patrick Kincaid!"

His words were cut off by the metal door slamming shut.

Damn, damn, damn! He'd scared her, and that made him feel like shit.

He ran after her.

As soon as he opened the door, he was hit over the head and pushed down, and something hard was pressed against his back.

Solely on instinct, he kicked his legs, rolled over, and flipped his attacker, his hand grabbing the wrist that held the weapon he knew wasn't a gun.

It was a cell phone.

"Dammit, Gabrielle! It's Patrick Kincaid."

She stared at him blankly. He jumped up, holding out his hand for her. She didn't take it.

"The cell phone would protect you better if you called nine-one-one."

Recognition crossed her stunned expression, and she got up on her own and grabbed her phone from his hand. "Patrick? *Kincaid*? What the *hell* are you doing here? And in my apartment?"

"The door was unlocked."

"So you just walked in?"

"Your mother sent me."

"My mother?"

He rolled his eyes and brushed off his slacks. "Can I come in?"

"You already have." She glared at him and opened the door.

He followed her. "Gabrielle—I'm sorry, but—"

"Elle."

"Excuse me?"

"Only my family calls me Gabrielle. As soon as I went to college, I changed my name. It's Elle."

"Like the letter 'L.' "

"Like the last syllable of my name," she snapped.

"Elle, I'm sorry. Really. Your mother was worried because she couldn't reach you—"

"And you came all the way from San Diego? No—wait—you live cross country now, don't you?"

"Washington. But I was in Sacramento."

"So you drove two hours just to check on me?"

"Your mother is worried—" he said again.

"Because I said I couldn't come home for Christmas? Jeez!" She tossed her hands in the air, then scratched the back of her head as if she was still confused.

"*Because*," Patrick said, "she's left a dozen messages and you haven't called her back. And your employer said you took vacation time."

"I'm thirty-two years old and my mother is sending a cop after me because I don't answer my phone."

"I'm not a cop. I'm a family friend."

"Tell her I'm fine. Thank you. Good-bye."

Elle seemed agitated, over and beyond her irritation that Patrick had been in her apartment.

"What's wrong?"

She gave him a puzzled look. "What's wrong?"

"Why do you do that?"

"Do what?"

"Deflect. I ask questions. You don't answer them."

"I have a lot going on, Patrick." She spread her arms wide and spun in a circle. "Take a good look. Tell my mother I'm alive and well."

"Call her."

"I will."

"Now."

She scrunched up her nose. "I haven't seen you in, like, ten, twelve years and you break into my house and order me to call my mother?" She laughed, but it sounded strained.

Patrick didn't want to get in the middle of a family squabble, because he was getting the distinct impression that this was all about family, and family—even a close clan like the Kincaids or the Santanas—could drive anyone crazy.

When she realized that he was serious and that she was still holding her phone, she made a production of punching the buttons. A moment later Patrick could hear a loud *Gabrielle!* on the other end of the line.

"Mama, I can't believe you sent Patrick Kincaid to track me down. I am so embarrassed!"

She didn't look embarrassed; she looked pissed.

"I told you, I have to work. It's an important case, I can't take the time off."

Patrick raised his eyebrow, but Elle wasn't paying attention. She listened to her mother talk, then both of them started talking in rapid Spanish. Patrick wasn't as conversational in the language as his younger sister, but he'd been raised by a Cuban mother so he had a grasp of Spanish. And the conversation was rapidly deteriorating as Elle explained why she had to spend Christmas preparing for a case, and why it was important, and that she couldn't do it in San Diego because she needed access to her law office.

And the entire time, Patrick had the strong impression that she was lying. And not just because her employer had said she had taken vacation time.

"I love you, too, Mama. I'm sorry—I'll visit as soon as I can. I know it's not the same as Christmas—I know, it's been two years—Mama, *please*, I feel bad already. Yes. I promise." She hung up. "There," she said to Patrick. "Satisfied?"

"I did my job," he said. "But why did you lie to your mother?"

"What? I didn't. I am working."

"Your law firm said you were on vacation."

"I don't need to explain myself to you—look, Patrick, I *really* have to go."

"You just got home."

"Because I needed to get some things."

The buzzer rang and Elle briefly looked like a deer caught in headlights. She ran to her front door and pressed a button on the panel. A screen with a black-and-white image popped up. An Asian woman in jeans and a long, wool coat was at the door. She rang the buzzer again.

"Shit, what's she doing here?" Elle backed away from the door as if it were about to attack.

"Who is she?"

"A social worker. Damn, I have to wait until she leaves. This is the *worst* day in my life!"

Patrick knew he was going to regret it, but he said, "Can I help?"

"No!"

"What does she want?"

"Something I can't give her." Her cell phone rang and Elle looked at it. "She's calling me now. Dammit!" She then glanced at Patrick and said, "Tell her we're not here."

"We?"

"She's going to ask about Jami. Tell her Jami and I went out and you don't know when we'll be back. Look, I can't lie to her, but you can!" She tossed Patrick her phone.

Skeptical, and wholly uncomfortable with what Elle asked him to do, he answered the phone. "Santana residence."

"Is Gabrielle Santana there?"

"I'm sorry, who's calling?"

"Lea Chin, I need to come up."

"I'm sorry, I'm not supposed to let anyone inside while Gabrielle isn't home."

"Who's this?"

"Who's this?"

"Lea Chin, with the San Francisco Department of Child Welfare. I need to inspect the apartment, and Ms. Santana has been avoiding me. Where's Jami?"

Elle had leaned close to him to hear both sides of the conversation better. Lea Chin had a much softer voice than Mrs. Santana.

"Not here either."

"And you are?"

"A friend."

"Ms. Santana didn't inform us that a man was living with her."

"I'm just visiting."

"Jami's curfew is ten p.m. I expect to hear from Ms. Santana by then, or Jami will be placed in custody." She cut off the call.

Patrick had no idea what that conversation was about. "Elle, what just happened?"

She glanced at her watch, then grabbed her phone back from Patrick. "I have two hours to find Jami. I've been looking for her since noon!"

"Who's Jami?"

"A fifteen-year-old who's in deep trouble and will be in deeper trouble if she doesn't show up in court Tuesday morning. Something spooked her when I went out for groceries. I know it. She wouldn't just leave. She knows how important this is!"

Elle ran into the kitchen, opened the freezer, and took a can of coffee from the freezer. But there was no coffee inside—only money. Roughly a thousand dollars in fives, tens, and twenties.

"I've never known anyone who keeps money in her freezer."

"My mom," she said. She counted out three hundred dollars and pocketed it, then put the can back. She ran upstairs and came back a minute later with a bag filled with clothes, and a heavier jacket with a hole in the elbow. "Thanks for covering with Lea for me."

Patrick was going to regret this. But he said, "Let me help."

She stared at him as if surprised by the offer. "Don't you have someplace to be?"

"My flight doesn't leave until tomorrow."

"It's nice of you. Really. But no one is going to trust you. You look—well, you look like a cop. I know where she hangs out. They don't like cops. Especially cops who dress like kids from a rich prep school."

Patrick glanced down at his khaki Dockers slacks and leather loafers. Rich prep kid? Hardly.

He said, "You've been looking for her all day and couldn't find her."

"I have to convince the right people that they can trust me, and I'll be able to find her." She didn't sound optimistic, just determined.

"You need help. I have the time. And the training."

Her expression showed her inner battle, but she finally said, "Okay, fine, thanks. But just trust me out there, okay? Don't do anything, well, *cop-like.*"

"I haven't been a cop in nearly eight years." She glared at him. "All right, I'll try not to act like one." They walked out. He motioned to the door. "Aren't you going to lock it?"

"Jami has the downstairs door code, if she comes back she needs to be able to get in." She waved her hand dismissively. "It's not like I have anything valuable in there, except my computer."

They walked down the metal stairs to the lobby. "Are you going to tell me what's going on with this kid?"

"There's nothing to tell. She's a witness and I need to keep her safe until Tuesday morning."

Warning bells rang in his head. "A witness? Why aren't the cops watching her?"

"Because no one realizes that she could be in danger. They wanted to 'protect' her by putting her in juvenile hall, and that's exactly where Lorenzo's crew could get to her. I promised the judge that she'd be in court on Tuesday morning to testify—it's required for her plea arrangement— and everything was going great until this afternoon. I gave her a phone, but she's not answering it." Elle went out not the front door, but down a hall and through a door marked FIRE EXIT. No alarms went off. "It's disabled," she said dismissively. "If Lea is hanging around, I don't want her to see me."

Patrick realized then that something much, much bigger was going on. "Why not call the cops and have them help you?"

She spun around. "Look, you're going to have to trust me on this. If I tell anyone she ran away, they'll put a bench warrant out for her and she'll not only go to jail before she testifies, but her plea deal is off. She's *fifteen.* She's been on and off the streets since she was eleven. I got her a great arrangement, and if she testifies, the day after Christmas she'll be put in a group home that can protect her, send her to school, make sure she has a real shot at a future. And that's why I'm not going to San Diego."

Patrick had a dozen questions—was Jami a client of hers? What kind of law firm did she work for? Why would she agree to bring a client to live with her? Who was the girl testifying against? Did she leave the apartment willingly? Had she been coerced?

Elle led the way to a carport in the building next to hers. "I don't have my own spot, but my best friend is a flight attendant and she's gone half the time and lets me park in hers." She looked back at Patrick as she headed for the car. "I'm going to retrace my steps, but she's probably hiding out in the Haight."

"The infamous Haight Ashbury?"

Elle rolled her eyes as she stopped next to an older Honda Civic. She put the bag of clothes in the backseat, which was packed with blankets and boxes of granola bars and Gatorade bottles. "Just get in."

"Santana!" a voice shouted from behind them.

Patrick turned and saw two men rapidly approaching.

"Get in!" she shouted. She was already turning the key to the ignition before she'd closed her door.

Patrick did. "More social workers?"

A gunshot rang out.

"That's a warning, bitch!"

Elle pulled out of the carport and sideswiped one of the guys. He shouted profanities at them and his partner fired another shot, this time at the car. It missed.

"How did they know where I live?" Elle glanced over her shoulder, eyes wide, knuckles white on the steering wheel. She turned onto Howard from the alley and sped up.

"Who are they?"

"I think they work for Richie Lorenzo."

"Who the hell is that?" Patrick was getting testy, because

he really hated being shot at—especially when he didn't have a gun on him.

"A drug dealer. Jami used to work for him. That's what got her in trouble with the police."

"Is that who she's testifying against?"

"No," she said in a tone that made Patrick feel like he'd missed several conversations. But she didn't clarify as she turned onto another street and started winding through hills.

"Elle, talk to me! Who is this kid testifying against? Does Lorenzo work for him?"

"Lorenzo works for no one. He's a twenty-three-year-old punk who takes runaways and has them sell his trash."

"And the case? The trial?"

Elle hesitated, then said, "Jami is testifying against a prominent businessman who is running a sweatshop down in Dogpatch—over near the old Candlestick Park. Without her, the guy walks, and he'll just set up somewhere else." She bit her lip. "But I think Lorenzo has been helping him, and Lorenzo wants Jami back in his stable, or dead. Maybe they cut a deal or something."

She bit her lip and glanced at Patrick. Though there were tears in her eyes, her jaw was clenched in anger. "I have to find her, Patrick. I can't lose another kid to those bastards."